Benito Perez Galdos,

best novels

In this book:

Dona Perfecta

Translator:

Mary J. Serrano

Trafalgar

Translator:

Clara Bell

The Novel on the Tram

Translator:

Michael Wooff

Benito Pérez Galdós (1843 –1920) was a Spanish realist novelist. Some authorities consider him second only to Cervantes in stature as a Spanish novelist. He was the leading literary figure in 19th century Spain.
Galdós was a prolific writer, publishing 31 novels, 46 Episodios Nacionales (National Episodes), 23 plays, and the equivalent of 20 volumes of shorter fiction, journalism and other writings. He remains popular in Spain, and is considered as equal to Dickens, Balzac and Tolstoy. As recently as 1950, few of his works were available translated to English, although he has slowly become popular in the Anglophone world.

In this book:

Dona Perfecta

CHAPTER I

VILLAHORRENDA! FIVE MINUTES!

When the down train No. 65—of what line it is unnecessary to say—stopped at the little station between kilometres 171 and 172, almost all the second-and third-class passengers remained in the cars, yawning or asleep, for the penetrating cold of the early morning did not invite to a walk on the unsheltered platform. The only first-class passenger on the train alighted quickly, and addressing a group of the employes asked them if this was the Villahorrenda station.

"We are in Villahorrenda," answered the conductor whose voice was drowned by the cackling of the hens which were at that moment being lifted into the freight car. "I forgot to call you, Senor de Rey. I think they are waiting for you at the station with the beasts."

"Why, how terribly cold it is here!" said the traveller, drawing his cloak more closely about him. "Is there no place in the station where I could rest for a while, and get warm, before undertaking a journey on horseback through this frozen country?"

Before he had finished speaking the conductor, called away by the urgent duties of his position, went off, leaving our unknown cavalier's question unanswered. The latter saw that another employe was coming toward him, holding a lantern in his right hand, that swung back and forth as he walked, casting the light on the platform of the station in a series of zigzags, like those described by the shower from a watering-pot.

"Is there a restaurant or a bedroom in the station of Villahorrenda?" said the traveller to the man with the lantern.

"There is nothing here," answered the latter brusquely, running toward the men who were putting the freight on board the cars, and assuaging them with such a volley of oaths, blasphemies, and abusive epithets that the very chickens, scandalized by his brutality, protested against it from their baskets.

"The best thing I can do is to get away from this place as quickly as possible," said the gentlemen to himself. "The conductor said that the beasts were here."

Just as he had come to this conclusion he felt a thin hand pulling him gently and respectfully by the cloak. He turned round and saw a figure enveloped in a gray cloak, and out of whose voluminous folds peeped the shrivelled and astute countenance of a Castilian peasant. He looked at the ungainly figure, which reminded one of the black poplar among trees; he observed the shrewd eyes that shone from beneath the wide brim of the old velvet hat; the sinewy brown hand that grasped a green switch, and the broad foot that, with every movement, made the iron spur jingle.

"Are you Senor Don Jose de Rey?" asked the peasant, raising his hand to his hat.

"Yes; and you, I take it," answered the traveller joyfully, "are Dona Perfecta's servant, who have come to the station to meet me and show me the way to Orbajosa?"

"The same. Whenever you are ready to start. The pony runs like the wind. And Senor Don Jose, I am sure, is a good rider. For what comes by race—"

"Which is the way out?" asked the traveller, with impatience. "Come, let us start, senor—What is your name?"

"My name is Pedro Lucas," answered the man of the gray cloak, again making a motion to take off his hat; "but they call me Uncle Licurgo. Where is the young gentleman's baggage?"

"There it is—there under the cloak. There are three pieces—two portmanteaus and a box of books for Senor Don Cayetano. Here is the check."

A moment later cavalier and squire found themselves behind the barracks called a depot, and facing a road which, starting at this point, disappeared among the neighboring hills, on whose naked slopes could be vaguely distinguished the miserable hamlet of Villahorrenda. There were three animals to carry the men and the luggage. A not ill-looking nag was destined for the cavalier; Uncle

Licurgo was to ride a venerable hack, somewhat loose in the joints, but sure-footed; and the mule, which was to be led by a stout country boy of active limbs and fiery blood, was to carry the luggage.

Before the caravan had put itself in motion the train had started, and was now creeping along the road with the lazy deliberation of a way train, awakening, as it receded in the distance, deep subterranean echoes. As it entered the tunnel at kilometre 172, the steam issued from the steam whistle with a shriek that resounded through the air. From the dark mouth of the tunnel came volumes of whitish smoke, a succession of shrill screams like the blasts of a trumpet followed, and at the sound of its stentorian voice villages, towns, the whole surrounding country awoke. Here a cock began to crow, further on another. Day was beginning to dawn.

CHAPTER II

A JOURNEY IN THE HEART OF SPAIN

When they had proceeded some distance on their way and had left behind them the hovels of Villahorrenda, the traveller, who was young and handsome spoke thus:

"Tell me, Senor Solon—"

"Licurgo, at your service."

"Senor Licurgo, I mean. But I was right in giving you the name of a wise legislator of antiquity. Excuse the mistake. But to come to the point. Tell me, how is my aunt?"

"As handsome as ever," answered the peasant, pushing his beast forward a little. "Time seems to stand still with Senora Dona Perfecta. They say that God gives long life to the good, and if that is so that angel of the Lord ought to live a thousand years. If all the blessings that are showered on her in this world were feathers, the senora would need no other wings to go up to heaven with."

"And my cousin, Senorita Rosario?"

"The senora over again!" said the peasant. "What more can I tell you of Dona Rosarito but that that she is the living image of her mother? You will have a treasure, Senor Don Jose, if it is true, as I hear, that you have come to be married to her. She will be a worthy mate for you, and the young lady will have nothing to complain of, either. Between Pedro and Pedro the difference is not very great."

"And Senor Don Cayetano?"

"Buried in his books as usual. He has a library bigger than the cathedral; and he roots up the earth, besides, searching for stones covered with fantastical scrawls, that were written, they say, by the Moors."

"How soon shall we reach Orbajosa?"

"By nine o'clock, God willing. How delighted the senora will be when she sees her nephew! And yesterday, Senorita Rosario was putting the room you are to have in order. As they have never seen you, both mother and daughter think of nothing else but what Senor Don Jose is like, or is not like. The time has now come for letters to be silent and tongues to talk. The young lady will see her cousin and all will be joy and merry-making. If God wills, all will end happily, as the saying is."

"As neither my aunt nor my cousin has yet seen me," said the traveller smiling, "it is not wise to make plans."

"That's true; for that reason it was said that the bay horse is of one mind and he who saddles him of another," answered the peasant. "But the face does not lie. What a jewel you are getting! and she, what a handsome man!"

The young man did not hear Uncle Licurgo's last words, for he was preoccupied with his own thoughts. Arrived at a bend in the road, the peasant turned his horse's head in another direction, saying:

"We must follow this path now. The bridge is broken, and the river can only be forded at the Hill of the Lilies."

"The Hill of the Lilies," repeated the cavalier, emerging from his revery. "How abundant beautiful names are in these unattractive localities! Since I have been travelling in this part of the country the terrible irony of the names is a constant surprise to me. Some place that is remarkable for its barren aspect and the desolate sadness of the landscape is called Valleameno (Pleasant Valley). Some wretched mud-walled village stretched on a barren plain and proclaiming its poverty in diverse ways has the insolence to call itself Villarica (Rich Town); and some arid and stony ravine, where not even the thistles can find nourishment, calls itself, nevertheless, Valdeflores (Vale of Flowers). That hill in front of us is the Hill of the Lilies? But where, in Heaven's name, are the lilies? I see nothing but stones and withered grass. Call it Hill of Desolation, and you will be right. With the exception of Villahorrenda, whose appearance corresponds with its name, all is irony here. Beautiful words, a prosaic and mean reality. The blind would be happy in this country, which for the tongue is a Paradise and for the eyes a hell."

Senor Licurgo either did not hear the young man's words, or, hearing, he paid no attention to them. When they had forded the river, which, turbid and impetuous, hurried on with impatient haste, as if fleeing from its own hands, the peasant pointed with outstretched arm to some barren and extensive fields that were to be seen on the left, and said:

"Those are the Poplars of Bustamante."

"My lands!" exclaimed the traveller joyfully, gazing at the melancholy fields illumined by the early morning light. "For the first time, I see the patrimony which I inherited from my mother. The poor woman used to praise this country so extravagantly, and tell me so many marvellous things about it when I was a child, that I thought that to be here was to be in heaven. Fruits, flowers, game, large and small; mountains, lakes, rivers, romantic streams, pastoral hills, all were to be found in the Poplars of Bustamante; in this favored land, the best and most beautiful on the earth. But what is to be said? The people of this place live in their imaginations. If I had been brought here in my youth, when I shared the ideas and the enthusiasm of my dear mother, I suppose that I, too, would have been enchanted with these bare hills, these arid or marshy plains, these dilapidated farmhouses, these rickety norias, whose buckets drip water enough to sprinkle half a dozen cabbages, this wretched and barren desolation that surrounds me."

"It is the best land in the country," said Senor Licurgo; "and for the chick-pea, there is no other like it."

"I am delighted to hear it, for since they came into my possession these famous lands have never brought me a penny."

The wise legislator of Sparta scratched his ear and gave a sigh.

"But I have been told," continued the young man, "that some of the neighboring proprietors have put their ploughs in these estates of mine, and that, little by little, they are filching them from me. Here there are neither landmarks nor boundaries, nor real ownership, Senor Licurgo."

The peasant, after a pause, during which his subtle intellect seemed to be occupied in profound disquisitions, expressed himself as follows:

"Uncle Paso Largo, whom, for his great foresight, we call the Philosopher, set his plough in the Poplars, above the hermitage, and bit by bit, he has gobbled up six fanegas."

"What an incomparable school!" exclaimed the young man, smiling. "I wager that he has not been the only—philosopher?"

"It is a true saying that one should talk only about what one knows, and that if there is food in the dove-cote, doves won't be wanting. But you, Senor Don Jose, can apply to your own cause the saying that the eye of the master fattens the ox, and now that you are here, try and recover your property."

"Perhaps that would not be so easy, Senor Licurgo," returned the young man, just as they were entering a path bordered on either side by wheat-fields, whose luxuriance and early ripeness gladdened the eye. "This field appears to be better cultivated. I see that all is not dreariness and misery in the Poplars."

The peasant assumed a melancholy look, and, affecting something of disdain for the fields that had been praised by the traveller, said in the humblest of tones:

"Senor, this is mine."

"I beg your pardon," replied the gentleman quickly; "now I was going to put my sickle in your field. Apparently the philosophy of this place is contagious."

They now descended into a canebrake, which formed the bed of a shallow and stagnant brook, and, crossing it, they entered a field full of stones and without the slightest trace of vegetation.

"This ground is very bad," said the young man, turning round to look at his companion and guide, who had remained a little behind. "You will hardly be able to derive any profit from it, for it is all mud and sand."

Licurgo, full of humility, answered:

"This is yours."

"I see that all the poor land is mine," declared the young man, laughing good-humoredly.

As they were thus conversing, they turned again into the high-road. The morning sunshine, pouring joyously through all the gates and balconies of the Spanish horizon, had now inundated the fields with brilliant light. The wide sky, undimmed by a single cloud, seemed to grow wider and to recede further from the earth, in order to contemplate it, and rejoice in the contemplation, from a greater height. The desolate, treeless land, straw-colored at intervals, at intervals of the color of chalk, and all cut up into triangles and quadrilaterals, yellow or black, gray or pale green, bore a fanciful resemblance to a beggar's cloak spread out in the sun. On that miserable cloak Christianity and Islamism had fought with each other epic battles. Glorious fields, in truth, but the combats of the past had left them hideous!

"I think we shall have a scorching day, Senor Licurgo," said the young man, loosening his cloak a little. "What a dreary road! Not a single tree to be seen, as far as the eye can reach. Here everything is in contradiction. The irony does not cease. Why, when there are no poplars here, either large or small, should this be called The Poplars?"

Uncle Licurgo did not answer this question because he was listening with his whole soul to certain sounds which were suddenly heard in the distance, and with an uneasy air he stopped his beast, while he explored the road and the distant hills with a gloomy look.

"What is the matter?" asked the traveller, stopping his horse also.

"Do you carry arms, Don Jose?"

"A revolver—ah! now I understand. Are there robbers about?"

"Perhaps," answered the peasant, with visible apprehension. "I think I heard a shot."

"We shall soon see. Forward!" said the young man, putting spurs to his nag. "They are not very terrible, I dare say."

"Keep quiet, Senor Don Jose," exclaimed the peasant, stopping him. "Those people are worse than Satan himself. The other day they murdered two gentlemen who were on their way to take the train. Let us leave off jesting. Gasparon el Fuerte, Pepito Chispillas, Merengue, and Ahorca Suegras shall not see my face while I live. Let us turn into the path."

"Forward, Senor Licurgo!"

"Back, Senor Don Jose," replied the peasant, in distressed accents. "You don't know what kind of people those are. They are the same men who stole the chalice, the Virgin's crown, and two candlesticks from the church of the Carmen last month; they are the men who robbed the Madrid train two years ago."

Don Jose, hearing these alarming antecedents, felt his courage begin to give way.

"Do you see that great high hill in the distance? Well, that is where those rascals hide themselves; there in some caves which they call the Retreat of the Cavaliers."

"Of the Cavaliers?"

"Yes, senor. They come down to the high-road when the Civil Guards are not watching, and rob all they can. Do you see a cross beyond the bend of the road? Well, that was erected in remembrance of the death of the Alcalde of Villahorrenda, whom they murdered there at the time of the elections."

"Yes, I see the cross."

"There is an old house there, in which they hide themselves to wait for the carriers. They call that place The Pleasaunce."

"The Pleasaunce?"

"If all the people who have been murdered and robbed there were to be restored they would form an army."

While they were thus talking shots were again heard, this time nearer than before, which made the valiant hearts of the travellers quake a little, but not that of the country lad, who, jumping about for joy, asked Senor Licurgo's permission to go forward to watch the conflict which was taking place so near them. Observing the courage of the boy Don Jose felt a little ashamed of having been frightened, or at least a little disturbed, by the proximity of the robbers, and cried, putting spurs to his nag:

"We will go forward, then. Perhaps we may be able to lend assistance to the unlucky travellers who find themselves in so perilous a situation, and give a lesson besides to those cavaliers."

The peasant endeavored to convince the young man of the rashness of his purpose, as well as of the profitlessness of his generous design, since those who had been robbed were robbed and perhaps dead also, and not in a condition to need the assistance of any one.

The gentleman insisted, in spite of these sage counsels; the peasant reiterated his objections more strongly than before; when the appearance of two or three carters, coming quietly down the road driving a wagon, put an end to the controversy. The danger could not be very great when these men were coming along so unconcernedly, singing merry songs; and such was in fact the case, for the shots, according to what the carters said, had not been fired by the robbers, but by the Civil Guards, who desired in this way to prevent the escape of half a dozen thieves whom they were taking, bound together, to the town jail.

"Yes, I know now what it was," said Licurgo, pointing to a light cloud of smoke which was to be seen some distance off, to the right of the road. "They have peppered them there. That happens every other day."

The young man did not understand.

"I assure you, Senor Don Jose," added the Lacedaemonian legislator, with energy, "that it was very well done; for it is of no use to try those rascals. The judge cross-questions them a little and then lets them go. If at the end of a trial dragged out for half a dozen years one of them is sent to jail, at the moment least expected he escapes, and returns to the Retreat of the Cavaliers. That is the best thing to do—shoot them! Take them to prison, and when you are passing a suitable place—Ah, dog, so you want to escape, do you? pum! pum! The indictment is drawn up, the witnesses summoned, the trial ended, the sentence pronounced—all in a minute. It is a true saying that the fox is very cunning, but he who catches him is more cunning still."

"Forward, then, and let us ride faster, for this road, besides being a long one, is not at all a pleasant one," said Rey.

As they passed The Pleasaunce, they saw, a little in from the road, the guards who a few minutes before had executed the strange sentence with which the reader has been made acquainted. The country boy was inconsolable because they rode on and he was not allowed to get a nearer view of the palpitating bodies of the robbers, which could be distinguished forming a horrible group in the distance. But they had not proceeded twenty paces when they heard the sound of a horse galloping after them at so rapid a pace that he gained upon them every moment. Our traveller turned round and saw a man, or rather a Centaur, for the most perfect harmony imaginable existed between horse and rider. The latter was of a robust and plethoric constitution, with large fiery eyes, rugged features, and a black mustache. He was of middle age and had a general air of rudeness and aggressiveness, with indications of strength in his whole person. He was mounted on a superb horse with a muscular chest, like the horses of the Parthenon, caparisoned in the picturesque fashion of the country, and carrying on the crupper a great leather bag on the cover of which was to be seen, in large letters, the word Mail.

"Hello! Good-day, Senor Caballuco," said Licurgo, saluting the horseman when the latter had come up with them. "How is it that we got so far ahead of you? But you will arrive before us, if you set your mind to it."

"I will rest a little," answered Senor Caballuco, adapting his horse's pace to that of our travellers' beasts, and attentively observing the most distinguished of the three, "since there is such good company."

"This gentleman," said Licurgo, smiling, "is the nephew of Dona Perfecta."

"Ah! At your service, senor."

The two men saluted each other, it being noticeable that Caballuco performed his civilities with an expression of haughtiness and superiority that revealed, at the very least, a consciousness of great importance, and of a high standing in the district. When the arrogant horseman rode aside to stop and talk for a moment with two Civil Guards who passed them on the road, the traveller asked his guide:

"Who is that odd character?"

"Who should it be? Caballuco."

"And who is Caballuco?"

"What! Have you never heard of Caballuco?" said the countryman, amazed at the crass ignorance of Dona Perfecta's nephew. "He is a very brave man, a fine rider, and the best connoisseur of horses in all the surrounding country. We think a great deal of him in Orbajosa; and he is well worthy of it. Just as you see him, he is a power in the place, and the governor of the province takes off his hat to him."

"When there is an election!"

"And the Governor of Madrid writes official letters to him with a great many titles in the superscription. He throws the bar like a St. Christopher, and he can manage every kind of weapon as easily as we manage our fingers. When there was market inspection here, they could never get the best of him, and shots were to be heard every night at the city gates. He has a following that is worth any money, for they are ready for anything. He is good to the poor, and any stranger who should come here and attempt to touch so much as a hair of the head of any native of Orbajosa would have him to settle with. It is very seldom that soldiers come here from Madrid, but whenever they do come, not a day passes without blood being shed, for Caballuco would pick a quarrel with them, if not for one thing for another. At present it seems that he is fallen into poverty and he is employed to carry the mail. But he is trying hard to persuade the Town Council to have a market-inspector's office here again and to put him in charge of it. I don't know how it is that you have never heard him mentioned in Madrid, for he is the son of a famous Caballuco who was in the last rebellion, and who was himself the son of another Caballuco, who was also in the rebellion of that day. And as there is a rumor now that there is going to be another insurrection—for the whole country is in a ferment—we are afraid that Caballuco will join that also, following in the illustrious footsteps of his father and his grandfather, who, to our glory be it said, were born in our city."

Our traveller was surprised to see the species of knight-errantry that still existed in the regions which he had come to visit, but he had no opportunity to put further questions, for the man who was the object of them now joined them, saying with an expression of ill-humor:

"The Civil Guard despatched three. I have already told the commander to be careful what he is about. To-morrow we will speak to the governor of the province, and I——"

"Are you going to X.?"

"No; but the governor is coming here, Senor Licurgo; do you know that they are going to send us a couple of regiments to Orbajosa?"

"Yes," said the traveller quickly, with a smile. "I heard it said in Madrid that there was some fear of a rising in this place. It is well to be prepared for what may happen."

"They talk nothing but nonsense in Madrid," exclaimed the Centaur violently, accompanying his affirmation with a string of tongue-blistering vocables. "In Madrid there is nothing but rascality. What do they send us soldiers for? To squeeze more contributions out of us and a couple of conscriptions afterward. By all that's holy! if there isn't a rising there ought to be. So you"—he ended, looking banteringly at the young man—"so you are Dona Perfecta's nephew?"

This abrupt question and the insolent glance of the bravo annoyed the young man.

"Yes, senor, at your service."

"I am a friend of the senora's, and I love her as I do the apple of my eye," said Caballuco. "As you are going to Orbajosa we shall see each other there."

And without another word he put spurs to his horse, which, setting off at a gallop, soon disappeared in a cloud of dust.

After half an hour's ride, during which neither Senor Don Jose nor Senor Licurgo manifested much disposition to talk, the travellers came in sight of an ancient-looking town seated on the slope of a hill, from the midst of whose closely clustered houses arose many dark towers, and, on a height above it, the ruins of a dilapidated castle. Its base was formed by a mass of shapeless walls, of mud hovels, gray and dusty looking as the soil, together with some fragments of turreted walls, in whose shelter about a thousand humble huts raised their miserable adobe fronts, like anaemic and hungry faces demanding an alms from the passer-by. A shallow river surrounded the town, like a girdle of tin, refreshing, in its course, several gardens, the only vegetation that cheered the eye. People were going into and coming out of the town, on horseback and on foot, and the human movement, although not great, gave some appearance of life to that great dwelling place whose architectural aspect was rather that of ruin and death than of progress and life. The innumerable and repulsive-looking beggars who dragged themselves on either side of the road, asking the obolus from the passer-by, presented a pitiful spectacle. It would be impossible to see beings more in harmony with, or better suited to the fissures of that sepulchre in which a city was not only buried but gone to decay. As our travellers approached the town, a discordant peal of bells gave token, with their expressive sound, that that mummy had still a soul.

It was called Orbajosa, a city that figures, not in the Chaldean or Coptic geography, but in that of Spain, with 7324 inhabitants, a town-hall, an episcopal seat, a court-house, a seminary, a stock farm, a high school, and other official prerogatives.

"The bells are ringing for high mass in the cathedral," said Uncle Licurgo. "We have arrived sooner than I expected."

"The appearance of your native city," said the young man, examining the panorama spread out before him, "could not be more disagreeable. The historic city of Orbajosa, whose name is no doubt a corruption of Urbs Augusta, looks like a great dunghill."

"All that can be seen from here is the suburbs," said the guide, in an offended tone. "When you enter the Calle Real and the Calle de Condestable, you will see handsome buildings, like the cathedral."

"I don't want to speak ill of Orbajosa before seeing it," said the young man. "And you must not take what I have said as a mark of contempt, for whether humble and mean, or stately and handsome, that city will always be very dear to me, not only is it my mother's native place, but because there are persons living in it whom I love without seeing them. Let us enter the august city, then."

They were now ascending a road on the outskirts of the town, and passing close to the walls of the gardens.

"Do you see that great house at the end of this large garden whose wall we are now passing?" said Uncle Licurgo, pointing to a massive, whitewashed wall belonging to the only dwelling in view which had the appearance of a cheerful and comfortable habitation.

"Yes; that is my aunt's house?"

"Exactly so! What we are looking at is the rear of the house. The front faces the Calle del Condestable, and it has five iron balconies that look like five castles. The fine garden behind the wall belongs to the house, and if you rise up in your stirrups you will be able to see it all from here."

"Why, we are at the house, then!" cried the young man. "Can we not enter from here?"

"There is a little door, but the senora had it condemned."

The young man raised himself in his stirrups and, stretching his neck as far as he could, looked over the wall.

"I can see the whole of the garden," he said. "There, under the trees, there is a woman, a girl, a young lady."

"That is Senorita Rosario," answered Licurgo.

And at the same time he also raised himself in his stirrups to look over the wall.

"Eh! Senorita Rosario!" he cried, making energetic signs with his right hand. "Here we are; I have brought your cousin with me."

"She has seen us," said the young man, stretching out his neck as far as was possible. "But if I am not mistaken, there is an ecclesiastic with her—a priest."

"That is the Penitentiary," answered the countryman, with naturalness.

"My cousin has seen us—she has left the priest, and is running toward the house. She is beautiful."

"As the sun!"

"She has turned redder than a cherry. Come, come, Senor Licurgo."

CHAPTER III

PEPE REY

Before proceeding further, it will be well to tell who Pepe Rey was, and what were the affairs which had brought him to Orbajosa.

When Brigadier Rey died in 1841, his two children, Juan and Perfecta, had just married: the latter the richest land-owner of Orbajosa, the former a young girl of the same city. The husband of Perfecta was called Don Manuel Maria Jose de Polentinos, and the wife of Juan, Maria Polentinos; but although they had the same surname, their relationship was somewhat distant and not very easy to make out. Juan Rey was a distinguished jurisconsult who had been graduated in Seville and had practised law in that city for thirty years with no less honor than profit. In 1845 he was left a widower with a son who was old enough to play mischievous pranks; he would sometimes amuse himself by constructing viaducts, mounds, ponds, dikes, and trenches of earth, in the yard of the house, and then flooding those fragile works with water. His father let him do so, saying, "You will be an engineer."

Perfecta and Juan had ceased to see each other from the time of their marriage, because the sister had gone to Madrid with her husband, the wealthy Polentinos, who was as rich as he was extravagant. Play and women had so completely enslaved Manuel Maria Jose that he would have dissipated all his fortune, if death had not been beforehand with him and carried him off before he had had time to squander it. In a night of orgy the life of the rich provincial, who had been sucked so voraciously by the leeches of the capital and the insatiable vampire of play, came to a sudden termination. His sole heir was a daughter a few months old. With the death of Perfecta's husband the terrors of the family were at an end, but the great struggle began. The house of Polentinos was ruined; the estates were in danger of being seized by the money-lenders; all was in confusion: enormous debts, lamentable management in Orbajosa, discredit and ruin in Madrid.

Perfecta sent for her brother, who, coming to the distressed widow's assistance, displayed so much diligence and skill that in a short time the greater part of the dangers that threatened her had disappeared. He began by obliging his sister to live in Orbajosa, managing herself her vast estates, while he faced the formidable pressure of the creditors in Madrid. Little by little the house freed itself from the enormous burden of its debts, for the excellent Don Juan Rey, who had the best way in the world for managing such matters, pleaded in the court, made settlements with the principal creditors and arranged to pay them by instalments, the result of this skilful management being that the rich patrimony of Polentinos was saved from ruin and might continue, for many years to come, to bestow splendor and glory on that illustrious family.

Perfecta's gratitude was so profound that in writing to her brother from Orbajosa, where she determined to reside until her daughter should be grown up, she said to him, among other affectionate things: "You have been more than a brother to me, more than a father to my daughter. How can either of us ever repay you for services so great? Ah, my dear brother? from the moment in which my daughter can reason and pronounce a name I will teach her to bless yours. My gratitude will end only with my life. Your unworthy sister regrets only that she can find no opportunity of showing you how much she loves you and of recompensing you in a manner suited to the greatness of your soul and the boundless goodness of your heart."

At the same time when these words were written Rosarito was two years old. Pepe Rey, shut up in a school in Seville, was making lines on paper, occupied in proving that "the sum of all the interior angles of any polygon is equal to twice as many right angles, wanting four, as the figure has sides." These vexatious commonplaces of the school kept him very busy. Year after year passed. The boy grew up, still continuing to make lines. At last, he made one which is called "From Tarragona to Montblanch." His first serious toy was the bridge, 120 metres in length, over the River Francoli.

During all this time Dona Perfecta continued to live in Orbajosa. As her brother never left Seville, several years passed without their seeing each other. A quarterly letter, as punctually written as it was punctually answered, kept in communication these two hearts, whose affection neither time nor distance could cool. In 1870, when Don Juan Rey, satisfied with having fulfilled his mission in society, retired from it and went to live in his fine house in Puerto Real, Pepe, who had been employed for several years in the works of various rich building companies, set out on a tour through Germany and England, for the purpose of study. His father's fortune, (as large as it is possible for a fortune which has only an honorable law-office for its source to be in Spain), permitted him to free himself in a short time from the yoke of material labor. A man of exalted ideas and with an ardent love for science, he found his purest enjoyment in the observation and study of the marvels by means of which the genius of the age furthers at the same time the culture and material comfort and the moral progress of man.

On returning from his tour his father informed him that he had an important project to communicate to him. Pepe supposed that it concerned some bridge, dockyard, or, at the least, the draining of some marsh, but Don Juan soon dispelled his error, disclosing to him his plan in the following words:

"This is March, and Perfecta's quarterly letter has not failed to come. Read it, my dear boy, and if you can agree to what that holy and exemplary woman, my dear sister, says in it, you will give me the greatest happiness I could desire in my old age. If the plan does not please you, reject it without hesitation, for, although your refusal would grieve me, there is not in it the shadow of constraint on my part. It would be unworthy of us both that it should be realized through the coercion of an obstinate father. You are free either to accept or to reject it, and if there is in your mind the slightest repugnance to it, arising either from your inclinations or from any other cause, I do not wish you to do violence to your feelings on my account."

Pepe laid the letter on the table after he had glanced through it, and said quietly:

"My aunt wishes me to marry Rosario!"

"She writes accepting joyfully my idea," said his father, with emotion. "For the idea was mine. Yes, it is a long time, a very long time since it occurred to me; but I did not wish to say anything to you until I knew what your sister might think about it. As you see, Perfecta receives my plan with joy; she says that she too had thought of it, but that she did not venture to mention it to me, because you are—you have seen what she says—because you are a young man of very exceptional merit and her daughter is a country girl, without either a brilliant education or worldly attractions. Those are her words. My poor sister! How good she is! I see that you are not displeased; I see that this project of mine, resembling a little the officious prevision of the fathers of former times who married their children without consulting their wishes in the matter, and making generally inconsiderate and unwise matches, does not seem absurd to you. God grant that this may be, as it seems to promise, one of the happiest. It is true that you have never seen your cousin, but we are both aware of her virtue, of her discretion, of her modest and noble simplicity. That nothing may be wanting, she is even beautiful. My opinion is," he added gayly, "that you should at once start for that out-of-the-way episcopal city, that Urbs Augusta, and there, in the presence of my sister and her charming Rosarito, decide whether the latter is to be something more to me or not, than my niece."

Pepe took up the letter again and read it through carefully. His countenance expressed neither joy nor sorrow. He might have been examining some plan for the junction of two railroads.

"In truth," said Don Juan, "in that remote Orbajosa, where, by the way, you have some land that you might take a look at now, life passes with the tranquillity and the sweetness of an idyl. What patriarchal customs! What noble simplicity! What rural and Virgilian peace! If, instead of being a mathematician, you were a Latinist, you would repeat, as you enter it, the *ergo tua rura manebunt*. What an admirable place in which to commune with one's own soul and to prepare one's self for good works. There all is kindness and goodness; there the deceit and hypocrisy of our great cities are unknown; there the holy inclinations which the turmoil of modern life stifles spring into being again; there dormant faith reawakens and one feels within the breast an impulse, vague but keen, like the impatience of youth, that from the depths of the soul cries out: 'I wish to live!'"

A few days after this conference Pepe left Puerto Real. He had refused, some months before, a commission from the government to survey, in its mineralogical aspects, the basin of the River Nahara, in the valley of Orbajosa; but the plans to which the conference above recorded gave rise, caused him to say to himself: "It will be as well to make use of the time. Heaven only knows how long this courtship may last, or what hours of weariness it may bring with it." He went, then, to Madrid, solicited the commission to explore the basin of the Nahara, which he obtained without difficulty, although he did not belong officially to the mining corps, set out shortly afterward, and, after a second change of trains, the mixed train No. 65 bore him, as we have seen, to the loving arms of Uncle Licurgo.

The age of our hero was about thirty-four years. He was of a robust constitution, of athletic build, and so admirably proportioned and of so commanding an appearance that, if he had worn a uniform, he would have presented the most martial air and figure that it is possible to imagine. His hair and beard were blond in color, but in his countenance there was none of the phlegmatic imperturbability of the Saxon, but, on the contrary, so much animation that his eyes, although they were not black, seemed to be so. His figure would have served as a perfect and beautiful model for a statue, on the pedestal of which the sculptor might engrave the words: "Intellect, strength." If not in visible characters, he bore them vaguely expressed in the brilliancy of his glance, in the potent attraction with which his person was peculiarly endowed, and in the sympathy which his cordial manners inspired.

He was not very talkative—only persons of inconstant ideas and unstable judgment are prone to verbosity. His profound moral sense made him sparing of words in the disputes in which the men of the day are prone to engage on any and every subject, but in polite conversation he displayed an eloquence full of wit and intelligence, emanating always from good sense and a temperate and just appreciation of worldly matters. He had no toleration for those sophistries, and mystifications, and quibbles of the understanding with which persons of intelligence, imbued with affected culture, sometimes amuse themselves; and in defence of the truth Pepe Rey employed at times, and not always with moderation, the weapon of ridicule. This was almost a defect in the eyes of many people who esteemed him, for our hero thus appeared wanting in respect for a multitude of things commonly accepted and believed. It must be acknowledged, although it may lessen him in the opinion of many, that Rey did not share the mild toleration of the compliant age which has invented strange disguises of words and of acts to conceal what to the general eye might be disagreeable.

Such was the man, whatever slanderous tongues may say to the contrary, whom Uncle Licurgo introduced into Orbajosa just as the cathedral bells were ringing for high mass. When, looking over the garden wall, they saw the young girl and the Penitentiary, and then the flight of the former toward the house, they put spurs to their beasts and entered the Calle Real, where a great many idlers stood still to gaze at the traveller, as if he were a stranger and an intruder in the patriarchal city. Turning presently to the right and riding in the direction of the cathedral, whose massive bulk dominated the town, they entered the Calle del Condestable, in which, being narrow and paved, the hoofs of the animals clattered noisily, alarming the people of the neighborhood, who came to the windows and to the balconies to satisfy their curiosity. Shutters opened with a grating sound and various faces, almost all feminine, appeared above and below. By the time Pepe Rey had reached the threshold of the house of Polentinos many and diverse comments had been already made on his person.

CHAPTER IV

THE ARRIVAL OF THE COUSIN

When Rosarito left him so abruptly the Penitentiary looked toward the garden wall, and seeing the faces of Licurgo and his companion, said to himself:

"So the prodigy is already here, then."

He remained thoughtful for some moments, his cloak, grasped with both hands, folded over his abdomen, his eyes fixed on the ground, his gold-rimmed spectacles slipping gently toward the point of his nose, his under-lip moist and projecting, and his iron-gray eyebrows gathered in a slight frown. He was a pious and holy man, of uncommon learning and of irreproachable clerical habits, a little past his sixtieth year, affable in his manners, courteous and kind, and greatly addicted to giving advice and counsel to both men and women. For many years past he had been master of Latin and rhetoric in the Institute, which noble profession had supplied him with a large fund of quotations from Horace and of florid metaphors, which he employed with wit and opportuneness. Nothing more need be said regarding this personage, but that, as soon as he heard the trot of the animals approaching the Calle del Condestable, he arranged the folds of his cloak, straightened his hat, which was not altogether correctly placed upon his venerable head, and, walking toward the house, murmured:

"Let us go and see this paragon."

Meanwhile Pepe was alighting from his nag, and Dona Perfecta, her face bathed in tears and barely able to utter a few trembling words, the sincere expression of her affection, was receiving him at the gate itself in her loving arms.

"Pepe—but how tall you are! And with a beard. Why, it seems only yesterday that I held you in my lap. And now you are a man, a grown-up man. Well, well! How the years pass! This is my daughter Rosario."

As she said this they reached the parlor on the ground floor, which was generally used as a reception-room, and Dona Perfecta presented her daughter to Pepe.

Rosario was a girl of delicate and fragile appearance, that revealed a tendency to pensive melancholy. In her delicate and pure countenance there was something of the soft, pearly pallor which most novelists attribute to their heroines, and without which sentimental varnish it appears that no Enriquieta or Julia can be interesting. But what chiefly distinguished Rosario was that her face expressed so much sweetness and modesty that the absence of the perfections it lacked was not observed. This is not to say that she was plain; but, on the other hand, it is true that it would be an exaggeration to call her beautiful in the strictest meaning of the word. The real beauty of Dona Perfecta's daughter consisted in a species of transparency, different from that of pearl, alabaster, marble, or any of the other substances used in descriptions of the human countenance; a species of transparency through which the inmost depths of her soul were clearly visible; depths not cavernous and gloomy, like those of the sea, but like those of a clear and placid river. But the material was wanting there for a complete personality. The channel was wanting, the banks were wanting. The vast wealth of her spirit overflowed, threatening to wash away the narrow borders. When her cousin saluted her she blushed crimson, and uttered only a few unintelligible words.

"You must be fainting with hunger," said Dona Perfecta to her nephew. "You shall have your breakfast at once."

"With your permission," responded the traveller, "I will first go and get rid of the dust of the journey."

"That is a sensible idea," said the senora. "Rosario, take your cousin to the room that we have prepared for him. Don't delay, nephew. I am going to give the necessary orders."

Rosario took her cousin to a handsome apartment situated on the ground floor. The moment he entered it Pepe recognized in all the details of the room the diligent and loving hand of a woman. All was arranged with perfect taste, and the purity and freshness of everything in this charming nest invited to repose. The guest observed minute details that made him smile.

"Here is the bell," said Rosario, taking in her hand the bell-rope, the tassel of which hung over the head of the bed. "All you have to do is to stretch out your hand. The writing-table is placed so that you will have the light from the left. See, in this basket you can throw the waste papers. Do you smoke?"

"Unfortunately, yes," responded Pepe Rey.

"Well, then, you can throw the ends of your cigars here," she said, touching with the tip of her shoe a utensil of gilt-brass filled with sand. "There is nothing uglier than to see the floor covered with cigar-ends. Here is the washstand. For your clothes you have a wardrobe and a bureau. I think this is a bad place for the watch-case; it would be better beside the bed. If the light annoys you, all you have to do is to lower the shade with this cord; see, this way."

The engineer was enchanted.

Rosarito opened one of the windows.

"Look," she said, "this window opens into the garden. The sun comes in here in the afternoon. Here we have hung the cage of a canary that sings as if he was crazy. If his singing disturbs you we will take it away."

She opened another window on the opposite side of the room.

"This other window," she continued, "looks out on the street. Look; from here you can see the cathedral; it is very handsome, and full of beautiful things. A great many English people come to see it. Don't open both windows at the same time, because draughts are very bad."

"My dear cousin," said Pepe, his soul inundated with an inexplicable joy; "in all that is before my eyes I see an angel's hand that can be only yours. What a beautiful room this is! It seems to me as if I had lived in it all my life. It invites to peace."

Rosarito made no answer to these affectionate expressions, and left the room, smiling.

"Make no delay," she said from the door; "the dining-room too is down stairs—in the centre of this hall."

Uncle Licurgo came in with the luggage. Pepe rewarded him with a liberality to which the countryman was not accustomed, and the latter, after humbly thanking the engineer, raised his hand to his head with a hesitating movement, and in an embarrassed tone, and mumbling his words, he said hesitatingly:

"When will it be most convenient for me to speak to Senor Don Jose about a—a little matter of business?"

"A little matter of business? At once," responded Pepe, opening one of his trunks.

"This is not a suitable time," said the countryman. "When Senor Don Jose has rested it will be time enough. There are more days than sausages, as the saying is; and after one day comes another. Rest now, Senor Don Jose. Whenever you want to take a ride—the nag is not bad. Well, good-day, Senor Don Jose. I am much obliged to you. Ah! I had forgotten," he added, returning a few moments later. "If you have any message for the municipal judge—I am going now to speak to him about our little affair."

"Give him my compliments," said Pepe gayly, no better way of getting rid of the Spartan legislator occurring to him.

"Good-by, then, Senor Don Jose."

"Good-by."

The engineer had not yet taken his clothes out of the trunk when for the third time the shrewd eyes and the crafty face of Uncle Licurgo appeared in the door-way.

"I beg your pardon, Senor Don Jose," he said, displaying his brilliantly white teeth in an affected smile, "but—I wanted to say that if you wish to settle the matter by means of friendly arbitrations—

— Although, as the saying is, 'Ask other people's opinion of something that concerns only yourself, and some will say it is white and others black.'"

"Will you get away from here, man?"

"I say that, because I hate the law. I don't want to have anything to do with the law. Well, good-by, again, Senor Don Jose. God give you long life to help the poor!"

"Good-by, man, good-by."

Pepe turned the key in the lock of the door, saying to himself:

"The people of this town appear to be very litigious."

CHAPTER V

WILL THERE BE DISSENSION?

A little later Pepe made his appearance in the dining-room.

"If you eat a hearty breakfast," said Dona Perfecta to him, in affectionate accents, "you will have no appetite for dinner. We dine here at one. Perhaps you may not like the customs of the country."

"I am enchanted with them, aunt."

"Say, then, which you prefer—to eat a hearty breakfast now, or to take something light, and keep your appetite for dinner."

"I prefer to take something light now, in order to have the pleasure of dining with you. But not even if I had found anything to eat in Villahorrenda, would I have eaten any thing at this early hour."

"Of course, I need not tell you that you are to treat us with perfect frankness. You may give your orders here as if you were in your own house."

"Thanks, aunt."

"But how like your father you are!" said the senora, regarding the young man, as he ate, with real delight. "I can fancy I am looking now at my dear brother Juan. He sat just as you are sitting and ate as you are eating. In your expression, especially, you are as like as two drops of water."

Pepe began his frugal breakfast. The words, as well as the manner and the expression, of his aunt and cousin inspired him with so much confidence that he already felt as if he were in his own house.

"Do you know what Rosario was saying to me this morning?" said Dona Perfecta, looking at her nephew. "Well, she was saying that, as a man accustomed to the luxuries and the etiquette of the capital and to foreign ways, you would not be able to put up with the somewhat rustic simplicity and the lack of ceremony of our manner of life; for here every thing is very plain."

"What a mistake!" responded Pepe, looking at his cousin. "No one abhors more than I do the falseness and the hypocrisy of what is called high society. Believe me, I have long wished to give myself a complete bath in nature, as some one has said; to live far from the turmoil of existence in the solitude and quiet of the country. I long for the tranquillity of a life without strife, without anxieties; neither envying nor envied, as the poet has said. For a long time my studies at first, and my work afterward, prevented me from taking the rest which I need, and which my mind and my body both require; but ever since I entered this house, my dear aunt, my dear cousin, I have felt myself surrounded by the peaceful atmosphere which I have longed for. You must not talk to me, then, of society, either high or low; or of the world, either great or small, for I would willingly exchange them all for this peaceful retreat."

While he was thus speaking, the glass door which led from the dining-room into the garden was obscured by the interposition between it and the light of a dark body. The glasses of a pair of spectacles, catching a sunbeam, sent forth a fugitive gleam; the latch creaked, the door opened, and the Penitentiary gravely entered the room. He saluted those present, taking off his broad-brimmed hat and bowing until its brim touched the floor.

"It is the Senor Penitentiary, of our holy cathedral," said Dona Perfecta: "a person whom we all esteem greatly, and whose friend you will, I hope, be. Take a seat, Senor Don Inocencio."

Pepe shook hands with the venerable canon, and both sat down.

"If you are accustomed to smoke after meals, pray do so," said Dona Perfecta amiably; "and the Senor Penitentiary also."

The worthy Don Inocencio drew from under his cassock a large leather cigar-case, which showed unmistakable signs of long use, opened it, and took from it two long cigarettes, one of which he offered to our friend. Rosario took a match from a little leaf-shaped matchbox, which the Spaniards ironically call a wagon, and the engineer and the canon were soon puffing their smoke over each other.

"And what does Senor Don Jose think of our dear city of Orbajosa?" asked the canon, shutting his left eye tightly, according to his habit when he smoked.

"I have not yet been able to form an idea of the town," said Pepe. "From the little I have seen of it, however, I think that half a dozen large capitalists disposed to invest their money here, a pair of intelligent heads to direct the work of renovating the place, and a couple of thousands of active hands to carry it out, would not be a bad thing for Orbajosa. Coming from the entrance to the town to the door of this house, I saw more than a hundred beggars. The greater part of them are healthy, and even robust men. It is a pitiable army, the sight of which oppresses the heart."

"That is what charity is for," declared Don Inocencio. "Apart from that, Orbajosa is not a poor town. You are already aware that the best garlic in all Spain is produced here. There are more than twenty rich families living among us."

"It is true," said Dona Perfecta, "that the last few years have been wretched, owing to the drought; but even so, the granaries are not empty, and several thousands of strings of garlic were recently carried to market."

"During the many years that I have lived in Orbajosa," said the priest, with a frown, "I have seen innumerable persons come here from the capital, some brought by the electoral hurly-burly, others to visit some abandoned site, or to see the antiquities of the cathedral, and they all talk to us about the English ploughs and threshing-machines and water-power and banks, and I don't know how many other absurdities. The burden of their song is that this place is very backward, and that it could be improved. Let them keep away from us, in the devil's name! We are well enough as we are, without the gentlemen from the capital visiting us; a great deal better off without hearing that continual clamor about our poverty and the grandeurs and the wonders of other places. The fool in his own house is wiser than the wise man in another's. Is it not so, Senor Don Jose? Of course, you mustn't imagine, even remotely, that I say this on your account. Not at all! Of course not! I know that we have before us one of the most eminent young men of modern Spain, a man who would be able to transform into fertile lands our arid wastes. And I am not at all angry because you sing us the same old song about the English ploughs and arboriculture and silviculture. Not in the least. Men of such great, such very great merit, may be excused for the contempt which they manifest for our littleness. No, no, my friend; no, no, Senor Don Jose! you are entitled to say any thing you please, even to tell us that we are not much better than Kaffirs."

This philippic, concluded in a marked tone of irony, and all of it impertinent enough, did not please the young man; but he refrained from manifesting the slightest annoyance and continued the conversation, endeavoring to avoid as far as possible the subjects in which the over-sensitive patriotism of the canon might find cause of offence. The latter rose when Dona Perfecta began to speak to her nephew about family matters, and took a few turns about the room.

This was a spacious and well-lighted apartment, the walls of which were covered with an old-fashioned paper whose flowers and branches, although faded, preserved their original pattern, thanks to the cleanliness which reigned in each and every part of the dwelling. The clock, from the case of which hung, uncovered, the apparently motionless weights and the voluble pendulum, perpetually repeating No, no, occupied, with its variegated dial, the most prominent place among the solid pieces of furniture of the dining-room, the adornment of the walls being completed by a series of French engravings representing the exploits of the conqueror of Mexico, with prolix explanations at the foot of each concerning a Ferdinand Cortez, and a Donna Marine, as little true to nature as were the figures delineated by the ignorant artist. In the space between the two glass doors which communicated with the garden was an apparatus of brass, which it is not necessary to describe further than to say that it served to support a parrot, which maintained itself on it with the air of gravity and circumspection peculiar to those animals, taking note of everything that went on. The hard and ironical expression of the parrot tribe, their green coats, their red caps, their yellow boots, and finally, the hoarse, mocking words which they generally utter, give them a strange and repulsive aspect, half serious, half-comic. There is in their air an indescribable something of the stiffness of diplomats. At times they remind one of buffoons, and they always resemble those absurdly conceited people who, in their desire to appear very superior, look like caricatures.

The Penitentiary was very fond of the parrot. When he left Dona Perfecta and Rosario conversing with the traveller, he went over to the bird, and, allowing it to bite his forefinger with the greatest good humor, said to it:

"Rascal, knave, why don't you talk? You would be of little account if you weren't a prater. The world of birds, as well as men, is full of praters."

Then, with his own venerable hand, he took some peas from the dish beside him, and gave them to the bird to eat. The parrot began to call to the maid, asking her for some chocolate, and its words diverted the two ladies and the young man from a conversation which could not have been very engrossing.

CHAPTER VI

IN WHICH IT IS SEEN THAT DISAGREEMENT MAY ARISE WHEN LEAST EXPECTED

Suddenly Don Cayetano Polentinos, Dona Perfecta's brother-in-law, appeared at the door, and entering the room with outstretched arms, cried:

"Let me embrace you, my dear Don Jose."

They embraced each other cordially. Don Cayetano and Pepe were already acquainted with each other, for the eminent scholar and bibliophile was in the habit of making a trip to Madrid whenever an executor's sale of the stock of some dealer in old books was advertised. Don Cayetano was tall and thin, of middle age, although constant study or ill-health had given him a worn appearance; he expressed himself with a refined correctness which became him admirably, and he was affectionate and amiable in his manners, at times to excess. With respect to his vast learning, what can be said but that he was a real prodigy? In Madrid his name was always mentioned with respect, and if Don Cayetano had lived in the capital, he could not have escaped becoming a member, in spite of his modesty, of every academy in it, past, present, and to come. But he was fond of quiet and retirement, and the place which vanity occupies in the souls of others, a pure passion for books, a love of solitary and secluded study, without any other aim or incentive than the books and the study themselves, occupied in his.

He had formed in Orbajosa one of the finest libraries that is to be found in all Spain, and among his books he passed long hours of the day and of the night, compiling, classifying, taking notes, and selecting various sorts of precious information, or composing, perhaps, some hitherto unheard-of and undreamed-of work, worthy of so great a mind. His habits were patriarchal; he ate little, drank less, and his only dissipations consisted of a luncheon in the Alamillos on very great occasions, and daily walks to a place called Mundogrande, where were often disinterred from the accumulated dust of twenty centuries, medals, bits of architecture, and occasionally an amphora or cubicularia of inestimable value.

Don Cayetano and Dona Perfecta lived in such perfect harmony that the peace of Paradise was not to be compared to it. They never disagreed. It is true that Don Cayetano never interfered in the affairs of the house nor Dona Perfecta in those of the library, except to have it swept and dusted every Saturday, regarding with religious respect the books and papers that were in use on the table or anywhere else in the room.

After the questions and answers proper to the occasion had been interchanged Don Cayetano said:

"I have already looked at the books. I am very sorry that you did not bring me the edition of 1527. I shall have to make a journey to Madrid myself. Are you going to remain with us long? The longer the better, my dear Pepe. How glad I am to have you here! Between us both we will arrange a part of my library and make an index of the writers on the Art of Horsemanship. It is not always one has at hand a man of your talents. You shall see my library. You can take your fill of reading there—as often as you like. You will see marvels, real marvels, inestimable treasures, rare works that no one but myself has a copy of. But I think it must be time for dinner, is it not, Jose? Is it not, Perfecta? Is it not, Rosarito? Is it not, Senor Don Inocencio? To-day you are doubly a Penitentiary—I mean because you will accompany us in doing penance."

The canon bowed and smiled, manifesting his pleased acquiescence. The dinner was substantial, and in all the dishes there was noticeable the excessive abundance of country banquets, realized at the expense of variety. There was enough to surfeit twice as many persons as sat down to table. The conversation turned on various subjects.

"You must visit our cathedral as soon as possible," said the canon. "There are few cathedrals like ours, Senor Don Jose! But of course you, who have seen so many wonders in foreign countries, will find nothing remarkable in our old church. We poor provincials of Orbajosa, however, think it divine. Master Lopez of Berganza, one of the prebendaries of the cathedral, called it in the sixteenth century *pulchra augustissima*. But perhaps for a man of your learning it would possess no merit, and some market constructed of iron would seem more beautiful."

The ironical remarks of the wily canon annoyed Pepe Rey more and more every moment, but, determined to control himself and to conceal his anger, he answered only with vague words. Dona Perfecta then took up the theme and said playfully:

"Take care, Pepito; I warn you that if you speak ill of our holy church we shall cease to be friends. You know a great deal, you are a man eminent for your knowledge on every subject, but if you are going to discover that that grand edifice is not the eighth wonder of the world you will do well to keep your knowledge to yourself and leave us in our ignorance."

"Far from thinking that the building is not handsome," responded Pepe, "the little I have seen of its exterior has seemed to me of imposing beauty. So there is no need for you to be alarmed, aunt. And I am very far from being a savant."

"Softly; softly," said the canon, extending his hand and giving his mouth a truce from eating in order to talk. "Stop there—don't come now pretending modesty, Senor Don Jose; we are too well aware of your great merit, of the high reputation you enjoy and the important part you play wherever you are, for that. Men like you are not to be met with every day. But now that I have extolled your merits in this way——"

He stopped to eat a mouthful, and when his tongue was once more at liberty he continued thus:

"Now that I have extolled your merits in this way, permit me to express a different opinion with the frankness which belongs to my character. Yes, Senor Don Jose, yes, Senor Don Cayetano; yes, senora and senorita, science, as the moderns study and propagate it, is the death of sentiment and of every sweet illusion. Under its influence the life of the spirit declines, every thing is reduced to fixed rules, and even the sublime charms of nature disappear. Science destroys the marvellous in the arts, as well as faith in the soul. Science says that every thing is a lie, and would reduce every thing to figures and lines, not only *maria ac terras*, where we are, but *coelumque profundum*, where God is. The wonderful visions of the soul, its mystic raptures, even the inspiration of the poets, are all a lie. The heart is a sponge; the brain, a place for breeding maggots."

Every one laughed, while the canon took a draught of wine.

"Come, now, will Senor Don Jose deny," continued the ecclesiastic, "that science, as it is taught and propagated to-day, is fast making of the world and of the human race a great machine?"

"That depends," said Don Cayetano. "Every thing has its *pro* and its *contra*."

"Take some more salad, Senor Penitentiary," said Dona Perfecta; "it is just as you like it—with a good deal of mustard."

Pepe Rey was not fond of engaging in useless discussions; he was not a pedant, nor did he desire to make a display of his learning, and still less did he wish to do so in the presence of women, and in a private re-union; but the importunate and aggressive verbosity of the canon required, in his opinion, a corrective. To flatter his vanity by agreeing with his views would, he thought, be a bad way to give it to him, and he determined therefore to express only such opinions as should be most directly opposed to those of the sarcastic Penitentiary and most offensive to him.

"So you wish to amuse yourself at my expense," he said to himself. "Wait, and you will see what a fine dance I will lead you."

Then he said aloud:

"All that the Senor Penitentiary has said ironically is the truth. But it is not our fault if science overturns day after day the vain idols of the past: its superstitions, its sophisms, its innumerable fables—beautiful, some of them, ridiculous others—for in the vineyard of the Lord grow both good fruit and bad. The world of illusions, which is, as we might say, a second world, is tumbling about us in ruins. Mysticism in religion, routine in science, mannerism in art, are falling, as the Pagan gods fell, amid jests. Farewell, foolish dreams! the human race is awakening and its eyes behold the light. Its vain sentimentalism, its mysticism, its fevers, its hallucination, its delirium are passing away, and he who was before sick is now well and takes an ineffable delight in the just appreciation of things. Imagination, the terrible madwoman, who was the mistress of the house, has become the servant. Look around you, Senor Penitentiary, and you will see the admirable aggregation of truths which has taken the place of fable. The sky is not a vault; the stars are not little lamps; the moon is not a sportive huntress, but an opaque mass of stone; the sun is not a gayly adorned and vagabond charioteer but a fixed fire; Scylla and Charybdis are not nymphs but sunken rocks; the sirens are seals; and in the order of personages, Mercury is Manzanedo; Mars is a clean-shaven old man, the Count von Moltke; Nestor may be a gentleman in an overcoat, who is called M. Thiers; Orpheus is Verdi; Vulcan is Krupp; Apollo is any poet. Do you wish more? Well, then, Jupiter, a god who, if he were living now, would deserve to be put in jail, does not launch the thunderbolt, but the thunderbolt falls when electricity wills it. There is no Parnassus; there is no Olympus; there is no Stygian lake; nor are there any other Elysian Fields than those of Paris. There is no other descent to hell than the descents of Geology, and this traveller, every time he returns from it, declares that there are no damned souls in the centre of the earth. There are no other ascents to heaven than those of Astronomy, and she, on her return, declares that she has not seen the six or seven circles of which Dante and the mystical dreamers of the Middle Ages speak. She finds only stars and distances, lines, vast spaces, and nothing more. There are now no false computations of the age of the earth, for paleontology and prehistoric research have counted the teeth of this skull in which we live and discovered the true age. Fable, whether it be called paganism or Christian idealism, exists no longer, and imagination plays only a secondary part. All the miracles possible are such as I work, whenever I desire to do so, in my laboratory, with my Bunsen pile, a conducting wire, and a magnetized needle. There are now no other multiplications of loaves and fishes than those which Industry makes, with her moulds and her machines, and those of the printing press, which imitates Nature, taking from a single type millions of copies. In short, my dear canon, orders have been given to put on the retired list all the absurdities, lies, illusions, dreams, sentimentalities, and prejudices which darken the understanding of man. Let us rejoice at the fact."

When Pepe finished speaking, a furtive smile played upon the canon's lips and his eyes were extraordinarily animated. Don Cayetano busied himself in giving various forms—now rhomboidal, now prismatic—to a little ball of bread. But Dona Perfecta was pale and kept her eyes fixed on the canon with observant insistence. Rosarito looked with amazement at her cousin. The latter, bending toward her, whispered under his breath:

"Don't mind me, little cousin; I am talking all this nonsense only to enrage the canon."

CHAPTER VII

THE DISAGREEMENT INCREASES

"Perhaps you think," said Dona Perfecta, with a tinge of conceit in her tones, "that Senor Don Inocencio is going to remain silent and not give you an answer to each and every one of those points."

"Oh, no!" exclaimed the canon, arching his eyebrows. "I will not attempt to measure my poor abilities with a champion so valiant and at the same time so well armed. Senor Don Jose knows every thing; that is to say, he has at his command the whole arsenal of the exact sciences. Of course I know that the doctrines he upholds are false; but I have neither the talent nor the eloquence to combat them. I would employ theological arguments, drawn from revelation, from faith, from the Divine Word; but alas! Senor Don Jose, who is an eminent savant, would laugh at theology, at faith, at revelation, at the holy prophets, at the gospel. A poor ignorant priest, an unhappy man who knows neither mathematics, nor German philosophy with its *ego* and its *non ego*, a poor dominie, who knows only the science of God and something of the Latin poets, cannot enter into combat with so valiant a champion."

Pepe Rey burst into a frank laugh.

"I see that Senor Don Inocencio," he said, "has taken seriously all the nonsense I have been talking. Come, Senor Canon, regard the whole matter as a jest, and let it end there. I am quite sure that my opinions do not in reality differ greatly from yours. You are a pious and learned man; it is I who am ignorant. If I have allowed myself to speak in jest, pardon me, all of you—that is my way."

"Thanks!" responded the presbyter, visibly annoyed. "Is that the way you want to get out of it now? I am well aware, we are all well aware, that the views you have sustained are your own. It could not be otherwise. You are the man of the age. It cannot be denied that you have a wonderful, a truly wonderful intellect. While you were talking, at the same time that I inwardly deplored errors so great, I could not but admire, I will confess it frankly, the loftiness of expression, the prodigious fluency, the surprising method of your reasoning, the force of your arguments. What a head, Senora Dona Perfecta, what a head your young nephew has! When I was in Madrid and they took me to the Atheneum, I confess that I was amazed to see the wonderful talent which God has bestowed on the atheists and the Protestants."

"Senor Don Inocencio," said Dona Perfecta, looking alternately at her nephew and her friend, "I think that in judging this boy you are more than benevolent. Don't get angry, Pepe, or mind what I say, for I am neither a savante, nor a philosopher, nor a theologian; but it seems to me that Senor Don Inocencio has just given a proof of his great modesty and Christian charity in not crushing you as he could have done if he had wished."

"Oh, senora!" said the ecclesiastic.

"That is the way with him," continued Dona Perfecta, "always pretending to know nothing. And he knows more than the seven doctors put together. Ah, Senor Don Inocencio, how well the name you have suits you! But don't affect an unseasonable humility now. Why, my nephew has no pretensions. All he knows is what he has been taught. If he has been taught error, what more can he desire than that you should enlighten him and take him out of the limbo of his false doctrines?"

"Just so; I desire nothing more than that the Senor Penitentiary should take me out,"—murmured Pepe, comprehending that without intending it, he had got himself into a labyrinth.

"I am a poor priest, whose only learning is some knowledge of the ancients," responded Don Inocencio. "I recognize the immense value, from a worldly point of view, of Senor Don Jose's scientific knowledge, and before so brilliant an oracle I prostrate myself and am silent."

So saying, the canon folded his hands across his breast and bent his head. Pepe Rey was somewhat disturbed because of the turn which his mind had chosen to give to an idle discussion jestingly followed up, and in which he had engaged only to enliven the conversation a little. He thought that the most prudent course to pursue would be to end at once so dangerous a debate, and for this purpose he addressed a question to Senor Don Cayetano when the latter, shaking off the drowsiness which had overcome him after the dessert, offered the guests the indispensable toothpicks stuck in a china peacock with outspread tail.

"Yesterday I discovered a hand grasping the handle of an amphora, on which there are a number of hieratic characters. I will show it to you," said Don Cayetano, delighted to introduce a favorite theme.

"I suppose that Senor de Rey is very expert in archaeological matters also," said the canon, who, still implacable, pursued his victim to his last retreat.

"Of course," said Dona Perfecta. "What is there that these clever children of our day do not understand? They have all the sciences at their fingers' ends. The universities and the academics teach them every thing in a twinkling, giving them a patent of learning."

"Oh, that is unjust!" responded the canon, observing the pained expression of the engineer's countenance.

"My aunt is right," declared Pepe. "At the present day we learn a little of every thing, and leave school with the rudiments of various studies."

"I was saying," continued the canon, "that you are no doubt a great archaeologist."

"I know absolutely nothing of that science," responded the young man. "Ruins are ruins, and I have never cared to cover myself with dust going among them."

Don Cayetano made an expressive grimace.

"That is not to say that I condemn archaeology," said Dona Perfecta's nephew quickly, observing with pain that he could not utter a word without wounding some one. "I know that from that dust issues history. Those studies are delightful and very useful."

"You," said the Penitentiary, putting his toothpick into the last of his back teeth, "are no doubt more inclined to controversial studies. An excellent idea has just occurred to me, Senor Don Jose; you ought to be a lawyer."

"Law is a profession which I abhor," replied Pepe Rey. "I know many estimable lawyers, among them my father, who is the best of men; but, in spite of so favorable a specimen, I could never had brought myself to practise a profession which consists in defending with equal readiness the *pro* and the *contra* of a question. I know of no greater misjudgment, no greater prejudice, no greater blindness, than parents show in their eagerness to dedicate their sons to the law. The chief and the most terrible plague of Spain is the crowd of our young lawyers, for whose existence a fabulous number of lawsuits are necessary. Lawsuits multiply in proportion to the demand. And even thus, numbers are left without employment, and, as a jurisconsult cannot put his hand to the plough or seat himself at the loom, the result is that brilliant squadron of idlers full of pretensions, who clamor for places, embarrass the administration, agitate public opinion, and breed revolutions. In some way they must make a living. It would be a greater misfortune if there were lawsuits enough for all of them."

"Pepe, for Heaven's sake, take care what you say," said Dona Perfecta, in a tone of marked severity. "But excuse him, Senor Don Inocencio, for he is not aware that you have a nephew who, although he has only lately left the university, is a prodigy in the law."

"I speak in general terms," said Pepe, with firmness. "Being, as I am, the son of a distinguished lawyer, I cannot be ignorant of the fact that there are many men who practise that noble profession with honor to themselves."

"No; my nephew is only a boy yet," said the canon, with affected humility. "Far be it from me to assert that he is a prodigy of learning, like Senor de Rey. In time, who can tell? His talents are neither brilliant nor seductive. Of course, Jacinto's ideas are solid and his judgment is sound. What he knows he knows thoroughly. He is unacquainted with sophistries and hollow phrases."

Pepe Rey appeared every moment more and more disturbed. The idea that, without desiring it, his opinions should be in opposition to those of the friends of his aunt, vexed him, and he resolved to remain silent lest he and Don Inocencio should end by throwing the plates at each other's heads. Fortunately the cathedral bell, calling the canon to the important duties of the choir, extricated him from his painful position. The venerable ecclesiastic rose and took leave of every one, treating Rey with as much amiability and kindness as if they had been old and dear friends. The canon, after offering his services to Pepe for all that he might require, promised to present his nephew to him in order that the young man might accompany him to see the town, speaking in the most affectionate terms and deigning, on leaving the room, to pat him on the shoulder. Pepe Rey, accepting with pleasure these formulas of concord, nevertheless felt indescribably relieved when the priest had left the dining-room and the house.

CHAPTER VIII

IN ALL HASTE

A little later the scene had changed. Don Cayetano, finding rest from his sublime labors in a gentle slumber that had overcome him after dinner, reclined comfortably in an arm-chair in the dining-room. Rosarito, seated at one of the windows that opened into the garden, glanced at her cousin, saying to him with the mute eloquence of her eyes:

"Cousin, sit down here beside me and tell me every thing you have to say to me."

Her cousin, mathematician though he was, understood.

"My dear cousin," said Pepe, "how you must have been bored this afternoon by our disputes! Heaven knows that for my own pleasure I would not have played the pedant as I did; the canon was to blame for it. Do you know that that priest appears to me to be a singular character?"

"He is an excellent person!" responded Rosarito, showing the delight she felt at being able to give her cousin all the data and the information that he might require.

"Oh, yes! An excellent person. That is very evident!"

"When you know him a little better, you will see that."

"That he is beyond all price! But it is enough for him to be your friend and your mamma's to be my friend also," declared the young man. "And does he come here often?"

"Every day. He spends a great deal of his time with us," responded Rosarito ingenuously. "How good and kind he is! And how fond he is of me!"

"Come! I begin to like this gentleman."

"He comes in the evening, besides, to play tresillo," continued the young girl; "for every night some friends meet here—the judge of the lower court, the attorney-general, the dean, the bishop's secretary, the alcalde, the collector of taxes, Don Inocencio's nephew——"

"Ah! Jacintito, the lawyer."

"Yes; he is a simple-hearted boy, as good as gold. His uncle adores him. Since he returned from the university with his doctor's tassel—for he is a doctor in two sciences, and he took honors besides—what do you think of that?—well, as I was saying, since his return, he has come here very often with his uncle. Mamma too is very fond of him. He is a very sensible boy. He goes home early with his uncle; he never goes at night to the Casino, nor plays nor squanders money, and he is employed in the office of Don Lorenzo Ruiz, who is the best lawyer in Orbajosa. They say Jacinto will be a great lawyer, too."

"His uncle did not exaggerate when he praised him, then," said Pepe. "I am very sorry that I talked all that nonsense I did about lawyers. I was very perverse, was I not, my dear cousin?"

"Not at all; for my part, I think you were quite right."

"But, really, was I not a little—"

"Not in the least, not in the least!"

"What a weight you have taken off my mind! The truth is that I found myself constantly, and without knowing why, in distressing opposition to that venerable priest. I am very sorry for it."

"What I think," said Rosarito, looking at him with eyes full of affection, "is that you will not find yourself at home among us."

"What do you mean by that?"

"I don't know whether I can make myself quite clear, cousin. I mean that it will not be easy for you to accustom yourself to the society and the ideas of the people of Orbajosa. I imagine so—it is a supposition."

"Oh, no! I think you are mistaken."

"You come from a different place, from another world, where the people are very clever, and very learned, and have refined manners, and a witty way of talking, and an air—perhaps I am not making myself clear. I mean that you are accustomed to live among people of refinement; you know a great deal. Here there is not what you need; here the people are not learned or very polished. Every thing is plain, Pepe. I imagine you will be bored, terribly bored, and that in the end you will have to go away."

The expression of sadness which was natural in Rosarito's countenance here became so profound that Pepe Rey was deeply moved.

"You are mistaken, my dear cousin. I did not come here with the ideas you fancy, nor is there between my character and my opinions and the character and opinions of the people here the want of harmony you imagine. But let us suppose for a moment that there were."

"Let us suppose it."

"In that case I have the firm conviction that between you and me, between us two, dear Rosarito, perfect harmony would still exist. On this point I cannot be mistaken. My heart tells me that I am not mistaken."

Rosarito blushed deeply, but making an effort to conceal her embarrassment under smiles and fugitive glances, she said:

"Come, now, no pretences. But if you mean that I shall always approve of what you say, you are right."

"Rosario," exclaimed the young man, "the moment I saw you my soul was filled with gladness; I felt at the same time a regret that I had not come before to Orbajosa."

"Now, that I am not going to believe," she said, affecting gayety to conceal her emotion. "So soon? Don't begin to make protestations already. See, Pepe, I am only a country girl, I can talk only about common things; I don't know French; I don't dress with elegance; all I know is how to play the piano; I——"

"Oh, Rosario!" cried the young man, with ardor; "I believed you to be perfect before; now I am sure you are so."

Her mother at this moment entered the room. Rosarito, who did not know what to say in answer to her cousin's last words, was conscious, however, of the necessity of saying something, and, looking at her mother, she cried:

"Ah! I forgot to give the parrot his dinner."

"Don't mind that now. But why do you stay in here? Take your cousin for a walk in the garden."

Dona Perfecta smiled with maternal kindness at her nephew, as she pointed toward the leafy avenue which was visible through the glass door.

"Let us go there," said Pepe, rising.

Rosarito darted, like a bird released from its cage, toward the glass door.

"Pepe, who knows so much and who must understand all about trees," said Dona Perfecta, "will teach you how to graft. Let us see what he thinks of those young pear-trees that they are going to transplant."

"Come, come!" called Rosarito to her cousin impatiently from the garden.

Both disappeared among the foliage. Dona Perfecta watched them until they were out of sight and then busied herself with the parrot. As she changed its food she said to herself with a contemplative air:

"How different he is! He has not even given a caress to the poor bird."

Then, thinking it possible that she had been overheard by her brother-in-law, she said aloud:

"Cayetano, what do you think of my nephew? Cayetano!"

A low grunt gave evidence that the antiquary was returning to the consciousness of this miserable world.

"Cayetano!"

"Just so, just so!" murmured the scientist in a sleepy voice. "That young gentleman will maintain, as every one does, that the statues of Mundogrande belong to the first Phoenician immigration. But I will convince him—"

"But, Cayetano!"

"But, Perfecta! There! Now you will insist upon it again that I have been asleep."

"No, indeed; how could I insist upon any thing so absurd! But you haven't told me what you think about that young man."

Don Cayetano placed the palm of his hand before his mouth to conceal a yawn; then he and Dona Perfecta entered upon a long conversation. Those who have transmitted to us the necessary data for a compilation of this history omit this dialogue, no doubt because it was entirely confidential. As for what the engineer and Rosarito said in the garden that afternoon, it is evident that it was not worthy of mention.

On the afternoon of the following day, however, events took place which, being of the gravest importance, ought not to be passed over in silence. Late in the afternoon the two cousins found themselves alone, after rambling through different parts of the garden in friendly companionship and having eyes and ears only for each other.

"Pepe," Rosario was saying, "all that you have been telling me is pure fancy, one of those stories that you clever men know so well how to put together. You think that because I am a country girl I believe every thing I am told."

"If you understood me as well as I think I understand you, you would know that I never say any thing I do not mean. But let us have done with foolish subtleties and lovers' sophistries, that lead only to misunderstandings. I will speak to you only in the language of truth. Are you by chance a young lady whose acquaintance I have made on the promenade or at a party, and with whom I propose to spend a pleasant hour or two? No, you are my cousin. You are something more. Rosario, let us at once put things on their proper footing. Let us drop circumlocutions. I have come here to marry you."

Rosario felt her face burning, and her heart was beating violently.

"See, my dear cousin," continued the young man. "I swear to you that if you had not pleased me I should be already far away from this place. Although politeness and delicacy would have obliged me to make an effort to conceal my disappointment, I should have found it hard to do so. That is my character."

"Cousin, you have only just arrived," said Rosarito laconically, trying to laugh.

"I have only just arrived, and I already know all that I wanted to know; I know that I love you; that you are the woman whom my heart has long been announcing to me, saying to me night and day, 'Now she is coming, now she is near; now you are burning.'"

These words served Rosario as an excuse for breaking into the laugh that had been dimpling her lips. Her soul swelled with happiness; she breathed an atmosphere of joy.

"You persist in depreciating yourself," continued Pepe, "but for me you possess every perfection. You have the admirable quality of radiating on all around you the divine light of your soul. The moment one sees you one feels instinctively the nobility of your mind and the purity of your heart. To see you is to see a celestial being who, through the forgetfulness of Heaven, remains upon the earth; you are an angel, and I adore you."

When he had said this it seemed as if he had fulfilled an important mission. Rosarito, overcome by the violence of her emotion, felt her scant strength suddenly fail her; and, half-fainting, she sank on a stone that in those pleasant solitudes served as a seat. Pepe bent over her. Her eyes were closed, her forehead rested on the palm of her hand. A few moments later the daughter of Dona Perfecta Polentinos gave her cousin, amid happy tears, a tender glance followed by these words:

"I loved you before I had ever seen you."

Placing her hands in those of the young man she rose to her feet, and their forms disappeared among the leafy branches of an oleander walk. Night was falling and soft shadows enveloped the lower end of the garden, while the last rays of the setting sun crowned the tree-tops with fleeting splendors. The noisy republic of the birds kept up a deafening clamor in the upper branches. It was the hour in which, after flitting about in the joyous regions of the sky, they were all going to rest, and they were disputing with one another the branches they had selected for sleeping-places. Their chatter at times had a sound of recrimination and controversy, at times of mockery and merriment. In their voluble twitter the little rascals said the most insulting things to each other, pecking at each other and flapping their wings, as orators wave their arms when they want to make their hearers believe the lies they are telling them. But words of love were to be heard there too, for the peace of the hour and the beauty of the spot invited to it. A sharp ear might have distinguished the following:

"I loved you before I had even seen you, and if you had not come I should have died of grief. Mamma used to give me your father's letters to read, and he praised you so much in them that I used to say, 'That is the man who ought to be my husband.' For a long time your father said nothing about our marrying, which seemed to me great negligence. Uncle Cayetano, whenever he spoke of you, would say, 'There are not many men like him in the world. The woman who gets him for a husband may think herself fortunate.' At last your father said what he could not avoid saying. Yes, he could not avoid saying it—I was expecting it every day."

Shortly after these words the same voice added uneasily: "Some one is following us."

Emerging from among the oleanders, Pepe, turning round, saw two men approaching them, and touching the leaves of a young tree near by, he said aloud to his companion:

"It is not proper to prune young trees like this for the first time until they have taken firm root. Trees recently planted have not sufficient strength to bear the operation. You know that the roots can grow only by means of the leaves, so that if you take the leaves from a tree—"

"Ah, Senor Don Jose," cried the Penitentiary, with a frank laugh, approaching the two young people and bowing to them, "are you giving lessons in horticulture? *Insere nunc Meliboee piros; pone ordine vites*, as the great singer of the labors of the field said. 'Graft the pear-tree, dear Meliboeus, trim the vines.' And how are we now, Senor Don Jose?"

The engineer and the canon shook hands. Then the latter turned round, and indicating by a gesture a young man who was behind him, said, smiling:

"I have the pleasure of presenting to you my dear Jacintillo—a great rogue, a feather-head, Senor Don Jose."

CHAPTER IX

THE DISAGREEMENT CONTINUES TO INCREASE, AND THEREAFTER TO BECOME DISCORD

Close beside the black cassock was a fresh and rosy face, that seemed fresher and rosier from the contrast. Jacinto saluted our hero, not without some embarrassment.

He was one of those precocious youths whom the indulgent university sends prematurely forth into the arena of life, making them fancy that they are men because they have received their doctor's degree. Jacinto had a round, handsome face with rosy cheeks, like a girl's, and without any beard save the down which announced its coming. In person he was plump and below the medium height. His age was a little over twenty. He had been educated from childhood under the direction of his excellent and learned uncle, which is the same as saying that the twig had not become crooked in the growing. A severe moral training had kept him always straight, and in the fulfilment of his scholastic duties he had been almost above reproach. Having concluded his studies at the university with astonishing success, for there was scarcely a class in which he did not take the highest honors, he entered on the practice of his profession, promising, by his application and his aptitude for the law, to maintain fresh and green in the forum the laurels of the lecture-hall.

At times he was as mischievous as a boy, at times as sedate as a man. In very truth, if Jacinto had not had a little, and even a great deal of liking for pretty girls, his uncle would have thought him perfect. The worthy man preached to him unceasingly on this point, hastening to clip the wings of every audacious fancy. But not even this mundane inclination of the young man could cool the great affection which our worthy canon bore the charming offspring of his dear niece, Maria Remedios. Where the young lawyer was concerned, every thing else must give way. Even the grave and methodical habits of the worthy ecclesiastic were altered when they interfered with the affairs of his precocious pupil. That order and regularity, apparently as fixed as the laws of a planetary system, were interrupted whenever Jacinto was ill or had to take a journey. Useless celibacy of the clergy! The Council of Trent prohibits them from having children of their own, but God—and not the Devil, as the proverb says—gives them nephews and nieces in order that they may know the tender anxieties of paternity.

Examining impartially the qualities of this clever boy, it was impossible not to recognize that he was not wanting in merit. His character was in the main inclined to uprightness, and noble actions awakened a frank admiration in his soul. With respect to his intellectual endowments and his social knowledge, they were sufficient to enable him to become in time one of those notabilities of whom there are so many in Spain; he might be what we take delight in calling hyperbolically a distinguished patrician, or an eminent public man; species which, owing to their great abundance, are hardly appreciated at their just value. In the tender age in which the university degree serves as a sort of solder between boyhood and manhood, few young men—especially if they have been spoiled by their masters—are free from an offensive pedantry, which, if it gives them great importance beside their mamma's arm-chair, makes them very ridiculous when they are among grave and experienced men. Jacinto had this defect, which was excusable in him, not only because of his youth, but also because his worthy uncle stimulated his puerile vanity by injudicious praise.

When the introduction was over they resumed their walk. Jacinto was silent. The canon, returning to the interrupted theme of the *pyros* which were to be grafted and the*vites* which were to be trimmed, said:

"I am already aware that Senor Don Jose is a great agriculturist."

"Not at all; I know nothing whatever about the subject," responded the young man, observing with no little annoyance the canon's mania of supposing him to be learned in all the sciences.

"Oh, yes! a great agriculturist," continued the Penitentiary; "but on agricultural subjects, don't quote the latest treatises to me. For me the whole of that science, Senor de Rey, is condensed in what I call the Bible of the Field, in the 'Georgics' of the immortal Roman. It is all admirable, from that grand sentence, *Nec vero terroe ferre omnes omnia possunt*—that is to say, that not every soil is suited to every tree, Senor Don Jose—to the exhaustive treatise on bees, in which the poet describes the habits of those wise little animals, defining the drone in these words:

"'Ille horridus alter
Desidia, latamque trahens inglorius alvum.'

"'Of a horrible and slothful figure, dragging along the ignoble weight of the belly,' Senor Don Jose."

"You do well to translate it for me," said Pepe, "for I know very little Latin."

"Oh, why should the men of the present day spend their time in studying things that are out of date?" said the canon ironically. "Besides, only poor creatures like Virgil and Cicero and Livy wrote in Latin. I, however, am of a different way of thinking; as witness my nephew, to whom I have taught that sublime language. The rascal knows it better than I do. The worst of it is, that with his modern reading he is forgetting it; and some fine day, without ever having suspected it, he will find out that he is an ignoramus. For, Senor Don Jose, my nephew has taken to studying the newest books and the most extravagant theories, and it is Flammarion here and Flammarion there, and nothing will do him but that the stars are full of people. Come, I fancy that you two are going to be very good friends. Jacinto, beg this gentleman to teach you the higher mathematics, to instruct you concerning the German philosophers, and then you will be a man."

The worthy ecclesiastic laughed at his own wit, while Jacinto, delighted to see the conversation turn on a theme so greatly to his taste, after excusing himself to Pepe Rey, suddenly hurled this question at him:

"Tell me, Senor Don Jose, what do you think of Darwinism?"

Our hero smiled at this inopportune pedantry, and he felt almost tempted to encourage the young man to continue in this path of childish vanity; but, judging it more prudent to avoid intimacy, either with the nephew or the uncle, he answered simply:

"I can think nothing at all about the doctrines of Darwin, for I know scarcely any thing about him. My professional labors have not permitted me to devote much of my time to those studies."

"Well," said the canon, laughing, "it all reduces itself to this, that we are descended from monkeys. If he had said that only in the case of certain people I know, he would have been right."

"The theory of natural selection," said Jacinto emphatically, "has, they say, a great many partisans in Germany."

"I do not doubt it," said the ecclesiastic. "In Germany they would have no reason to be sorry if that theory were true, as far as Bismarck is concerned."

Dona Perfecta and Senor Don Cayetano at this moment made their appearance.

"What a beautiful evening!" said the former. "Well, nephew, are you getting terribly bored?"

"I am not bored in the least," responded the young man.

"Don't try to deny it. Cayetano and I were speaking of that as we came along. You are bored, and you are trying to hide it. It is not every young man of the present day who would have the self-denial to spend his youth, like Jacinto, in a town where there are neither theatres, nor opera bouffe, nor dancers, nor philosophers, nor athenaeums, nor magazines, nor congresses, nor any other kind of diversions or entertainments."

"I am quite contented here," responded Pepe. "I was just now saying to Rosario that I find this city and this house so pleasant that I would like to live and die here."

Rosario turned very red and the others were silent. They all sat down in a summer-house, Jacinto hastening to take the seat on the left of the young girl.

"See here, nephew, I have a piece of advice to give you," said Dona Perfecta, smiling with that expression of kindness that seemed to emanate from her soul, like the aroma from the flower. "But don't imagine that I am either reproving you or giving you a lesson—you are not a child, and you will easily understand what I mean."

"Scold me, dear aunt, for no doubt I deserve it," replied Pepe, who was beginning to accustom himself to the kindnesses of his father's sister.

"No, it is only a piece of advice. These gentlemen, I am sure, will agree that I am in the right."

Rosario was listening with her whole soul.

"It is only this," continued Dona Perfecta, "that when you visit our beautiful cathedral again, you will endeavor to behave with a little more decorum while you are in it."

"Why, what have I done?"

"It does not surprise me that you are not yourself aware of your fault," said his aunt, with apparent good humor. "It is only natural; accustomed as you are to enter athenaeums and clubs, and academies and congresses without any ceremony, you think that you can enter a temple in which the Divine Majesty is in the same manner."

"But excuse me, senora," said Pepe gravely, "I entered the cathedral with the greatest decorum."

"But I am not scolding you, man; I am not scolding you. If you take it in that way I shall have to remain silent. Excuse my nephew, gentlemen. A little carelessness, a little heedlessness on his part is not to be wondered at. How many years is it since you set foot in a sacred place before?"

"Senora, I assure you——But, in short, let my religious ideas be what they may, I am in the habit of observing the utmost decorum in church."

"What I assure you is——There, if you are going to be offended I won't go on. What I assure you is that a great many people noticed it this morning. The Senores de Gonzalez, Dona Robustiana, Serafinita—in short, when I tell you that you attracted the attention of the bishop——His lordship complained to me about it this afternoon when I was at my cousin's. He told me that he did not order you to be put out of the church only because you were my nephew."

Rosario looked anxiously at her cousin, trying to read in his countenance, before he uttered it, the answer he would make to these charges.

"No doubt they mistook me for some one else."

"No, no! it was you. But there, don't get angry! We are talking here among friends and in confidence. It was you. I saw you myself."

"You saw me!"

"Just so. Will you deny that you went to look at the pictures, passing among a group of worshippers who were hearing mass? I assure you that my attention was so distracted by your comings and goings that—well, you must not do it again. Then you went into the chapel of San Gregorio. At the elevation of the Host at the high altar you did not even turn around to make a gesture of reverence. Afterward you traversed the whole length of the church, you went up to the tomb of the Adelantado, you touched the altar with your hands, then you passed a second time among a group of worshippers, attracting the notice of every one. All the girls looked at you, and you seemed pleased at disturbing so finely the devotions of those good people."

"Good Heavens! How many things I have done!" exclaimed Pepe, half angry, half amused. "I am a monster, it seems, without ever having suspected it."

"No, I am very well aware that you are a good boy," said Dona Perfecta, observing the canon's expression of unalterable gravity, which gave his face the appearance of a pasteboard mask. "But, my dear boy, between thinking things and showing them in that irreverent manner, there is a distance which a man of good sense and good breeding should never cross. I am well aware that your ideas are——Now, don't get angry! If you get angry, I will be silent. I say that it is one thing to have certain ideas about religion and another thing to express them. I will take good care not to reproach you because you believe that God did not create us in his image and likeness, but that we are descended from the monkeys; nor because you deny the existence of the soul, asserting that it is a drug, like the little papers of rhubarb and magnesia that are sold at the apothecary's—"

"Senora, for Heaven's sake!" exclaimed Pepe, with annoyance. "I see that I have a very bad reputation in Orbajosa."

The others remained silent.

"As I said, I will not reproach you for entertaining those ideas. And, besides, I have not the right to do so. If I should undertake to argue with you, you, with your wonderful talents, would confute me a thousand times over. No, I will not attempt any thing of that kind. What I say is that these poor and humble inhabitants of Orbajosa are pious and good Christians, although they know nothing about German philosophy, and that, therefore, you ought not publicly to manifest your contempt for their beliefs."

"My dear aunt," said the engineer gravely, "I have shown no contempt for any one, nor do I entertain the ideas which you attribute to me. Perhaps I may have been a little wanting in reverence in the church. I am somewhat absent-minded. My thoughts and my attention were engaged with the architecture of the building and, frankly speaking, I did not observe——But this was no reason for the bishop to think of putting me out of the church, nor for you to suppose me capable of attributing to a paper from the apothecary's the functions of the soul. I may tolerate that as a jest, but only as a jest."

The agitation of Pepe Rey's mind was so great that, notwithstanding his natural prudence and moderation, he was unable to conceal it.

"There! I see that you are angry," said Dona Perfecta, casting down her eyes and clasping her hands. "I am very sorry. If I had known that you would have taken it in that way, I should not have spoken to you. Pepe, I ask your pardon."

Hearing these words and seeing his kind aunt's deprecating attitude, Pepe felt ashamed of the sternness of his last words, and he made an effort to recover his serenity. The venerable Penitentiary extricated him from his embarrassing position, saying with his accustomed benevolent smile:

"Senora Dona Perfecta, we must be tolerant with artists. Oh, I have known a great many of them! Those gentlemen, when they have before them a statue, a piece of rusty armor, a mouldy painting, or an old wall, forget every thing else. Senor Don Jose is an artist, and he has visited our cathedral as the English visit it, who would willingly carry it away with them to their museums, to its last tile, if they could. That the worshippers were praying, that the priest was elevating the Sacred Host, that the moment of supreme piety and devotion had come—what of that? What does all that matter to an artist? It is true that I do not know what art is worth, apart from the sentiments which it expresses, but, in fine, at the present day, it is the custom to adore the form, not the idea. God preserve me from undertaking to discuss this question with Senor Don Jose, who knows so much, and who, reasoning with the admirable subtlety of the moderns, would instantly confound my mind, in which there is only faith."

"The determination which you all have to regard me as the most learned man on earth annoys me exceedingly," said Pepe, speaking in his former hard tone. "Hold me for a fool; for I would rather be regarded as a fool than as the possessor of that Satanic knowledge which is here attributed to me."

Rosarito laughed, and Jacinto thought that a highly opportune moment had now arrived to make a display of his own erudition.

"Pantheism or panentheism," he said, "is condemned by the Church, as well as by the teachings of Schopenhauer and of the modern Hartmann."

"Ladies and gentlemen," said the canon gravely, "men who pay so fervent a worship to art, though it be only to its form, deserve the greatest respect. It is better to be an artist, and delight in the contemplation of beauty, though this be only represented by nude nymphs, than to be indifferent and incredulous in every thing. The mind that consecrates itself to the contemplation of beauty, evil will not take complete possession of. *Est Deus in nobis*. *Deus*, be it well understood. Let Senor Don Jose, then, continue to admire the marvels of our church; I, for one, will willingly forgive him his acts of irreverence, with all due respect for the opinions of the bishop."

"Thanks, Senor Don Inocencio," said Pepe, feeling a bitter and rebellious sentiment of hostility springing up within him toward the canon, and unable to conquer his desire to mortify him. "But let none of you imagine, either, that it was the beauties of art, of which you suppose the temple to be full, that engaged my attention. Those beauties, with the exception of the imposing architecture of a portion of the edifice and of the three tombs that are in the chapel of the apse, I do not see. What occupied my mind was the consideration of the deplorable decadence of the religious arts; and the innumerable monstrosities, of which the cathedral is full, caused me not astonishment, but disgust."

The amazement of all present was profound.

"I cannot endure," continued Pepe, "those glazed and painted images that resemble so much—God forgive me for the comparison—the dolls that little girls pay with. And what am I to say of the theatrical robes that cover them? I saw a St. Joseph with a mantle whose appearance I will not describe, out of respect for the holy patriarch and for the church of which he is the patron. On the altar are crowded together images in the worst possible taste; and the innumerable crowns, branches, stars, moons, and other ornaments of metal or gilt paper have an air of an ironmongery that offends the religious sentiment and depresses the soul. Far from lifting itself up to religious contemplation, the soul sinks, and the idea of the ludicrous distracts it. The great works of art which give sensible form to ideas, to dogmas, to religious faith, to mystic exaltation, fulfil a noble mission. The caricatures, the aberrations of taste, the grotesque works with which a mistaken piety fills the church, also fulfil their object; but this is a sad one enough: They encourage superstition, cool enthusiasm, oblige the eyes of the believer to turn away from the altar, and, with the eyes, the souls that have not a very profound and a very firm faith turn away also."

"The doctrine of the iconoclasts, too," said Jacinto, "has, it seems, spread widely in Germany."

"I am not an iconoclast, although I would prefer the destruction of all the images to the exhibition of buffooneries of which I speak," continued the young man. "Seeing it, one may justly advocate a return of religious worship to the august simplicity of olden times. But no; let us not renounce the admirable aid which all the arts, beginning with poetry and ending with music, lend to the relations between man and God. Let the arts live; let the utmost pomp be displayed in religious ceremonies. I am a partisan of pomp."

"An artist, an artist, and nothing more than an artist!" exclaimed the canon, shaking his head with a sorrowful air. "Fine pictures, fine statues, beautiful music; pleasure for the senses, and let the devil take the soul!"

"Apropos of music," said Pepe Rey, without observing the deplorable effect which his words produced on both mother and daughter, "imagine how disposed my mind would be to religious contemplation on entering the cathedral, when just at that moment, and precisely at the offertory at high mass, the organist played a passage from 'Traviata.'"

"Senor de Rey is right in that," said the little lawyer emphatically. "The organist played the other day the whole of the drinking song and the waltz from the same opera, and afterward a rondeau from the 'Grande Duchesse.'"

"But when I felt my heart sink," continued the engineer implacably, "was when I saw an image of the Virgin, which seems to be held in great veneration, judging from the crowd before it and the multitude of tapers which lighted it. They have dressed her in a puffed-out garment of velvet, embroidered with gold, of a shape so extraordinary that it surpasses the most extravagant of the fashions of the day. Her face is almost hidden under a voluminous frill, made of innumerable rows of lace, crimped with a crimping-iron, and her crown, half a yard in height, surrounded by golden rays, looks like a hideous catafalque erected over her head. Of the same material, and embroidered in the same manner, are the trousers of the Infant Jesus. I will not go on, for to describe the Mother and the Child might perhaps lead me to commit some irreverence. I will only say that it was impossible for me to keep from smiling, and for a short time I contemplated the profaned image, saying to myself: 'Mother and Lady mine, what a sight they have made of you!'"

As he ended Pepe looked at his hearers, and although, owing to the gathering darkness, he could not see their countenances distinctly, he fancied that in some of them he perceived signs of angry consternation.

"Well, Senor Don Jose!" exclaimed the canon quickly, smiling with a triumphant expression, "that image, which to your philosophy and pantheism appears so ridiculous, is Our Lady of Help, patroness and advocate of Orbajosa, whose inhabitants regard her with so much veneration that they would be quite capable of dragging any one through the streets who should speak ill of her. The chronicles and history, Senor Don Jose, are full of the miracles which she has wrought, and even at the present day we receive constantly incontrovertible proofs of her protection. You must know also that your aunt, Dona Perfecta, is chief lady in waiting to the Most Holy Virgin of Help, and that the dress that to you appears so grotesque—went out from this house, and that the trousers of the Infant are the work of the skilful needle and the ardent piety combined of your cousin Rosarito, who is now listening to us."

Pepe Rey was greatly disconcerted. At the same instant Dona Perfecta rose abruptly from her seat, and, without saying a word, walked toward the house, followed by the Penitentiary. The others rose also. Recovering from his stupefaction, the young man was about to beg his cousin's pardon for his irreverence, when he observed that Rosarito was weeping. Fixing on her cousin a look of friendly and gentle reproof, she said:

"What ideas you have!"

The voice of Dona Perfecta was heard crying in an altered accent:

"Rosario! Rosario!"

The latter ran toward the house.

CHAPTER X

THE EVIDENCE OF DISCORD IS EVIDENT

Pepe Rey was disturbed and perplexed, enraged with himself and every one else; he tried in vain to imagine what could be the conflict that had arisen, in spite of himself, between his ideas and the ideas of his aunt's friends. Thoughtful and sad, foreseeing future discord, he remained for a short time sitting on the bench in the summer-house, his chin resting on his breast, his forehead gathered in a frown, his hands clasped. He thought himself alone.

Suddenly he heard a gay voice humming the refrain of a song from a zarzuela. He looked up and saw Don Jacinto sitting in the opposite corner of the summer-house.

"Ah, Senor de Rey!" said the youth abruptly, "one does not offend with impunity the religious sentiments of the great majority of a nation. If you doubt it, consider what happened in the first French revolution."

When Pepe heard the buzzing of this insect his irritation increased. Nevertheless there was no anger in his soul toward the youthful doctor of laws. The latter annoyed him, as a fly might annoy him, but nothing more. Rey felt the irritation which every importunate being inspires, and with the air of one who brushes away a buzzing drone, he answered:

"What has the French revolution to do with the robe of the Virgin?"

He got up and walked toward the house, but he had not taken half a dozen steps before he heard again beside him the buzzing of the mosquito, saying:

"Senor Don Jose, I wish to speak to you about an affair in which you are greatly interested and which may cause you some trouble."

"An affair?" said the young man, drawing back. "Let us hear what affair is that."

"You suspect what it is, perhaps," said Jacinto, approaching Pepe, and smiling with the air of a man of business who has some unusually important matter on hand; "I want to speak to you about the lawsuit."

"The lawsuit! My friend, I have no lawsuits. You, as a good lawyer, dream of lawsuits and see stamped paper everywhere."

"What! You have not heard of your lawsuit?" exclaimed the youth, with amazement.

"Of my lawsuit! But I have no lawsuits, nor have I ever had any."

"Well, if you have not heard of it, I am all the better pleased to have spoken to you about it, so that you may be on your guard. Yes, senor, you are going to have a suit at law."

"And with whom?"

"With Uncle Licurgo and other land-owners whose property borders on the estate called The Poplars."

Pepe Rey was astounded.

"Yes, senor," continued the little lawyer. "To-day Uncle Licurgo and I had a long conference. As I am such a friend of the family, I wanted to let you know about it, so that, if you think well of it, you may hasten to arrange the matter."

"But what have I to arrange? What do those rascals claim from me?"

"It seems that a stream of water which rises in your property has changed its course and flows over some tile-works of the aforesaid Uncle Licurgo and the mill of another person, occasioning considerable damage. My client—for he is determined that I shall get him out of this difficulty—my client, as I said, demands that you shall restore the water to its former channel, so as to avoid fresh injuries, and that you shall indemnify him for the damage which his works have already sustained through the neglect of the superior proprietor."

"And I am the superior proprietor! If I engage in a lawsuit, that will be the first fruit that those famous Poplars, which were mine and which now, as I understand, belong to everybody, will have ever produced me, for Licurgo, as well as some of the other farmers of the district, have been filching from me, little by little, year after year, pieces of land, and it will be very difficult to re-establish the boundaries of my property."

"That is a different question."

"That is not a different question. The real suit," exclaimed the engineer, unable to control his anger, "will be the one that I will bring against that rabble who no doubt propose to themselves to tire me out and drive me to desperation—so that I may abandon every thing and let them continue in possession of what they have stolen. We shall see if there are lawyers and judges who will uphold the infamous conduct of those village legists, who are forever at law, and who waste and consume the property of others. I am obliged to you, young gentleman, for having informed me of the villanous intentions of those boors, who are more perverse than Satan himself. When I tell you that that very tile-yard and that very mill on which Licurgo bases his claim are mine—"

"The title-deeds of the property ought to be examined, to see if possession may not constitute a title in this case."

"Possession! Those scoundrels are not going to have the pleasure of laughing at me in that way. I suppose that justice is honestly and faithfully administered in the city of Orbajosa."

"Oh, as to that!" exclaimed the little lawyer, with an approving look, "the judge is an excellent person! He comes here every evening. But it is strange that you should have received no notice of Senor Licurgo's claims. Have you not yet been summoned to appear before the tribunal of arbitration?"

"No."

"It will be to-morrow, then. Well, I am very sorry that Senor Licurgo's precipitation has deprived me of the pleasure and honor of defending you, but what is to be done? Licurgo was determined that I should take him out of his troubles. I will study the matter with the greatest care. This vile slavery is the great drawback of jurisprudence."

Pepe entered the dining-room in a deplorable state of mind. Dona Perfecta was talking with the Penitentiary, as he entered, and Rosarito was sitting alone, with her eyes fixed on the door. She was no doubt waiting for her cousin.

"Come here, you rascal," said his aunt, smiling with very little spontaneity. "You have insulted us, you great atheist! but we forgive you. I am well aware that my daughter and myself are two rustics who are incapable of soaring to the regions of mathematics where you dwell, but for all that it is possible that you may one day get down on your knees to us and beg us to teach you the Christian doctrine."

Pepe answered with vague phrases and formulas of politeness and repentance.

"For my part," said Don Inocencio, with an affected air of meekness and amiability, "if in the course of these idle disputes I have said any thing that could offend Senor Don Jose, I beg his pardon for it. We are all friends here."

"Thanks. It is of no consequence."

"In spite of every thing," said Dona Perfecta, smiling with more naturalness than before, "I shall always be the same for my dear nephew; in spite of his extravagant and anti-religious ideas. In what way do you suppose I am going to spend this evening? Well, in trying to make Uncle Licurgo give up those obstinate notions which would otherwise cause you annoyance. I sent for him, and he is waiting for me now in the hall. Make yourself easy, I will arrange the matter; for although I know that he is not altogether without right on his side—"

"Thanks, dear aunt," responded the young man, his whole being invaded by a wave of the generous emotion which was so easily aroused in his soul.

Pepe Rey looked in the direction of his cousin, intending to join her, but some wily questions of the canon retained him at Dona Perfecta's side. Rosario looked dejected, and was listening with an air of melancholy indifference to the words of the little lawyer, who, having installed himself at her side, kept up a continuous stream of fulsome flatteries, seasoned with ill-timed jests and fatuous remarks in the worst possible taste.

"The worst of it is," said Dona Perfecta to her nephew—surprising the glance which he cast in the direction of the ill-assorted pair—"the worst of it is, that you have offended poor Rosario. You must do all in your power to make your peace with her. The poor child is so good!"

"Oh, yes! so good," added the canon, "that I have no doubt that she will forgive her cousin."

"I think that Rosario has already forgiven me," affirmed Rey.

"And if not, angelic breasts do not harbor resentment long," said Don Inocencio mellifluously. "I have a great deal of influence with the child, and I will endeavor to dissipate in her generous soul whatever prejudice may exist there against you. As soon as I say a word or two to her——"

Pepe Rey felt a cloud darken his soul and he said with meaning:

"Perhaps it may not be necessary."

"I will not speak to her now," added the capitular, "because she is listening entranced to Jacinto's nonsense. Ah, those children! When they once begin there is no stopping them."

The judge of the lower court, the alcalde's lady, and the dean of the cathedral now made their appearance. They all saluted the engineer, manifesting in their words and manner, on seeing him, the satisfaction of gratified curiosity. The judge was one of those clever and intelligent young men who every day spring into notice in official circles; aspiring, almost before they are out of the shell, to the highest political and administrative positions. He gave himself airs of great importance, and in speaking of himself and of his juvenile toga, he seemed indirectly to manifest great offence because he had not been all at once made president of the supreme court. In such inexpert hands, in a brain thus swollen with vanity, in this incarnation of conceit, had the state placed the most delicate and the most difficult functions of human justice. His manners were those of a perfect courtier, and revealed a scrupulous and minute attention to all that concerned his own person. He had the insufferable habit of taking off and putting on every moment his gold eye-glasses, and in his conversation he manifested with frequency the strong desire which he had to be transferred to Madrid, in order that he might give his invaluable services to the Department of Grace and Justice.

The alcalde's lady was a good-natured woman, whose only weakness was to fancy that she had a great many acquaintances at the court. She asked Pepe Rey various questions about the fashions, mentioning establishments in which she had had a mantle or a skirt made on her last journey to the capital, contemporaneous with the visit of Muley-Abbas, and she also mentioned the names of a dozen duchesses and marchionesses; speaking of them with as much familiarity as if they had been friends of her school-days. She said also that the Countess of M. (famous for her parties) was a friend of hers and that in '60 she had paid her a visit, when the countess had invited her to her box at the Teatro Real, where she saw Muley-Abbas in Moorish dress and accompanied by his retinue of Moors. The alcalde's wife talked incessantly and was not wanting in humor.

The dean was a very old man, corpulent and red-faced, plethoric and apoplectic looking, a man so obese that he seemed bursting out of his skin. He had belonged to one of the suppressed religious orders; he talked only of religious matters; and from the very first manifested the most profound contempt for Pepe Rey. The latter appeared every moment more unable to accommodate himself to a society so little to his taste. His disposition—not at all malleable, hard, and very little flexible—rejected the duplicities and the compromises of language to simulate concord when it did not exist. He remained, then, very grave during the whole of the tiresome evening, obliged as he was to endure the oratorical vehemence of the alcalde's wife, who, without being Fame, had the privilege of fatiguing with a hundred tongues the ears of men. If, in some brief respite which this lady gave her hearers, Pepe Rey made an attempt to approach his cousin, the Penitentiary attached himself to him instantly, like the mollusk to the rock; taking him apart with a mysterious air to propose to him an excursion with Senor Don Cayetano to Mundogrande, or a fishing party on the clear waters of the Nahara.

At last the evening came to an end, as every thing does in this world. The dean retired, leaving the house, as it seemed, empty, and very soon there remained of the alcalde's wife only an echo, like the buzz which remains in the air after a storm has passed away. The judge also deprived the company of his presence, and at last Don Inocencio gave his nephew the signal for departure.

"Come, boy, come; for it is late," he said, smiling. "How you have tormented poor Rosarito, has he not, child? Home, you rogue, home, without delay."

"It is time to go to bed," said Dona Perfecta.

"Time to go to work," responded the little lawyer.

"I am always telling him that he ought to get through with his business in the day-time, but he will not mind me."

"There is so much, so very much business to be got through."

"No, say rather, that confounded work which you have undertaken. He does not wish to say it, Senor Don Jose, but the truth is that he is writing a book on 'The Influence of Woman in Christian Society,' and, in addition to that, 'A Glance at the Catholic Movement in'—somewhere or other. What do you know about glances or influences? But these youths of the present day have audacity enough for any thing. Oh, what boys! Well, let us go home. Good-night, Senora Dona Perfecta—good-night, Senor Don Jose—Rosarito."

"I will wait for Senor Don Cayetano," said Jacinto, "to ask him to give me the Augusto Nicolas."

"Always carrying books. Why, sometimes you come into the house laden like a donkey. Very well, then, let us wait."

"Senor Don Jacinto does not write hastily," said Pepe Rey; "he prepares himself well for his work, so that his books may be treasures of learning."

"But that boy will injure his brain," objected Dona Perfecta. "For Heaven's sake be careful! I would set a limit to his reading."

"Since we are going to wait," said the little doctor, in a tone of insufferable conceit, "I will take with me also the third volume of Concilios. What do you think, uncle?"

"Take that, of course. It would never do to leave that behind you."

Fortunately Senor Don Cayetano (who generally spent his evenings at the house of Don Lorenzo Ruiz) soon arrived, and the books being received, uncle and nephew left the house.

Rey read in his cousin's sad countenance a keen desire to speak to him. He approached her while Dona Perfecta and Don Cayetano were discussing some domestic matter apart.

"You have offended mamma," said Rosarito.

Her features expressed something like terror.

"It is true," responded the young man; "I have offended your mamma—I have offended you."

"No, not me. I already imagined that the Infant Jesus ought not to wear trousers."

"But I hope that you will both forgive me. Your mamma was so kind to me a little while ago."

Dona Perfecta's voice suddenly vibrated through the dining-room, with so discordant a tone that her nephew started as if he had heard a cry of alarm. The voice said imperiously:

"Rosario, go to bed!"

Startled, her mind filled with anxious fears, the girl lingered in the room, going here and there as if she was looking for something. As she passed her cousin she whispered softly and cautiously these words:

"Mamma is angry."

"But—"

"She is angry—be on your guard, be on your guard."

Then she left the room. Her mother, for whom Uncle Licurgo was waiting, followed her, and for some time the voices of Dona Perfecta and the countryman were heard mingled together in familiar conference. Pepe was left with Don Cayetano, who, taking a light, said;

"Good-night, Pepe. But don't suppose that I am going to sleep, I am going to work. But why are you so thoughtful? What is the matter with you?—Just as I say, to work. I am making notes for a 'Memorial Discourse on the Genealogies of Orbajosa.' I have already found data and information of the utmost value. There can be no dispute about it. In every period of our history the Orbajosans have been distinguished for their delicate sense of honor, their chivalry, their valor, their intellectuality. The conquest of Mexico, the wars of the Emperor, the wars of Philip against the heretics, testify to this. But are you ill? What is the matter with you? As I say, eminent theologians, valiant warriors, conquerors, saints, bishops, statesmen—all sorts of illustrious men—have flourished in this humble land of the garlic. No, there is not in Christendom a more illustrious city than ours. Its virtues and its glories are in themselves enough and more than enough to fill all the pages of our country's history. Well, I see that it is sleepy you are—good-night. As I say, I would not exchange the glory of being a son of this noble city for all the gold in the world. Augusta, the ancients called it; Augustissima, I call it now; for now, as then, high-mindedness, generosity, valor, magnanimity, are the patrimony of all. Well, good-night, dear Pepe. But I fancy you are not well.

Has the supper disagreed with you?—Alonzo Gonzalez de Bustamante was right when he said in his 'Floresta Amena' that the people of Orbajosa suffice in themselves to confer greatness and honor on a kingdom. Don't you think so?"

"Oh, yes, senor; undoubtedly," responded Pepe Rey, going abruptly toward his room.

CHAPTER XI

THE DISCORD GROWS

During the following days Pepe Rey made the acquaintance of several of the people of the place; he visited the Casino, and formed friendships with some of the individuals who spend their lives in the rooms of that corporation.

But the youth of Orbajosa did not spend all their time in the Casino, as evil-minded people might imagine. In the afternoons there were to be seen at the corner of the cathedral, and in the little plaza formed by the intersection of the Calle del Condestable and the Calle de la Triperia, several gentlemen who, gracefully enveloped in their cloaks, stood there like sentinels, watching the people as they passed by. If the weather was fine, those shining lights of the Urbs Augustan culture bent their steps, still enveloped in the indispensable cloak, toward the promenade called the Paseo de las Descalzas, which was formed by a double row of consumptive-looking elms and some withered bushes of broom. There the brilliant Pleiad watched the daughters of this fellow-townsman or that, who had also come there for a walk, and the afternoon passed tolerably. In the evening, the Casino filled up again; and while some of the members gave their lofty minds to the delights of monte, others read the newspapers, while the majority discussed in the coffee-room subjects of the various kinds, such as the politics, horses, bulls, or the gossip of the place. The result of every discussion was the renewed conviction of the supremacy of Orbajosa and its inhabitants over all the other towns and peoples on the face of the earth.

These distinguished men were the cream of the illustrious city; some rich landowners, others very poor, but all alike free from lofty aspirations. They had the imperturbable tranquillity of the beggar who desires nothing more so long as he has a crust of bread with which to cheat hunger, and the sun to warm him. What chiefly distinguished the Orbajosans of the Casino was a sentiment of bitter hostility toward all strangers, and whenever any stranger of note appeared in its august halls, they believed that he had come there to call in question the superiority of the land of the garlic, or to dispute with it, through envy, the incontestable advantages which nature had bestowed upon it.

When Pepe Rey presented himself in the Casino, they received him with something of suspicion, and as facetious persons abounded in it, before the new member had been there a quarter of an hour, all sorts of jokes had been made about him. When in answer to the reiterated questions of the members he said that he had come to Orbajosa with a commission to explore the basin of the Nahara for coal, and to survey a road, they all agreed that Senor Don Jose was a conceited fellow who wished to give himself airs, discovering coalbeds and planning railroads. Some one added:

"He has come to a bad place for that, then. Those gentlemen imagine that here we are all fools, and that they can deceive us with fine words. He has come to marry Dona Perfecta's daughter, and all that he says about coalbeds is only for the sake of appearances."

"Well, this morning," said another, a merchant who had failed, "they told me at the Dominguez' that the gentleman has not a peseta, and that he has come here in order to be supported by his aunt and to see if he can catch Rosarito."

"It seems that he is no engineer at all," added an olive-planter, whose plantations were mortgaged for double their value. "But it is as you say: those starvelings from Madrid think they are justified in deceiving poor provincials, and as they believe that here we all wear tails—"

"It is plain to be seen that he is penniless—"

"Well, half-jest and the whole earnest, he told us last night that we were lazy barbarians."

"That we spent our time sunning ourselves, like the Bedouins."

"That we lived with the imagination."

"That's it; that we lived with the imagination."

"And that this city was precisely like a city in Morocco."

"Well! one has no patience to listen to those things. Where else could he see (unless it might be in Paris) a street like the Calle del Condestable, that can show seven houses in a row, all of them magnificent, from Dona Perfecta's house to that of Nicolasita Hernandez? Does that fellow suppose that one has never seen any thing, or has never been in Paris?"

"He also said, with a great deal of delicacy, that Orbajosa was a city of beggars; and he gave us to understand that in his opinion we live in the meanest way here without being ourselves aware of it."

"What insolence! If he ever says that to me, there will be a scene in the Casino," exclaimed the collector of taxes. "Why didn't they tell him how many arrobas of oil Orbajosa produced last year? Doesn't the fool know that in good years Orbajosa produces wheat enough to supply all Spain, and even all Europe, with bread? It is true that the crops have been bad for several years past, but that is not the rule. And the crop of garlic! I wager the gentleman doesn't know that the garlic of Orbajosa made the gentleman of the jury in the Exposition of London stare!"

These and other conversations of a similar kind were to be heard in the rooms of the Casino in those days. Notwithstanding this boastful talk, so common in small towns, which, for the very reason that they are small, are generally arrogant, Rey was not without finding sincere friends among the members of the learned corporation, for they were not all gossips, nor were there wanting among them persons of good sense. But our hero had the misfortune—if misfortune it can be called—to be unusually frank in the manifestation of his feelings, and this awakened some antipathy toward him.

Days passed. In addition to the natural disgust which the social customs of the episcopal city produced in him, various causes, all of them disagreeable, began to develop in his mind a profound sadness, chief among these causes being the crowd of litigants that swarmed about him like voracious ants. Many others of the neighboring landowners besides Uncle Licurgo claimed damages from him, or asked him to render accounts for lands managed by his grandfather. A claim was also brought against him because of a certain contract of partnership entered into by his mother and which, as it appeared, had not been fulfilled; and he was required in the same way to acknowledge a mortgage on the estate of The Poplars executed in an irregular form by his uncle. Claims swarmed around him, multiplying with ant-like rapidity. He had come to the determination to renounce the ownership of his lands, but meanwhile his dignity required that he should not yield to the wily manoeuvres of the artful rustics; and as the town-council brought a claim against him also on account of a pretended confusion of the boundary lines of his estate with those of an adjoining wood belonging to the town-lands, the unfortunate young man found himself at every step obliged to prove his rights, which were being continually called in question. His honor was engaged, and he had no alternative but to defend his rights to the death.

Dona Perfecta had promised in her magnanimity to help him to free himself from these disgraceful plots by means of an amicable arrangement; but the days passed, and the good offices of the exemplary lady had produced no result whatever. The claims multiplied with the dangerous swiftness of a violent disease. Pepe Rey passed hour after hour at court, making declarations and answering the same questions over and over again, and when he returned home tired and angry, there appeared before him the sharp features and grotesque face of the notary, who had brought him a thick bundle of stamped papers full of horrible formulas—that he might be studying the question.

It will be easily understood that Pepe Rey was not a man to endure such annoyances when he might escape from them by leaving the town. His mother's noble city appeared to his imagination like a horrible monster which had fastened its ferocious claws in him and was drinking his blood. To free himself from this monster nothing more was necessary, he believed, than flight. But a weighty interest—an interest in which his heart was concerned—kept him where he was; binding him to the rock of his martyrdom with very strong bonds. Nevertheless, he had come to feel so dissatisfied with his position; he had come to regard himself as so utterly a stranger, so to say, in that gloomy city of lawsuits, of old-fashioned customs and ideas, of envy and of slander, that he resolved to leave it without further delay, without, however, abandoning the project which had brought him to it. One morning, finding a favorable occasion, he opened his mind to Dona Perfecta on this point.

"Nephew," responded that lady, with her accustomed gentleness, "don't be rash. Why! you are like fire. Your father was just the same—what a man he was! You are like a flash—I have already told you that I will be very glad to call you my son. Even if you did not possess the good qualities and the talents which distinguish you (in spite of some little defects, for you have those, too); even if you were not as good as you are; it is enough that this union has been proposed by your father, to whom both my daughter and myself owe so much, for me to accept it. And Rosarito will not oppose it since I wish it. What is wanting, then? Nothing; there is nothing wanting but a little time. The marriage cannot be concluded with the haste you desire and which might, perhaps, give ground for interpretations discreditable to my dear daughter's reputation. But as you think of nothing but machines, you want every thing done by steam. Wait, man, wait; what hurry are you in? This hatred that you have taken to our poor Orbajosa is nothing but a caprice. But of course you can only live among counts and marquises and orators and diplomats—all you want is to get married and separate me forever from my daughter," she added, wiping away a tear. "Since that is the case, inconsiderate boy, at least have the charity to delay for a little this marriage, for which you are so eager. What impatience! What ardent love! I did not suppose that a poor country girl like my daughter could inspire so violent a passion."

The arguments of his aunt did not convince Pepe Rey, but he did not wish to contradict her. A fresh cause of anxiety was soon added to those which already embittered his existence. He had now been in Orbajosa for two weeks, and during that time he had received no letter from his father. This could not be attributed to carelessness on the part of the officials of the post-office of Orbajosa, for the functionary who had charge of that service being the friend and *protégé* of Dona Perfecta, the latter every day recommended him to take the greatest care that the letters addressed to her nephew did not go astray. The letter-carrier, named Cristoval Ramos, and nicknamed Caballuco—a personage whose acquaintance we have already made—also visited the house, and to him Dona Perfecta was accustomed to address warnings and reprimands as energetic as the following:

"A pretty mail service you have! How is it that my nephew has not received a single letter since he has been in Orbajosa? When the carrying of the mail is entrusted to such a giddy-pate, how can things be expected to go well? I will speak to the governor of the province so that he may be careful what kind of people he puts in the post-office."

Caballuco, shrugging his shoulders, looked at Rey with the most complete indifference.

One day he entered the house with a letter in his hand.

"Thank Heaven!" said Dona Perfecta to her nephew. "Here are letters from your father. Rejoice, man! A pretty fright we have had through my brother's laziness about writing. What does he say? He is well, no doubt," she added, seeing that Pepe Rey opened the letter with feverish impatience.

The engineer turned pale as he glanced over the first lines.

"Good Heavens! Pepe, what is the matter?" exclaimed Dona Perfecta, rising in alarm. "Is your father ill?"

"This letter is not from my father," responded Pepe, revealing in his countenance the greatest consternation.

"What is it, then?"

"An order from the Minister of Public Works, relieving me from the charge which was confided to me."

"What! Can it be possible!"

"A dismissal pure and simple, expressed in terms very little flattering to me."

"Was there ever any thing so unjust!" exclaimed Dona Perfecta, when she had recovered from her amazement.

"What a humiliation!" exclaimed the young man. "It is the first time in my life that I have received an affront like this."

"But the Government is unpardonable! To put such a slight upon you! Do you wish me to write to Madrid? I have very good friends there, and I may be able to obtain satisfaction for you from the Government and reparation for this brutal affront."

"Thanks, senora, I desire no recommendations," said the young man, with ill-humor.

"But what a piece of injustice! what a high-handed proceeding! To discharge in this way a young man of your merit, an eminent scientist. Why, I cannot contain my anger!"

"I will find out," said Pepe, with energy, "who it is that occupies himself in injuring me."

"That minister—but what is to be expected from those infamous politicasters?"

"In this there is the hand of some one who is determined to drive me to desperation," declared the young man, visibly disturbed. "This is not the act of the minister; this and other contrarieties that I am experiencing are the result of a revengeful plot, of a secret and well-laid plan of some implacable enemy, and this enemy is here in Orbajosa, this plot has been hatched in Orbajosa, doubt it not, dear aunt."

"You are out of your mind," replied Dona Perfecta, with a look of compassion. "You have enemies in Orbajosa, you say? Some one wishes to revenge himself upon you? Come, Pepillo, you have lost your senses. The reading of those books in which they say that we have for ancestors monkeys or parrots has turned your brain."

She smiled sweetly as she uttered the last words, and taking a tone of familiar and affectionate admonition, she added:

"My dear boy, the people of Orbajosa may be rude and boorish rustics, without learning, or polish, or fine manners; but in loyalty and good faith we yield to no one—to no one, I say, no one."

"Don't suppose," said the young man, "that I accuse any one in this house. But that my implacable and cruel enemy is in this city, I am persuaded."

"I wish you would show me that stage villain," responded Dona Perfecta, smiling again. "I suppose you will not accuse Uncle Licurgo, nor any of the others who have brought suits against you; for the poor people believe they are only defending their rights. And between ourselves, they are not altogether wanting in reason in this case. Besides, Uncle Licurgo likes you greatly. He has told me so himself. From the moment he saw you, you took his fancy, and the poor old man has conceived such an affection for you—"

"Oh, yes—a profound affection!" murmured Pepe.

"Don't be foolish," continued his aunt, putting her hand on his shoulder and looking at him closely. "Don't imagine absurdities; convince yourself that your enemy, if you have one, is in Madrid, in that centre of corruption, of envy and rivalry, not in this peaceful and tranquil corner, where all is good-will and concord. Some one, no doubt, who is envious of your merit——There is one thing I wish to say now—and that is, that if you desire to go there to learn the cause of this affront and ask an explanation of it from the Government, you must not neglect doing so on our account."

Pepe Rey fixed his eyes on his aunt's countenance, as if he wished to penetrate with his glance the inmost depths of her soul.

"I say that if you wish to go, do so," repeated Dona Perfecta, with admirable serenity, while her countenance expressed the most complete and unaffected sincerity.

"No, senora: I do not wish to go."

"So much the better; I think you are right. You are more tranquil here, notwithstanding the suspicions with which you are tormenting yourself. Poor Pepillo! We poor rustics of Orbajosa live happy in our ignorance. I am very sorry that you are not contented here. But is it my fault if you vex and worry yourself without a cause? Do I not treat you like a son? Have I not received you as the hope of my house? Can I do more for you? If in spite of all this you do not like us, if you show so much indifference toward us, if you ridicule our piety, if you insult our friends, is it by chance because we do not treat you well?"

Dona Perfecta's eyes grew moist.

"My dear aunt," said Pepe, feeling his anger vanish, "I too have committed some faults since I have been a guest in this house."

"Don't be foolish. Don't talk about committing faults. Among the persons of the same family every thing is forgiven."

"But Rosarito—where is she?" asked the young man, rising. "Am I not to see her to-day, either?"

"She is better. Do you know that she did not wish to come down stairs?"

"I will go up to her then."

"No, it would be of no use. That girl has some obstinate notions—to-day she is determined not to leave her room. She has locked herself in."

"What a strange idea!"

"She will get over it. Undoubtedly she will get over it. We will see to-night if we cannot put these melancholy thoughts out of her head. We will get up a party to amuse her. Why don't you go to Don Inocencio's and ask him to come here to-night and bring Jacintillo with him?"

"Jacintillo!"

"Yes, when Rosarito has these fits of melancholy, the only one who can divert her is that young man."

"But I will go upstairs——"

"No, you must not."

"What etiquette there is in this house!"

"You are ridiculing us. Do as I ask you."

"But I wish to see her."

"But you cannot see her. How little you know the girl!"

"I thought I knew her well. I will stay here, then. But this solitude is horrible."

"There comes the notary."

"Maledictions upon him!"

"And I think the attorney-general has just come in too—he is an excellent person."

"He be hanged with his goodness!"

"But business affairs, when they are one's own, serve as a distraction. Some one is coming. I think it is the agricultural expert. You will have something to occupy you now for an hour or two."

"An hour or two of hell!"

"Ah, ha! if I am not mistaken Uncle Licurgo and Uncle Paso Largo have just entered. Perhaps they have come to propose a compromise to you."

"I would throw myself into the pond first!"

"How unnatural you are! For they are all very fond of you. Well, so that nothing may be wanting, there comes the constable too. He is coming to serve a summons on you."

"To crucify me."

All the individuals named were now entering the parlor one by one.

"Good-by, Pepe; amuse yourself," said Dona Perfecta.

"Earth, open and swallow me!" exclaimed the young man desperately.

"Senor Don Jose."

"My dear Don Jose."

"Esteemed Don Jose."

"My dearest Don Jose."

"My respected friend, Don Jose."

Hearing these honeyed and insinuating preliminaries, Pepe Rey exhaled a deep sigh and gave himself up. He gave himself up, soul and body, to the executioners, who brandished horrible leaves of stamped paper while the victim, raising his eyes to heaven with a look of Christian meekness, murmured:

"Father, why hast thou forsaken me?"

CHAPTER XII

HERE WAS TROY

Love, friendship, a wholesome moral atmosphere, spiritual light, sympathy, an easy interchange of ideas and feelings, these were what Pepe Rey's nature imperatively demanded. Deprived of them, the darkness that shrouded his soul grew deeper, and his inward gloom imparted a tinge of bitterness and discontent to his manner. On the day following the scenes described in the last chapter, what vexed him more than any thing was the already prolonged and mysterious seclusion of his cousin, accounted for at first by a trifling indisposition and then by caprices and nervous feelings difficult of explanation.

Rey was surprised by conduct so contrary to the idea which he had formed of Rosarito. Four days had passed during which he had not seen her; and certainly it was not because he did not desire to be at her side; and his situation threatened soon to become humiliating and ridiculous, if, by boldly taking the initiative, he did not at once put an end to it.

"Shall I not see my cousin to-day, either?" he said to his aunt, with manifest ill-humor, when they had finished dining.

"No, not to-day, either. Heaven knows how sorry I am for it. I gave her a good talking to this morning. This afternoon we will see what can be done."

The suspicion that in this unreasonable seclusion his adorable cousin was rather the helpless victim than the free and willing agent, induced him to control himself and to wait. Had it not been for this suspicion he would have left Orbajosa that very day. He had no doubt whatever that Rosario loved him, but it was evident that some unknown influence was at work to separate them, and it seemed to him to be the part of an honorable man to discover whence that malign influence proceeded and to oppose it, as far as it was in his power to do so.

"I hope that Rosarito's obstinacy will not continue long," he said to Dona Perfecta, disguising his real sentiments.

On this day he received a letter from his father in which the latter complained of having received none from Orbajosa, a circumstance which increased the engineer's disquietude, perplexing him still further. Finally, after wandering about alone in the garden for a long time, he left the house and went to the Casino. He entered it with the desperate air of a man about to throw himself into the sea.

In the principal rooms he found various people talking and discussing different subjects. In one group they were solving with subtle logic difficult problems relating to bulls; in another, they were discussing the relative merits of different breeds of donkeys of Orbajosa and Villahorrenda. Bored to the last degree, Pepe Rey turned away from these discussions and directed his steps toward the reading-room, where he looked through various reviews without finding any distraction in the reading, and a little later, passing from room to room, he stopped, without knowing why, at the gaming-table. For nearly two hours he remained in the clutches of the horrible yellow demon, whose shining eyes of gold at once torture and charm. But not even the excitement of play had power to lighten the gloom of his soul, and the same tedium which had impelled him toward the green cloth sent him away from it. Shunning the noise, he found himself in an apartment used as an assembly-room, in which at the time there was not a living soul, and here he seated himself wearily at a window overlooking the street.

This was very narrow, with more corners and salient angles than houses, and was overshaded throughout its whole extent by the imposing mass of the cathedral that lifted its dark and time-corroded walls at one end of it. Pepe Rey looked up and down and in every direction; no sign of life—not a footstep, not a voice, not a glance, disturbed the stillness, peaceful as that of a tomb, that reigned everywhere. Suddenly strange sounds, like the whispering of feminine voices, fell on his ear, and then the rustling of curtains that were being drawn, a few words, and finally the humming of a song, the bark of a lap-dog, and other signs of social life, which seemed very strange in such a place. Observing attentively, Pepe Rey perceived that these noises proceeded from an enormous balcony with blinds which displayed its corpulent bulk in front of the window at which he was sitting. Before he had concluded his observations, a member of the Casino suddenly appeared beside him, and accosted him laughingly in this manner:

"Ah, Senor Don Pepe! what a rogue you are! So you have shut yourself in here to ogle the girls, eh?"

The speaker was Don Juan Tafetan, a very amiable man, and one of the few members of the Casino who had manifested for Pepe Rey cordial friendship and genuine admiration. With his red cheeks, his little dyed mustache, his restless laughing eyes, his insignificant figure, his hair carefully combed to hide his baldness, Don Juan Tafetan was far from being an Antinous in appearance, but he was very witty and very agreeable and he had a happy gift for telling a good story. He was much given to laughter, and when he laughed his face, from his forehead to his chin, became one mass of grotesque wrinkles. In spite of these qualities, and of the applause which might have stimulated his taste for spicy jokes, he was not a scandal-monger. Every one liked him, and Pepe Rey spent with him many pleasant hours. Poor Tafetan, formerly an employe in the civil department of the government of the capital of the province, now lived modestly on his salary as a clerk in the bureau of charities; eking out his income by gallantly playing the clarionet in the processions, in the solemnities of the cathedral, and in the theatre, whenever some desperate company of players made their appearance in those parts with the perfidious design of giving representations in Orbajosa.

But the most curious thing about Don Juan Tafetan was his liking for pretty girls. He himself, in the days when he did not hide his baldness with half a dozen hairs plastered down with pomade, when he did not dye his mustache, when, in the freedom from care of youthful years, he walked with shoulders unstooped and head erect, had been a formidable *Tenorio*. To hear him recount his conquests was something to make one die laughing; for there are *Tenorios* and *Tenorios*, and he was one of the most original.

"What girls? I don't see any girls," responded Pepe Rey.

"Yes, play the anchorite!"

One of the blinds of the balcony was opened, giving a glimpse of a youthful face, lovely and smiling, that disappeared instantly, like a light extinguished by the wind.

"Yes, I see now."

"Don't you know them?"

"On my life I do not."

"They are the Troyas—the Troya girls. Then you don't know something good. Three lovely girls, the daughters of a colonel of staff, who died in the streets of Madrid in '54."

The blind opened again, and two faces appeared.

"They are laughing at me," said Tafetan, making a friendly sign to the girls.

"Do you know them?"

"Why, of course I know them. The poor things are in the greatest want. I don't know how they manage to live. When Don Francisco Troya died a subscription was raised for them, but that did not last very long."

"Poor girls! I imagine they are not models of virtue."

"And why not? I do not believe what they say in the town about them."

Once more the blinds opened.

"Good-afternoon, girls!" cried Don Juan Tafetan to the three girls, who appeared, artistically grouped, at the window. "This gentleman says that good things ought not to hide themselves, and that you should throw open the blinds."

But the blind was closed and a joyous concert of laughter diffused a strange gayety through the gloomy street. One might have fancied that a flock of birds was passing.

"Shall we go there?" said Tafetan suddenly.

His eyes sparkled and a roguish smile played on his discolored lips.

"But what sort of people are they, then?"

"Don't be afraid, Senor de Rey. The poor things are honest. Bah! Why, they live upon air, like the chameleons. Tell me, can any one who doesn't eat sin? The poor girls are virtuous enough. And even if they did sin, they fast enough to make up for it."

"Let us go, then."

A moment later Don Juan Tafetan and Pepe Rey were entering the parlor of the Troyas. The poverty he saw, that struggled desperately to disguise itself, afflicted the young man. The three girls were very lovely, especially the two younger ones, who were pale and dark, with large black eyes and slender figures. Well-dressed and well shod they would have seemed the daughters of a duchess, and worthy to ally themselves with princes.

When the visitors entered, the three girls were for a moment abashed: but very soon their naturally gay and frivolous dispositions became apparent. They lived in poverty, as birds live in confinement, singing behind iron bars as they would sing in the midst of the abundance of the forest. They spent the day sewing, which showed at least honorable principles; but no one in Orbajosa, of their own station in life, held any intercourse with them. They were, to a certain extent, proscribed, looked down upon, avoided, which also showed that there existed some cause for scandal. But, to be just, it must be said that the bad reputation of the Troyas consisted, more than in any thing else, in the name they had of being gossips and mischief-makers, fond of playing practical jokes, and bold and free in their manners. They wrote anonymous letters to grave personages; they gave nicknames to every living being in Orbajosa, from the bishop down to the lowest vagabond; they threw pebbles at the passers-by; they hissed behind the window bars, in order to amuse themselves with the perplexity and annoyance of the startled passer-by; they found out every thing that occurred in the neighborhood; to which end they made constant use of every window and aperture in the upper part of the house; they sang at night in the balcony; they masked themselves during the Carnival, in order to obtain entrance into the houses of the highest families; and they played many other mischievous pranks peculiar to small towns. But whatever its cause, the fact was that on the Troya triumvirate rested one of those stigmas that, once affixed on any one by a susceptible community, accompanies that person implacably even beyond the tomb.

"This is the gentleman they say has come to discover the gold-mines?" said one of the girls.

"And to do away with the cultivation of garlic in Orbajosa to plant cotton or cinnamon trees in its stead?"

Pepe could not help laughing at these absurdities.

"All he has come for is to make a collection of pretty girls to take back with him to Madrid," said Tafetan.

"Ah! I'll be very glad to go!" cried one.

"I will take the three of you with me," said Pepe. "But I want to know one thing; why were you laughing at me when I was at the window of the Casino?"

These words were the signal for fresh bursts of laughter.

"These girls are silly things," said the eldest.

"It was because we said you deserved something better than Dona Perfecta's daughter."

"It was because this one said that you are only losing your time, for Rosarito cares only for people connected with the Church."

"How absurd you are! I said nothing of the kind! It was you who said that the gentleman was a Lutheran atheist, and that he enters the cathedral smoking and with his hat on."

"Well, I didn't invent it; that is what Suspiritos told me yesterday."

"And who is this Suspiritos who says such absurd things about me?"

"Suspiritos is—Suspiritos."

"Girls," said Tafetan, with smiling countenance, "there goes the orange-vender. Call him; I want to invite you to eat oranges."

One of the girls called the orange-vender.

The conversation started by the Troyas displeased Pepe Rey not a little, dispelling the slight feeling of contentment which he had experienced at finding himself in such gay and communicative company. He could not, however, refrain from smiling when he saw Don Juan Tafetan take down a guitar and begin to play upon it with all the grace and skill of his youthful years.

"I have been told that you sing beautifully," said Rey to the girls.

"Let Don Juan Tafetan sing."

"I don't sing."

"Nor I," said the second of the girls, offering the engineer some pieces of the skin of the orange she had just peeled.

"Maria Juana, don't leave your sewing," said the eldest of the Troyas. "It is late, and the cassock must be finished to-night."

"There is to be no work to-day. To the devil with the needles!" exclaimed Tafetan.

And he began to sing a song.

"The people are stopping in the street," said the second of the girls, going out on the balcony. "Don Juan Tafetan's shouts can be heard in the Plaza—Juana, Juana!"

"Well?"

"Suspiritos is walking down the street."

"Throw a piece of orange-peel at her."

Pepe Rey looked out also; he saw a lady walking down the street at whom the youngest of the Troyas, taking a skilful aim, threw a large piece of orange-peel, which struck her straight on the back of the head. Then they hastily closed the blinds, and the three girls tried to stifle their laughter so that it might not be heard in the street.

"There is no work to-day," cried one, overturning the sewing-basket with the tip of her shoe.

"That is the same as saying, to-morrow there is to be no eating," said the eldest, gathering up the sewing implements.

Pepe Rey instinctively put his hand into his pocket. He would gladly have given them an alms. The spectacle of these poor orphans, condemned by the world because of their frivolity, saddened him beyond measure. If the only sin of the Troyas, if the only pleasure which they had to compensate them for solitude, poverty, and neglect, was to throw orange-peels at the passers-by, they might well be excused for doing it. The austere customs of the town in which they lived had perhaps preserved them from vice, but the unfortunate girls lacked decorum and good-breeding, the common and most visible signs of modesty, and it might easily be supposed that they had thrown out of the window something more than orange-peels. Pepe Rey felt profound pity for them. He noted their shabby dresses, made over, mended, trimmed, and retrimmed, to make them look like new; he noted their broken shoes—and once more he put his hand in his pocket.

"Vice may reign here," he said to himself, "but the faces, the furniture, all show that this is the wreck of a respectable family. If these poor girls were as bad as it is said they are, they would not live in such poverty and they would not work. In Orbajosa there are rich men."

The three girls went back and forward between him and the window, keeping up a gay and sprightly conversation, which indicated, it must be said, a species of innocence in the midst of all their frivolity and unconventionality.

"Senor Don Jose, what an excellent lady Dona Perfecta is!"

"She is the only person in Orbajosa who has no nickname, the only person in Orbajosa who is not spoken ill of."

"Every one respects her."

"Every one adores her."

To these utterances the young man responded by praises of his aunt, but he had no longer any inclination to take money from his pocket and say, "Maria Juana, take this for a pair of boots." "Pepa, take this to buy a dress for yourself." "Florentina, take this to provide yourself with a week's provisions," as he had been on the point of doing. At a moment when the three girls had run out to the balcony to see who was passing, Don Juan Tafetan approached Rey and whispered to him:

"How pretty they are! Are they not? Poor things! It seems impossible that they should be so gay when it may be positively affirmed that they have not dined to-day."

"Don Juan, Don Juan!" cried Pepilla. "Here comes a friend of yours, Nicolasito Hernandez, in other words, Cirio Pascual, with this three-story hat. He is praying to himself, no doubt, for the souls of those whom he has sent to the grave with his extortion."

"I wager that neither of you will dare to call him by his nickname."

"It is a bet."

"Juana, shut the blinds, wait until he passes, and when he is turning the corner, I will call out, 'Cirio, Cirio Pascual!'"

Don Juan Tafetan ran out to the balcony.

"Come here, Don Jose, so that you may know this type," he called.

Pepe Rey, availing himself of the moment in which the three girls and Don Juan were making merry in the balcony, calling Nicolasito Hernandez the nickname which so greatly enraged him, stepped cautiously to one of the sewing baskets in the room and placed in it a half ounce which he had left after his losses at play.

Then he hurried out to the balcony just as the two youngest cried in the midst of wild bursts of laughter, "Cirio, Cirio Pascual!"

CHAPTER XIII

A CASUS BELLI

After this prank the Troyas commenced a conversation with their visitors about the people and the affairs of the town. The engineer, fearing that his exploit might be discovered while he was present, wished to go, which displeased the Troyas greatly. One of them who had left the room now returned, saying:

"Suspiritos is now in the yard; she is hanging out the clothes."

"Don Jose will wish to see her," said another of the girls.

"She is a fine-looking woman. And now she arranges her hair in the Madrid fashion. Come, all of you."

They took their visitors to the dining-room—an apartment very little used—which opened on a terrace, where there were a few flowers in pots and many broken and disused articles of furniture. The terrace overlooked the yard of an adjoining house, with a piazza full of green vines and plants in pots carefully cultivated. Every thing about it showed it to be the abode of neat and industrious people of modest means.

The Troyas, approaching the edge of the roof, looked attentively at the neighboring house, and then, imposing silence by a gesture on their cavaliers, retreated to a part of the terrace from which they could not see into the yard, and where there was no danger of their being seen from it.

"She is coming out of the kitchen now with a pan of peas," said Maria Juana, stretching out her neck to look.

"There goes!" cried another, throwing a pebble into the yard.

The noise of the projectile striking against the glass of the piazza was heard, and then an angry voice crying:

"Now they have broken another pane of glass!"

The girls, hidden, close beside the two men, in a corner of the terrace, were suffocating with laughter.

"Senora Suspiritos is very angry," said Rey. "Why do they call her by that name?"

"Because, when she is talking, she sighs after every word, and although she has every thing she wants, she is always complaining."

There was a moment's silence in the house below. Pepita Troya looked cautiously down.

"There she comes again," she whispered, once more imposing silence by a gesture. "Maria, give me a pebble. Give it here—bang! there it goes!"

"You didn't hit her. It struck the ground."

"Let me see if I can. Let us wait until she comes out of the pantry again."

"Now, now she is coming out. Take care, Florentina."

"One, two, three! There it goes!"

A cry of pain was heard from below, a malediction, a masculine exclamation, for it was a man who uttered it. Pepe Rey could distinguish clearly these words:

"The devil! They have put a hole in my head, the——Jacinto, Jacinto! But what an abominable neighborhood this is!"

"Good Heavens! what have I done!" exclaimed Florentina, filled with consternation. "I have struck Senor Don Inocencio on the head."

"The Penitentiary?" said Pepe Rey.

"Yes."

"Does he live in that house?"

"Why, where else should he live?"

"And the lady of the sighs——"

"Is his niece, his housekeeper, or whatever else she may be. We amuse ourselves with her because she is very tiresome, but we are not accustomed to play tricks on his reverence, the Penitentiary."

While this dialogue was being rapidly carried on, Pepe Rey saw, in front of the terrace and very near him, a window belonging to the bombarded house open; he saw a smiling face appear at it—a familiar face—a face the sight of which stunned him, terrified him, made him turn pale and tremble. It was that of Jacinto, who, interrupted in his grave studies, appeared at it with his pen behind his ear. His modest, fresh, and smiling countenance, appearing in this way, had an auroral aspect.

"Good-afternoon, Senor Don Jose," he said gayly.

"Jacinto, Jacinto, I say!"

"I am coming. I was saluting a friend."

"Come away, come away!" cried Florentina, in alarm. "The Penitentiary is going up to Don Nominative's room and he will give us a blessing."

"Yes, come away; let us close the door of the dining-room."

They rushed pell-mell from the terrace.

"You might have guessed that Jacinto would see you from his temple of learning," said Tafetan to the Troyas.

"Don Nominative is our friend," responded one of the girls. "From his temple of science he says a great many sweet things to us on the sly, and he blows us kisses besides."

"Jacinto?" asked the engineer. "What the deuce is that name you gave him?"

"Don Nominative."

The three girls burst out laughing.

"We call him that because he is very learned."

"No, because when we were little he was little too. But, yes, now I remember. We used to play on the terrace, and we could hear him studying his lessons aloud."

"Yes, and the whole blessed day he used to spend singling."

"Declining, girl! That is what it was. He would go like this: 'Nominative, rosa, Genitive, Dative, Accusative.'"

"I suppose that I have my nickname too," said Pepe Rey.

"Let Maria Juana tell you what it is," said Florentina, hiding herself.

"I? Tell it to him you, Pepa."

"You haven't any name yet, Don Jose."

"But I shall have one. I promise you that I will come to hear what it is and to receive confirmation," said the young man, making a movement to go.

"What, are you going?"

"Yes. You have lost time enough already. To work, girls! Throwing stones at the neighbors and the passers-by is not the most suitable occupation for girls as pretty and as clever as you are. Well, good-by."

And without waiting for further remonstrances, or answering the civilities of the girls, he left the house hastily, leaving Don Juan Tafetan behind him.

The scene which he had just witnessed, the indignity suffered by the canon, the unexpected appearance of the little doctor of laws, added still further to the perplexities, the anxieties, and the disagreeable presentiments that already disturbed the soul of the unlucky engineer. He regretted with his whole soul having entered the house of the Troyas, and, resolving to employ his time better while his hypochondriasm lasted, he made a tour of inspection through the town.

He visited the market, the Calle de la Triperia, where the principal stores were; he observed the various aspects presented by the industry and commerce of the great city of Orbajosa, and, finding only new motives of weariness, he bent his steps in the direction of the Paseo de las Descalzas; but he saw there only a few stray dogs, for, owing to the disagreeable wind which prevailed, the usual promenaders had remained at home. He went to the apothecary's, where various species of ruminant friends of progress, who chewed again and again the cud of the same endless theme, were accustomed to meet, but there he was still more bored. Finally, as he was passing the cathedral, he heard the strains of the organ and the beautiful chanting of the choir. He entered, knelt before the high altar, remembering the warnings which his aunt had given him about behaving with decorum in church; then visited a chapel, and was about to enter another when an acolyte, warden, or beadle approached him, and with the rudest manner and in the most discourteous tone said to him:

"His lordship says that you are to get out of the church."

The engineer felt the blood rush to his face. He obeyed without a word. Turned out everywhere, either by superior authority or by his own tedium, he had no resource but to return to his aunt's house, where he found waiting for him:

First, Uncle Licurgo, to announce a second lawsuit to him; second, Senor Don Cayetano, to read him another passage from his discourse on the "Genealogies of Orbajosa"; third, Caballuco, on some business which he had not disclosed; fourth, Dona Perfecta and her affectionate smile, for what will appear in the following chapter.

CHAPTER XIV

THE DISCORD CONTINUES TO INCREASE

A fresh attempt to see his cousin that evening failed, and Pepe Rey shut himself up in his room to write several letters, his mind preoccupied with one thought.

"To-night or to-morrow," he said to himself, "this will end one way or another."

When he was called to supper Dona Perfecta, who was already in the dining-room, went up to him and said, without preface:

"Dear Pepe, don't distress yourself, I will pacify Senor Don Inocencio. I know every thing already. Maria Remedios, who has just left the house, has told me all about it."

Dona Perfecta's countenance radiated such satisfaction as an artist, proud of his work, might feel.

"About what?"

"Set your mind at rest. I will make an excuse for you. You took a few glasses too much in the Casino, that was it, was it not? There you have the result of bad company. Don Juan Tafetan, the Troyas! This is horrible, frightful. Did you consider well?"

"I considered every thing," responded Pepe, resolved not to enter into discussions with his aunt.

"I shall take good care not to write to your father what you have done."

"You may write whatever you please to him."

"You will exculpate yourself by denying the truth of this story, then?"

"I deny nothing."

"You confess then that you were in the house of those——"

"I was."

"And that you gave them a half ounce; for, according to what Maria Remedios has told me, Florentina went down to the shop of the Extramaduran this afternoon to get a half ounce changed. They could not have earned it with their sewing. You were in their house to-day; consequently—"

"Consequently I gave it to her. You are perfectly right."

"You do not deny it?"

"Why should I deny it? I suppose I can do whatever I please with my money?"

"But you will surely deny that you threw stones at the Penitentiary."

"I do not throw stones."

"I mean that those girls, in your presence—"

"That is another matter."

"And they insulted poor Maria Remedios, too."

"I do not deny that, either."

"And how do you excuse your conduct! Pepe in Heaven's name, have you nothing to say? That you are sorry, that you deny—"

"Nothing, absolutely nothing, senora!"

"You don't even give me any satisfaction."

"I have done nothing to offend you."

"Come, the only thing there is left for you to do now is—there, take that stick and beat me!"

"I don't beat people."

"What a want of respect! What, don't you intend to eat any supper?"

"I intend to take supper."

For more than a quarter of an hour no one spoke. Don Cayetano, Dona Perfecta, and Pepe Rey ate in silence. This was interrupted when Don Inocencio entered the dining-room.

"How sorry I was for it, my dear Don Jose! Believe me, I was truly sorry for it," he said, pressing the young man's hand and regarding him with a look of compassion.

The engineer was so perplexed for a moment that he did not know what to answer.

"I refer to the occurrence of this afternoon."

"Ah, yes!"

"To your expulsion from the sacred precincts of the cathedral."

"The bishop should consider well," said Pepe Rey, "before he turns a Christian out of the church."

"That is very true. I don't know who can have put it into his lordship's head that you are a man of very bad habits; I don't know who has told him that you make a boast of your atheism everywhere; that you ridicule sacred things and persons, and even that you are planning to pull down the cathedral to build a large tar factory with the stones. I tried my best to dissuade him, but his lordship is a little obstinate."

"Thanks for so much kindness."

"And it is not because the Penitentiary has any reason to show you these considerations. A little more, and they would have left him stretched on the ground this afternoon."

"Bah!" said the ecclesiastic, laughing. "But have you heard of that little prank already? I wager Maria Remedios came with the story. And I forbade her to do it—I forbade her positively. The thing in itself is of no consequence, am I not right, Senor de Rey?"

"Since you think so——"

"That is what I think. Young people's pranks! Youth, let the moderns say what they will, is inclined to vice and to vicious actions. Senor de Rey, who is a person of great endowments, could not be altogether perfect—why should it be wondered at that those pretty girls should have captivated him, and, after getting his money out of him, should have made him the accomplice of their shameless and criminal insults to their neighbors? My dear friend, for the painful part that I had in this afternoon's sport," he added, raising his hand to the wounded spot, "I am not offended, nor will I distress you by even referring to so disagreeable an incident. I am truly sorry to hear that Maria Remedios came here to tell all about it. My niece is so fond of gossiping! I wager she told too about the half ounce, and your romping with the girls on the terrace, and your chasing one another about, and the pinches and the capers of Don Juan Tafetan. Bah! those things ought not to be told."

Pepe Rey did not know which annoyed him most—his aunt's severity or the hypocritical condescension of the canon.

"Why should they not be told?" said Dona Perfecta. "He does not seem ashamed of his conduct himself. I assure you all that I keep this from my dear daughter only because, in her nervous condition, a fit of anger might be dangerous to her."

"Come, it is not so serious as all that, senora," said the Penitentiary. "I think the matter should not be again referred to, and when the one who was stoned says that, the rest may surely be satisfied. And the blow was no joke, Senor Don Jose. I thought they had split my head open and that my brains were oozing out."

"I am truly sorry for the occurrence!" stammered Pepe Rey. "It gives me real pain, although I had no part in it—"

"Your visit to those Senoras Troyas will be talked about all over the town," said the canon. "We are not in Madrid, in that centre of corruption, of scandal—"

"There you can visit the vilest places without any one knowing it," said Dona Perfecta.

"Here we are very observant of one another," continued Don Inocencio. "We take notice of everything our neighbors do, and with such a system of vigilance public morals are maintained at a proper height. Believe me, my friend, believe me,—and I do not say this to mortify you,—you are the first gentleman of your position who, in the light of day—the first, yes, senor—*Trojoe qui primus ab oris*."

And bursting into a laugh, he clapped the engineer on the back in token of amity and good-will.

"How grateful I ought to be," said the young man, concealing his anger under the sarcastic words which he thought the most suitable to answer the covert irony of his interlocutors, "to meet with so much generosity and tolerance, when my criminal conduct would deserve—"

"What! Is a person of one's own blood, one who bears one's name," said Dona Perfecta, "to be treated like a stranger? You are my nephew, you are the son of the best and the most virtuous of men, of my dear brother Juan, and that is sufficient. Yesterday afternoon the secretary of the bishop came here to tell me that his lordship is greatly displeased because I have you in my house."

"And that too?" murmured the canon.

"And that too. I said that in spite of the respect which I owe the bishop, and the affection and reverence which I bear him, my nephew is my nephew, and I cannot turn him out of my house."

"This is another singularity which I find in this place," said Pepe Rey, pale with anger. "Here, apparently, the bishop governs other people's houses."

"He is a saint. He is so fond of me that he imagines—he imagines that you are going to contaminate us with your atheism, your disregard for public opinion, your strange ideas. I have told him repeatedly that, at bottom, you are an excellent young man."

"Some concession must always be made to superior talent," observed Don Inocencio.

"And this morning, when I was at the Cirujedas'—oh, you cannot imagine in what a state they had my head! Was it true that you had come to pull down the cathedral; that you were commissioned by the English Protestants to go preaching heresy throughout Spain; that you spent the whole night gambling in the Casino; that you were drunk in the streets? 'But, senoras,' I said to them, 'would you have me send my nephew to the hotel?' Besides, they are wrong about the drunkenness, and as for gambling—I have never yet heard that you gambled."

Pepe Rey found himself in that state of mind in which the calmest man is seized by a sudden rage, by a blind and brutal impulse to strangle some one, to strike some one in the face, to break some one's head, to crush some one's bones. But Dona Perfecta was a woman and was, besides, his aunt; and Don Inocencio was an old man and an ecclesiastic. In addition to this, physical violence is in bad taste and unbecoming a person of education and a Christian. There remained the resource of giving vent to his suppressed wrath in dignified and polite language; but this last resource seemed to him premature, and only to be employed at the moment of his final departure from the house and from Orbajosa. Controlling his fury, then, he waited.

Jacinto entered as they were finishing supper.

"Good-evening, Senor Don Jose," he said, pressing the young man's hand. "You and your friends kept me from working this afternoon. I was not able to write a line. And I had so much to do!"

"I am very sorry for it, Jacinto. But according to what they tell me, you accompany them sometimes in their frolics."

"I!" exclaimed the boy, turning scarlet. "Why, you know very well that Tafetan never speaks a word of truth. But is it true, Senor de Rey, that you are going away?"

"Is that the report in the town?"

"Yes. I heard it in the Casino and at Don Lorenzo Ruiz's."

Rey contemplated in silence for a few moments the fresh face of Don Nominative. Then he said:

"Well, it is not true; my aunt is very well satisfied with me; she despises the calumnies with which the Orbajosans are favoring me—and she will not turn me out of her house, even though the bishop himself should try to make her do so."

"As for turning you out of the house—never. What would your father say?"

"Notwithstanding all your kindness, dearest aunt, notwithstanding the cordial friendship of the reverend canon, it is possible that I may myself decide to go away."

"To go away!"

"To go away—you!"

A strange light shone in Dona Perfecta's eyes. The canon, experienced though he was in dissimulation, could not conceal his joy.

"Yes, and perhaps this very night."

"Why, man, how impetuous you are; Why don't you at least wait until morning? Here—Juan, let some one go for Uncle Licurgo to get the nag ready. I suppose you will take some luncheon with you. Nicolasa, that piece of veal that is on the sideboard! Librada, the senorito's linen."

"No, I cannot believe that you would take so rash a resolution," said Don Cayetano, thinking himself obliged to take some part in the question.

"But you will come back, will you not?" asked the canon.

"At what time does the morning train pass?" asked Dona Perfecta, in whose eyes was clearly discernible the feverish impatience of her exaltation.

"I am going away to-night."

"But there is no moon."

In the soul of Dona Perfecta, in the soul of the Penitentiary, in the little doctor's youthful soul echoed like a celestial harmony the word, "To-night!"

"Of course, dear Pepe, you will come back. I wrote to-day to your father, your excellent father," exclaimed Dona Perfecta, with all the physiognomic signs that make their appearance when a tear is about to be shed.

"I will trouble you with a few commissions," said the savant.

"A good opportunity to order the volume that is wanting in my copy of the Abbe Gaume's work," said the youthful lawyer.

"You take such sudden notions, Pepe; you are so full of caprices," murmured Dona Perfecta, smiling, with her eyes fixed on the door of the dining-room. "But I forgot to tell you that Caballuco is waiting to speak to you."

CHAPTER XV

DISCORD CONTINUES TO GROW UNTIL WAR IS DECLARED

Every one looked toward the door, at which appeared the imposing figure of the Centaur, serious-looking and frowning; embarrassed by his anxiety to salute the company politely; savagely handsome, but disfigured by the violence which he did himself in smiling civilly and treading softly and holding his herculean arms in a correct posture.

"Come in, Senor Ramos," said Pepe Rey.

"No, no!" objected Dona Perfecta. "What he has to say to you is an absurdity."

"Let him say it."

"I ought not to allow such ridiculous questions to be discussed in my house."

"What is Senor Ramos' business with me?"

Caballuco uttered a few words.

"Enough, enough!" exclaimed Dona Perfecta. "Don't trouble my nephew any more. Pepe, don't mind this simpleton. Do you wish me to tell you the cause of the great Caballuco's anger?" she said, turning to the others.

"Anger? I think I can imagine," said the Penitentiary, leaning back in his chair and laughing with boisterous hilarity.

"I wanted to say to Senor Don Jose—" growled the formidable horseman.

"Hold your tongue, man, for Heaven's sake! And don't tire us any more with that nonsense."

"Senor Caballuco," said the canon, "it is not to be wondered at that gentlemen from the capital should cut out the rough riders of this savage country."

"In two words, Pepe, the question is this: Caballuco is—"

She could not go on for laughing.

"Is—I don't know just what," said Don Inocencio, "of one of the Troya girls, of Mariquita Juana, if I am not mistaken."

"And he is jealous! After his horse, the first thing in creation for him is Mariquilla Troya."

"A pretty insinuation that!" exclaimed Dona Perfecta. "Poor Cristobal! Did you suppose that a person like my nephew—let us hear, what were you going to say to him? Speak."

"Senor Don Jose and I will talk together presently," responded the bravo of the town brusquely.

And without another word he left the room.

Shortly afterward Pepe Rey left the dining-room to retire to his own room. In the hall he found himself face to face with his Trojan antagonist, and he could not repress a smile at the sight of the fierce and gloomy countenance of the offended lover.

"A word with you," said the latter, planting himself insolently in front of the engineer. "Do you know who I am?"

As he spoke he laid his heavy hand on the young man's shoulder with such insolent familiarity that the latter, incensed, flung him off with violence, saying:

"It is not necessary to crush one to say that."

The bravo, somewhat disconcerted, recovered himself in a moment, and looking at Rey with provoking boldness, repeated his refrain:

"Do you know who I am?"

"Yes; I know now that you are a brute."

He pushed the bully roughly aside and went into his room. As traced on the excited brain of our unfortunate friend at this moment, his plan of action might be summed up briefly and definitely as follows: To break Caballuco's head without loss of time; then to take leave of his aunt in severe but polite words which should reach her soul; to bid a cold adieu to the canon and give an embrace to the inoffensive Don Cayetano; to administer a thrashing to Uncle Licurgo, by way of winding up the entertainment, and leave Orbajosa that very night, shaking the dust from his shoes at the city gates.

But in the midst of all these mortifications and persecutions the unfortunate young man had not ceased to think of another unhappy being, whom he believed to be in a situation even more painful and distressing than his own. One of the maid-servants followed the engineer into his room.

"Did you give her my message?" he asked.

"Yes, senor, and she gave me this."

Rey took from the girl's hand a fragment of a newspaper, on the margin of which he read these words:

"They say you are going away. I shall die if you do."

When he returned to the dining-room Uncle Licurgo looked in at the door and asked:

"At what hour do you want the horse?"

"At no hour," answered Rey quickly.

"Then you are not going to-night?" said Dona Perfecta. "Well, it is better to wait until to-morrow."

"I am not going to-morrow, either."

"When are you going, then?"

"We will see presently," said the young man coldly, looking at his aunt with imperturbable calmness. "For the present I do not intend to go away."

His eyes flashed forth a fierce challenge.

Dona Perfecta turned first red, then pale. She looked at the canon, who had taken off his gold spectacles to wipe them, and then fixed her eyes successively on each of the other persons in the room, including Caballuco, who, entering shortly before, had seated himself on the edge of a chair. Dona Perfecta looked at them as a general looks at his trusty body-guard. Then she studied the thoughtful and serene countenance of her nephew—of that enemy, who, by a strategic movement, suddenly reappeared before her when she believed him to be in shameful flight.

Alas! Bloodshed, ruin, and desolation! A great battle was about to be fought.

CHAPTER XVI

NIGHT

Orbajosa slept. The melancholy street-lamps were shedding their last gleams at street-corners and in by-ways, like tired eyes struggling in vain against sleep. By their dim light, wrapped in their cloaks, glided past like shadows, vagabonds, watchmen, and gamblers. Only the hoarse shout of the drunkard or the song of the serenader broke the peaceful silence of the historic city. Suddenly the "Ave Maria Purisima" of some drunken watchman would be heard, like a moan uttered in its sleep by the town.

In Dona Perfecta's house also silence reigned, unbroken but for a conversation which was taking place between Don Cayetano and Pepe Rey, in the library of the former. The savant was seated comfortably in the arm-chair beside his study table, which was covered with papers of various kinds containing notes, annotations, and references, all arranged in the most perfect order. Rey's eyes were fixed on the heap of papers, but his thoughts were doubtless far away from this accumulated learning.

"Perfecta," said the antiquary, "although she is an excellent woman, has the defect of allowing herself to be shocked by any little act of folly. In these provincial towns, my dear friend, the slightest slip is dearly paid for. I see nothing particular in your having gone to the Troyas' house. I fancy that Don Inocencio, under his cloak of piety, is something of a mischief-maker. What has he to do with the matter?"

"We have reached a point, Senor Don Cayetano, in which it is necessary to take a decisive resolution. I must see Rosario and speak with her."

"See her, then!"

"But they will not let me," answered the engineer, striking the table with his clenched hand. "Rosario is kept a prisoner."

"A prisoner!" repeated the savant incredulously. "The truth is that I do not like her looks or her hair, and still less the vacant expression in her beautiful eyes. She is melancholy, she talks little, she weeps—friend Don Jose, I greatly fear that the girl may be attacked by the terrible malady to which so many of the members of my family have fallen victims."

"A terrible malady! What is it?"

"Madness—or rather mania. Not a single member of my family has been free from it. I alone have escaped it."

"You! But leaving aside the question of madness," said Rey, with impatience, "I wish to see Rosario."

"Nothing more natural. But the isolation in which her mother keeps her is a hygienic measure, dear Pepe, and the only one that has been successfully employed with the various members of my family. Consider that the person whose presence and voice would make the strongest impression on Rosarillo's delicate nervous system is the chosen of her heart."

"In spite of all that," insisted Pepe, "I wish to see her."

"Perhaps Perfecta will not oppose your doing so," said the savant, giving his attention to his notes and papers. "I don't want to take any responsibility in the matter."

The engineer, seeing that he could obtain nothing from the good Polentinos, rose to retire.

"You are going to work," he said, "and I will not trouble you any longer."

"No, there is time enough. See the amount of precious information that I collected to-day. Listen: 'In 1537 a native of Orbajosa, called Bartolome del Hoyo, went to Civita-Vecchia in one of the galleys of the Marquis of Castel Rodrigo.' Another: 'In the same year two brothers named Juan and Rodrigo Gonzalez del Arco embarked in one of the six ships which sailed from Maestricht on the 20th of February, and which encountered in the latitude of Calais an English vessel and the Flemish fleet commanded by Van Owen.' That was truly an important exploit of our navy. I have discovered that it was an Orbajosan, one Mateo Diaz Coronel, an ensign in the guards, who, in 1709, wrote and published in Valencia the 'Metrical Encomium, Funeral Chant, Lyrical Eulogy, Numerical Description, Glorious Sufferings, and Sorrowful Glories of the Queen of the Angels.' I possess a most precious copy of this work, which is worth the mines of Peru. Another Orbajosan was the author of that famous 'Treatise on the Various Styles of Horsemanship' which I showed you yesterday; and, in short, there is not a step I take in the labyrinth of unpublished history that I do not stumble against some illustrious compatriot. It is my purpose to draw all these names out of the unjust obscurity and oblivion in which they have so long lain. How pure a joy, dear Pepe, to restore all their lustre to the glories, epic and literary, of one's native place! And how could a man better employ the scant intellect with which Heaven has endowed him, the fortune which he has inherited, and the brief period of time on earth allowed to even the longest life. Thanks to me it will be seen that Orbajosa is the illustrious cradle of Spanish genius. But what do I say? Is not its illustrious ancestry evident in the nobleness and high-mindedness of the present Urbs Augustan generation? We know few places where all the virtues, unchoked by the malefic weeds of vice, grow more luxuriantly. Here all is peace, mutual respect, Christian humility. Charity is practised here as it was in Biblical times; here envy is unknown; here the criminal passions are unknown, and if you hear thieves and murderers spoken of, you may be sure that they are not the children of this noble soil; or, that if they are, they belong to the number of unhappy creatures perverted by the teachings of demagogues. Here you will see the national character in all its purity—upright, noble, incorruptible, pure, simple, patriarchal, hospitable, generous. Therefore it is that I live so happy in this solitude far from the turmoil of cities where, alas! falsehood and vice reign. Therefore it is that the many friends whom I have in Madrid have not been able to tempt me from this place; therefore it is that I spend my life in the sweet companionship of my faithful townspeople and my books, breathing the wholesome atmosphere of integrity, which is gradually becoming circumscribed in our Spain to the humble and Christian towns that have preserved it with the emanations of their virtues. And believe me, my dear Pepe, this peaceful isolation has greatly contributed to preserve me from the terrible malady connatural in my family. In my youth I suffered, like my brothers and my father, from a lamentable propensity to the most absurd manias; but here you have me so miraculously cured that all I know of the malady is what I see of it in others. And it is for that reason that I am so uneasy about my little niece."

"I am rejoiced that the air of Orbajosa has proved so beneficial to you," said Rey, unable to resist the jesting mood that, by a strange contradiction, came over him in the midst of his sadness. "With me it has agreed so badly that I think I shall soon become mad if I remain in it. Well, good-night, and success to your labors."

"Good-night."

Pepe went to his room, but feeling neither a desire for sleep or the need of physical repose,—on the contrary, a violent excitation of mind which impelled him to move, to act,—he walked up and down the room, torturing himself with useless cavilling. After a time he opened the window which overlooked the garden and, leaning his elbows on the parapet, he gazed out on the limitless darkness of the night. Nothing could be seen, but he who is absorbed in his own thoughts sees with the mental vision, and Pepe Rey, his eyes fixed on the darkness, saw the varied panorama of his misfortunes unroll itself upon it before him. The obscurity did not permit him to see the flowers of the earth, nor those of the heavens, which are the stars. The very absence of light produced the effect of an illusory movement in the masses of foliage, which seemed to stretch away, to recede slowly, and come curling back like the waves of a shadowy sea. A vast flux and reflux, a strife between forces vaguely comprehended, agitated the silent sky. The mathematician, contemplating this strange projection of his soul upon the night, said to himself:

"The battle will be terrible. Let us see who will come out of it victorious."

The nocturnal insects whispered in his ear mysterious words. Here a shrill chirp; there a click, like the click made with the tongue; further on, plaintive murmurs; in the distance a tinkle like that of the bell on the neck of the wandering ox. Suddenly Rey heard a strange sound, a rapid note, that could be produced only by the human tongue and lips. This sibilant breathing passed through the young man's brain like a flash of lightning. He felt that swift "s-s-s" dart snake-like through him, repeated again and then again, with augmented intensity. He looked all around, then he looked toward the upper part of the house, and he fancied that in one of the windows he could distinguish an object like a white bird flapping its wings. Through Pepe Rey's excited mind flashed instantly the idea of the phoenix, of the dove, of the regal heron, and yet the bird he saw was noting more than a handkerchief.

The engineer sprang from the balcony into the garden. Observing attentively, he saw the hand and the face of his cousin. He thought he could perceive the gesture commonly employed of imposing silence by laying the finger on the lips. Then the dear shade pointed downward and disappeared. Pepe Rey returned quickly to this room, entered the hall noiselessly, and walked slowly forward. He felt his heart beat with violence. He waited for a few moments, and at last he heard distinctly light taps on the steps of the stairs. One, two, three—the sounds were produced by a pair of little shoes.

He walked in the direction whence they proceeded, and stretched out his hands in the obscurity to assist the person who was descending the stairs. In his soul there reigned an exalted and profound tenderness, but—why seek to deny it—mingling with this tender feeling, there suddenly arose within him, like an infernal inspiration, another sentiment, a fierce desire for revenge. The steps continued to descend, coming nearer and nearer. Pepe Rey went forward, and a pair of hands, groping in the darkness, came in contact with his own. The two pairs of hands were united in a close clasp.

CHAPTER XVII

LIGHT IN THE DARKNESS

The hall was long and broad. At one end of it was the door of the room occupied by the engineer, in the centre that of the dining-room, and at the other end were the staircase and a large closed door reached by a step. This door opened into a chapel in which the Polentinos performed their domestic devotions. Occasionally the holy sacrifice of the mass was celebrated in it.

Rosario led her cousin to the door of the chapel and then sank down on the doorstep.

"Here?" murmured Pepe Rey.

From the movements of Rosarito's right hand he comprehended that she was blessing herself.

"Rosario, dear cousin, thanks for allowing me to see you!" he exclaimed, embracing her ardently.

He felt the girl's cold fingers on his lips, imposing silence. He kissed them rapturously.

"You are frozen. Rosario, why do you tremble so?"

Her teeth were chattering, and her whole frame trembled convulsively. Rey felt the burning heat of his cousin's face against his own, and he cried in alarm:

"Your forehead is burning! You are feverish."

"Very."

"Are you really ill?"

"Yes."

"And you have left your room——"

"To see you."

The engineer wrapped his arms around her to protect her from the cold, but it was not enough.

"Wait," he said quickly, rising. "I am going to my room to bring my travelling rug."

"Put out the light, Pepe."

Rey had left the lamp burning in his room, through the door of which issued a faint streak of light, illuminating the hall. He returned in an instant. The darkness was now profound. Groping his way along the wall he reached the spot where his cousin was sitting, and wrapped the rug carefully around her.

"You are comfortable now, my child."

"Yes, so comfortable! With you!"

"With me—and forever!" exclaimed the young man, with exaltation.

But he observed that she was releasing herself from his arms and was rising.

"What are you doing?"

A metallic sound was heard. Rosario had put the key into the invisible lock and was cautiously opening the door on the threshold of which they had been sitting. The faint odor of dampness, peculiar to rooms that have been long shut up, issued from the place, which was as dark as a tomb. Pepe Rey felt himself being guided by the hand, and his cousin's voice said faintly:

"Enter!"

They took a few steps forward. He imagined himself being led to an unknown Elysium by the angel of night. Rosario groped her way. At last her sweet voice sounded again, murmuring:

"Sit down."

They were beside a wooden bench. Both sat down. Pepe Rey embraced Rosario again. As he did so, his head struck against a hard body.

"What is this?" he asked.

"The feet."

"Rosario—what are you saying?"

"The feet of the Divine Jesus, of the image of Christ crucified, that we adore in my house."

Pepe Rey felt a cold chill strike through him.

"Kiss them," said the young girl imperiously.

The mathematician kissed the cold feet of the holy image.

"Pepe," then cried the young girl, pressing her cousin's hand ardently between her own, "do you believe in God?"

"Rosario! What are you saying? What absurdities are you imagining?" responded her cousin, perplexed.

"Answer me."

Pepe Rey felt drops of moisture on his hands.

"Why are you crying?" he said, greatly disturbed. "Rosario, you are killing me with your absurd doubts. Do I believe in God? Do you doubt it?"

"I do not doubt it; but they all say that you are an atheist."

"You would suffer in my estimation, you would lose your aureole of purity—your charm—if you gave credit to such nonsense."

"When I heard them accuse you of being an atheist, although I could bring no proof to the contrary, I protested from the depths of my soul against such a calumny. You cannot be an atheist. I have within me as strong and deep a conviction of your faith as of my own."

"How wisely you speak! Why, then, do you ask me if I believe in God?"

"Because I wanted to hear it from your own lips, and rejoice in hearing you say it. It is so long since I have heard the sound of your voice! What greater happiness than to hear it again, saying: 'I believe in God?'"

"Rosario, even the wicked believe in him. If there be atheists, which I doubt, they are the calumniators, the intriguers with whom the world is infested. For my part, intrigues and calumnies matter little to me; and if you rise superior to them and close your heart against the discord which a perfidious hand would sow in it, nothing shall interfere with our happiness."

"But what is going on around us? Pepe, dear Pepe, do you believe in the devil?"

The engineer was silent. The darkness of the chapel prevented Rosario from seeing the smile with which her cousin received this strange question.

"We must believe in him," he said at last.

"What is going on? Mamma forbids me to see you; but, except in regard to the atheism, she does not say any thing against you. She tells me to wait, that you will decide; that you are going away, that you are coming back——Speak to me with frankness—have you formed a bad opinion of my mother?"

"Not at all," replied Rey, urged by a feeling of delicacy.

"Do you not believe, as I do, that she loves us both, that she desires only our good, and that we shall in the end obtain her consent to our wishes?"

"If you believe it, I do too. Your mama adores us both. But, dear Rosario, it must be confessed that the devil has entered this house."

"Don't jest!" she said affectionately. "Ah! Mamma is very good. She has not once said to me that you were unworthy to be my husband. All she insists upon is the atheism. They say, besides, that I have manias, and that I have the mania now of loving you with all my soul. In our family it is a rule not to oppose directly the manias that are hereditary in it, because to oppose them aggravates them."

"Well, I believe that there are skilful physicians at your side who have determined to cure you, and who will, in the end, my adored girl, succeed in doing so."

"No, no; a thousand times no!" exclaimed Rosario, leaning her forehead on her lover's breast. "I am willing to be mad if I am with you. For you I am suffering, for you I am ill; for you I despise life and I risk death. I know it now—to-morrow I shall be worse, I shall be dangerously ill, I shall die. What does it matter to me?"

"You are not ill," he responded, with energy; "there is nothing the matter with you but an agitation of mind which naturally brings with it some slight nervous disturbances; there is nothing the matter with you but the suffering occasioned by the horrible coercion which they are using with you. Your simple and generous soul does not comprehend it. You yield; you forgive those who injure you; you torment yourself, attributing your suffering to baleful, supernatural influences; you suffer in silence; you give your innocent neck to the executioner, you allow yourself to be slain, and the very knife which is plunged into your breast seems to you the thorn of a flower that has pierced you in passing. Rosario, cast those ideas from your mind; consider our real situation, which is serious; seek its cause where it really is, and do not give way to your fears; do not yield to the tortures which are inflicted upon you, making yourself mentally and physically ill. The courage which you lack would restore you to health, because you are not really ill, my dear girl, you are—do you wish me to say it?—you are frightened, terrified. You are under what the ancients, not knowing how to express it, called an evil spell. Courage, Rosario, trust in me! Rise and follow me. That is all I will say."

"Ah, Pepe—cousin! I believe that you are right," exclaimed Rosario, drowned in tears. "Your words resound within my heart, arousing in it new energy, new life. Here in this darkness, where we cannot see each other's faces, an ineffable light emanates from you and inundates my soul. What power have you to transform me in this way? The moment I saw you I became another being. In the days when I did not see you I returned to my former insignificance, my natural cowardice. Without you, my Pepe, I live in Limbo. I will do as you tell me, I will arise and follow you. We will go together wherever you wish. Do you know that I feel well? Do you know that I have no fever: that I have recovered my strength; that I want to run about and cry out; that my whole being is renewed and enlarged, and multiplied a hundred-fold in order to adore you? Pepe, you are right. I am not sick, I am only afraid; or rather, bewitched."

"That is it, bewitched."

"Bewitched! Terrible eyes look at me, and I remain mute and trembling. I am afraid, but of what? You alone have the strange power of calling me back to life. Hearing you, I live again. I believe if I were to die and you were to pass by my grave, that deep under the ground I should feel your footsteps. Oh, if I could see you now! But you are here beside me, and I cannot doubt that it is you. So many days without seeing you! I was mad. Each day of solitude appeared to me a century. They said to me, to-morrow and to-morrow, and always to-morrow. I looked out of the window at night, and the light of the lamp in your room served to console me. At times your shadow on the window was for me a divine apparition. I stretched out my arms to you, I shed tears and cried out inwardly, without daring to do so with my voice. When I received the message you sent me with the maid, when I received your letter telling me that you were going away, I grew very sad, I thought my soul was leaving my body and that I was dying slowly. I fell, like the bird wounded as it flies, that falls and, falling, dies. To-night, when I saw that you were awake so late, I could not resist the longing I had to speak to you; and I came down stairs. I believe that all the courage of my life has been used up in this single act, and that now I can never be any thing again but a coward. But you will give me courage; you will give me strength; you will help me, will you not? Pepe, my dear cousin, tell me that you will; tell me that I am strong, and I will be strong; tell me that I am not ill, and I will not be ill. I am not ill now. I feel so well that I could laugh at my ridiculous maladies."

As she said this she felt herself clasped rapturously in her cousin's arms. An "Oh!" was heard, but it came, not from her lips, but from his, for in bending his head, he had struck it violently against the feet of the crucifix. In the darkness it is that the stars are seen.

In the exalted state of his mind, by a species of hallucination natural in the darkness, it seemed to Pepe Rey not that his head had struck against the sacred foot, but that this had moved, warning him in the briefest and most eloquent manner. Raising his head he said, half seriously, half gayly:

"Lord, do not strike me; I will do nothing wrong."

At the same moment Rosario took the young man's hand and pressed it against her heart. A voice was heard, a pure, grave, angelic voice, full of feeling, saying:

"Lord whom I adore, Lord God of the world, and guardian of my house and of my family; Lord whom Pepe also adores; holy and blessed Christ who died on the cross for our sins; before thee, before thy wounded body, before thy forehead crowned with thorns, I say that this man is my husband, and that, after thee, he is the being whom my heart loves most; I say that I declare him to be my husband, and that I will die before I belong to another. My heart and my soul are his. Let not the world oppose our happiness, and grant me the favor of this union, which I swear to be true and good before the world, as it is in my conscience."

"Rosario, you are mine!" exclaimed Pepe Rey, with exaltation. "Neither your mother nor any one else shall prevent it."

Rosario sank powerless into her cousin's arms. She trembled in his manly embrace, as the dove trembles in the talons of the eagle.

Through the engineer's mind the thought flashed that the devil existed; but the devil then was he. Rosario made a slight movement of fear; she felt the thrill of surprise, so to say, that gives warning that danger is near.

"Swear to me that you will not yield to them," said Pepe Rey, with confusion, observing the movement.

"I swear it to you by my father's ashes that are—"

"Where?"

"Under our feet."

The mathematician felt the stone rise under his feet—but no, it was not rising; he only fancied, mathematician though he was, that he felt it rise.

"I swear it to you," repeated Rosario, "by my father's ashes, and by the God who is looking at us——May our bodies, united as they are, repose under those stones when God wills to take us out of this world."

"Yes," repeated the Pepe Rey, with profound emotion, feeling his soul filled with an inexplicable trouble.

Both remained silent for a short time. Rosario had risen.

"Already?" he said.

She sat down again.

"You are trembling again," said Pepe. "Rosario, you are ill; your forehead is burning."

"I think I am dying," murmured the young girl faintly. "I don't know what is the matter with me."

She fell senseless into her cousin's arms. Caressing her, he noticed that her face was covered with a cold perspiration.

"She is really ill," he said to himself. "It was a piece of great imprudence to have come down stairs."

He lifted her up in his arms, endeavoring to restore her to consciousness, but neither the trembling that had seized her nor her insensibility passed away; and he resolved to carry her out of the chapel, in the hope that the fresh air would revive her. And so it was. When she recovered consciousness Rosario manifested great disquietude at finding herself at such an hour out of her own room. The clock of the cathedral struck four.

"How late it is!" exclaimed the young girl. "Release me, cousin. I think I can walk. I am really very ill."

"I will go upstairs with you."

"Oh, no; on no account! I would rather drag myself to my room on my hands and feet. Don't you hear a noise?"

Both were silent. The anxiety with which they listened made the silence intense.

"Don't you hear any thing, Pepe?"

"Absolutely nothing."

"Pay attention. There, there it is again. It is a noise that sounds as if it might be either very, very distant, or very near. It might either be my mother's breathing or the creaking of the vane on the tower of the cathedral. Ah! I have a very fine ear."

"Too fine! Well, dear cousin, I will carry you upstairs in my arms."

"Very well; carry me to the head of the stairs. Afterward I can go alone. As soon as I rest a little I shall be as well as ever. But don't you hear?"

They stopped on the first step.

"It is a metallic sound."

"Your mother's breathing?"

"No, it is not that. The noise comes from a great distance. Perhaps it is the crowing of a cock?"

"Perhaps so."

"It sounds like the words, 'I am going there, I am going there!'"

"Now, now I hear," murmured Pepe Rey.

"It is a cry."

"It is a cornet."

"A cornet!"

"Yes. Let us hurry. Orbajosa is going to wake up. Now I hear it clearly. It is not a trumpet but a clarionet. The soldiers are coming."

"Soldiers!"

"I don't know why I imagine that this military invasion is going to be advantageous to me. I feel glad. Up, quickly, Rosario!"

"I feel glad, too. Up, up!"

In an instant he had carried her upstairs, and the lovers took a whispered leave of each other.

"I will stand at the window overlooking the garden, so that you may know I have reached my room safely. Good-by."

"Good-by, Rosario. Take care not to stumble against the furniture."

"I can find my way here perfectly, cousin. We shall soon see each other again. Stand at your window if you wish to receive my telegraphic despatch."

Pepe Rey did as he was bade; but he waited a long time, and Rosario did not appear at the window. The engineer fancied he heard agitated voices on the floor above him.

CHAPTER XVIII

THE SOLDIERS

The inhabitants of Orbajosa heard in the twilight vagueness of their morning slumbers the same sonorous clarionet, and they opened their eyes, saying:

"The soldiers!"

Some murmured to themselves between sleeping and waking:

"At last they have sent us that rabble."

Others got out of bed hastily, growling:

"Let us go take a look at those confounded soldiers."

Some soliloquized in this way:

"It will be necessary to hurry up matters. They say drafts and contributions; we will say blows and more blows."

In another house were heard these words uttered joyfully:

"Perhaps my son is coming! Perhaps my brother is coming!"

Everywhere people were springing out of bed, dressing hastily, opening the windows to see the regiment that caused all this excitement entering the city in the early dawn. The city was gloom, silence, age; the army gayety, boisterousness, youth. As the army entered the city it seemed as if the mummy received by some magic art the gift of life and sprang with noisy gayety from its damp sarcophagus to dance around it. What movement, what shouting, what laughter, what merriment! There is nothing so interesting as a regiment. It is our country in its youthful and vigorous aspect. All the ineptitude, the turbulence, the superstition at times, and at times the impiety of the country as represented in the individual, disappears under the iron rule of discipline, which of so many insignificant figures makes an imposing whole. The soldier, or so to say, the corpuscle, separating at the command "Break ranks!" from the mass in which he has led a regular and at times a sublime life, occasionally preserves some of the qualities peculiar to the army. But this is not the general rule. The separation is most often accompanied by a sudden deterioration, with the result that if an army is the glory and honor of a nation, an assemblage of soldiers may be an insupportable calamity; and the towns that shed tears of joy and enthusiasm when they see a victorious battalion enter their precincts, groan with terror and tremble with apprehension when they see the same soldiers separate and off duty.

This last was what happened in Orbajosa, for in those days there were no glorious deeds to celebrate, nor was there any motive for weaving wreaths or tracing triumphal inscriptions, or even for making mention of the exploits of our brave soldiers, for which reason all was fear and suspicion in the episcopal city, which, although poor, did not lack treasures in chickens, fruits, money, and maidenhood, all of which ran great risk from the moment when the before-mentioned sons of Mars entered it. In addition to this, the native town of Polentinos, as a city remote from the movement and stir brought with them by traffic, the newspapers, railroads, and other agents which it is unnecessary now to specify, did not wish to be disturbed in its tranquil existence.

Besides which, it manifested on every favorable occasion a strong aversion to submitting to the central authority which, badly or well, governs us; and calling to mind its former privileges and ruminating upon them anew, as the camel chews the cud of the grass which it ate yesterday, it would occasionally display a certain rebellious independence, and vicious tendencies much to be deplored, which at times gave no little anxiety to the governor of the province.

It must also be taken into account that Orbajosa had rebellious antecedents, or rather ancestry. Doubtless it still retained some of those energetic fibres which, in remote ages, according to the enthusiastic opinion of Don Cayetano, impelled it to unexampled epic deeds; and, even in its decadence, occasionally felt an eager desire to do great things, although they might be only barbarities and follies. As it had given to the world so many illustrious sons, it desired, no doubt, that its actual scions, the Caballucos, Merengues, and Pelosmalos, should renew the glorious *Gesta* of their predecessors.

Whenever there was disaffection in Spain, Orbajosa gave proof that it was not in vain that it existed on the face of the earth, although it is true that it was never the theatre of a real war. The spirit of the town, its situation, its history, all reduced it to the secondary part of raising guerillas. It bestowed upon the country this national product in 1827, at the time of the Apostolics, during the Seven Years' War, in 1848, and at other epochs of less resonance in the national history. The guerillas and their chiefs were always popular, a fatal circumstance due to the War of Independence, one of those good things which have been the origin of an infinite number of detestable things. *Corruptio optimi pessima.* And with the popularity of the guerillas and their chiefs coincided, in ever-increasing proportion, the unpopularity of every one who entered Orbajosa in the character of a delegate or instrument of the central power. The soldiers were held in such disrepute there that, whenever the old people told of any crime, any robbery, assassination, or the like atrocity, they added: "This happened when the soldiers were here."

And now that these important observations have been made, it will be well to add that the battalions sent there during the days in which the events of our story took place did not go to parade through the streets, but for another purpose which will be clearly and minutely set forth later on. As a detail of no little interest, it may be noted that the events here related took place at a period neither very remote nor very recent. It may also be said that Orbajosa (called by the Romans Urbs Augusta, although some learned moderns, enquiring into the etymology of the termination *ajosa*[*] are of the opinion that it comes by it from being the richest garlic-growing country in the world) is neither very near Madrid nor very far from it; nor can we say whether its glorious foundations are laid toward the north or toward the south, toward the east or toward the west; but that it may be supposed to be in any part of Spain where the pungent odor of its garlic is to be perceived.

[*] Rich in garlic.

The billets of residence being distributed by the authorities, each soldier went to seek his borrowed home. They were received by their hosts with a very ill grace and assigned the most atrociously uninhabitable parts of the houses. The girls of the city were not indeed among those who were most dissatisfied, but a strict watch was kept over them, and it was considered not decent to show pleasure at the visit of such rabble. The few soldiers who were natives of the district only were treated like kings. The others were regarded as invaders.

At eight in the morning a lieutenant-colonel of cavalry entered the house of Dona Perfecta Polentinos with his billet. He was received by the servants, by order of its mistress, who, being at the time in a deplorable state of mind, did not wish to go down stairs to meet the soldier, and by them he was shown to the only room in the house which, it seemed, was disposable, the room occupied by Pepe Rey.

"Let them settle themselves as best they can," said Dona Perfecta, with an expression of gall and vinegar. "And if they have not room enough, let them go into the street."

Was it her intention to annoy in this way her detested nephew, or was there really no other unoccupied room in the house? This we do not know, nor do the chronicles from which this true history is taken say a word on this important point. What we know positively is that, far from displeasing the two guests to be thus boxed up together, it gave them great pleasure, as they happened to be old friends. They were greatly surprised and delighted when they met, and they were never tired of asking each other questions and uttering exclamations, dwelling on the strange chance that had brought them together in such a place and on such an occasion.

"Pinzon—you here! Why, what is this? I had no suspicion that you were in this neighborhood."

"I heard that you were in this part of the country, Pepe; but I had no idea, either, that I should meet you in this horrible, this barbarous Orbajosa."

"But what a fortunate chance! For this chance is most fortunate—providential. Pinzon, between us both we are going to do a great thing in this wretched town."

"And we shall have time enough to consult about it," answered the other, seating himself on the bed in which the engineer was lying, "for it appears that we are both to occupy this room. What the devil sort of a house is this?"

"Why, man, it is my aunt's. Speak with more respect about it. Have you not met my aunt? But I am going to get up."

"I am very glad of it, for then I can lie down and rest; and badly I need it. What a road, friend Pepe, what a road, and what a town!"

"Tell me, have you come to set fire to Orbajosa?"

"Fire!"

"I ask you because, in that case, I might help you."

"What a town! But what a town!" exclaimed the soldier, removing his shako, and laying aside sword and shoulder-belt, travelling case and cloak. "This is the second time they have sent us here. I swear to you that the third time I will ask my discharge."

"Don't talk ill of these good people! But you have come in the nick of time. It seems as if Providence has sent you to my aid, Pinzon. I have a terrible project on hand, an adventure,—a plot, if you wish to call it so, my friend,—and it would have been difficult for me to carry it through without you. A moment ago I was in despair, wondering how I should manage, and saying to myself anxiously, 'If I only had a friend here, a good friend!'"

"A project, a plot, an adventure! One of two things, Senor Mathematician: it is either the discovery of aerial navigation, or else some love affair."

"It is serious, very serious. Go to bed, sleep a while, and afterward we will talk about it."

"I will go to bed, but I will not sleep. You may say all you wish to me. All that I ask is that you will say as little as possible about Orbajosa."

"It is precisely about Orbajosa that I wish to speak to you. But have you also an antipathy to this cradle of illustrious men?"

"These garlic-venders—we call them the garlic-venders—may be as illustrious as you choose, but to me they are as irritating as the product of the country. This is a town ruled by people who teach distrust, superstition, and hatred of the whole human race. When we have leisure I will relate to you an occurrence—an adventure, half-comic, half-tragic—that happened to me here last year. When I tell it to you, you will laugh and I shall be fuming. But, in fine, what is past is past."

"In what is happening to me there is nothing comic."

"But I have various reasons for hating this wretched place. You must know that my father was assassinated here in '48 by a party of barbarous guerillas. He was a brigadier, and he had left the service. The Government sent for him, and he was passing through Villahorrenda on his way to Madrid, when he was captured by half a dozen ruffians. Here there are several dynasties of guerilla chiefs—the Aceros, the Caballucos, the Pelosmalos—a periodical eruption, as some one has said who knew very well what he was talking about."

"I suppose that two infantry regiments and some cavalry have not come here solely for the pleasure of visiting these delightful regions."

"Certainly not! We have come to survey the country. There are many deposits of arms here. The Government does not venture, as it desires, to remove from office the greater number of the municipal councils without first distributing a few companies of soldiers through these towns. As there is so much disturbance in this part of the country, as two of the neighboring provinces are already infested, and as this municipal district of Orbajosa has, besides, so brilliant a record in all the civil wars, there are fears that the bravos of the place may take to the roads and rob all they can lay hands on."

"A good precaution! But I am firmly convinced that not until these people die and are born over again, not until the very stones have changed their form, will there be peace in Orbajosa."

"That is my opinion too," said the officer, lighting a cigarette. "Don't you see that the guerilla chiefs are the pets of this place? Those who desolated the district in 1848 and at other epochs, or, if not they, their sons, are employed in the market inspector's office, at the town gates, in the town-hall, in the post-office; among them are constables, sacristans, bailiffs. Some have become powerful party leaders and they are the ones who manage the elections, have influence in Madrid, bestow places—in short, this is terrible."

"And tell me, is there no hope of the guerilla chiefs performing some exploit in these days? If that should happen, you could destroy the town, and I would help you."

"If it depended upon me——They will play their usual pranks no doubt," said Pinzon, "for the insurrection in the two neighboring provinces is spreading like wildfire. And between ourselves, friend Rey, I think this is going to last for a long time. Some people smile and say that it would be impossible that there should be another insurrection like the last one. They don't know the country; they don't know Orbajosa and its inhabitants. I believe that the war that is now beginning will have serious consequences, and that we shall have another cruel and bloody struggle, that will last Heaven knows how long. What is your opinion?"

"Well, in Madrid I laughed at any one who spoke of the possibility of a civil war as long and as terrible as the Seven Years' War; but since I have been here——"

"One must come to the heart of this enchanting country, see the people at home, and hear them talk, to know what the real state of affairs is."

"Just so. Without knowing precisely on what I base my opinion, the fact is that here I see things in a different light, and I now believe that it is possible that there may be a long and bloody war."

"Exactly so."

"But at present my thoughts are occupied less by the public war than by a private war in which I am engaged and which I declared a short time ago."

"You said this was your aunt's house. What is her name?"

"Dona Perfecta Rey de Polentinos."

"Ah! I know her by reputation. She is an excellent person, and the only one of whom I have not heard the garlic-venders speak ill. When I was here before I heard her goodness, her charity, her innumerable virtues, everywhere extolled."

"Yes, my aunt is very kind, very amiable," said Rey.

Then he fell into a thoughtful silence.

"But now I remember!" exclaimed Pinzon suddenly. "How one thing fits in with another! Yes, I heard in Madrid that you were going to be married to a cousin of yours. All is clear now. Is it that beautiful and heavenly Rosario?"

"Pinzon, we must have a long talk together."

"I imagine that there are difficulties."

"There is something more; there is violent opposition. I have need of a determined friend—a friend who is prompt to act, fruitful in resource, of great experience in emergencies, astute and courageous."

"Why, this is even more serious than a challenge."

"A great deal more serious. It would be easy to fight with another man. With women, with unseen enemies who work in the dark, it is impossible."

"Come, I am all ears."

Lieutenant-colonel Pinzon lay stretched at full length upon the bed. Pepe Rey drew a chair up to the bedside and, leaning his elbow on the bed and his head on his hand, began his conference, consultation, exposition of plan, or whatever else it might be called, and continued talking for a long time. Pinzon listened to him with profound attention and without interrupting him, except to ask an occasional question for the purpose of obtaining further details or additional light upon some obscure point. When Pepe Rey ended, Pinzon looked grave. He stretched himself, yawning with the satisfaction of one who has not slept for three nights, and then said:

"You plan is dangerous and difficult."

"But not impossible."

"Oh, no! for nothing is impossible. Reflect well about it."

"I have reflected."

"And you are resolved to carry it through? Consider that these things are not now in fashion. They generally turn out badly and throw discredit on those who undertake them."

"I am resolved."

"For my part, then, although the business is dangerous and serious—very serious—I am ready to aid you in all things and for all things."

"Can I rely upon you?"

"To the death."

CHAPTER XIX

A TERRIBLE BATTLE-STRATEGY

The opening of hostilities could not long be delayed. When the hour of dinner arrived, after coming to an agreement with Pinzon regarding the plan to be pursued, the first condition of which was that the friends should pretend not to know each other, Pepe Rey went to the dining-room. There he found his aunt, who had just returned from the cathedral where she had spent the morning as was her habit. She was alone, and appeared to be greatly preoccupied. The engineer observed that on that pale and marble-like countenance, not without a certain beauty, there rested a mysterious shadow. When she looked up it recovered its sinister calmness, but she looked up seldom, and after a rapid examination of her nephew's countenance, that of the amiable lady would again take on its studied gloom.

They awaited dinner in silence. They did not wait for Don Cayetano, for he had gone to Mundogrande. When they sat down to table Dona Perfecta said:

"And that fine soldier whom the Government has sent us, is he not coming to dinner?"

"He seems to be more sleepy than hungry," answered the engineer, without looking at his aunt.

"Do you know him?"

"I have never seen him in all my life before."

"We are nicely off with the guests whom the Government sends us. We have beds and provisions in order to keep them ready for those vagabonds of Madrid, whenever they may choose to dispose of them."

"There are fears of an insurrection," said Pepe Rey, with sudden heat, "and the Government is determined to crush the Orbajosans—to crush them, to grind them to powder."

"Stop, man, stop, for Heaven's sake; don't crush us!" cried Dona Perfecta sarcastically. "Poor we! Be merciful, man, and allow us unhappy creatures to live. And would you, then, be one of those who would aid the army in the grand work of crushing us?"

"I am not a soldier. I will do nothing but applaud when I see the germs of civil war; of insubordination, of discord, of disorder, of robbery, and of barbarism that exist here, to the shame of our times and of our country, forever extirpated."

"All will be as God wills."

"Orbajosa, my dear aunt, has little else than garlic and bandits; for those who in the name of some political or religious idea set out in search of adventures every four or five years are nothing but bandits."

"Thanks, thanks, my dear nephew!" said Dona Perfecta, turning pale. "So Orbajosa has nothing more than that? Yet there must be something else here—something that you do not possess, since you have come to look for it among us."

Rey felt the cut. His soul was on fire. He found it very difficult to show his aunt the consideration to which her sex, her rank, and her relation to himself entitled her. He was on the verge of a violent outbreak, and a force that he could not resist was impelling him against his interlocutor.

"I came to Orbajosa," he said, "because you sent for me; you arranged with my father—"

"Yes, yes; it is true," she answered, interrupting him quickly and making an effort to recover her habitual serenity. "I do not deny it. I am the one who is really to blame. I am to blame for your ill-humor, for the slights you put upon us, for every thing disagreeable that has been happening in my house since you entered it."

"I am glad that you are conscious of it."

"In exchange, you are a saint. Must I also go down on my knees to your grace and ask your pardon?"

"Senora," said Pepe Rey gravely, laying down his knife and fork, "I entreat you not to mock me in so pitiless a manner. I cannot meet you on equal ground. All I have said is that I came to Orbajosa at your invitation."

"And it is true. Your father and I arranged that you should marry Rosario. You came in order to become acquainted with her. I accepted you at once as a son. You pretended to love Rosario—"

"Pardon me," objected Pepe; "I loved and I love Rosario; you pretended to accept me as a son; receiving me with deceitful cordiality, you employed from the very beginning all the arts of cunning to thwart me and to prevent the fulfilment of the proposals made to my father; you determined from the first day to drive me to desperation, to tire me out; and with smiles and affectionate words on your lips you have been killing me, roasting me at the slow fire; you have let loose upon me in the dark and from behind an ambush a swarm of lawsuits; you have deprived me of the official commission which I brought to Orbajosa; you have brought me into disrepute in the town; you have had me turned out of the cathedral; you have kept me constantly separated from the chosen of my heart; you have tortured your daughter with an inquisitorial imprisonment which will cause her death, unless God interposes to prevent it."

Dona Perfecta turned scarlet. But the flush of offended pride passed away quickly, leaving her face of a greenish pallor. Her lips trembled. Throwing down the knife and fork with which she had been eating, she rose swiftly to her feet. Her nephew rose also.

"My God! Holy Virgin of Succor!" she cried, raising both her hands to her head and pressing it between them with the gesture indicative of desperation, "is it possible that I deserve such atrocious insults? Pepe, my son, is it you who speak to me in this way? If I have done what you say, I am indeed very wicked."

She sank on the sofa and covered her face with her hands. Pepe, approaching her slowly, saw that his aunt was sobbing bitterly and shedding abundant tears. In spite of his conviction he could not altogether conquer the feeling of compassion which took possession of him; and while he condemned himself for his cowardice he felt something of remorse for the severity and the frankness with which he had spoken.

"My dear aunt," he said, putting his hand on her shoulder, "if you answer me with tears and sighs, you will not convince me. Proofs, not emotions, are what I require. Speak to me, tell me that I am mistaken in thinking what I think; then prove it to me, and I will acknowledge my error."

"Leave me, you are not my brother's son! If you were, you would not insult me as you have insulted me. So, then, I am an intriguer, an actress, a hypocritical harpy, a domestic plotter?"

As she spoke, Dona Perfecta uncovered her face and looked at her nephew with a martyr-like expression. Pepe was perplexed. The tears as well as the gentle voice of his father's sister could not be insignificant phenomena for the mathematician's soul. Words crowded to his lips to ask her pardon. A man of great firmness generally, any appeal to his emotions, any thing which touched his heart, converted him at once into a child. Weaknesses of a mathematician! It is said that Newton was the same.

"I will give you the proofs you ask," said Dona Perfecta, motioning him to a seat beside her. "I will give you satisfaction. You shall see whether I am kind, whether I am indulgent, whether I am humble. Do you think that I am going to contradict you; to deny absolutely the acts of which you have accused me? Well, then, no; I do not deny them."

The engineer was astounded.

"I do not deny them," continued Dona Perfecta. "What I deny is the evil intention which you attribute to them. By what right do you undertake to judge of what you know only from appearances and by conjecture? Have you the supreme intelligence which is necessary to judge justly the actions of others and pronounce sentence upon them? Are you God, to know the intentions?"

Pepe was every moment more amazed.

"Is it not allowable at times to employ indirect means to attain a good and honorable end? By what right do you judge actions of mine that you do not clearly understand? I, my dear nephew, manifesting a sincerity which you do not deserve, confess to you that I have indeed employed subterfuges to attain a good end, to attain what was at the same time beneficial to you and to my daughter. You do not comprehend? You look bewildered. Ah! your great mathematician's and German philosopher's intellect is not capable of comprehending these artifices of a prudent mother."

"I am more and more astounded every moment," said the engineer.

"Be as astounded as you choose, but confess your barbarity," said the lady, with increasing spirit; "acknowledge your hastiness and your brutal conduct toward me in accusing me as you have done. You are a young man without any experience or any other knowledge than that which is derived from books, which teach nothing about the world or the human heart. All you know is how to make roads and docks. Ah, my young gentleman! one does not enter into the human heart through the tunnel of a railroad, or descend into its depths through the shaft of a mine. You cannot read in the conscience of another with the microscope of a naturalist, nor decide the question of another's culpability measuring ideas with a theodolite."

"For God's sake, dear aunt!"

"Why do you pronounce the name of God when you do not believe in him?" said Dona Perfecta, in solemn accents. "If you believed in him, if you were a good Christian, you would not dare to form evil judgments about my conduct. I am a devout woman, do you understand? I have a tranquil conscience, do you understand? I know what I am doing and why I do it, do you understand?"

"I understand, I understand, I understand!"

"God in whom you do not believe, sees what you do not see and what you cannot see—the intention. I will say no more; I do not wish to enter into minute explanations, for I do not need to do so. Nor would you understand me if I should tell you that I desired to attain my object without scandal, without offending your father, without offending you, without giving cause for people to talk by an explicit refusal—I will say nothing of all this to you, for you would not understand it, either, Pepe. You are a mathematician. You see what is before your eyes, and nothing more; brute matter and nothing more. You see the effect, and not the cause. God is the supreme intention of the world. He who does not know this must necessarily judge things as you judge them—foolishly. In the tempest, for instance, he sees only destruction; in the conflagration, ruin; in the drought, famine; in the earthquake, desolation; and yet, arrogant young man, in all those apparent calamities we are to seek the good intentions—yes, senor, the intention, always good, of Him who can do nothing evil."

This confused, subtle, and mystic logic did not convince Pepe Rey; but he did not wish to follow his aunt in the tortuous path of such a method of reasoning, and he said simply:

"Well, I respect intentions."

"Now that you seem to recognize your error," continued the pious lady, with ever-increasing confidence, "I will make another confession to you, and that is that I see now that I did wrong in adopting the course I did, although my object was excellent. In view of your impetuous disposition, in view of your incapacity to comprehend me, I should have faced the situation boldly and said to you, 'Nephew, I do not wish that you should be my daughter's husband.'"

"That is the language you should have used to me from the beginning," said the engineer, drawing a deep breath, as if his mind had been relieved from an enormous weight. "I am greatly obliged to you for those words. After having been stabbed in the dark, this blow on the face in the light of day is a great satisfaction to me."

"Well, I will repeat the blow, nephew," declared Dona Perfecta, with as much energy as displeasure. "You know it now—I do not wish you to marry Rosario!"

Pepe was silent. There was a long pause, during which the two regarded each other attentively, as if the face of each was for the other the most perfect work of art.

"Don't you understand what I have said to you?" she repeated. "That every thing is at an end, that there is to be no marriage."

"Permit me, dear aunt," said the young man, with composure, "not to be terrified by the intimation. In the state at which things have arrived your refusal has little importance for me."

"What are you saying?" cried Dona Perfecta violently.

"What you hear. I will marry Rosario!"

Dona Perfecta rose to her feet, indignant, majestic, terrible. Her attitude was that of anathema incarnated in a woman. Rey remained seated, serene, courageous, with the passive courage of a profound conviction and an immovable resolve. The whole weight of his aunt's wrath, threatening to overwhelm him, did not make him move an eyelash. This was his character.

"You are mad. Marry my daughter, you! Marry her against my will!"

Dona Perfecta's trembling lips articulated these words in a truly tragic tone.

"Against your will! She is of a different way of thinking."

"Against my will!" repeated Dona Perfecta. "Yes, and I repeat it again and again. I do not wish it, I do not wish it!"

"She and I wish it."

"Fool! Is nothing else in the world to be considered but her and you? Are there not parents; is there not society; is there not a conscience; is there not a God?"

"Because there is society, because there is a conscience, because there is a God," affirmed Rey gravely, rising to his feet, and pointing with outstretched arm to the heavens, "I say and I repeat that I will marry her."

"Wretch! arrogant man! And if you would dare to trample every thing under your feet, do you think there are not laws to prevent your violence?"

"Because there are laws, I say and I repeat that I will marry her."

"You respect nothing!"

"Nothing that is unworthy of respect."

"And my authority, my will, I—am I nothing?"

"For me your daughter is every thing—the rest is nothing."

Pepe Rey's composure was, so to say, the arrogant display of invincible and conscious strength. The blows he gave were hard and crushing in their force, without any thing to mitigate their severity. His words, if the comparison may be allowed, were like a pitiless discharge of artillery.

Dona Perfecta sank again on the sofa; but she shed no tears, and a convulsive tremor agitated her frame.

"So that for this infamous atheist," she exclaimed, with frank rage, "there are no social conventionalities, there is nothing but caprice. This is base avarice. My daughter is rich!"

"If you think to wound me with that treacherous weapon, evading the question and giving a distorted meaning to my sentiments in order to offend my dignity, you are mistaken, dear aunt. Call me mercenary, if you choose. God knows what I am."

"You have no dignity!"

"That is an opinion, like any other. The world may hold you to be infallible. I do not. I am far from believing that from your judgments there is no appeal to God."

"But is what you say true? But do you persist in your purpose, after my refusal? You respect nothing, you are a monster, a bandit."

"I am a man."

"A wretch! Let us end this at once. I refuse to give my daughter to you; I refuse her to you!"

"I will take her then! I shall take only what is mine."

"Leave my presence!" exclaimed Dona Perfecta, rising suddenly to her feet. "Coxcomb, do you suppose that my daughter thinks of you?"

"She loves me, as I love her."

"It is a lie! It is a lie!"

"She herself has told me so. Excuse me if, on this point, I put more faith in her words than in her mother's."

"How could she have told you so, when you have not seen her for several days?"

"I saw her last night, and she swore to me before the crucifix in the chapel that she would be my wife."

"Oh, scandal; oh, libertinism! But what is this? My God, what a disgrace!" exclaimed Dona Perfecta, pressing her head again between her hands and walking up and down the room. "Rosario left her room last night?"

"She left it to see me. It was time."

"What vile conduct is yours! You have acted like a thief; you have acted like a vulgar seducer!"

"I have acted in accordance with the teachings of your school. My intention was good."

"And she came down stairs! Ah, I suspected it! This morning at daybreak I surprised her, dressed, in her room. She told me she had gone out, I don't know for what. You were the real criminal, then. This is a disgrace! Pepe, I expected any thing from you rather than an outrage like this. Every thing is at an end! Go away! You are dead to me. I forgive you, provided you go away. I will not say a word about this to your father. What horrible selfishness! No, there is no love in you. You do not love my daughter!"

"God knows that I love her, and that is sufficient for me."

"Be silent, blasphemer! and don't take the name of God upon your lips!" exclaimed Dona Perfecta. "In the name of God, whom I can invoke, for I believe in him, I tell you that my daughter will never be your wife. My daughter will be saved, Pepe; my daughter shall not be condemned to a living hell, for a union with you would be a hell!"

"Rosario will be my wife," repeated the mathematician, with pathetic calmness.

The pious lady was still more exasperated by her nephew's calm energy. In a broken voice she said:

"Don't suppose that your threats terrify me. I know what I am saying. What! are a home and a family to be outraged like this? Are human and divine authority to be trampled under foot in this way?"

"I will trample every thing under foot," said the engineer, beginning to lose his composure and speaking with some agitation.

"You will trample every thing under foot! Ah! it is easy to see that you are a barbarian, a savage, a man who lives by violence."

"No, dear aunt; I am mild, upright, honorable, and an enemy to violence; but between you and me—between you who are the law and I who am to honor it—is a poor tormented creature, one of God's angels, subjected to iniquitous tortures. The spectacle of this injustice, this unheard-of violence, is what has converted my rectitude into barbarity; my reason into brute force; my honor into violence, like an assassin's or a thief's; this spectacle, senora, is what impels me to disregard your law, what impels me to trample it under foot, braving every thing. This which appears to you lawlessness is obedience to an unescapable law. I do what society does when a brutal power, as illogical as irritating, opposes its progress. It tramples it under foot and destroys it in an outburst of frenzy. Such am I at this moment—I do not recognize myself. I was reasonable, and now I am a brute; I was respectful, and now I am insolent; I was civilized, and now I am a savage. You have brought me to this horrible extremity; infuriating me and driving me from the path of rectitude which I was tranquilly pursuing. Who is to blame—I or you?"

"You, you!"

"Neither you nor I can decide the question. I think we are both to blame: you for your violence and injustice, I for my injustice and violence. We have both become equally barbarous, and we struggle with and wound each other without compassion. God has permitted that it should be so; my blood will be upon your conscience, yours will be upon mine. Enough now, senora. I do not wish to trouble you with useless words. We will now proceed to acts."

"To acts, very well!" said Dona Perfecta, roaring rather than speaking. "Don't suppose that in Orbajosa there is no civil guard!"

"Good-by, senora. I will now leave this house. I think we shall meet again."

"Go, go! go now!" she cried, pointing with an energetic gesture to the door.

Pepe Rey left the room. Dona Perfecta, after pronouncing a few incoherent words, which were the clearest expression of her anger, sank into a chair, with indications of fatigue, or of a coming attack of nerves. The maids came running in.

"Go for Senor Don Inocencio!" she cried. "Instantly—hurry! Ask him to come here!"

Then she tore her handkerchief with her teeth.

CHAPTER XX

RUMORS—FEARS

On the day following that of this lamentable quarrel, various rumors regarding Pepe Rey and his conduct spread through Orbajosa, going from house to house, from club to club, from the Casino to the apothecary's and from the Paseo de las Descalzes to the Puerta de Baidejos. They were repeated by every body, and so many were the comments made that, if Don Cayetano had collected and compiled them, he might have formed with them a rich "Thesaurus" of Orbajosan benevolence. In the midst of the diversity of the reports circulated, there was agreement in regard to certain important particulars, one of which was the following:

That the engineer, enraged at Dona Perfecta's refusal to marry Rosario to an atheist, had raised his hand to his aunt.

The young man was living in the widow De Cusco's hotel, an establishment mounted, as they say now, not at the height, but at the depth of the superlative backwardness of the town. Lieutenant-colonel Pinzon visited him with frequency, in order that they might discuss together the plot which they had on hand, and for the successful conduct of which the soldier showed the happiest dispositions. New artifices and stratagems occurred to him at every instant, and he hastened to put them into effect with excellent humor, although he would often say to his friend:

"The role I am playing, dear Pepe, is not a very dignified one; but to give an annoyance to the Orbajosans I would walk on my hands and feet."

We do not know what cunning stratagems the artful soldier, skilled in the wiles of the world, employed; but certain it is that before he had been in the house three days he had succeeded in making himself greatly liked by every body in it. His manners were very pleasing to Dona Perfecta, who could not hear unmoved his flattering praises of the elegance of the house, and of the nobility, piety, and august magnificence of its mistress. With Don Inocencio he was hand and glove. Neither her mother nor the Penitentiary placed any obstacle in the way of his speaking with Rosario (who had been restored to liberty on the departure of her ferocious cousin); and, with his delicate compliments, his skilful flattery, and great address, he had acquired in the house of Polentinos considerable ascendency, and he had even succeeded in establishing himself in it on a footing of familiarity. But the object of all his arts was a servant maid named Librada, whom he had seduced (chastely speaking) that she might carry messages and notes to Rosario, of whom he pretended to be enamored. The girl allowed herself to be bribed with persuasive words and a good deal of money, because she was ignorant of the source of the notes and of the real meaning of the intrigue, for had she known that it was all a diabolical plot of Don Jose, although she liked the latter greatly, she would not have acted with treachery toward her mistress for all the money in the world.

One day Dona Perfecta, Don Inocencio, Jacinto, and Pinzon were conversing together in the garden. They were talking about the soldiers and the purpose for which they had been sent to Orbajosa, in which the Penitentiary found motive for condemning the tyrannical conduct of the Government; and, without knowing how it came about, Pepe Rey's name was mentioned.

"He is still at the hotel," said the little lawyer. "I saw him yesterday, and he gave me remembrances for you, Dona Perfecta."

"Was there ever seen such insolence! Ah, Senor Pinzon! do not be surprised at my using this language, speaking of my own nephew—that young man, you remember, who had the room which you occupy."

"Yes, I know. I am not acquainted with him, but I know him by sight and by reputation. He is an intimate friend of our brigadier."

"An intimate friend of the brigadier?"

"Yes, senor; of the commander of the brigade that has just arrived in this district, and which is quartered in the neighboring villages."

"And where is he?" asked the lady.

"In Orbajosa."

"I think he is stopping at Polavieja's," observed Jacinto.

"Your nephew and Brigadier Batalla are intimate friends," continued Pinzon; "they are always to be seen together in the streets."

"Well, my friend, that gives me a bad idea of your chief," said Dona Perfecta.

"He is—he is very good-natured," said Pinzon, in the tone of one who, through motives of respect, did not venture to use a harsher word.

"With your permission, Senor Pinzon, and making an honorable exception in your favor, it must be said that in the Spanish army there are some curious types——"

"Our brigadier was an excellent soldier before he gave himself up to spiritualism."

"To spiritualism!"

"That sect that calls up ghosts and goblins by means of the legs of a table!" said the canon, laughing.

"From curiosity, only from curiosity," said Jacintillo, with emphasis, "I ordered Allan Kardec's book from Madrid. It is well to know something about every thing."

"But is it possible that such follies—Heavens! Tell me, Pinzon, does my nephew too belong to that sect of table-tippers?"

"I think it was he who indoctrinated our valiant Brigadier Batalla."

"Good Heavens!"

"Yes; and whenever he chooses," said Don Inocencio, unable to contain his laughter, "he can speak to Socrates, St. Paul, Cervantes, or Descartes, as I speak to Librada to ask her for a match. Poor Senor de Rey! I was not mistaken in saying that there was something wrong in his head."

"Outside that," continued Pinzon, "our brigadier is a good soldier. If he errs at all, it is on the side of severity. He takes the orders of the Government so literally that, if he were to meet with much opposition here, he would be capable of not leaving one stone upon another in Orbajosa. Yes, I advise you all to be on your guard."

"But is that monster going to cut all our heads off, then? Ah, Senor Don Inocencio! these visits of the army remind me of what I have read in the lives of the martyrs about the visits of the Roman proconsuls to a Christian town."

"The comparison is not wanting in exactness," said the Penitentiary, looking at the soldier over his spectacles.

"It is not very agreeable, but if it is the truth, why should it not be said?" observed Pinzon benevolently. "Now you all are at our mercy."

"The authorities of the place," objected Jacinto, "still exercise their functions as usual."

"I think you are mistaken," responded the soldier, whose countenance Dona Perfecta and the Penitentiary were studying with profound interest. "The alcalde of Orbajosa was removed from office an hour ago."

"By the governor of the province?"

"The governor of the province has been replaced by a delegate from the Government, who was to arrive this morning. The municipal councils will all be removed from office to-day. The minister has so ordered because he suspected, I don't know on what grounds, that they were not supporting the central authority."

"This is a pretty state of things!" murmured the canon, frowning and pushing out his lower lip.

Dona Perfecta looked thoughtful.

"Some of the judges of the primary court, among them the judge of Orbajosa, have been deprived of office."

"The judge! Periquito—Periquito is no longer judge!" exclaimed Dona Perfecta, in a voice and with the manner of a person who has just been stung by a snake.

"The person who was judge in Orbajosa is judge no longer," said Pinzon. "To-morrow the new judge will arrive."

"A stranger!"

"A stranger."

"A rascal, perhaps. The other was so honorable!" said Dona Perfecta, with alarm. "I never asked any thing from him that he did not grant it to me at once. Do you know who will be the new alcalde?"

"They say a corregidor is coming."

"There, say at once that the Deluge is coming, and let us be done with it," said the canon, rising.

"So that we are at the brigadier's mercy!"

"For a few days only. Don't be angry with me. In spite of my uniform I am an enemy of militarism; but we are ordered to strike—and we strike. There could not be a viler trade than ours."

"That it is, that it is!" said Dona Perfecta, with difficulty concealing her fury. "Now that you have confessed it——So, then, neither alcalde nor judge——"

"Nor governor of the province."

"Let them take the bishop from us also and send us a choir boy in his stead."

"That is all that is wanting—if the people here will allow them to do it," murmured Don Inocencio, lowering his eyes. "They won't stop at trifles."

"And it is all because they are afraid of an insurrection in Orbajosa," exclaimed Dona Perfecta, clasping her hands and waving them up and down. "Frankly, Pinzon, I don't know why it is that even the very stones don't rise up in rebellion. I wish you no harm; but it would be a just judgment on you if the water you drink turned into mud. You say that my nephew is the intimate friend of the brigadier?"

"So intimate that they are together all day long; they were school-fellows. Batalla loves him like a brother, and would do anything to please him. In your place, senora, I would be uneasy."

"Oh, my God! I fear there will be an attack on the house!"

"Senora," declared the canon, with energy, "before I would consent that there should be an attack on this honorable house—before I would consent that the slightest harm should be done to this noble family—I, my nephew, all the people of Orbajosa——"

Don Inocencio did not finish. His anger was so great that the words refused to come. He took a few steps forward with a martial air, then returned to his seat.

"I think that your fears are not idle," said Pinzon. "If it should be necessary, I——"

"And I——" said Jacinto.

Dona Perfecta had fixed her eyes on the glass door of the dining-room, through which could be seen a graceful figure. As she looked at it, it seemed as if the cloud of apprehension which rested on her countenance grew darker.

"Rosario! come in here, Rosario!" she said, going to meet the young girl. "I fancy you look better to-day, and that you are more cheerful. Don't you think that Rosario looks better? She seems a different being."

They all agreed that the liveliest happiness was depicted on her countenance.

CHAPTER XXI

"DESPERTA FERRO"

About this time the following items of news appeared in the Madrid newspapers:

"There is no truth whatever in the report that there has been an insurrection in the neighborhood of Orbajosa. Our correspondent in that place informs us that the country is so little disposed for adventures that the further presence of the Batalla brigade in that locality is considered unnecessary."

"It is said that the Batalla brigade will leave Orbajosa, as troops are not required there, to go to Villajuan de Nahara, where guerillas have made their appearance."

"The news has been confirmed that the Aceros, with a number of mounted followers, are ranging the district of Villajuan, adjacent to the judicial district of Orbajosa. The governor of the province of X. has telegraphed to the Government that Francisco Acero entered Las Roquetas, where he demanded provisions and money. Domingo Acero (Faltriquera), was ranging the Jubileo mountains, actively pursued by the Civil Guards, who killed one of his men and captured another. Bartolome Acero is the man who burned the registry office of Lugarnoble and carried away with him as hostages the alcalde and two of the principal landowners."

"Complete tranquillity reigns in Orbajosa, according to a letter which we have before us, and no one there thinks of anything but cultivating the garlic fields, which promise to yield a magnificent crop. The neighboring districts, however, are infested with guerillas, but the Batalla brigade will make short work of these."

Orbajosa was, in fact, tranquil. The Aceros, that warlike dynasty, worthy, in the opinion of some, of figuring in the "Romancero," had taken possession of the neighboring province; but the insurrection was not spreading within the limits of the episcopal city. It might be supposed that modern culture had at last triumphed in its struggle with the turbulent habits of the great city of disorder, and that the latter was tasting the delights of a lasting peace. So true is this that Caballuco himself, one of the most important figures of the historic rebellion of Orbajosa, said frankly to every one that he did not wish to quarrel with the Government nor involve himself in a business which might cost him dear.

Whatever may be said to the contrary, the impetuous nature of Ramos had quieted down with years, and the fiery temper which he had received with life from the ancestral Caballucos, the most valiant race of warriors that had ever desolated the earth, had grown cooler. It is also related that in those days the new governor of the province held a conference with this important personage, and received from his lips the most solemn assurances that he would contribute as far as in him lay to the tranquillity of the country, and would avoid doing any thing that might give rise to disturbances. Reliable witnesses declare that he was to be seen in friendly companionship with the soldiers, hobnobbing with this sergeant or the other in the tavern, and it was even said that an important position in the town-hall of the capital of the province was to be given him. How difficult it is for the historian who tries to be impartial to arrive at the exact truth in regard to the sentiments and opinions of the illustrious personages who have filled the world with their fame! He does not know what to hold by, and the absence of authentic records often gives rise to lamentable mistakes. Considering events of such transcendent importance as that of the 18th Brumaire, the sack of Rome by Bourbon, or the destruction of Jerusalem—where is the psychologist or the historian who would be able to determine what were the thoughts which preceded or followed them in the minds of Bonaparte, of Charles V., and of Titus? Ours is an immense responsibility. To discharge it in part we will report words, phrases, and even discourses of the Orbajosan emperor himself; and in this way every one will be able to form the opinion which may seem to him most correct.

It is beyond a doubt that Cristobal Ramos left his house just after dark, crossed the Calle del Condestable, and, seeing three countrymen mounted on powerful mules coming toward him, asked them where they were going, to which they answered that they were going to Senora Dona Perfecta's house to take her some of the first fruits of their gardens and a part of the rent that had fallen due. They were Senor Paso Largo, a young man named Frasquito Gonzales, and a third, a man of medium stature and robust make, who was called Vejarruco, although his real name was Jose Esteban Romero. Caballuco turned back, tempted by the agreeable society of these persons, who were old and intimate friends of his, and accompanied them to Dona Perfecta's house. This took place, according to the most reliable accounts, at nightfall, and two days after the day on which Dona Perfecta and Pinzon held the conversation which those who have read the preceding chapter will have seen recorded there. The great Ramos stopped for a moment to give Librada certain messages of trifling importance, which a neighbor had confided to his good memory, and when he entered the dining-room he found the three before-mentioned countrymen and Senor Licurgo, who by a singular coincidence was also there, conversing about domestic matters and the crops. The Senora was in a detestable humor; she found fault with every thing, and scolded them harshly for the drought of the heavens and the barrenness of the earth, phenomena for which they, poor men! were in no wise to blame. The Penitentiary was also present. When Caballuco entered, the good canon saluted him affectionately and motioned him to a seat beside himself.

"Here is the individual," said the mistress of the house disdainfully. "It seems impossible that a man of such little account should be so much talked about. Tell me, Caballuco, is it true that one of the soldiers slapped you on the face this morning?"

"Me! me!" said the Centaur, rising indignantly, as if he had received the grossest insult.

"That is what they say," said Dona Perfecta. "Is it not true? I believed it; for any one who thinks so little of himself—they might spit in your face and you would think yourself honored with the saliva of the soldiers."

"Senora!" vociferated Ramos with energy, "saving the respect which I owe you, who are my mother, my mistress, my queen—saving the respect, I say, which I owe to the person who has given me all that I possess—saving the respect—"

"Well? One would think you were going to say something."

"I say then, that saving the respect, that about the slap is a slander," he ended, expressing himself with extraordinary difficulty. "My affairs are in every one's mouth—whether I come in or whether I go out, where I am going and where I have come from—and why? All because they want to make me a tool to raise the country. Pedro is contented in his own house, ladies and gentlemen. The troops have come? Bad! but what are we going to do about it? The alcalde and the secretary and the judge have been removed from office? Very bad! I wish the very stones of Orbajosa might rise up against them; but I have given my word to the governor, and up to the present—-"

He scratched his head, gathered his gloomy brows in a frown, and with ever-increasing difficulty of speech continued:

"I may be brutal, disagreeable, ignorant, quarrelsome, obstinate, and every thing else you choose, but in honor I yield to no one."

"What a pity of the Cid Campeador!" said Dona Perfecta contemptuously. "Don't you agree with me, Senor Penitentiary, that there is not a single man left in Orbajosa who has any shame in him?"

"That is a serious view to take of the case," responded the capitular, without looking at his friend, or removing from his chin the hand on which he rested his thoughtful face; "but I think this neighborhood has accepted with excessive submission the heavy yoke of militarism."

Licurgo and the three countrymen laughed boisterously.

"When the soldiers and the new authorities," said Dona Perfecta, "have taken from us our last real, when the town has been disgraced, we will send all the valiant men of Orbajosa in a glass case to Madrid to be put in the museum there or exhibited in the streets."

"Long life to the mistress!" cried the man called Vejarruco demonstratively. "What she says is like gold. It won't be said on my account that there are no brave men here, for if I am not with the

Aceros it is only because I have a wife and three children, and if any thing was to happen—if it wasn't for that—"

"But haven't you given your word to the governor, too?" said Dona Perfecta.

"To the governor?" cried the man named Frasquito Gonzalez. "There is not in the whole country a scoundrel who better deserves a bullet. Governor and Government, they are all of a piece. Last Sunday the priest said so many rousing things in his sermon about the heresies and the profanities of the people of Madrid—oh! it was worth while hearing him! Finally, he shouted out in the pulpit that religion had no longer any defenders."

"Here is the great Cristobal Ramos!" said Dona Perfecta, clapping the Centaur on the back. "He mounts his horse and rides about in the Plaza and up and down the high-road to attract the attention of the soldiers; when they see him they are terrified at the fierce appearance of the hero, and they all run away, half-dead with fright."

Dona Perfecta ended with an exaggerated laugh, which the profound silence of her hearers made still more irritating. Caballuco was pale.

"Senor Paso Largo," continued the lady, becoming serious, "when you go home to-night, send me your son Bartolome to stay here. I need to have brave people in the house; and even with that it may very well happen that, some fine morning, my daughter and myself will be found murdered in our beds."

"Senora!" exclaimed every one.

"Senora!" cried Caballuco, rising to his feet, "is that a jest, or what is it?"

"Senor Vejarruco, Senor Paso Largo," continued Dona Perfecta, without looking at the bravo of the place, "I am not safe in my own house. No one in Orbajosa is, and least of all, I. I live with my heart in my mouth. I cannot close my eyes in the whole night."

"But who, who would dare——"

"Come," exclaimed Licurgo with fire, "I, old and sick as I am, would be capable of fighting the whole Spanish army if a hair of the mistress' head should be touched!"

"Senor Caballuco," said Frasquito Gonzalez, "will be enough and more than enough."

"Oh, no," responded Dona Perfecta, with cruel sarcasm, "don't you see that Ramos has given his word to the governor?"

Caballuco sat down again, and, crossing one leg over the other, clasped his hands on them.

"A coward will be enough for me," continued the mistress of the house implacably, "provided he has not given his word to any one. Perhaps I may come to see my house assaulted, my darling daughter torn from my arms, myself trampled under foot and insulted in the vilest manner——"

She was unable to continue. Her voice died away in her throat, and she burst into tears.

"Senora, for Heaven's sake calm yourself! Come, there is no cause yet!" said Don Inocencio hastily, and manifesting the greatest distress in his voice and his countenance. "Besides, we must have a little resignation and bear patiently the calamities which God sends us."

"But who, senora, who would dare to commit such outrages?" asked one of the four countrymen. "Orbajosa would rise as one man to defend the mistress."

"But who, who would do it?" they all repeated.

"There, don't trouble yourselves asking useless questions," said the Penitentiary officiously. "You may go."

"No, no, let them stay," said Dona Perfecta quickly, drying her tears. "The company of my loyal servants is a great consolation to me."

"May my race be accursed!" said Uncle Licurgo, striking his knee with his clenched hand, "if all this mess is not the work of the mistress' own nephew."

"Of Don Juan Rey's son?"

"From the moment I first set eyes on him at the station at Villahorrenda, and he spoke to me with his honeyed voice and his mincing manners," declared Licurgo, "I thought him a great—I will not say what, through respect for the mistress. But I knew him—I put my mark upon him from that moment, and I make no mistakes. A thread shows what the ball is, as the saying goes; a sample tells what the cloth is, and a claw what the lion is."

"Let no one speak ill of that unhappy young man in my presence," said Senora de Polentinos severely. "No matter how great his faults may be, charity forbids our speaking of them and giving them publicity."

"But charity," said Don Inocencio, with some energy, "does not forbid us protecting ourselves against the wicked, and that is what the question is. Since character and courage have sunk so low in unhappy Orbajosa; since our town appears disposed to hold up its face to be spat upon by half a dozen soldiers and a corporal, let us find protection in union among ourselves."

"I will protect myself in whatever way I can," said Dona Perfecta resignedly, clasping her hands. "God's will be done!"

"Such a stir about nothing! By the Lord! In this house they are all afraid of their shadows," exclaimed Caballuco, half seriously, half jestingly. "One would think this Don Pepito was a legion of devils. Don't be frightened, senora. My little nephew Juan, who is thirteen, will guard the house, and we shall see, nephew for nephew, which is the best man."

"We all know already what your boasting and bragging signify," replied Dona Perfecta. "Poor Ramos! You want to pretend to be very brave when we have already had proof that you are not worth any thing."

Ramos turned slightly pale, while he fixed on Dona Perfecta a strange look in which terror and respect were blended.

"Yes, man; don't look at me in that way. You know already that I am not afraid of bugaboos. Do you want me to speak plainly to you now? Well, you are a coward."

Ramos, moving about restlessly in his chair, like one who is troubled with the itch, seemed greatly disturbed. His nostrils expelled and drew in the air, like those of a horse. Within that massive frame a storm of rage and fury, roaring and destroying, struggled to escape. After stammering a few words and muttering others under his breath, he rose to his feet and bellowed:

"I will cut off the head of Senor Rey!"

"What folly! You are as brutal as you are cowardly," said Dona Perfecta, turning pale. "Why do you talk about killing? I want no one killed, much less my nephew—a person whom I love, in spite of his wickedness."

"A homicide! What an atrocity!" exclaimed Don Inocencio, scandalized. "The man is mad!"

"To kill! The very idea of killing a man horrifies me, Caballuco," said Dona Perfecta, closing her mild eyes. "Poor man! Ever since you have been wanting to show your bravery, you have been howling like a ravening wolf. Go away, Ramos; you terrify me."

"Doesn't the mistress say she is afraid? Doesn't she say that they will attack the house; that they will carry off the young lady?"

"Yes, I fear so."

"And one man is going to do that," said Ramos contemptuously, sitting down again, "Don Pepe Poquita Cosa, with his mathematics, is going to do that. I did wrong in saying I would slit his throat. A doll of that kind one takes by the ear and ducks in the river."

"Yes, laugh now, you fool! It is not my nephew alone who is going to commit the outrages you have mentioned and which I fear; if it were he alone I should not fear him. I would tell Librada to stand at the door with a broom—and that would be sufficient. It is not he alone, no!"

"Who then?"

"Pretend you don't understand! Don't you know that my nephew and the brigadier who commands that accursed troop have been confabulating?"

"Confabulating!" repeated Caballuco, as if puzzled by the word.

"That they are bosom friends," said Licurgo. "Confabulate means to be like bosom friends. I had my suspicions already of what the mistress says."

"It all amounts to this—that the brigadier and the officers are hand and glove with Don Jose, and what he wants those brave soldiers want; and those brave soldiers will commit all kinds of outrages and atrocities, because that is their trade."

"And we have no alcalde to protect us."

"Nor judge."

"Nor governor. That is to say that we are at the mercy of that infamous rabble."

"Yesterday," said Vejarruco, "some soldiers enticed away Uncle Julian's youngest daughter, and the poor thing was afraid to go back home; they found her standing barefooted beside the old fountain, crying and picking up the pieces of her broken jar."

"Poor Don Gregorio Palomeque, the notary of Naharilla Alta!" said Frasquito. "Those rascals robbed him of all the money he had in his house. And all the brigadier said, when he was told about it, was it was a lie."

"Tyrants! greater tyrants were never born," said the other. "When I say that it is through punctilio that I am not with the Aceros!"

"And what news is there of Francisco Acero?" asked Dona Perfecta gently. "I should be sorry if any mischance were to happen to him. Tell me, Don Inocencio, was not Francisco Acero born in Orbajosa?"

"No; he and his brother are from Villajuan."

"I am sorry for it, for Orbajosa's sake," said Dona Perfecta. "This poor city has fallen into misfortune. Do you know if Francisco Acero gave his word to the governor not to trouble the poor soldiers in their abductions, in their impious deeds, in their sacrilegious acts, in their villanies?"

Caballuco sprang from his chair. He felt himself now not stung, but cut to the quick by a cruel stroke, like that of a sabre. With his face burning and his eyes flashing fire he cried:

"I gave my word to the governor because the governor told me that they had come for a good purpose."

"Barbarian, don't shout! Speak like other people, and we will listen to you."

"I promised that neither I nor any of my friends would raise guerillas in the neighborhood of Orbajosa. To those who wanted to take up arms because they were itching to fight I said: 'Go to the Aceros, for here we won't stir.' But I have a good many honest men, yes, senora; and true men, yes, senora; and valiant men, yes, senora; scattered about in the hamlets and villages and in the suburbs and the mountains, each in his own house, eh? And so soon as I say a quarter of a word to them, eh? they will be taking down their guns, eh? and setting out on horseback or on foot, for whatever place I tell them. And don't keep harping on words, for if I gave my word it was because I don't wish to fight; and if I want guerillas there will be guerillas; and if I don't there won't, for I am who I am, the same man that I always was, as every one knows very well. And I say again don't keep harping on words, eh? and don't let people say one thing to me when they mean another, eh? and if people want me to fight, let them say so plainly, eh? for that is what God has given us tongues for, to say this thing or that. The mistress knows very well who I am, as I know that I owe to her the shirt on my back, and the bread I eat to-day, and the first pea I sucked after I was weaned, and the coffin in which my father was buried when he died, and the medicines and the doctor that cured me when I was sick; and the mistress knows very well that if she says to me, 'Caballuco, break your head,' I will go there to the corner and dash it against the wall; the mistress knows very well that if she tells me now that it is day, although I see that it is night, I will believe that I am mistaken, and that it is broad day; the mistress knows very well that she and her interests are for me before my own life, and that if a mosquito stings her in my presence, I pardon it, because it is a mosquito; the mistress knows very well that she is dearer to me than all there is besides under the sun. To a man of heart like me one says, 'Caballuco, you stupid fellow, do this or do that.' And let there be an end to sarcasms, and beating about the bush, and preaching one thing and meaning another, and a stab here and a pinch there."

"There, man, calm yourself," said Dona Perfecta kindly. "You have worked yourself into a heat like those republican orators who came here to preach free religion, free love, and I don't know how many other free things. Let them bring you a glass of water."

Caballuco, twisting his handkerchief into a ball, wiped with it his broad forehead and his neck, which were bathed in perspiration. A glass of water was brought to him and the worthy canon, with a humility that was in perfect keeping with his sacerdotal character, took it from the servant's hand to give it to him himself, and held the plate while he drank. Caballuco gulped down the water noisily.

"Now bring another glass for me, Senora Librada," said Don Inocencio. "I have a little fire inside me too."

CHAPTER XXII

"DESPERTA!"

"With regard to the guerillas," said Dona Perfecta, when they had finished drinking, "all I will say is—do as your conscience dictates to you."

"I know nothing about dictations," cried Ramos. "I will do whatever the mistress pleases!"

"I can give you no advice on so important a matter," answered Dona Perfecta with the cautiousness and moderation which so well became her. "This is a very serious business, and I can give you no advice about it."

"But your opinion——"

"My opinion is that you should open your eyes and see, that you should open your ears and hear. Consult your own heart—I will grant that you have a great heart. Consult that judge, that wise counsellor, and do as it bids you."

Caballuco reflected; he meditated as much as a sword can meditate.

"We counted ourselves yesterday in Naharilla Alta," said Vejarruco, "and we were thirteen—ready for any little undertaking. But as we were afraid the mistress might be vexed, we did nothing. It is time now for the shearing."

"Don't mind about the shearing," said Dona Perfecta. "There will be time enough for it. It won't be left undone for that."

"My two boys quarrelled with each other yesterday," said Licurgo, "because one of them wanted to join Francisco Acero and the other didn't. 'Easy, boys, easy,' I said to them; 'all in good time. Wait; we know how to fight here as well as they do anywhere else.'"

"Last night," said Uncle Paso Largo, "Roque Pelosmalos told me that the moment Senor Ramos said half a word they would all be ready, with their arms in their hands. What a pity that the two Burguillos brothers went to work in the fields in Lugarnoble!"

"Go for them you," said the mistress quickly. "Senor Lucas, do you provide Uncle Paso Largo with a horse."

"And if the mistress tells me to do so, and Senor Ramos agrees," said Frasquito Gonzalez, "I will go to Villahorrenda to see if Robustiano, the forester, and his brother Pedro will also—"

"I think that is a good idea. Robustiano will not venture to come to Orbajosa, because he owes me a trifle. You can tell him that I forgive him the six dollars and a half. These poor people who sacrifice themselves with so little. Is it not so, Senor Don Inocencio?"

"Our good Ramos here tells me," answered the canon, "that his friends are displeased with him for his lukewarmness; but that, as soon as they see that he has decided, they will all put the cartridge-box in their belts."

"What, have you decided to take to the roads?" said the mistress. "I have not advised you to do any such thing, and if you do it, it is of your own free-will. Neither has Senor Don Inocencio said a word to you to that effect. But if that is your decision, you have no doubt strong reasons for coming to it. Tell me, Cristobal, will you have some supper? Will you take something—speak frankly."

"As far as my advising Senor Ramos to take the field is concerned," said Don Inocencio, looking over his spectacles, "Dona Perfecta is quite right. I, as an ecclesiastic, could advise nothing of the kind. I know that some priests do so, and even themselves take up arms; but that seems to me improper, very improper, and I for one will not follow their example. I carry my scrupulosity so far as not to say a word to Senor Ramos about the delicate question of his taking up arms. I know that Orbajosa desires it; I know that all the inhabitants of this noble city would bless him for it; I know that deeds are going to be done here worthy of being recorded in history; but notwithstanding, let me be allowed to maintain a discreet silence."

"Very well said," said Dona Perfecta. "I don't approve of ecclesiastics taking any part in such matters. That is the way an enlightened priest ought to act. Of course we know that on serious and solemn occasions, as when our country and our faith are in danger, for instance, it is within the province of an ecclesiastic to incite men to the conflict and even to take a part in it. Since God himself has taken part in celebrated battles, under the form of angels and saints, his ministers may very well do so also. During the wars against the infidels how many bishops headed the Castilian troops!"

"A great many, and some of them were illustrious warriors. But these times are not like those senora. It is true that, if we examine the matter closely, the faith is in greater danger now than it was then. For what do the troops that occupy our city and the surrounding villages represent? What do they represent? Are they any thing else but the vile instruments of which the atheists and Protestants who infest Madrid make use for their perfidious conquests and the extermination of the faith? In that centre of corruption, of scandal, of irreligion and unbelief, a few malignant men, bought by foreign gold, occupy themselves in destroying in our Spain the deeds of faith. Why, what do you suppose? They allow us to say mass and you to hear it through the remnant of consideration, for shame's sake—but, the day least expected—For my part, I am tranquil. I am not a man to disturb myself about any worldly and temporal interest. Dona Perfecta is well aware of that; all who know me are aware of it. My mind is at rest, and the triumph of the wicked does not terrify me. I know well that terrible days are in store for us; that all of us who wear the sacerdotal garb have our lives hanging by a hair, for Spain, doubt it not, will witness scenes like those of the French Revolution, in which thousands of pious ecclesiastics perished in a single day. But I am not troubled. When the hour to kill strikes, I will present my neck. I have lived long enough. Of what use am I? None, none!"

"May I be devoured by dogs," exclaimed Vejarruco, shaking his fist, which had all the hardness and the strength of a hammer, "if we do not soon make an end of that thievish rabble!"

"They say that next week they will begin to pull down the cathedral," observed Frasquito.

"I suppose they will pull it down with pickaxes and hammers," said the canon, smiling. "There are artificers who, without those implements, can build more rapidly than they can pull down. You all know that, according to holy tradition, our beautiful chapel of the Sagrario was pulled down by the Moors in a month, and immediately afterward rebuilt by the angels in a single night. Let them pull it down; let them pull it down!"

"In Madrid, as the curate of Naharilla told us the other night," said Vejarruco, "there are so few churches left standing that some of the priests say mass in the middle of the street, and as they are beaten and insulted and spat upon, there are many who don't wish to say it."

"Fortunately here, my children," observed Don Inocencio, "we have not yet had scenes of that nature. Why? Because they know what kind of people you are; because they have heard of your ardent piety and your valor. I don't envy the first ones who lay hands on our priests and our religion. Of course it is not necessary to say that, if they are not stopped in time, they will commit atrocities. Poor Spain, so holy and so meek and so good! Who would have believed she would ever arrive at such extremities! But I maintain that impiety will not triumph, no. There are courageous people still; there are people still like those of old. Am I not right, Senor Ramos?"

"Yes, senor, that there are," answered the latter.

"I have a blind faith in the triumph of the law of God. Some one must stand up in defence of it. If not one, it will be another. The palm of victory, and with it eternal glory, some one must bear. The wicked will perish, if not to-day, to-morrow. That which goes against the law of God will fall irremediably. Let it be in this manner or in that, fall it must. Neither its sophistries, nor its evasions, nor its artifices will save it. The hand of God is raised against it and will infallibly strike it. Let us pity them and desire their repentance. As for you, my children, do not expect that I shall say a word to you about the step which you are no doubt going to take. I know that you are good; I know that your generous determination and the noble end which you have in view will wash away from you all the stain of the sin of shedding blood. I know that God will bless you; that your victory, the same as your death, will exalt you in the eyes of men and in the eyes of God. I know that you deserve palms and glory and all sorts of honors; but in spite of this, my children, my lips will not incite you to the combat. They have never done it, and they will not do it now. Act according to the impulse of your own noble hearts. If they bid you to remain in your houses, remain in them; if they bid you to leave them—why, then, leave them. I will resign myself to be a martyr and to bow my neck to the executioner, if that vile army remains here. But if a noble and ardent and pious impulse of the sons of Orbajosa contributes to the great work of the extirpation of our country's ills, I shall hold myself the happiest of men, solely in being your fellow-townsman; and all my life of study, of penitence, of resignation, will seem to me less meritorious, less deserving of heaven, than a single one of your heroic days."

"Impossible to say more or to say it better!" exclaimed Dona Perfecta, in a burst of enthusiasm.

Caballuco had leaned forward in his chair and was resting his elbows on his knees; when the canon ended he took his hand and kissed it with fervor.

"A better man was never born," said Uncle Licurgo, wiping, or pretending to wipe away a tear.

"Long life to the Senor Penitentiary!" cried Frasquito Gonzalez, rising to his feet and throwing his cap up to the ceiling.

"Silence!" said Dona Perfecta. "Sit down, Frasquito! You are one of those with whom it is always much cry and little wool."

"Blessed be God who gave you that eloquent tongue!" exclaimed Cristobal, inflamed with admiration. "What a pair I have before me! While these two live what need is there of any one else? All the people in Spain ought to be like them. But how could that be, when there is nothing in it but roguery! In Madrid, which is the capital where the law and the mandarins come from, every thing is robbery and cheating. Poor religion, what a state they have brought it to! There is nothing to be seen but crimes. Senor Don Inocencio, Senora Dona Perfecta, by my father's soul, by the soul of my grandfather, by the salvation of my own soul, I swear that I wish to die!"

"To die!"

"That I wish those rascally dogs may kill me, and I say that I wish they may kill me, because I cannot cut them in quarters. I am very little."

"Ramos, you are great," said Dona Perfecta solemnly.

"Great? Great? Very great, as far as my courage is concerned; but have I fortresses, have I cavalry, have I artillery?"

"That is a thing, Ramos," said Dona Perfecta, smiling, "about which I would not concern myself. Has not the enemy what you lack?"

"Yes."

"Take it from him, then."

"We will take it from him, yes, senora. When I say that we will take it from him—"

"My dear Ramos," exclaimed Don Inocencio, "yours is an enviable position. To distinguish yourself, to raise yourself above the base multitude, to put yourself on an equality with the greatest heroes of the earth, to be able to say that the hand of God guides your hand—oh, what grandeur and honor! My friend, this is not flattery. What dignity, what nobleness, what magnanimity! No; men of such a temper cannot die. The Lord goes with them, and the bullet and the steel of the enemy are arrested in their course; they do not dare—how should they dare—to touch them, coming from the musket and the hand of heretics? Dear Caballuco, seeing you, seeing your bravery and your nobility, there come to my mind involuntarily the verses of that ballad on the conquest of the Empire of Trebizond:

"'Came the valiant Roland

Armed at every point,
On his war-horse mounted,
The gallant Briador;
His good sword Durlindana
Girded to his side,
Couched for the attack his lance,
On his arm his buckler stout,
Through his helmet's visor
Flashing fire he came;
Quivering like a slender reed
Shaken by the wind his lance,
And all the host united
Defying haughtily.'"

"Very good," exclaimed Licurgo, clapping his hands. "And I say like Don Renialdos:

"'Let none the wrath of Don Renialdos
Dare brave and hope to escape unscathed;
For he who seeks with him a quarrel,
Shall pay so dearly for his rashness
That he, and all his cause who champion,
Shall at my hand or meet destruction
Or chastisement severe shall suffer.'"

"Ramos, you will take some supper, you will eat something; won't you?" said the mistress of the house.

"Nothing, nothing;" answered the Centaur. "Or if you give me any thing, let it be a plate of gunpowder."

And bursting into a boisterous laugh, he walked up and down the room several times, attentively observed by every one; then, stopping beside the group, he looked fixedly at Dona Perfecta and thundered forth these words:

"I say that there is nothing more to be said. Long live Orbajosa! death to Madrid!"

And he brought his hand down on the table with such violence that the floor shook.

"What a valiant spirit!" said Don Inocencio.

"What a fist you have!"

Every one was looking at the table, which had been split in two by the blow.

Then they looked at the never-enough-to-be-admired Renialdos or Caballuco. Undoubtedly there was in his handsome countenance, in his green eyes animated by a strange, feline glow, in his black hair, in his herculean frame, a certain expression and air of grandeur—a trace, or rather a memory, of the grand races that dominated the world. But his general aspect was one of pitiable degeneration, and it was difficult to discover the noble and heroic filiation in the brutality of the present. He resembled Don Cayetano's great men as the mule resembles the horse.

CHAPTER XXIII

MYSTERY

The conference lasted for some time longer, but we omit what followed as not being necessary to a clear understanding of our story. At last they separated, Senor Don Inocencio remaining to the last, as usual. Before the canon and Dona Perfecta had had time to exchange a word, an elderly woman, Dona Perfecta's confidential servant and her right hand, entered the dining-room, and her mistress, seeing that she looked disturbed and anxious, was at once filled with disquietude, suspecting that something wrong was going on in the house.

"I can't find the senorita anywhere," said the servant, in answer to her mistress' questions.

"Good Heavens—Rosario! Where is my daughter?"

"Virgin of Succor protect us!" cried the Penitentiary, taking up his hat and preparing to hurry out with Dona Perfecta.

"Search for her well. But was she not with you in her room?"

"Yes, senora," answered the old woman, trembling, "but the devil tempted me, and I fell asleep."

"A curse upon your sleep! What is this? Rosario, Rosario! Librada!"

They went upstairs and came down again, they went up a second time and came down again; carrying a light and looking carefully in all the rooms. At last the voice of the Penitentiary was heard saying joyfully from the stairs:

"Here she is, here she is! She has been found."

A moment later mother and daughter were standing face to face in the hall.

"Where were you?" asked Dona Perfecta, in a severe voice, scrutinizing her daughter's face closely.

"In the garden," answered the girl, more dead than alive.

"In the garden at this hour? Rosario!"

"I was warm, I went to the window, my handkerchief dropped out, and I came down stairs for it!"

"Why didn't you ask Librada to get it for you? Librada! Where is that girl? Has she fallen asleep too?"

Librada at last made her appearance. Her pale face revealed the consternation and the apprehension of the delinquent.

"What is this? Where were you?" asked her mistress, with terrible anger.

"Why, senora, I came down stairs to get the clothes out of the front room—and I fell asleep."

"Every one here seems to have fallen asleep to-night. Some of you, I fancy, will not sleep in my house to-morrow night. Rosario, you may go."

Comprehending that it was necessary to act with promptness and energy, Dona Perfecta and the canon began their investigations without delay. Questions, threats, entreaties, promises, were skilfully employed to discover the truth regarding what had happened. Not even the shadow of guilt was found to attach to the old servant; but Librada confessed frankly between tears and sighs all her delinquencies, which we will sum up as follows:

Shortly after his arrival in the house Senor Pinzon had begun to cast loving glances at Senorita Rosario. He had given money to Librada, according to what the latter said, to carry messages and love-letters to her. The young lady had not seemed angry, but, on the contrary, pleased, and several days had passed in this manner. Finally, the servant declared that Rosario and Senor Pinzon had agreed to meet and talk with each other on this night at the window of the room of the latter, which opened on the garden. They had confided their design to the maid, who promised to favor it, in consideration of a sum which was at once given her. It had been agreed that Senor Pinzon was to leave the house at his usual hour and return to it secretly at nine o'clock, go to his room, and leave it and the house again, clandestinely also, a little later, to return, without concealment, at his usual late hour. In this way no suspicion would fall upon him. Librada had waited for Pinzon, who had entered the house closely enveloped in his cloak, without speaking a word. He had gone to his room at the same moment in which the young lady descended to the garden. During the interview, at which she was not present, Librada had remained on guard in the hall to warn Pinzon, if any danger should threaten; and at the end of an hour the latter had left the house enveloped in his cloak, as before, and without speaking a word. When the confession was ended Don Inocencio said to the wretched girl:

"Are you sure that the person who came into and went out of the house was Senor Pinzon?"

The culprit answered nothing, but her features expressed the utmost perplexity.

Her mistress turned green with anger.

"Did you see his face?"

"But who else could it be but he?" answered the maid. "I am certain that it was he. He went straight to his room—he knew the way to it perfectly well."

"It is strange," said the canon. "Living in the house there was no need for him to use such mystery. He might have pretended illness and remained in the house. Does it not seem so to you, senora?"

"Librada," exclaimed the latter, in a paroxysm of anger, "I vow that you shall go to prison."

And clasping her hands, she dug the nails of the one into the other with such force as almost to draw blood.

"Senor Don Inocencio," she exclaimed, "let us die—there is no remedy but to die."

Then she burst into a fit of inconsolable weeping.

"Courage, senora," said the priest, in a moved voice. "Courage—now it is necessary to be very brave. This requires calmness and a great deal of courage.

"Mine is immense," said Senora de Polentinos, in the midst of her sobs.

"Mine is very small," said the canon; "but we shall see, we shall see."

CHAPTER XXIV

THE CONFESSION

Meanwhile Rosario—with her heart torn and bleeding, unable to shed tears, unable to be at peace or rest, transpierced by grief as by a sharp sword, with her thoughts passing swiftly from the world to God and from God to the world, bewildered and half-crazed, her hands clasped, her bare feet resting on the floor—was kneeling, late in the evening, in her own room, beside her bed, on the edge of which she rested her burning forehead, in darkness, in solitude, and in silence. She was careful not to make the slightest noise, in order not to attract the attention of her mother, who was asleep, or seemed to be asleep, in the adjoining room. She lifted up her distracted thoughts to Heaven in this form:

"Lord, my God, why is it that before I did not know how to lie, and now I know? Why did I not know before how to deceive, and now I deceive? Am I a vile woman? Is this that I feel, is this that is happening to me, a fall from which there can be no arising? Have I ceased to be virtuous and good? I do not recognize myself. Is it I or is it some one else who is in this place? How many terrible things in a few days! How many different sensations! My heart is consumed with all it has felt. Lord, my God, dost thou hear my voice, or am I condemned to pray eternally without being heard? I am good, nothing will convince me that I am not good. To love, to love boundlessly, is that wickedness? But no—it is no illusion, no error—I am worse than the worst woman on earth. A great serpent is within me, and has fastened his poisonous fangs in my heart. What is this that I feel? My God, why dost thou not kill me? Why dost thou not plunge me forever into the depths of hell? It is frightful, but I confess it to the priest—I hate my mother. Why is this? I cannot explain it to myself. He has not said a word to me against my mother. I do not know how this is come to pass. How wicked I am! The demons have taken possession of me. Lord, come to my help, for with my own strength alone I cannot vanquish myself. A terrible impulse urges me to leave this house. I wish to escape, to fly from it. If he does not take me, I will drag myself after him through the streets. What divine joy is this that mingles in my breast with so cruel a grief? Lord God, my father, illumine me. I desire only to love. I was not born for this hatred that is consuming me. I was not born to deceive, to lie, to cheat. To-morrow I will go out into the streets and cry aloud to all the passers-by: 'I love! I hate!' My heart will relieve itself in this way. What happiness it would be to be able to reconcile every thing, to love and respect every one! May the Most Holy Virgin protect me. Again that terrible idea! I don't wish to think it, and I think it. Ah! I cannot deceive myself in regard to this. I can neither destroy it nor diminish it—but I can confess it; and I confess it, saying to thee: 'Lord, I hate my mother!'"

At last she fell into a doze. In her uneasy sleep her imagination reproduced in her mind all she had done that night, distorting it, without altering it in substance. She heard again the clock of the cathedral striking nine; she saw with joy the old servant fall into a peaceful sleep; and she left the room very slowly, in order to make no noise; she descended the stairs softly, step by step and on tiptoe, in order to avoid making the slightest sound. She went into the garden, going around through the servants' quarters and the kitchen; in the garden she paused for a moment to look up at the sky, which was dark and studded with stars. The wind was hushed. Not a breath disturbed the profound stillness of the night. It seemed to maintain a fixed and silent attention—the attention of eyes that look without winking and ears that listen attentively, awaiting a great event. The night was watching.

She then approached the glass door of the dining-room and looked cautiously through it, from a little distance, fearing that those within might perceive her. By the light of the dining-room lamp she saw her mother sitting with her back toward her. The Penitentiary was on her right, and his profile seemed to undergo a strange transformation, his nose grew larger and larger, seeming like the beak of some fabulous bird; and his whole face became a black silhouette with angles here and there, sharp derisive, irritating. In front of him sat Caballuco, who resembled a dragon rather than a man. Rosario could see his green eyes, like two lanterns of convex glass. This glow, and the imposing figure of the animal, inspired her with fear. Uncle Licurgo and the other three men appeared to her imagination like grotesque little figures. She had seen somewhere, doubtless in some of the clay figures at the fairs, that foolish smile, those coarse faces, that stupid look. The dragon moved his arms which, instead of gesticulating, turned round, like the arms of a windmill, and the green globes, like the lights of a pharmacy, moved from side to side. His glance was blinding. The conversation appeared to be interesting. The Penitentiary was flapping his wings. He was a presumptuous bird, who tried to fly and could not. His beak lengthened itself, twisting round and round. His feathers stood out, as if with rage; and then, collecting himself and becoming pacified, he hid his bald head under his wings. Then the little clay figures began to move, wishing to be persons, and Frasquito Gonzalez was trying to pass for a man.

Rosario felt an inexplicable terror, witnessing this friendly conference. She went away from the door and advanced, step by step, looking around her to see if she was observed. Although she saw no one, she fancied that a million eyes were fastened upon her. But suddenly her fears and her shame were dispelled. At the window of the room occupied by Senor Pinzon appeared a man, dressed in blue; the buttons on his coat shone like rows of little lights. She approached. At the same instant she felt a pair of arms with galloons lift her up as if she were a feather and with a swift movement place her in the room. All was changed. Suddenly a crash was heard, a violent blow that shook the house to its foundations. Neither knew the cause of the noise. They trembled and were silent.

It was the moment in which the dragon had broken the table in the dining-room.

CHAPTER XXV

UNFORESEEN EVENTS—A PASSING DISAGREEMENT

The scene changes. We see before us a handsome room, bright, modest, gay, comfortable, and surprisingly clean. A fine matting covers the floor, and the white walls are covered with good prints of saints and some sculptures of doubtful artistic value. The old mahogany of the furniture shines with the polish of many Saturday rubbings, and the altar, on which a magnificent Virgin, dressed in blue and silver, receives domestic worship, is covered with innumerable pretty trifles, half sacred, half profane. There are on it, besides, little pictures in beads, holy-water fonts, a watch-case with an Agnes Dei, a Palm Sunday palm-branch, and not a few odorless artificial flowers. A number of oaken bookshelves contain a rich and choice library, in which Horace, the Epicurean and Sybarite, stands side by side with the tender Virgil, in whose verses we see the heart of the enamored Dido throbbing and melting; Ovid the large-nosed, as sublime as he is obscene and sycophantic, side by side with Martial, the eloquent and witty vagabond; Tibullus the impassioned, with Cicero the grand; the severe Titus Livius with the terrible Tacitus, the scourge of the Caesars; Lucretius the pantheist; Juvenal, who flayed with his pen; Plautus, who composed the best comedies of antiquity while turning a mill-wheel; Seneca the philosopher, of whom it is said that the noblest act of his life was his death; Quintilian the rhetorician; the immoral Sallust, who speaks so eloquently of virtue; the two Plinys; Suetonius and Varro—in a word, all the Latin letters from the time when they stammered their first word with Livius Andronicus until they exhaled their last sigh with Rutilius.

But while making this unnecessary though rapid enumeration, we have not observed that two women have entered the room. It is very early, but the Orbajosans are early risers. The birds are singing to burst their throats in their cages; the church-bells are ringing for mass, and the goats, going from house to house to be milked, are tinkling their bells gayly.

The two ladies whom we see in the room that we have described have just come back from hearing mass. They are dressed in black, and each of them carries in her right hand her little prayer-book, and the rosary twined around her fingers.

"Your uncle cannot delay long now," said one of them. "We left him beginning mass; but he gets through quickly, and by this time he will be in the sacristy, taking off his chasuble. I would have stayed to hear him say mass, but to-day is a very busy day for me."

"I heard only the prebendary's mass to-day," said the other, "and he says mass in a twinkling; and I don't think it has done me any good, for I was greatly preoccupied. I could not get the thought of the terrible things that are happening to us out of my head."

"What is to be done? We must only have patience. Let us see what advice your uncle will give us."

"Ah!" exclaimed the other, heaving a deep and pathetic sigh; "I feel my blood on fire."

"God will protect us."

"To think that a person like you should be threatened by a ——. And he persists in his designs! Last night Senora Dona Perfecta, I went back to the widow De Cuzco's hotel, as you told me, and asked her for later news. Don Pepito and the brigadier Batalla are always consulting together—ah, my God! consulting about their infernal plans, and emptying bottle after bottle of wine. They are a pair of rakes, a pair of drunkards. No doubt they are plotting some fine piece of villany together. As I take such an interest in you, last night, seeing Don Pepito having the hotel while I was there, I followed him——"

"And where did you go?"

"To the Casino; yes, senora, to the Casino," responded the other, with some confusion. "Afterward he went back to his hotel. And how my uncle scolded me because I remained out so late, playing the spy in that way! But I can't help it, and to see a person like you threatened by such dangers makes me wild. For there is no use in talking; I foresee that the day we least expect it those villains will attack the house and carry off Rosarito."

Dona Perfecta, for she it was, bending her eyes on the floor, remained for a long time wrapped in thought. She was pale, and her brows were gathered in a frown. At last she exclaimed:

"Well, I see no way of preventing it!"

"But I see a way," quickly said the other woman, who was the niece of the Penitentiary and Jacinto's mother; "I see a very simple way, that I explained to you, and that you do not like. Ah, senora! you are too good. On occasions like this it is better to be a little less perfect—to lay scruples aside. Why, would that be an offence to God?"

"Maria Remedios," said Dona Perfecta haughtily, "don't talk nonsense."

"Nonsense! You, with all your wisdom, cannot make your nephew do as you wish. What could be simpler than what I propose? Since there is no justice now to protect us, let us do a great act of justice ourselves. Are there not men in your house who are ready for any thing? Well, call them and say to them: 'Look, Caballuco, Paso Largo,' or whoever it may be, 'to-night disguise yourself well, so that you may not be recognized; take with you a friend in whom you have confidence, and station yourself at the corner of the Calle de Santa Faz. Wait a while, and when Don Jose Rey passes through the Calle de la Triperia on his way to the Casino,—for he will certainly go to the Casino, understand me well,—when he is passing you will spring out on him and give him a fright.'"

"Maria Remedios, don't be a fool!" said Dona Perfecta with magisterial dignity.

"Nothing more than a fright, senora; attend well to what I say, a fright. Why! Do you suppose I would advise a crime? Good God! the very idea fills me with horror, and I fancy I can see before my eyes blood and fire! Nothing of the sort, senora. A fright—nothing but a fright, which will make that ruffian understand that we are well protected. He goes alone to the Casino, senora, entirely alone;

and there he meets his valiant friends, those of the sabre and the helmet. Imagine that he gets the fright and that he has a few bones broken, in addition—without any serious wounds, of course. Well, in that case, either his courage will fail him and he will leave Orbajosa, or he will be obliged to keep his bed for a fortnight. But they must be told to make the fright a good one. No killing, of course; they must take care of that, but just a good beating."

"Maria," said Dona Perfecta haughtily, "you are incapable of a lofty thought, of a great and saving resolve. What you advise me is an unworthy piece of cowardice."

"Very well, I will be silent. Poor me! what a fool I am!" exclaimed the Penitentiary's niece with humility. "I will keep my follies to console you after you have lost your daughter."

"My daughter! Lose my daughter!" exclaimed Dona Perfecta, with a sudden access of rage. "Only to hear you puts me out of my senses. No, they shall not take her from me! If Rosario does not abhor that ruffian as I wish her to do, she shall abhor him. For a mother's authority must have some weight. We will tear this passion, or rather this caprice, from her heart, as a tender plant is torn out of the ground before it has had time to cast roots. No, this cannot be, Remedios. Come what may, it shall not be! Not even the most infamous means he could employ will avail that madman. Rather than see her my nephew's wife, I would accept any evil that might happen to her, even death!"

"Better dead, better buried and food for worms," affirmed Remedios, clasping her hands as if she were saying a prayer—"than see her in the power of—ah, senora, do not be offended if I say something to you, and that is, that it would be a great weakness to yield merely because Rosarito has had a few secret interviews with that audacious man. The affair of the night before last, as my uncle related it to me, seems to me a vile trick on Don Jose to obtain his object by means of a scandal. A great many men do that. Ah, Divine Saviour, I don't know how there are women who can look any man in the face unless it be a priest."

"Be silent, be silent!" said Dona Perfecta, with vehemence. "Don't mention the occurrence of the night before last to me. What a horrible affair! Maria Remedios, I understand now how anger can imperil the salvation of a soul. I am burning with rage—unhappy that I am, to see such things and not to be a man! But to speak the truth in regard to the occurrence of the night before last—I still have my doubts. Librada vows and declares that Pinzon was the man who came into the house. My daughter denies every thing; my daughter has never told me a lie! I persist in my suspicions. I think that Pinzon is a hypocritical go-between, but nothing more."

"We come back to the same thing—that the author of all the trouble is the blessed mathematician. Ah! my heart did not deceive me when I first saw him. Well, then senora! resign yourself to see something still more terrible, unless you make up your mind to call Caballuco and say to him, 'Caballuco, I hope that—'"

"The same thing again; what a simpleton you are!"

"Oh yes! I know I am a great simpleton; but how can I help it if I am not any wiser? I say what comes into my head, without any art."

"What you think of—that silly and vulgar idea of the beating and the fright—is what would occur to any one. You have not an ounce of brains, Remedios; to solve a serious question you can think of nothing better than a piece of folly like that. I have thought of a means more worthy of noble-minded and well-bred persons. A beating! What stupidity! Besides, I would not on any account have my nephew receive even so much as a scratch by an order of mine. God will send him his punishment through some one of the wonderful ways which he knows how to choose. All we have to do is to work in order that the designs of God may find no obstacle. Maria Remedios, it is necessary in matters of this kind to go directly to the causes of things. But you know nothing about causes—you can see only trifles."

"That may be so," said the priest's niece, with humility. "I wonder why God made me so foolish that I can understand nothing of those sublime ideas!"

"It is necessary to go to the bottom—to the bottom, Remedios. Don't you understand yet?"

"No."

"My nephew is not my nephew, woman; he is blasphemy, sacrilege, atheism, demagogy. Do you know what demagogy is?"

"Something relating to those people who burned Paris with petroleum; and those who pull down the churches and fire on the images. So far I understand very well."

"Well, my nephew is all that! Ah! if he were alone in Orbajosa—but no, child. My nephew, through a series of fatalities, which are trials, the transitory evils that God permits for our chastisement, is equivalent to an army; is equivalent to the authority of the government; equivalent to the alcalde; equivalent to the judge. My nephew is not my nephew; he is the official nation, Remedios—that second nation composed of the scoundrels who govern in Madrid, and who have made themselves masters of its material strength; of that apparent nation—for the real nation is the one that is silent, that pays and suffers; of that fictitious nation that signs decrees and pronounces discourses and makes a farce of government, and a farce of authority, and a farce of every thing. That is what my nephew is to-day; you must accustom yourself to look under the surface of things. My nephew is the government, the brigadier, the new alcalde, the new judge—for they all protect him, because of the unanimity of their ideas; because they are chips of the same block, birds of a feather. Understand it well; we must defend ourselves against them all, for they are all one, and one is all; we must attack them all together; and not by beating a man as he turns a corner, but as our forefathers attacked the Moors—the Moors, Remedios. Understand this well, child; open your understanding and allow an idea that is not vulgar to enter it—rise above yourself; think lofty thoughts, Remedios!"

Don Inocencio's niece was struck dumb by so much loftiness of soul. She opened her mouth to say something that should be in consonance with so sublime an idea, but she only breathed a sigh.

"Like the Moors," repeated Dona Perfecta. "It is a question of Moors and Christians. And did you suppose that by giving a fright to my nephew all would be ended? How foolish you are! Don't you see that his friends support him? Don't you see that you are at the mercy of that rabble? Don't you see that any little lieutenant can set fire to my house, if he takes it into his head to do so? But don't you know this? Don't you comprehend that it is necessary to go to the bottom of things? Don't you comprehend how vast, how tremendous is the power of my enemy, who is not a man, but a sect? Don't you comprehend that my nephew, as he confronts me to-day, is not a calamity, but a plague? Against this plague, dear Remedios, we shall have here a battalion sent by God that will annihilate the infernal militia from Madrid. I tell you that this is going to be great and glorious."

"If it were at last so!"

"But do you doubt it? To-day we shall see terrible things here," said Dona Perfecta, with great impatience. "To-day, to-day! What o'clock is it? Seven? So late, and nothing has happened!"

"Perhaps my uncle has heard something; he is here now, I hear him coming upstairs."

"Thank God!" said Dona Perfecta, rising to receive the Penitentiary. "He will have good news for us."

Don Inocencio entered hastily. His altered countenance showed that his soul, consecrated to religion and to the study of the classics, was not as tranquil as usual.

"Bad news!" he said, laying his hat on a chair and loosening the cords of his cloak.

Dona Perfecta turned pale.

"They are arresting people," added Don Inocencio, lowering his voice, as if there was a soldier hidden under every chair. "They suspect, no doubt, that the people here would not put up with their high-handed measures, and they have gone from house to house, arresting all who have a reputation for bravery."

Dona Perfecta threw herself into an easy chair and clutched its arms convulsively.

"It remains to be seen whether they have allowed themselves to be arrested," observed Remedios.

"Many of them have—a great many of them," said Don Inocencio, with an approving look, addressing Dona Perfecta, "have had time to escape, and have gone with arms and horses to Villahorrenda."

"And Ramos?"

"They told me in the cathedral that he is the one they are looking for most eagerly. Oh, my God! to arrest innocent people in that way, who have done nothing yet. Well, I don't know how good Spaniards can have patience under such treatment. Senora Dona Perfecta, when I was telling you about the arrests, I forgot to say that you ought to go home at once."

"Yes, I will go at once. Have those bandits searched my house?"

"It is possible. Senora, we have fallen upon evil days," said Don Inocencio, in solemn and feeling accents. "May God have pity upon us!"

"There are half a dozen well-armed men in my house," responded the lady, greatly agitated. "What iniquity! Would they be capable of wanting to carry them off too?"

"Assuredly Senor Pinzon will not have neglected to denounce them. Senora, I repeat that we have fallen upon evil days. But God will protect the innocent."

"I am going now. Don't fail to stop in at the house."

"Senora, as soon as the lesson is over—though I imagine that with the excitement that there is in the town, all the boys will play truant to-day——But in any case I will go to the house after class hours. I don't wish you to go out alone, senora. Those vagabond soldiers are strutting about the streets with such insolent airs. Jacinto, Jacinto!"

"It is not necessary. I will go alone."

"Let Jacinto go with you," said the young man's mother. "He must be up by this time."

They heard the hurried footsteps of the little doctor, who was coming down the stairs in the greatest haste. He entered the room with flushed face and panting for breath.

"What is the matter?" asked his uncle.

"In the Troyas' house," said the young man, "in the house of those—those girls—"

"Finish at once!"

"Caballuco is there!"

"Up there? In the house of the Troyas?"

"Yes, senor. He spoke to me from the terrace, and he told me he was afraid they were coming there to arrest him."

"Oh, what a fool! That idiot is going to allow himself to be arrested!" exclaimed Dona Perfecta, tapping the floor impatiently with her foot.

"He wants to come down and let us hide him in the house."

"Here?"

The canon and his niece exchanged a glance.

"Let him come down!" said Dona Perfecta vehemently.

"Here?" repeated Don Inocencio, with a look of ill-humor.

"Here," answered the lady. "I don't know of any house where he would be more secure."

"He can let himself down easily from the window of my room," said Jacinto.

"Well, if it is necessary——"

"Maria Remedios," said Dona Perfecta, "if they take that man, all is lost."

"I am a fool and a simpleton," answered the canon's niece, laying her hand on her breast and stifling the sigh that was doubtless about to escape from it; "but they shall not take him."

Dona Perfecta went out quickly, and shortly afterward the Centaur was making himself comfortable in the arm-chair in which Don Inocencio was accustomed to sit when he was writing his sermons.

We do not know how it reached the ears of Brigadier Batalla, but certain it is that this active soldier had had notice that the Orbajosans had changed their intentions; and on the morning of this day he had ordered the arrest of those whom in our rich insurrectional language we are accustomed to call marked. The great Caballuco escaped by a miracle, taking refuge in the house of the Troyas, but not thinking himself safe there he descended, as we have seen, to the holy and unsuspected mansion of the good canon.

At night the soldiers, established at various points of the town, kept a strict watch on all who came in and went out, but Ramos succeeded in making his escape, cheating or perhaps without cheating the vigilance of the military. This filled the measure of the rage of the Orbajosans, and numbers of people were conspiring in the hamlets near Villahorrenda; meeting at night to disperse in the morning and prepare in this way the arduous business of the insurrection. Ramos scoured the surrounding country, collecting men and arms; and as the flying columns followed the Aceros into the district of Villajuan de Nahara, our chivalrous hero made great progress in a very short time.

At night he ventured boldly into Orbajosa, employing stratagems and perhaps bribery. His popularity and the protection which he received in the town served him, to a certain extent, as a safeguard; and it would not be rash to affirm that the soldiers did not manifest toward this daring leader of the insurrection the same rigor as toward the insignificant men of the place. In Spain, and especially in time of war, which is here always demoralizing, these unworthy considerations toward the great are often seen, while the little are persecuted pitilessly. Favored then by his boldness, by bribery, or by we know not what, Caballuco entered Orbajosa, gained new recruits, and collected arms and money. Either for the great security of his person or in order to save appearances, he did not set foot in his own house; he entered Dona Perfecta's only for the purpose of treating of important affairs, and he usually supped in the house of some friend, preferring always the respected domicile of some priest, and especially that of Don Inocencio, where he had taken refuge on the fateful morning of the arrests.

Meanwhile Batalla had telegraphed to the Government the information that a plot of the rebels having been discovered its authors had been imprisoned, and the few who had succeeded in escaping had fled in various directions and were being actively pursued by the military.

CHAPTER XXVI

MARIA REMEDIOS

There is nothing more entertaining than to search for the cause of some interesting event which surprises or agitates us, and nothing more satisfactory than to discover it. When, seeing violent passions in open or concealed conflict, and led by the natural intuitive impulse which always accompanies human observation we succeed in discovering the hidden source from which that turbulent river had derived its waters, we experience a sensation very similar to the delight of the explorer or the discoverer of an unknown land.

This delight Providence has now bestowed upon us; for, exploring the hidden recesses of the hearts which beat in this story, we have discovered an event that is assuredly the source of the most important events that we have narrated; a passion which is the first drop of water of the impetuous current whose course we are observing.

Let us go on with our story, then. To do so, let us leave Senora de Polentinos, without concerning ourselves in regard to what may have happened to her on the morning of her conversation with Maria Remedios. Returning to her house, full of anxiety, she found herself obliged to endure the apologies and the civilities of Senor Pinzon, who assured her that while he lived her house should not be searched. Dona Perfecta responded haughtily, without deigning to look at him, for which reason he asked her politely for an explanation of her coldness, to which she replied requesting Senor Pinzon to leave her house, deferring to a future occasion the explanation which she would require from him of his perfidious conduct while in it. Don Cayetano arriving at this moment, words were exchanged between the two gentlemen, as between man and man; but as we are more interested at present in another matter, we will leave the Polentinos and the lieutenant-colonel to settle matters between them as best they can, and proceed to examine the question of the sources above mentioned.

Let us fix our attention on Maria Remedios, an estimable woman, to whom it is indispensably necessary to devote a few words. She was a lady, a real lady—for, notwithstanding her humble origin, the virtues of her uncle, Senor Don Inocencio, also of low origin, but elevated by his learning and his estimable qualities, had shed extraordinary lustre over the whole family.

The love of Remedios for Jacinto was one of the strongest passions of which the maternal heart is capable. She loved him with delirium; her son's welfare was her first earthly consideration; she regarded him as the most perfect type of beauty and talent ever created by God, and to see him happy and great and powerful she would have given her whole life and even a part of the life to come. The maternal sentiment is the only one which, because of its nobility and its sanctity, will admit of exaggeration; the only one which the delirium of passion does not debase. Nevertheless it is a singular phenomenon, frequently observed, that this exaltation of maternal affection, if not accompanied with absolute purity of heart and with perfect uprightness is apt to become perverted and transformed into a lamentable frenzy, which may lead, like any other ungoverned passion, to great errors and catastrophies.

In Orbajosa Maria Remedios passed for a model of virtue and a model niece—perhaps she was so in reality. She served with affection all who needed her services; she never gave occasion for gossip or for scandal; she never mixed herself up in intrigues. She carried her religion to the extreme of an offensive fanaticism; she practised charity; she managed her uncle's house with the utmost ability; she was well received, admired and kindly treated everywhere, in spite of the almost intolerable annoyance produced by her persistent habit of sighing and speaking always in a complaining voice.

But in Dona Perfecta's house this excellent lady suffered a species of *capitis diminutio*. In times far distant and very bitter for the family of the good Penitentiary, Maria Remedios (since it is the truth, why should it not be told?) had been a laundress in the house of Polentinos. And let it not be supposed that Dona Perfecta looked down upon her on this account—nothing of the kind. She behaved to her without any haughtiness; she felt a real sisterly affection for her; they ate together; they prayed together; they confided their troubles to each other; they aided each other in their charities and in their devotions as well as in domestic matters; but, truth to say, there was always a something, there was always a line, invisible but which could not be crossed between the improvised lady and the lady by birth and ancestry. Dona Perfecta addressed Maria as "thou," while the latter could never lay aside certain ceremonial forms. Maria Remedios always felt herself so insignificant in the presence of her uncle's friend that her natural humility had acquired through this feeling a strange tinge of sadness. She saw that the good canon was a species of perpetual Aulic councillor in the house; she saw her idolized Jacintillo mingling on terms of almost lover-like familiarity with the young lady, and nevertheless the poor mother and niece visited the house as little as possible. It is to be observed that Maria Remedios' dignity as a lady suffered not a little in Dona Perfecta's house, and this was disagreeable to her; for in this sighing spirit, too, there was, as there is in every living thing, a little pride. To see her son married to Rosarito, to see him rich and powerful; to see him related to Dona Perfecta, to the senora—ah! this was for Maria Remedios earth and heaven, this life and the next, the present and the future, the supreme totality of existence. For years her mind and her heart had been filled by the light of this sweet hope. Because of this hope she was good and she was bad; because of it she was religious and humble, or fierce and daring; because of it she was whatever she was—for without this idea Maria, who was the incarnation of her project, would not exist.

In person, Maria Remedios could not be more insignificant than she was. She was remarkable for a surprising freshness and robustness which made her look much younger than she really was, and she always dressed in mourning, although her widowhood was now of long standing.

Five days had passed since the entrance of Caballuco into the Penitentiary's house. It was evening. Remedios entered her uncle's room with the lighted lamp, which she placed on the table. She then seated herself in front of the old man, who, for a great part of the afternoon, had been sitting motionless and thoughtful in his easy chair. His fingers supported his chin, wrinkling up the brown skin, unshaven for the past three days.

"Did Caballuco say he would come here to supper to-night?" he asked his niece.

"Yes, senor, he will come. It is in a respectable house like this that the poor fellow is most secure."

"Well, I am not altogether easy in my mind, in spite of the respectability of the house," answered the Penitentiary. "How the brave Ramos exposes himself! And I am told that in Villahorrenda and the surrounding country there are a great many men. I don't know how many men——What have you heard?"

"That the soldiers are committing atrocities."

"It is a miracle that those Hottentots have not searched the house! I declare that if I see one of the red-trousered gentry enter the house, I shall fall down speechless."

"This is a nice condition of things!" said Remedios, exhaling half her soul in a sigh. "I cannot get out of my head the idea of the tribulation in which Senora Dona Perfecta finds herself. Uncle, you ought to go there."

"Go there to-night? The military are parading the streets! Imagine that some insolent soldier should take it into his head to——The senora is well protected. The other day they searched the house and they carried off the six armed men she had there; but afterward they sent them back to her. We have no one to protect us in case of an attack."

"I sent Jacinto to the senora's, to keep her company for a while. If Caballuco comes, we will tell him to stop in there, too. No one can put it out of my head but that those rascals are plotting some piece of villany against our friend. Poor senora, poor Rosarito! When one thinks that this might have been avoided by what I proposed to Dona Perfecta two days ago——"

"My dear niece," said the Penitentiary phlegmatically, "we have done all that it was in human power to do to carry out our virtuous purpose. More we cannot do. Convince yourself of this, and do not be obstinate. Rosarito cannot be the wife of our idolized Jacintillo. Your golden dream, your ideal of happiness, that at one time seemed attainable, and to which like a good uncle, I devoted all the powers of my understanding, has become chimerical, has vanished into smoke. Serious obstructions, the wickedness of a man, the indubitable love of the girl, and other things, regarding which I am silent, have altered altogether the condition of affairs. We were in a fair way to conquer, and suddenly we are conquered. Ah, niece! convince yourself of one thing. As matters are now, Jacinto deserves something a great deal better than that crazy girl."

"Caprices and obstinate notions!" responded Maria, with an ill-humor that was far from respectful. "That's a pretty thing to say now, uncle! The great minds are outshining themselves, now. Dona Perfecta with her lofty ideas, and you with your doubts and fears—of much use either of you is. It is a pity that God made me such a fool and gave me an understanding of brick and mortar, as the senora says, for if that wasn't the case I would soon settle the question."

"You?"

"If she and you had allowed me, it would be settled already."

"By the beating?"

"There's no occasion for you to be frightened or to open your eyes like that. There is no question of killing any body. What an idea!"

"Beating," said the canon, smiling, "is like scratching—when one begins one doesn't know when to leave off."

"Bah! say too that I am cruel and blood-thirsty. I wouldn't have the courage to kill a fly; it's not very likely that I should desire the death of a man."

"In fine, child, no matter what objections you may make, Senor Don Pepe Rey will carry off the girl. It is not possible now to prevent it. He is ready to employ every means, including dishonor. If Rosarito—how she deceived us with that demure little face and those heavenly eyes, eh!—if Rosarito, I say, did not herself wish it, then all might be arranged, but alas! she loves him as the sinner loves Satan; she is consumed with a criminal passion; she has fallen, niece, into the snares of the Evil One. Let us be virtuous and upright; let us turn our eyes away from the ignoble pair, and think no more about either of them."

"You know nothing about women, uncle," said Remedios, with flattering hypocrisy; "you are a holy man; you do not understand that Rosario's feeling is only a passing caprice, one of those caprices that are cured by a sound whipping."

"Niece," said Don Inocencio gravely and sententiously, "when serious things have taken place, caprices are not called caprices, but by another name."

"Uncle, you don't know what you are talking about," responded Maria Remedios, her face flushing suddenly. "What! would you be capable of supposing that Rosarito—what an atrocity! I will defend her; yes, I will defend her. She is as pure as an angel. Why, uncle, those things bring a blush to my cheek, and make me indignant with you."

As she spoke the good priest's face was darkened by a cloud of sadness that made him look ten years older.

"My dear Remedios," he said, "we have done all that is humanly possible, and all that in conscience we can or ought to do. Nothing could be more natural than our desire to see Jacintillo connected with that great family, the first in Orbajosa; nothing more natural than our desire to see him master of the seven houses in the town, the meadow of Mundogrande, the three gardens of the upper farm, La Encomienda, and the other lands and houses which that girl owns. Your son has great merit, every one knows it well. Rosarito liked him, and he liked Rosarito. The matter seemed settled. Dona Perfecta herself, without being very enthusiastic, doubtless on account of our origin, seemed favorably disposed toward it, because of her great esteem and veneration for me, as her confessor and friend. But suddenly this unlucky young man presents himself. The senora tells me that she has given her word to her brother, and that she cannot reject the proposal made by him. A difficult situation! But what do I do in view of all this? Ah, you don't know every thing! I will be frank with you. If I had found Senor de Rey to be a man of good principles, calculated to make Rosario happy, I would not have interfered in the matter; but the young man appeared to me to be a wretch, and, as the spiritual director of the house, it was my duty to take a hand in the business, and I took it. You know already that I determined to unmask him. I exposed his vices; I made manifest his atheism; I laid bare to the view of all the rottenness of that materialistic heart, and the senora was convinced that in giving her daughter to him, she would be delivering her up to vice. Ah, what anxieties I endured! The senora vacillated; I strengthened her wavering mind; I advised her concerning the means she might lawfully employ to send her nephew away without scandal. I suggested ingenious ideas to her; and as she often spoke to me of the scruples that troubled her tender conscience, I tranquillized her, pointing out to her how far it was allowable for us to go in our fight against that lawless enemy. Never did I counsel violent or sanguinary measures or base outrages, but always subtle artifices, in which there was no sin. My mind is tranquil, my dear niece. But you know that I struggled hard, that I worked like a negro. Ah! when I used to come home every night and say, 'Mariquilla, we are getting on well, we are getting on very well,' you used to be wild with delight, and you would kiss my hands again and again, and say I was the best man on earth. Why do you fly into a passion now, disfiguring your noble character and peaceable disposition? Why do you scold me? Why do you say that you are indignant, and tell me in plain terms that I am nothing better than an idiot?"

"Because," said the woman, without any diminution of her rage, "because you have grown faint-hearted all of a sudden."

"The thing is that every thing is going against us, woman. That confounded engineer, protected as he is by the army, is resolved to dare every thing. The girl loves him, the girl—I will say no more. It cannot be; I tell you that it cannot be."

"The army! But do you believe, like Dona Perfecta, that there is going to be a war, and that to drive Don Pepe from the town it will be necessary for one half of the nation to rise up against the other half? The senora has lost her senses, and you are in a fair way to lose yours."

"I believe as she does. In view of the intimate connection of Rey with the soldiers the personal question assumes larger proportions. But, ah, niece! if two days ago I entertained the hope that our valiant townsmen would kick the soldiers out of the town, since I have seen the turn things have taken, since I have seen that most of them have been surprised before fighting, and that Caballuco is in hiding and that the insurrection is going to the devil, I have lost confidence in every thing. The good doctrines have not yet acquired sufficient material force to tear in pieces the ministers and the emissaries of error. Ah, niece! resignation, resignation!"

And Don Inocencio, employing the method of expression which characterized his niece, heaved two or three profound sighs. Maria, contrary to what might have been expected, maintained absolute silence. She showed now neither anger nor the superficial sentimentality of her ordinary life; but only a profound and humble grief. Shortly after the good canon had ended his peroration two tears rolled down his niece's rosy cheeks; before long were heard a few half-suppressed sighs, and gradually, as the swell and tumult of a sea that is beginning to be stormy rise higher and higher and become louder and louder, so the surge of Maria Remedios' grief rose and swelled, until it at last broke forth in a flood of tears.

CHAPTER XXVII

A CANON'S TORTURE

"Resignation, resignation!" repeated Don Inocencio.

"Resignation, resignation!" repeated his niece, drying her tears. "If my dear son is doomed to be always a beggar, well, then, be it so. Lawsuits are becoming scarce; the day will soon come when the practice of the law will be the same as nothing. What is the use of all his talent? What is the use of his tiring his brain with so much study? Ah! We are poor. A day will come, Senor Don Inocencio, when my poor boy will not have a pillow on which to lay his head."

"Woman!"

"Man! can you deny it? Tell me, then, what inheritance are you going to leave him when you close your eyes on this world? A couple of rooms, half a dozen big books, poverty, and nothing more. What times are before us, uncle; what times! My poor boy is growing very delicate in his health, and he won't be able to work—it makes him dizzy now to read a book; he gets a headache and nausea whenever he works at night! He will have to beg a paltry situation; I shall have to take in sewing, and who knows, who knows but we may have to beg our bread!"

"Woman!"

"Oh, I know very well what I am talking about! Fine times before us!" added the excellent woman, forcing still more the lachrymose note in her diatribe. "My God! What is going to become of us? Ah, it is only a mother's heart that can feel these things! Only a mother is capable of suffering so much anxiety about a son's welfare. How should you understand it? No; it is one thing to have children and to suffer anxiety on their account and another to sing the *gori gori* in the cathedral and to teach Latin in the institute. Of great use is it for my son to be your nephew and to have taken so many honors and to be the pride and ornament of Orbajosa. He will die of starvation, for we already know what law brings; or else he will have to ask the deputies for a situation in Havana, where the yellow fever will kill him."

"But, niece—"

"No, I am not grieving, I am silent now; I won't annoy you any more. I am very troublesome, always crying and sighing; and I am not to be endured because I am a fond mother and I will look out for the good of my beloved son. I will die, yes, I will die in silence, and stifle my grief. I will swallow my tears, in order not to annoy his reverence the canon. But my idolized son will comprehend me and he won't put his hands to his ears as you are doing now. Woe is me! Poor Jacinto knows that I would die for him, and that I would purchase his happiness at the sacrifice of my life. Darling child of my soul! To be so deserving and to be forever doomed to mediocrity, to a humble station, for—don't get indignant, uncle—no matter what airs we put on, you will always be the son of Uncle Tinieblas, the sacristan of San Bernardo, and I shall never be any thing more than the daughter of Ildefonso Tinieblas, your brother, who used to sell crockery, and my son will be the grandson of the Tinieblas—for obscure we were born, and we shall never emerge from our obscurity, nor own a piece of land of which we can say, 'This is mine'; nor shall I ever plunge my arms up to the elbows in a sack of wheat threshed and winnowed on our own threshing-floor—all because of your cowardice, your folly, your soft-heartedness."

"But—but, niece!"

The canon's voice rose higher every time he repeated this phrase, and, with his hands to his ears, he shook his head from side to side with a look of mingled grief and desperation. The shrill complaint of Maria Remedios grew constantly shriller, and pierced the brain of the unhappy and now dazed priest like an arrow. But all at once the woman's face became transformed; her plaintive wail was changed to a hard, shrill scream; she turned pale, her lips trembled, she clenched her hands, a few locks of her disordered hair fell over her forehead, her eyes glittered, dried by the heat of the anger that glowed in her breast; she rose from her seat and, not like a woman, but like a harpy, cried:

"I am going away from here! I am going away from here with my son! We will go to Madrid; I don't want my son to fret himself to death in this miserable town! I am tired now of seeing that my son, under the protection of the cassock, neither is nor ever will be any thing. Do you hear, my reverend uncle? My son and I are going away! You will never see us again—never!"

Don Inocencio had clasped his hands and was receiving the thunderbolts of his niece's wrath with the consternation of a criminal whom the presence of the executioner has deprived of his last hope.

"In Heaven's name, Remedios," he murmured, in a pained voice; "in the name of the Holy Virgin——"

These fits of range of his niece, who was usually so meek, were as violent as they were rare, and five or six years would sometimes pass without Don Inocencio seeing Remedios transformed into a fury.

"I am a mother! I am a mother! and since no one else will look out for my son, I will look out for him myself!" roared the improvised lioness.

"In the name of the Virgin, niece, don't let your passion get the best of you! Remember that you are committing a sin. Let us say the Lord's Prayer and an Ave Maria, and you will see that this will pass away."

As he said this the Penitentiary trembled, and the perspiration stood on his forehead. Poor dove in the talons of the vulture! The furious woman completed his discomfiture with these words:

"You are good for nothing; you are a poltroon! My son and I will go away from this place forever, forever! I will get a position for my son, I will find him a good position, do you understand? Just as I would be willing to sweep the streets with my tongue if I could gain a living for him in no other way, so I will move heaven and earth to find a position for my boy in order that he may rise in the world and be rich, and a person of consequence, and a gentleman, and a lord and great, and all that there is to be—all, all!"

"Heaven protect me!" cried Don Inocencio, sinking into a chair and letting his head fall on his breast.

There was a pause during which the agitated breathing of the furious woman could be heard.

"Niece," said Don Inocencio at last, "you have shortened my life by ten years; you have set my blood on fire; you have put me beside myself. God give me the calmness that I need to bear with you! Lord, patience—patience is what I ask. And you, niece, do me the favor to sigh and cry to your heart's content for the next ten years; for your confounded mania of sniveling, greatly as it annoys me, is preferable to these mad fits of rage. If I did not know that you are good at heart——Well, for one who confessed and received communion this morning you are behaving—"

"Yes, but you are the cause of it—you!"

"Because in the matter of Rosario and Jacinto I say to you, resignation?"

"Because when every thing is going on well you turn back and allow Senor de Rey to get possession of Rosario."

"And how am I going to prevent it? Dona Perfecta is right in saying that you have an understanding of brick. Do you want me to go about the town with a sword, and in the twinkling of an eye to make mincemeat of the whole regiment, and then confront Rey and say to him, 'Leave the girl in peace or I will cut your throat'?"

"No, but when I advised the senora to give her nephew a fright, you opposed my advice, instead of supporting it."

"You are crazy with your talk about a fright."

"Because when the dog is dead the madness is at an end."

"I cannot advise what you call a fright, and what might be a terrible thing."

"Yes; because I am a cut-throat, am I not, uncle?"

"You know that practical jokes are vulgar. Besides, do you suppose that man would allow himself to be insulted? And his friends?"

"At night he goes out alone."

"How do you know that?"

"I know every thing; he does not take a step that I am not aware of; do you understand? The widow De Cuzco keeps me informed of every thing."

"There, don't set me crazy. And who is going to give him that fright? Let us hear."

"Caballuco."

"So that he is disposed—"

"No, but he will be if you command him."

"Come, niece, leave me in peace. I cannot command such an atrocity. A fright! And what is that? Have you spoken to him already?"

"Yes, senor; but he paid no attention to me, or rather he refused. There are only two people in Orbajosa who can make him do what they wish by a simple order—you and Dona Perfecta."

"Let Dona Perfecta order him to do it if she wishes, then. I will never advise the employment of violent and brutal measures. Will you believe that when Caballuco and some of his followers were talking of rising up in arms they could not draw a single word from me inciting them to bloodshed. No, not that. If Dona Perfecta wishes to do it—"

"She will not do it, either. I talked with her for two hours this afternoon and she said that she would preach war, and help it by every means in her power; but that she would not bid one man stab another in the back. She would be right in opposing it if anything serious were intended, but I don't want any wounds; all I want is to give him a fright."

"Well, if Dona Perfecta doesn't want to order a fright to be given to the engineer, I don't either, do you understand? My conscience is before every thing."

"Very well," returned his niece. "Tell Caballuco to come with me to-night—that is all you need say to him."

"Are you going out to-night?"

"Yes, senor, I am going out. Why, didn't I go out last night too?"

"Last night? I didn't know it; if I had known it I should have been angry; yes, senora."

"All you have to say to Caballuco is this: 'My dear Ramos, I will be greatly obliged to you if you will accompany my niece on an errand which she has to do to-night, and if you will protect her, if she should chance to be in any danger.'"

"I can do that. To accompany you, to protect you. Ah, rogue! you want to deceive me and make me your accomplice in some piece of villany."

"Of course—what do you suppose?" said Maria Remedios ironically. "Between Ramos and me we are going to slaughter a great many people to-night."

"Don't jest! I tell you again that I will not advise Ramos to do any thing that has the appearance of evil—I think he is outside."

A noise at the street-door was heard, then the voice of Caballuco speaking to the servant, and a little later the hero of Orbajosa entered the room.

"What is the news? Give us the news, Senor Ramos," said the priest. "Come! If you don't give us some hope in exchange for your supper and our hospitality——What is going on in Villahorrenda?"

"Something," answered the bravo, seating himself with signs of fatigue. "You shall soon see whether we are good for anything or not."

Like all persons who wish to make themselves appear important, Caballuco made a show of great reserve.

"To-night, my friend, you shall take with you, if you wish, the money they have given me for—"

"There is good need of it. If the soldiers should get scent of it, however, they won't let me pass," said Ramos, with a brutal laugh.

"Hold your tongue, man. We know already that you pass whenever you please. Why, that would be a pretty thing! The soldiers are not strait-laced gentry, and if they should become troublesome, with a couple of dollars, eh? Come, I see that you are not badly armed. All you want now is an eight-pounder. Pistols, eh? And a dagger too."

"For any thing that might happen," said Caballuco, taking the weapon from his belt and displaying its horrible blade.

"In the name of God and of the Virgin!" exclaimed Maria Remedios, closing her eyes and turning her face in terror, "put away that thing. The very sight of it terrifies me."

"If you won't take it ill of me," said Ramos, shutting the weapon, "let us have supper."

Maria Remedios prepared every thing quickly, in order that the hero might not become impatient.

"Listen to me a moment, Senor Ramos," said Don Inocencio to his guest, when they had sat down to supper. "Have you a great deal to do to-night?"

"Something there is to be done," responded the bravo. "This is the last night I shall come to Orbajosa—the last. I have to look up some boys who remained in the town, and we are going to see how we can get possession of the saltpetre and the sulphur that are in the house of Cirujeda."

"I asked you," said the curate amiably, filling his friend's plate, "because my niece wishes you to accompany her a short distance. She has some business or other to attend to, and it is a little late to be out alone."

"Is she going to Dona Perfecta's?" asked Ramos. "I was there a few moments ago, but I did not want to make any delay."

"How is the senora?"

"A little frightened. To-night I took away the six young men I had in the house."

"Why! don't you think they will be wanted there?" said Remedios, with alarm.

"They are wanted more in Villahorrenda. Brave men chafe at being kept in the house; is it not so, Senor Canon?"

"Senor Ramos, that house ought not to be left unprotected," said the Penitentiary.

"The servants are enough, and more than enough. But do you suppose, Senor Don Inocencio, that the brigadier employs himself in attacking the people's houses?"

"Yes, but you know very well that that diabolical engineer——"

"For that—there are not wanting brooms in the house," said Cristobal jovially. "For in the end, there will be no help for it but to marry them. After what has passed——"

"Senor Ramos," said Remedios, with sudden anger, "I imagine that all you know about marrying people is very little."

"I say that because a little while ago, when I was at the house, the mother and daughter seemed to be having a sort of reconciliation. Dona Perfecta was kissing Rosarito over and over again, and there was no end to their caresses and endearments."

"Reconciliation! With all these preparations for the war you have lost your senses. But, finally, are you coming with me or not?"

"It is not to Dona Perfecta's she wants to go," said the priest, "but to the hotel of the widow De Cuzco. She was saying that she does not dare to go alone, because she is afraid of being insulted."

"By whom?"

"It is easily understood. By that infernal engineer. Last night my niece met him there, and she gave him some plain talk; and for that reason she is not altogether easy in her mind to-night. The young fellow is revengeful and insolent."

"I don't know whether I can go," said Caballuco. "As I am in hiding now I cannot measure my strength against Don Jose Poquita Cosa. If I were not as I am—with half my face hidden, and the other half uncovered—I would have broken his back for him already twenty times over. But what happens if I attack him? He discovers who I am, he falls upon me with the soldiers, and good-bye to Caballuco. As for giving him a treacherous blow, that is something I couldn't do; nor would Dona Perfecta consent to it, either. For a stab in the dark Cristobal Ramos is not the man."

"But are you crazy, man? What are you thinking about?" said the Penitentiary, with unmistakable signs of astonishment. "Not even in thought would I advise you to do an injury to that gentleman. I would cut my tongue out before I would advise such a piece of villany. The wicked will fall, it is true; but it is God who will fix the moment, not I. And the question is not to give a beating, either. I would rather receive a hundred blows myself than advise the administration of such a medicine to any Christian. One thing only will I say to you," he ended, looking at the bravo over his spectacles, "and that is, that as my niece is going there; and as it is probable, very probable, is it not, Remedios? that she may have to say a few plain words to that man, I recommend you not to leave her unprotected, in case she should be insulted."

"I have something to do to-night," answered Caballuco, laconically and dryly.

"You hear what he says, Remedios. Leave your business for to-morrow."

"I can't do that. I will go alone."

"No, you shall not go alone, niece. Now let us hear no more about the matter. Senor Ramos has something to do, and he cannot accompany you. Fancy if you were to be insulted by that rude man!"

"Insulted! A lady insulted by that fellow!" exclaimed Caballuco. "Come that must not be."

"If you had not something to do—bah! I should be quite easy in my mind, then."

"I have something to do," said the Centaur, rising from the table, "but if you wish it——"

There was a pause. The Penitentiary had closed his eyes and was meditating.

"I wish it, Senor Ramos," he said at last.

"There is no more to be said then. Let us go, Senora Dona Maria."

"Now, my dear niece," said Don Inocencio, half seriously, half jestingly, "since we have finished supper bring me the basin."

He gave his niece a penetrating glance, and accompanying it with the corresponding action, pronounced these words:

"I wash my hands of the matter."

CHAPTER XXVIII

FROM PEPE REY TO DON JUAN REY

"ORBAJOSA, April 12.

"MY DEAR FATHER:

"Forgive me if for the first time in my life I disobey you in refusing to leave this place or to renounce my project. Your advice and your entreaty are what were to be expected from a kind, good father. My obstinacy is natural in an insensate son; but something strange is taking place within me; obstinacy and honor have become so blended and confounded in my mind that the bare idea of desisting from my purpose makes me ashamed. I have changed greatly. The fits of rage that agitate me now were formerly unknown to me. I regarded the violent acts, the exaggerated expressions of hot-tempered and impetuous men with the same scorn as the brutal actions of the wicked. Nothing of this kind surprises me any longer, for in myself I find at all times a certain terrible capacity for wickedness. I can speak to you as I would speak to God and to my conscience; I can tell you that I am a wretch, for he is a wretch who is wanting in that powerful moral force which enables him to chastise his passions and submit his life to the stern rule of conscience. I have been wanting in the Christian fortitude which exalts the spirit of the man who is offended above the offences which he receives and the enemies from whom he receives them. I have had the weakness to abandon myself to a mad fury, putting myself on a level with my detractors, returning them blow for blow, and endeavoring to confound them by methods learned in their own base school. How deeply I regret that you were not at my side to turn me from this path! It is now too late. The passions will not brook delay. They are impatient, and demand their prey with cries and with the convulsive eagerness of a fierce moral thirst. I have succumbed. I cannot forget what you so often said to me, that anger may be called the worst of the passions, since, suddenly transforming the character, it engenders all the others, and lends to each its own infernal fire.

"But it is not anger alone that has brought me to the state of mind which I have described. A more expansive and noble sentiment—the profound and ardent love which I have for my cousin, has also contributed to it, and this is the one thing that absolves me in my own estimation. But if love had not done so, pity would have impelled me to brave the fury and the intrigues of your terrible sister; for poor Rosario, placed between an irresistible affection and her mother, is at the present moment one of the most unhappy beings on the face of the earth. The love which she has for me, and which responds to mine—does it not give me the right to open, in whatever way I can, the doors of her house and take her out of it; employing the law, as far as the law reaches, and using force at the point where the law ceases to support me? I think that your rigid moral scrupulosity will not give an affirmative answer to this question; but I have ceased to be the upright and methodical character whose conscience was in exact conformity with the dictates of the moral law. I am no longer the man whom an almost perfect education enabled to keep his emotions under strict control. To-day I am a man like other men; at a single step I have crossed the line which separates the just and the good from the unjust and the wicked. Prepare yourself to hear of some dreadful act committed by me. I will take care to notify you of all my misdeeds.

"But the confession of my faults will not relieve me from the responsibility of the serious occurrences which have taken place and which are taking place, nor will this responsibility, no matter how much I may argue, fall altogether on your sister. Dona Perfecta's responsibility is certainly very great. What will be the extent of mine! Ah, dear father! believe nothing of what you hear about me; believe only what I shall tell you. If they tell you that I have committed a deliberate piece of villany, answer that it is a lie. It is difficult, very difficult, for me to judge myself, in the state of disquietude in which I am, but I dare assure you that I have not deliberately given cause for scandal. You know well to what extremes passion can lead when circumstances favor its fierce, its all-invading growth.

"What is most bitter to me is the thought of having employed artifice, deceit, and base concealments—I who was truth itself. I am humiliated in my own estimation. But is this the greatest perversity into which the soul can fall? Am I beginning now, or have I ended? I cannot tell. If Rosario with her angelic hand does not take me out of this hell of my conscience, I desire that you should come to take me out of it. My cousin is an angel, and suffering, as she has done, for my sake, she has taught me a great many things that I did not know before.

"Do not be surprised at the incoherence of what I write. Diverse emotions inflame me; thoughts at times assail me truly worthy of my immortal soul; but at times also I fall into a lamentable state of dejection, and I am reminded of the weak and degenerate characters whose baseness you have painted to me in such strong colors, in order that I might abhor them. In the state in which I am to-day I am ready for good or for evil. God have pity upon me! I already know what prayer is—a solemn and reflexive supplication, so personal that it is not compatible with formulas learned by heart; an expansion of the soul which dares to reach out toward its source; the opposite of remorse, in which the soul, at war with itself, seeks in vain to defend itself by sophisms and concealments. You have taught me many good things, but now I am practising; as we engineers say, I am studying on the ground; and in this way my knowledge will become broadened and confirmed. I begin to imagine now that I am not so wicked as I myself believe. Am I right?

"I end this letter in haste. I must send it with some soldiers who are going in the direction of the station at Villahorrenda, for the post-office of this place is not to be trusted."

"APRIL 14.

"It would amuse you, dear father, if I could make you understand the ideas of the people of this wretched town. You know already that almost all the country is up in arms. It was a thing to be anticipated, and the politicians are mistaken if they imagine that it will be over in a couple of days.

Hostility to us and to the Government is innate in the Orbajosan's mind, and forms a part of it as much as his religious faith. Confining myself to the particular question with my aunt, I will tell you a singular thing—the poor lady, who is penetrated by the spirit of feudalism to the marrow of her bones, has taken it into her head that I am going to attack her house and carry off her daughter, as the gentlemen of the Middle Ages attacked an enemy's castle to consummate some outrage. Don't laugh, for it is the truth—such are the ideas of these people. I need not tell you that she regards me as a monster, as a sort of heretic Moorish king, and of the officers here who are my friends she has no better opinion. In Dona Perfecta's house it is a matter of firm belief that the army and I have formed a diabolical and anti-religious coalition to rob Orbajosa of its treasures, its faith, and its maidens. I am sure that your sister firmly believes that I am going to take her house by assault, and there is not a doubt but that behind the door some barricade has been erected.

"But it could not be otherwise. Here they have the most antiquated ideas respecting society, religion, the state, property. The religious exaltation which impels them to employ force against the Government, to defend a faith which no one has attacked, and which, besides, they do not possess, revives in their mind the feudal sentiment; and as they would settle every question by brute force, with the sword and with fire, killing all who do not think as they do, they believe that no one in the world employs other methods.

"Far from intending to perform quixotic deeds in this lady's house, I have in reality saved her some annoyances from which the rest of the town have not escaped. Owing to my friendship with the brigadier she has not been obliged to present, as was ordered, a list of those of the men in her service who have joined the insurgents; and if her house was searched I have certain knowledge that it was only for form's sake; and if the six men there were disarmed, they have been replaced by six others, and nothing has been done to her. You see to what my hostility to that lady is reduced.

"It is true that I have the support of the military chiefs, but I make use of it solely to escape being insulted or ill-used by these implacable people. The probabilities of my success consist in the fact that the authorities recently appointed by the commander of the brigade are all my friends. I derive from them the moral force which enables me to intimidate these people. I don't know whether I shall find myself compelled to commit some violent action; but don't be alarmed, for the assault and the taking of the house is altogether a wild, feudal idea of your sister. Chance has placed me in an advantageous position. Rage, the passion that burns within me, will impel me to profit by it. I don't know how far I may go."

"APRIL 17.

"Your letter has given me great consolation. Yes; I can attain my object, employing only the resources of the law, which will be completely effectual for it. I have consulted the authorities of this place, and they all approve of the course you indicate. I am very glad of it. Since I have put into my cousin's mind the idea of disobedience, let it at least be under the protection of the law. I will do what you bid me, that is to say I will renounce the somewhat unworthy collaboration of Pinzon; I will break up the terrorizing solidarity which I established with the soldiers; I will cease to make a display of the power I derived from them; I will have done with adventures, and at the fitting moment I will act with calmness, prudence, and all the benignity possible. It is better so. My coalition, half-serious, half-jesting, with the army, had for its object to protect me against the violence of the Orbajosans and of the servants and the relations of my aunt. For the rest, I have always disapproved of the idea of what we call armed intervention.

"The friend who aided me has been obliged to leave the house; but I am not entirely cut off from communication with my cousin. The poor girl shows heroic valor in the midst of her sufferings, and will obey me blindly.

"Set your mind at rest about my personal safety. For my part, I have no fear and I am quite tranquil."

"APRIL 20.

"To-day I can write only a few lines. I have a great deal to do. All will be ended within two or three days. Don't write to me again to this miserable town. I shall soon have the happiness of embracing you.

"PEPE."

CHAPTER XXIX

FROM PEPE REY TO ROSARITO POLENTINOS

"Give Estebanillo the key of the garden and charge him to take care about the dog. The boy is mine, body and soul. Fear nothing! I shall be very sorry if you cannot come down stairs as you did the other night. Do all you can to manage it. I will be in the garden a little after midnight. I will then tell you what course I have decided upon, and what you are to do. Tranquillize your mind, my dear girl, for I have abandoned all imprudent or violent expedients. I will tell you every thing when I see you. There is much to tell; and it must be spoken, not written. I can picture to myself your terror and anxiety at the thought of my being so near you. But it is a week since I have seen you. I have sworn that this separation from you shall soon be ended, and it will be ended. My heart tells me that I shall see you. I swear that I will see you."

CHAPTER XXX

BEATING UP THE GAME

A man and a woman entered the hotel of the widow De Cuzco a little after ten o'clock, and left it at half-past eleven.

"Now, Senora Dona Maria," said the man, "I will take you to your house, for I have something to do."

"Wait, Senor Ramos, for the love of God!" she answered. "Why don't we go to the Casino to see if he comes out? You heard just now that Estebanillo, the boy that works in the garden, was talking with him this afternoon."

"But are you looking for Don Jose?" asked the Centaur, with ill-humor. "What have we to do with him? The courtship with Dona Rosario ended as it was bound to end, and now there is nothing for it but for my mother to marry them. That is my opinion."

"You are a fool!" said Remedios angrily.

"Senora, I am going."

"Why, you rude man, are you going to leave me alone in the street?"

"Yes, senora, unless you go home at once."

"That's right—leave me alone, exposed to be insulted! Listen to me, Senor Ramos. Don Jose will come out of the Casino in a moment, as usual. I want to see whether he goes into his hotel or goes past it. It is a fancy of mine, only a fancy."

"What I know is that I have something to do, and that it is near twelve o'clock."

"Silence!" said Remedios. "Let us hide ourselves around the corner. A man is coming down the Calle de la Triperia Alta. It is he!"

"Don Jose! I know him by his walk."

"Let us follow him," said Maria Remedios with anxiety. "Let us follow him at a little distance, Ramos."

"Senora—"

"Only a minute, then, Dona Remedios. After that I must go."

They walked on about thirty paces, keeping at a moderate distance behind the man they were watching. The Penitentiary's niece stopped then and said:

"He is not going into his hotel."

"He may be going to the brigadier's."

"The brigadier lives up the street, and Don Pepe is going down in the direction of the senora's house."

"Of the senora's house!" exclaimed Caballuco, quickening his steps.

But they were mistaken. The man whom they were watching passed the house of Polentinos and walked on.

"Do you see that you were wrong?"

"Senor Ramos, let us follow him!" said Remedios, pressing the Centaur's hand convulsively. "I have a foreboding."

"We shall soon know, for we are near the end of the town."

"Don't go so fast—he may see us. It is as I thought, Senor Ramos; he is going into the garden by the condemned door."

"Senora, you have lost your senses!"

"Come on, and we shall see."

The night was dark, and the watchers could not tell precisely at what point Senor de Rey had entered; but a grating of rusty hinges which they heard, and the circumstance of not meeting the young man in the whole length of the garden wall, convinced them that he had entered the garden. Caballuco looked at his companion with stupefaction. He seemed bewildered.

"What are you thinking about? Do you still doubt?"

"What ought I to do?" asked the bravo, covered with confusion. "Shall we give him a fright? I don't know what the senora would think about it. I say that because I was at her house this evening, and it seemed to me that the mother and daughter had become reconciled."

"Don't be a fool! Why don't you go in?"

"Now I remember that the armed men are not there; I told them to leave this evening."

"And this block of marble still doubts what he ought to do! Ramos, go into the garden and don't be a coward."

"How can I go in if the door is closed?"

"Get over the wall. What a snail! If I were a man——"

"Well, then, up! There are some broken bricks here where the boys climb over the wall to steal the fruit."

"Up quickly! I will go and knock at the front door to waken the senora, if she should be asleep."

The Centaur climbed up, not without difficulty. He sat astride on the wall for an instant, and then disappeared among the dark foliage of the trees. Maria Remedios ran desperately toward the Calle del Condestable, and, seizing the knocker of the front door, knocked—knocked three times with all her heart and soul.

CHAPTER XXXI

DONA PERFECTA

See with what tranquillity Senora Dona Perfecta pursues her occupation of writing. Enter her room, and, notwithstanding the lateness of the hour, you will surprise her busily engaged, her mind divided between meditation and the writing of several long and carefully worded epistles traced with a firm hand, every hair-stroke of every letter in which is correctly formed. The light of the lamp falls full upon her face and bust and hands, its shade leaving the rest of her person and almost the whole of the room in a soft shadow. She seems like a luminous figure evoked by the imagination from amid the vague shadows of fear.

It is strange that we should not have made before this a very important statement, which is that Dona Perfecta was handsome, or rather that she was still handsome, her face preserving the remains of former beauty. The life of the country, her total lack of vanity, her disregard for dress and personal adornment, her hatred of fashion, her contempt for the vanities of the capital, were all causes why her native beauty did not shine or shone very little. The intense shallowness of her complexion, indicating a very bilious constitution, still further impaired her beauty.

Her eyes black and well-opened, her nose finely and delicately shaped, her forehead broad and smooth, she was considered by all who saw her as a finished type of the human figure; but there rested on those features a certain hard and proud expression which excited a feeling of antipathy. As some persons, although ugly, attract; Dona Perfecta repelled. Her glance, even when accompanied by amiable words, placed between herself and those who were strangers to her the impassable distance of a mistrustful respect; but for those of her house—that is to say, for her relations, admirers, and allies—she possessed a singular attraction. She was a mistress in governing, and no one could equal her in the art of adapting her language to the person whom she was addressing.

Her bilious temperament and an excessive association with devout persons and things, which excited her imagination without object or result, had aged her prematurely, and although she was still young she did not seem so. It might be said of her that with her habits and manner of life she had wrought a sort of rind, a stony, insensible covering within which she shut herself, like the snail within his portable house. Dona Perfecta rarely came out of her shell.

Her irreproachable habits, and that outward amiability which we have observed in her from the moment of her appearance in our story, were the causes of the great prestige which she enjoyed in Orbajosa. She kept up relations, besides, with some excellent ladies in Madrid, and it was through their means that she obtained the dismissal of her nephew. At the moment which we have now arrived in our story, we find her seated at her desk, which is the sole confidant of her plans and the depository of her numerical accounts with the peasants, and of her moral accounts with God and with society. There she wrote the letters which her brother received every three months; there she composed the notes that incited the judge and the notary to embroil Pepe Rey in lawsuits; there she prepared the plot through which the latter lost the confidence of the Government; there she held long conferences with Don Inocencio. To become acquainted with the scene of others of her actions whose effects we have observed, it would be necessary to follow her to the episcopal palace and to the houses of various of her friends.

We do not know what Dona Perfecta would have been, loving. Hating, she had the fiery vehemence of an angel of hatred and discord among men. Such is the effect produced on a character naturally hard, and without inborn goodness, by religious exaltation, when this, instead of drawing its nourishment from conscience and from truth revealed in principles as simple as they are beautiful, seeks its sap in narrow formulas dictated solely by ecclesiastical interests. In order that religious fanaticism should be inoffensive, the heart in which it exists must be very pure. It is true that even in that case it is unproductive of good. But the hearts that have been born without the seraphic purity which establishes a premature Limbo on the earth, are careful not to become greatly inflamed with what they see in retables, in choirs, in locutories and sacristies, unless they have first erected in their own consciences an altar, a pulpit, and a confessional.

Dona Perfecta left her writing from time to time, to go into the adjoining room where her daughter was. Rosarito had been ordered to sleep, but, already precipitated down the precipice of disobedience, she was awake.

"Why don't you sleep?" her mother asked her. "I don't intend to go to bed to-night. You know already that Caballuco has taken away with him the men we had here. Something might happen, and I will keep watch. If I did not watch what would become of us both?"

"What time is it?" asked the girl.

"It will soon be midnight. Perhaps you are not afraid, but I am."

Rosarito was trembling, and every thing about her denoted the keenest anxiety. She lifted her eyes to heaven supplicatingly, and then turned them on her mother with a look of the utmost terror.

"Why, what is the matter with you?"

"Did you not say it was midnight?"

"Yes."

"Then——But is it already midnight?"

Rosario made an effort to speak, then shook her head, on which the weight of a world was pressing.

"Something is the matter with you; you have something on your mind," said her mother, fixing on her daughter her penetrating eyes.

"Yes—I wanted to tell you," stammered the girl, "I wanted to say——Nothing, nothing, I will go to sleep."

"Rosario, Rosario! your mother can read your heart like an open book," exclaimed Dona Perfecta with severity. "You are agitated. I have told you already that I am willing to pardon you if you will repent; if you are a good and sensible girl."

"Why, am I not good? Ah, mamma, mamma! I am dying!"

Rosario burst into a flood of bitter and disconsolate tears.

"What are these tears about?" said her mother, embracing her. "If they are tears of repentance, blessed be they."

"I don't repent, I can't repent!" cried the girl, in a burst of sublime despair.

She lifted her head and in her face was depicted a sudden inspired strength. Her hair fell in disorder over her shoulders. Never was there seen a more beautiful image of a rebellious angel.

"What is this? Have you lost your senses?" said Dona Perfecta, laying both her hands on her daughter's shoulders.

"I am going away, I am going away!" said the girl, with the exaltation of delirium.

And she sprang out of bed.

"Rosario, Rosario——My daughter! For God's sake, what is this?"

"Ah, mamma, senora!" exclaimed the girl, embracing her mother; "bind me fast!"

"In truth you would deserve it. What madness is this?"

"Bind me fast! I am going away—I am going away with him!"

Dona Perfecta felt a flood of fire surging from her heart up to her lips. She controlled herself, however, and answered her daughter only with her eyes, blacker than the night.

"Mamma, mamma, I hate all that is not he!" exclaimed Rosario. "Hear my confession, for I wish to confess it to every one, and to you first of all."

"You are going to kill me; you are killing me!"

"I want to confess it, so that you may pardon me. This weight, this weight that is pressing me down, will not let me live."

"The weight of a sin! Add to it the malediction of God, and see if you can carry that burden about with you, wretched girl! Only I can take it from you."

"No, not you, not you!" cried Rosario, with desperation. "But hear me; I want to confess it all, all! Afterward, turn me out of this house where I was born."

"I turn you out!"

"I will go away, then."

"Still less. I will teach you a daughter's duty, which you have forgotten."

"I will fly, then; he will take me with him!"

"Has he told you to do so? has he counselled you to do that? has he commanded you to do that?" asked the mother, launching these words like thunderbolts against her daughter.

"He has counselled me to do it. We have agreed to be married. We must be married, mamma, dear mamma. I will love you—I know that I ought to love you—I shall be forever lost if I do not love you."

She wrung her hands, and falling on her knees kissed her mother's feet.

"Rosario, Rosario!" cried Dona Perfecta, in a terrible voice, "rise!"

There was a short pause.

"This man—has he written to you?"

"Yes."

"And have you seen him again since that night?"

"Yes."

"And you have written to him!"

"I have written to him also. Oh, senora! why do you look at me in that way? You are not my mother.

"Would to God that I were not! Rejoice in the harm you are doing me. You are killing me; you have given me my death-blow!" cried Dona Perfecta, with indescribable agitation. "You say that this man—"

"Is my husband—I will be his wife, protected by the law. You are not a woman! Why do you look at me in that way? You make me tremble. Mother, mother, do not condemn me!"

"You have already condemned yourself—that is enough. Obey me, and I will forgive you. Answer me—when did you receive letters from that man?"

"To-day."

"What treachery! What infamy!" cried her mother, roaring rather than speaking. "Had you appointed a meeting?"

"Yes."

"When?"

"To-night."

"Where?"

"Here, here! I will confess every thing, every thing! I know it is a crime. I am a wretch; but you who are my mother will take me out of this hell. Give your consent. Say one word to me, only one word!"

"That man here in my house!" cried Dona Perfecta, springing back several paces from her daughter.

Rosario followed her on her knees. At the same instant three blows were heard, three crashes, three reports. It was the heart of Maria Remedios knocking at the door through the knocker. The house trembled with awful dread. Mother and daughter stood motionless as statues.

A servant went down stairs to open the door, and shortly afterward Maria Remedios, who was not now a woman but a basilisk enveloped in a mantle, entered Dona Perfecta's room. Her face, flushed with anxiety, exhaled fire.

"He is there, he is there!" she said, as she entered. "He got into the garden through the condemned door."

She paused for breath at every syllable.

"I know already," returned Dona Perfecta, with a sort of bellow.

Rosario fell senseless on the floor.

"Let us go down stairs," said Dona Perfecta, without paying any attention to her daughter's swoon.

The two women glided down stairs like two snakes. The maids and the man-servant were in the hall, not knowing what to do. Dona Perfecta passed through the dining-room into the garden, followed by Maria Remedios.

"Fortunately we have Ca-Ca-Ca-balluco there," said the canon's niece.

"Where?"

"In the garden, also. He cli-cli-climbed over the wall."

Dona Perfecta explored the darkness with her wrathful eyes. Rage gave them the singular power of seeing in the dark peculiar to the feline race.

"I see a figure there," she said. "It is going toward the oleanders."

"It is he!" cried Remedios. "But there comes Ramos—Ramos!"

The colossal figure of the Centaur was plainly distinguishable.

"Toward the oleanders, Ramos! Toward the oleanders!"

Dona Perfecta took a few steps forward. Her hoarse voice, vibrating with a terrible accent, hissed forth these words:

"Cristobal, Cristobal—kill him!"

A shot was heard. Then another.

CHAPTER XXXII
CONCLUSION

From Don Cayetano Polentinos to a friend in Madrid:

"ORBAJOSA, April 21.

"MY DEAR FRIEND:

"Send me without delay the edition of 1562 that you say you have picked up at the executor's sale of the books of Corchuelo. I will pay any price for that copy. I have been long searching for it in vain, and I shall esteem myself the most enviable of virtuosos in possessing it. You ought to find in the colophon a helmet with a motto over the word 'Tractado,' and the tail of the X of the date MDLXII ought to be crooked. If your copy agrees with these signs send me a telegraphic despatch at once, for I shall be very anxious until I receive it. But now I remember that, on account of these vexatious and troublesome wars, the telegraph is not working. I shall await your answer by return of mail.

"I shall soon go to Madrid for the purpose of having my long delayed work, the 'Genealogies of Orbajosa,' printed. I appreciate your kindness, my dear friend, but I cannot accept your too flattering expressions. My work does not indeed deserve the high encomiums you bestow upon it; it is a work of patience and study, a rude but solid and massive monument which I shall have erected to the past glories of my beloved country. Plain and humble in its form, it is noble in the idea that inspired it, which was solely to direct the eyes of this proud and unbelieving generation to the marvellous deeds and the pure virtues of our forefathers. Would that the studious youth of our country might take the step to which with all my strength I incite them! Would that the abominable studies and methods of reasoning introduced by philosophic license and erroneous doctrines might be forever cast into oblivion! Would that our learned men might occupy themselves exclusively in the contemplation of those glorious ages, in order that, this generation being penetrated with their essence and their beneficent sap, its insane eagerness for change, and its ridiculous mania for appropriating to itself foreign ideas which conflict with our beautiful national constitution, might disappear. I fear greatly that among the crowd of mad youth who pursue vain Utopias and heathenish novelties, my desires are not destined to be fulfilled, and that the contemplation of the illustrious virtues of the past will remain confined within the same narrow circle as to-day. What is to be done, my friend? I am afraid that very soon our poor Spain is doomed to be so disfigured that she will not be able to recognize herself, even beholding herself in the bright mirror of her stainless history.

"I do not wish to close this letter without informing you of a disagreeable event—the unfortunate death of an estimable young man, well known in Madrid, the civil engineer Don Jose de Rey, a nephew of my sister-in-law. This melancholy event occurred last night in the garden of our house, and I have not yet been able to form a correct judgment regarding the causes that may have impelled the unfortunate Rey to this horrible and criminal act. According to what Perfecta told me this morning, on my return from Mundo Grande, Pepe Rey at about twelve o'clock last night entered the garden of the house and shot himself in the right temple, expiring instantly. Imagine the consternation and alarm which such an event would produce in this peaceable and virtuous mansion. Poor Perfecta was so greatly affected that we were for a time alarmed about her; but she is better now, and this afternoon we succeeded in inducing her to take a little broth. We employ every means of consoling her, and as she is a good Christian, she knows how to support with edifying resignation even so great a misfortune as this.

"Between you and me, my friend, I will say here that in young Rey's fatal attempt upon his life, I believe the moving causes to have been an unfortunate attachment, perhaps remorse for his conduct, and the state of hypochondriasm into which he had fallen. I esteemed him greatly; I think he was not lacking in excellent qualities; but he was held in such disrepute here that never once have I heard any one speak well of him. According to what they say, he made a boast of the most extravagant ideas and opinions; he mocked at religion, entered the church smoking and with his hat on; he respected nothing, and for him there was neither modesty, nor virtue, nor soul, nor ideal, nor faith—nothing but theodolites, squares, rules, engines, pick-axes, and spades. What do you thing of that? To be just,

I must say that in his conversations with me he always concealed these ideas, doubtless through fear of being utterly routed by the fire of my arguments; but in public innumerable stories are told of his heretical ideas and his stupendous excesses.

"I cannot continue, my dear friend, for at this moment I hear firing. As I have no love for fighting, and as I am not a soldier, my pulse trembles a little. In due time I will give you further particulars of this war.

"Yours affectionately, etc., etc."

"APRIL 22. "MY EVER-REMEMBERED FRIEND:

"To-day we have had a bloody skirmish on the outskirts of Orbajosa. The large body of men raised in Villahorrenda were attacked by the troops with great fury. There was great loss in killed and wounded on both sides. After the combat the brave guerillas dispersed, but they are greatly encouraged, and it is possible that you may hear of wonderful things. Cristobal Caballuco, the son of the famous Caballuco whom you will remember in the last war, though suffering from a wound in the arm, how or when received is not known, commanded them. The present leader has eminent qualifications for the command; and he is, besides, an honest and simple-hearted man. As we must finally come to a friendly arrangement, I presume that Caballuco will be made a general in the Spanish army, whereby both sides will gain greatly.

"I deplore this war, which is beginning to assume alarming proportions; but I recognize that our valiant peasants are not responsible for it, since they have been provoked to the inhuman conflict by the audacity of the Government, by the demoralization of its sacrilegious delegates; by the systematic fury with which the representatives of the state attack what is most venerated by the people—their religious faith and the national spirit which fortunately still exists in those places that are not yet contaminated by the desolating pestilence. When it is attempted to take away the soul of a people to give it a different one; when it is sought to denationalize a people, so to say, perverting its sentiments, its customs, its ideas—it is natural that this people should defend itself, like the man who is attacked by highwaymen on a solitary road. Let the spirit and the pure and salutiferous substance of my work on the 'Genealogies'—excuse the apparent vanity—once reach the sphere of the Government and there will no longer be wars.

"To-day we have had here a very disagreeable question. The clergy, my friend, have refused to allow Rey to be buried in consecrated ground. I interfered in the matter, entreating the bishop to remove this heavy anathema, but without success. Finally, we buried the body of the young man in a grave made in the field of Mundo Grande, where my patient explorations have discovered the archaeological treasures of which you know. I spent some very sad hours, and the painful impression which I received has not yet altogether passed away. Don Juan Tafetan and ourselves were the only persons who accompanied the funeral cortege. A little later, strange to say, the girls whom they call here the Troyas went to the field, and prayed for a long time beside the rustic tomb of the mathematician. Although this seemed a ridiculous piece of officiousness it touched me.

"With respect to the death of Rey, the rumor circulates throughout the town that he was assassinated, but by whom is not known. It is asserted that he declared this to be the case, for he lived for about an hour and a half. According to what they say, he refused to reveal the name of his murderer. I repeat this version, without either contradicting or supporting it. Perfecta does not wish this matter to be spoken of, and she becomes greatly distressed whenever I allude to it.

"Poor woman! no sooner had one misfortune occurred than she met with another, which has grieved us all deeply. My friend, the fatal malady that has been for so many generations connatural in our family has now claimed another victim. Poor Rosario, who, thanks to our cares, was improving gradually in her health, has entirely lost her reason. Her incoherent words, her frenzy, her deadly pallor, bring my mother and my sister forcibly to my mind. This is the most serious case that I have witnessed in our family, for the question here is not one of mania but of real insanity. It is sad, terribly sad that out of so many I should be the only one to escape, preserving a sound mind with all my faculties unimpaired and entirely free from any sign of that fatal malady.

"I have not been able to give your remembrances to Don Inocencio, for the poor man has suddenly fallen ill and refuses to see even his most intimate friends. But I am sure that he would return your remembrances, and I do not doubt that he could lay his hand instantly on the translation of the collection of Latin epigrams which you recommend to him. I hear firing again. They say that we shall have a skirmish this afternoon. The troops have just been called out."

"BARCELONA, June 1.

"I have just arrived here after leaving my niece in San Baudilio de Llobregat. The director of the establishment has assured me that the case is incurable. She will, however, have the greatest care in that cheerful and magnificent sanitarium. My dear friend, if I also should ever succumb, let me be taken to San Baudilio. I hope to find the proofs of my 'Genealogies' awaiting me on my return. I intend to add six pages more, for it would be a great mistake not to publish my reasons for maintaining that Mateo Diez Coronel, author of the 'Metrico Encomio,' is descended, on the mother's side, from the Guevaras, and not from the Burguillos, as the author of the 'Floresta Amena' erroneously maintains.

"I write this letter principally for the purpose of giving you a caution. I have heard several persons here speaking of Pepe Rey's death, and they describe it exactly as it occurred. The secret of the manner of his death, which I learned some time after the event, I revealed to you in confidence when we met in Madrid. It has appeared strange to me that having told it to no one but yourself, it should be known here in all its details—how he entered the garden; how he fired on Caballuco when the latter attacked him with his dagger; how Ramos then fired on him with so sure an aim that he fell to the ground mortally wounded. In short, my dear friend, in case you should have inadvertently spoken of this to any one, I will remind you that it is a family secret, and that will be sufficient for a person as prudent and discreet as yourself.

"Joy! joy! I have just read in one of the papers here that Caballuco had defeated Brigadier Batalla."

"ORBAJOSA, December 12.

"I have a sad piece of news to give you. The Penitentiary has ceased to exist for us; not precisely because he has passed to a better life, but because the poor man has been, ever since last April, so grief-stricken, so melancholy, so taciturn that you would not know him. There is no longer in him even a trace of that Attic humor, that decorous and classic joviality which made him so pleasing. He shuns every body; he shuts himself up in his house and receives no one; he hardly eats any thing, and he has broken off all intercourse with the world. If you were to see him now you would not recognize him, for he is reduced to skin and bone. The strangest part of the matter is that he has quarreled with his niece and lives alone, entirely alone, in a miserable cottage in the suburb of Baidejos. They say now that he will resign his chair in the choir of the cathedral and go to Rome. Ah! Orbajosa will lose much in losing her great Latinist. I imagine that many a year will pass before we shall see such another. Our glorious Spain is falling into decay, declining, dying."

"ORBAJOSA, December 23.

"The young man who will present to you a letter of introduction from me is the nephew of our dear Penitentiary, a lawyer with some literary ability. Carefully educated by his uncle, he has very sensible ideas. How regrettable it would be if he should become corrupted in that sink of philosophy and incredulity! He is upright, industrious, and a good Catholic, for which reasons I believe that in an office like yours he will rise to distinction in his profession. Perhaps his ambition may lead him (for he has ambition, too) into the political arena, and I think he would not be a bad acquisition to the cause of order and tradition, now that the majority of our young men have become perverted and have joined the ranks of the turbulent and the vicious. He is accompanied by his mother, a commonplace woman without any social polish, but who has an excellent heart, and who is truly pious. Maternal affection takes in her the somewhat extravagant form of worldly ambition, and she declares that her son will one day be Minister. It is quite possible that he may.

"Perfecta desires to be remembered to you. I don't know precisely what is the matter with her; but the fact is, she gives us great uneasiness. She has lost her appetite to an alarming degree, and, unless

I am greatly mistaken in my opinion of her case, she shows the first symptoms of jaundice. The house is very sad without Rosarito, who brightened it with her smiles and her angelic goodness. A black cloud seems to rest now over us all. Poor Perfecta speaks frequently of this cloud, which is growing blacker and blacker, while she becomes every day more yellow. The poor mother finds consolation for her grief in religion and in devotional exercises, which each day she practises with a more exemplary and edifying piety. She passes almost the whole of the day in church, and she spends her large income in novenas and in splendid religious ceremonies. Thanks to her, religious worship has recovered in Orbajosa its former splendor. This is some consolation in the midst of the decay and dissolution of our nationality.

"To-morrow I will send the proofs. I will add a few pages more, for I have discovered another illustrious Orbajosan—Bernardo Amador de Sota, who was footman to the Duke of Osuna, whom he served during the period of the vice-royalty of Naples; and there is even good reason to believe that he had no complicity whatever in the conspiracy against Venice."

Our story is ended. This is all we have to say for the present concerning persons who seem, but are not good.

Trafalgar

CHAPTER I.

I TRUST that, before relating the important events of which I have been an eye-witness, I may be allowed to say a few words about my early life and to explain the singular accidents and circumstances which resulted in my being present at our great naval catastrophe.

In speaking of my birth I cannot follow the example of most writers who narrate the facts of their own lives, and who begin by naming their ancestry—usually of noble rank, *hidalgos* at the very least, if not actually descended from some royal or imperial progenitor. I cannot grace my opening page with high-sounding names, for, excepting my mother whom I remember for some few years, I know nothing of any of my forefathers, unless it be Adam from whom my descent would seem to be indisputable. In short, my history began in much the same way as that of Pablos, the brigand of Segovia; happily it pleased God that it should resemble it in no other particular.

I was born at Cadiz in the notorious quarter "de la Viña," which was not then, any more than at the present day, a good school of either morals or manners. My memory does not throw any light on the events of my infancy till I was six years old, and I remember that, only because I associate the idea of being six with an event I heard much talked about, the battle of Cape St. Vincent, which took place in 1797.

Endeavoring to see myself as I was at that time, with the curiosity and interest which must attach to self-contemplation, I am aware of a dim and hazy little figure in the picture of past events, playing in the creek with other small boys of the same age, more or less. This was to me the whole of life—as it was, at any rate, to our privileged class; those who did not live as I did appeared to me exceptional beings. In my childish ignorance of the world I firmly believed that man was made for the sea, Providence having created him to swim as being the noblest exercise of his limbs and body, and to dive for crabs as the highest use of his intelligence—and especially to fish up and sell the highly-esteemed crustacean known as *Bocas de la Isla*—as well as for his personal delectation and enjoyment, thus combining pleasure with profit.

The society into which I was born was indeed of the roughest, as ignorant and squalid as can well be imagined; so much so that the boys of our quarter of the town were regarded as even lower than those of the adjoining suburb of Puntales, whose occupations were the same and who defied the elements with equal devilry; the result of this invidious distinction was that each party looked upon the other as rivals, and the opposing forces would meet from time to time for a pitched battle with stones, when the earth was stained with heroic blood.

When I was old enough to begin to think that I might go into business on my own account, with a view to turning an honest penny, I remember that my sharpness stood me in good stead on the quay where I acted as*valet de place* to the numerous English who then, as now, disembarked there. The quay was a free academy peculiarly fitted to sharpen the wits and make the learner wide-awake, and I was not one of the least apt of its disciples in that wide branch of human experience; nor did I fail to distinguish myself in petty thefts, especially of fruit, an art for which the Plaza de San Juan offered an ample field, both for the experiments of the beginner and the exploits of the adept. But I have no wish to enlarge on this part of my history, for I blush with shame now, as I remember the depth to which I had sunk, and I thank God for having released me from it at an early period, and directed me into a better path.

Among the impressions which remain most vivid in my memory is the enthusiastic delight I felt at the sight of vessels of war, when they anchored outside Cadiz or in the cove of San

Fernando. As I had no means of satisfying my curiosity, when I saw these enormous structures I conceived the most absurd and fanciful ideas about them, imagining them as full of mysteries.

Always eager to mimic the greater world around us, we boys too had our squadrons of little ships, roughly hewn in wood, with sails of paper or of rag, which we navigated with the greatest deliberation and gravity in the pools of Puntales or La Caleta. To make all complete, whenever a few coppers came into our hands, earned by one or another of our small industries, we bought powder of old "Aunt Coscoja" in the street "del Torno de Santa María," and with this we could have a grand naval display. Our fleets sailed before the wind in an ocean three yards across, fired off their cannon, came alongside of each other to mimic a hand-to-hand fight—in which the imaginary crews valiantly held their own, and swarmed into the tops unfurling the flag, made of any scrap of colored rag we could pick up in a dust-heap—while we danced with ecstasy on the shore at the popping of the artillery, imagining ourselves to be the nationalities represented by our respective standards, and almost believing that in the world of grown-up men and great events the nations too would leap for joy, looking on at the victories of their splendid fleets. Boys see things through strange windows.

Those were times of great sea-fights, for there was one at least every year and a skirmish every month. I thought that fleets met in battle simply and solely because they enjoyed it, or to prove their strength and valor, like two bullies who meet outside the walls to stick knives into each other. I laugh when I recollect the wild ideas I had about the persons and events of the time. I heard a great deal about Napoleon and how do you think I had pictured him to myself! In every respect exactly like the smugglers whom we not unfrequently saw in our low quarter of the town: *Contrabandistas* from the lines at Gibraltar. I fancied him a man on horseback, on a Xerez nag, with a cloak, high boots, a broad felt-hat, and a blunderbuss of course. With these accoutrements, and followed by other adventurers on the same pattern, I supposed this man, whom all agreed in describing as most extraordinary, to have conquered Europe, which I fancied was a large island within which were other islands which were the different nations: England, Genoa, London, France, Malta, the land where the Moors lived, America, Gibraltar, Port Mahon, Russia, Toulon and so forth. This scheme of geography I had constructed on the basis of the names of the places from which the ships came whose passengers I had to deal with; and I need not say that of all these nations or islands Spain was the very best, for which reason the English—men after the likeness of highwaymen—wanted to get it for their own. Talking of these and similar matters I and my amphibious companions would give vent to sentiments and opinions inspired by the most ardent patriotism.

However, I need not weary the reader with trifles which relate only to my personal fancies, so I will say no more about myself. The one living soul that made up to me for the wretchedness of life by a wholly disinterested love for me, was my mother. All I can remember of her is that she was extremely pretty, or at any rate she seemed so to me. From the time when she was left a widow she maintained herself and me by doing washing, and mending sailors' clothes. She must have loved me dearly. I fell ill of yellow fever which was raging in Andalusia and when I got well she took me solemnly to mass at the old cathedral and made me kneel on the pavement for more than an hour, and then, as an *ex-voto* offering, she placed an image in wax of a child, which I believed to be an exact likeness of myself, at the foot of the altar where the service had been performed.

My mother had a brother, and if she was pretty, he was ugly and a cruel wretch into the bargain. I cannot think of my uncle without horror, and from one or two occurrences which I remember vividly I infer that this man must have committed some crime at the time I refer to. He was a sailor; when he was on shore and at Cadiz he would come home furiously drunk, and treat us brutally—his sister with words, calling her every abusive name, and me with deeds, beating me without any reason whatever.

My mother must have suffered greatly from her brother's atrocities, and these, added to severe labor for miserable pay, hastened her death which left an indelible impression on my feelings, though the details dwell but vaguely in my memory. During this period of misery and vagabondage my only occupations were playing by the sea-shore or running about the streets. My only troubles were a beating from my uncle, a frown from my mother, or some mishap in the conduct of my squadrons. I had never felt any really strong or deep emotion till the loss of my mother showed me life under a harder and clearer aspect than it had ever before presented to me. The shock it gave me has never faded from my mind. After all these years I still remember, as we remember the horrible pictures of a bad dream, that my mother lay prostrate from some sickness, I know not what; I remember women coming and going, whose names and purpose I cannot recall; I remember hearing cries of lamentation, and being placed in my mother's arms, and then I remember the shudder that ran through my whole body at the touch of a cold, cold hand. I think I was then taken away; but mixed up with these dim memories I can see the yellow tapers which gave a ghastly light at mid-day, I can hear the muttering of prayers, the hoarse whispers of the old gossips, the laughter of drunken sailors—and then came the lonely sense of orphanhood, the certainty that I was alone and abandoned in the world, which for a time absorbed me entirely.

I have no recollection of what my uncle was doing at that time; I only know that his brutality to me increased to such a point that, weary of his cruelty, I ran away, determined to seek my fortune. I fled to San Fernando and from thence to Puerto Real. I hung on to the lowest class that haunt the shore, which has always been a famous nest for gaol-birds. Why or wherefore I quite forget, but I found myself with a gang of these choice spirits at Medinasidonia when, one day, a tavern where we were sitting was entered by a press-gang and we promptly separated, each hiding himself as best he might. My good star led me to a house where the owners had pity on me, taking the greatest interest in me, no doubt by reason of the story I told, on my knees and drowned in tears, of my miserable plight, my past life and all my misfortunes.

These good people took me under their protection and saved me from the press-gang, and from that time I remained in their service. With them I went to Vejer de la Frontera where they lived; they had only been passing through Medinasidonia.

My guardian angels were Don Alonso Gutierrez de Cisniega, a ship's captain, and his wife, both advanced in years. They taught me much that I did not know, and as they took a great fancy to me before long I was promoted to be Don Alonso's page, accompanying him in his daily walks, for the worthy veteran could not use his right arm, and it was with difficulty that he moved his right leg. What they saw in me to arouse their interest I do not know; my tender years, my desolate circumstances and no doubt too my ready obedience may have contributed to win their benevolence, for which I have always been deeply grateful. I may also add—though I say it that should not—as explaining their kind feeling towards me, that although I had always lived among the lowest and most destitute class, I had a certain natural refinement of mind which enabled me very soon to improve in manners, and in a few years, notwithstanding I had no opportunities for learning, I could pass for a lad of respectable birth and training.

I had spent four years in this home when the events happened which I must now relate. The reader must not expect an accuracy of detail which is out of my power when speaking of events which happened in my tender youth, to be recalled in the evening of my existence when I am near the end of a long and busy life and already feel the slow poison of old age numbing the fingers that use the pen; while the torpid brain strives to cheat itself into transient return of youth, by conjuring up the sweet or ardent memories of the past. As some old men strive to revive the warm delights of the past by gazing at pictures of the beauties they have known, I will try to give some interest and vigor to the faded reminiscences of my long past days, and to warm them with the glow of a counterfeit presentment of departed glories.

The effect is magical! How marvellous are the illusions of fancy! I look back with curiosity and astonishment at the bygone years, as we look through the pages of a book we were reading, and left with a leaf turned down to mark the place; and so long as the charm works I feel as if some beneficent genius had suddenly relieved me of the weight of old age, mitigating the burden of years which crushes body and spirit alike. This blood—this tepid and languid ichor, which now scarcely lends warmth and life to my failing limbs, grows hot again, flows, boils, and fires my veins with a swifter course. A sudden light breaks in upon my brain, giving color and relief to numberless strange figures—just as the traveller's torch, blazing in some dark cavern, reveals the marvels of geology so unexpectedly that it seems as though they were then and there created. And my heart rises from the grave of past emotions—a Lazarus called by the voice of its Lord—and leaps in my breast with joy and pain at once.

I am young again; time has turned backwards, I stand in the presence of the events of my boyhood; I clasp the hands of old friends, the joys and griefs of my youth stir my soul once more—the fever of triumph, the anguish of defeat, intense delights, acute sorrows—all crowded and mixed in my memory as they were in life. But stronger than any other feeling one reigns supreme, one which guided all my actions during the fateful period between 1805 and 1834. As I approach the grave and reflect how useless I am among men—even now tears start to my eyes with the sacred love of country. I can only serve it with words—cursing the base scepticism which can deny it, and the corrupt philosophy which can treat it as a mere fashion of a day.

This was the passion to which I consecrated the vigor of my manhood, and to this I will devote the labors of my last years, enthroning it as the tutelary genius, the guiding spirit of my story as it has been of my existence. I have much to tell. Trafalgar, Bailén, Madrid, Zaragoza, Gerona, Arapiles!—I can tell you something of all these, if your patience does not fail. My story may not be as elegantly told as it should be but I will do my best to insure its being true.

CHAPTER II.

IT was on one of the early days of October in that fatal year, 1805, that my worthy master called me into his room and looked at me with the severity that was habitual to him—a severity that was only on the surface for his nature was gentleness itself—he said:

"Gabriel, are you a brave man?"

I did not know what to answer, for, to tell the truth, in my fourteen years of life no opportunity had ever presented itself for me to astonish the world with any deed of valor; still, it filled me with pride to hear myself called a man, and thinking it ill-judged to deny myself the credit of courage before any one who held it in such high estimation, I answered, with boyish boldness:

"Yes, sir, I am a brave man."

At this the noble gentleman, who had shed his blood in a hundred glorious fights and who nevertheless did not disdain to treat a faithful servant with frank confidence, smiled at me kindly, signed to me to take a seat, and seemed on the point of informing me of some business of importance, when his wife, my mistress, Doña Francisca entered the study, and, to give further interest to the discussion, began to declaim with vehemence.

"You are not to go," she said, "I declare you shall not join the fleet. What next will you be wanting to do?—at your age and when you have long retired as superannuated! No, no, Alonso my dear. You are past sixty and your dancing days are over."

I can see her now, that respectable and indignant dame—with her deep-bordered cap, her muslin dress, her white curls, and a hairy mole on one side of her chin. I describe these miscellaneous details, for they are inseparable from my recollection of her. She was pretty even in old age, like Murillo's Santa Anna, and her sober beauty would have justified the comparison if only the lady had been as silent as a picture. Don Alonso somewhat cowed, as he always was, by her flow of words, answered quietly:

"I must go, Paquita. From the letter I have just now received from my worthy friend Churruca, I learn that the united squadrons are either to sail from Cadiz and engage the English or to wait for them in the bay in case they are so bold as to enter. In either case it will be no child's play."

"That is well, and I am glad to hear it," replied Doña Francisca. "There are Gravina, Valdés, Cisneros, Churruca, Alcalá Galiano, and Alava; let them pound away at the English dogs. But you are a piece of useless lumber who can do no good if you go. Why you cannot move that left arm which they dislocated for you at Cape St. Vincent."

My master lifted his arm, with a stiff attempt at military precision, to show that he could use it. But his wife, not convinced by so feeble an argument, went on with shrill asseveration.

"No, you shall not go, what can they want of a piece of antiquity like you. If you were still forty as you were when you went to Tierra del Fuego and brought me back those green Indian necklaces.—Then indeed! But now!—I know, that ridiculous fellow Marcial fired your brain this morning with talking to you about battles. It seems to me that Señor Marcial and I will come to quarrelling.—Let him go to the ships if he likes and pay them out for the foot he lost! Oh! Saint Joseph the blessed! If I had known when I was a girl what you seamen were! Endless worry; never a day's peace! A woman marries to live with her husband and one fine day a dispatch comes from Madrid and he is sent off at two minutes notice to the Lord knows where—Patagonia or Japan or the infernal regions. For ten or twelve months she sees nothing of him and at last, if the savages have not eaten him meanwhile, he comes back again the picture of misery—so ill and yellow that she does not know what to do to restore him to his right color. But old birds are not to be caught in a trap, and then suddenly another dispatch comes from Madrid, with orders to go to Toulon or Brest or Naples—go here and go there—wherever it is necessary to meet the whims of that rascally First Consul...! If you would all do as I say, you would soon payout these gentlemen who keep the world in a turmoil!"

My master sat smiling and gazing at a cheap print, badly colored by some cheap artist, which was nailed against the wall, and which represented the Emperor Napoleon mounted on a green charger, in the celebrated "redingote" which was smeared with vermilion. It was no doubt the sight of this work of art, which I had seen daily for four years, which had modified my ideas with respect to the smuggler's costume of the great man of the day, and had fixed his image in my mind as dressed something like a cardinal and riding a green horse.

"This is not living!" Doña Francisca went on, throwing up her arms: "God forgive me, but I hate the sea, though they say it is one of His most glorious works. What is the use of the Holy Inquisition, will you tell me, if it is not to burn those diabolical ships of war to ashes? What is the good of this incessant firing of cannon,—balls upon balls, all directed against four boards, as you may say, which are soon smashed to leave hundreds of hapless wretches to drown in the sea? Is not that provoking God?—And yet you men are half-wild as soon as you hear a cannon fired! Merciful Heaven! my flesh creeps at the sound, and if every one was of my way of thinking, we should have no more sea-fights, and the cannon would be cast into bells. Look here, Alonso," she said, standing still in front of her husband, "it seems to me that they have done you damage enough already; what more do you want? You and a parcel of madmen like yourself,—had you not enough to satisfy you on the 14th?"

The battle of Cape St. Vincent was fought on February 14, 1797.

Don Alonso clenched his fists at this bitter reminiscence, and it was only out of consideration for his wife, to whom he paid the utmost respect, that he suppressed a good round oath.

"I lay all the blame of your absurd determination to join the fleet to that rascally Marcial," the lady went on, warming with her own eloquence; "that maniac for the sea who ought to have been drowned a hundred times and over, but that he escaped a hundred times to be the torment of my life. If he wants to join, with his wooden leg, his broken arm, his one eye, and his fifty wounds—let him go, by all means, and God grant he may never come back here again—but you shall not go, Alonso, for you are past service and have done enough for the King who has paid you badly enough in all conscience. If I were you, I would throw those captain's epaulettes you have worn these ten years in the face of the Generalissimo of the land and sea forces. My word! they ought have made you admiral, at least; you earned that when you went on that expedition to Africa and brought me back those blue beads which I gave with the Indian necklace to decorate the votive urn to the Virgin 'del Cármen.'"

"Admiral or not, it is my duty to join the fleet, Paquita," said my master. "I cannot be absent from this struggle. I feel that I must pay off some of my arrears to the English."

"Do you talk of paying off arrears!" exclaimed my mistress; "you—old, feeble, and half-crippled...."

"Gabriel will go with me," said Don Alonso, with a look at me which filled me with valor.

I bowed to signify that I agreed to this heroic scheme, but I took care not to be seen by my mistress, who would have let me feel the full weight of her hand if she had suspected my bellicose inclinations. Indeed, seeing that her husband was fully determined, she was more furious than ever, declaring that if she had to live her life again nothing should induce her to marry a sailor. She cursed the Emperor, abused our revered King, the Prince of Peace, and all those who had signed the Treaty of Subsidies, ending by threatening the brave old man with punishment from Heaven for his insane rashness.

During this dialogue, which I have reported with approximate exactness as I have to depend on my memory, a loud barking cough in the adjoining room revealed the fact that Marcial, the old sailor, could overhear with perfect ease, my mistress's vehement harangue, in which she had so frequently mentioned him in by no means flattering terms. Being now desirous of taking part in the conversation, as his intimacy in the house fully justified his doing, he opened the door and came into Don Alfonso's room. Before going any farther I must give some account of my master's former history, and of his worthy wife, that the reader may have a better understanding of what follows.

CHAPTER III.

DON ALFONSO GUTIERREZ DE CISNIEGA belonged to an old family of Vejer, where he lived. He had been devoted at an early age to a naval career and, while still quite young, had distinguished himself in defending Havana against the English in 1748. He was afterwards engaged in the expedition which sailed from Cartagena against the Algerines in 1775, and was present at the attack upon Gibraltar under the Duke de Crillon in 1782. He subsequently joined the expedition to the Straits of Magellan in the corvette *Santa María de la Cabeza*, commanded by Don Antonio de Córdova, and fought in the glorious engagements between the Anglo-Spanish fleet and the French before Toulon in 1793, terminating his career of glory at the disastrous battle of Cape St. Vincent, where he commanded the *Mejicano*, one of the ships which were forced to surrender.

From that time my master, whose promotion had been slower than his laborious and varied career had merited, retired from active service. He suffered much in body from the wounds he had received on that fatal day, and more in mind from the blow of such a defeat. His wife nursed and tended him with devotion though not in silence, for abuse of the navy and of seamen of every degree were as common in her mouth as the names of the saints in that of a bigot.

Doña Francisca was an excellent woman, of exemplary conduct and noble birth, devout and God-fearing—as all women were in those days, charitable and judicious, but with the most violent and diabolical temper I ever met with in the whole course of my life. Frankly I do not believe that this excessive irritability was natural to her, but the result and outcome of the worries in her life arising out of her husband's much-hated profession; it must be confessed that she did not complain wholly without reason, and every day of her life Doña Francisca addressed her prayers to Heaven for the annihilation of every fleet in Europe. This worthy couple had but one child, a daughter—the incomparable Rosita, of whom more anon.

The veteran, however, pined sadly at Vejer, seeing his laurels covered with dust and gnawed to powder by the rats, and all his thoughts and most of his discourse, morning, noon, and night, were based on the absorbing theme that if Córdova, the commander of the Spanish fleet, had only given the word "Starboard" instead of "Port" the good ships *Mejicano, San José, San Nicolás* and *San Isidro* would never have fallen into the hands of the English, and Admiral Jervis would have been defeated. His wife, Marcial, and even I myself, exceeding the limits of my duties—always assured him that there was no doubt of the fact, to see whether, if we acknowledged ourselves convinced, his vehemence would moderate—but no; his mania on that point only died with him.

Eight years had passed since that disaster, and the intelligence that the whole united fleet was to fight a decisive battle with the English had now roused my master to a feverish enthusiasm which seemed to have renewed his youth. He pictured to himself the inevitable rout of his mortal enemies; and although his wife tried to dissuade him, as has been said, it was impossible to divert him from his wild purpose. To prove how obstinate his determination was it is enough to mention that he dared to oppose his wife's strong will, though he avoided all discussion; and to give an adequate idea of all that his opposition implied I ought to mention that Don Alonso was afraid of no mortal thing or creature—neither of the English, the French, nor the savages of Magellan, not of the angry sea, nor of the monsters of the deep, nor of the raging tempest, nor of anything in the earth or sky—but only of his wife.

The last person I must mention is Marcial the sailor, the object of Doña Francisca's deepest aversion, though Don Alonso, under whom he had served, loved him as a brother.

Marcial—no one knew his other name—called by all the sailors "the Half a Man," had been boatswain on various men-of-war for forty years. At the time when my story begins this maritime hero's appearance was the strangest you can imagine. Picture to yourself an old man, tall rather than short, with a wooden leg, his left arm shortened to within a few inches of the elbow, minus an eye, and his face seamed with wounds in every direction—slashed by the various arms of the enemy; with his skin tanned brown, like that of all sea-faring men, and a voice so hoarse, hollow and slow, that it did not seem to belong to any rational human creature, and you have some idea of this eccentric personage. As I think of him I regret the narrow limits of my palette, for he deserves painting in more vivid colors and by a worthier artist. It was hard to say whether his appearance was most calculated to excite laughter or command respect—both at once I think, and according to the point of view you might adopt.

His life might be said to be an epitome of the naval history of Spain during the last years of the past century and the beginning of this—a history in whose pages the most splendid victories alternate with the most disastrous defeats. Marcial had served on board the *Conde de Regla*, the *San Joaquin*, the *Real Cárlos*, the*Trinidad* and other glorious but unfortunate vessels which, whether honorably defeated or perfidiously destroyed, carried with them to a watery grave the naval power of Spain. Besides the expeditions in which my master had taken part Marcial had been present at many others, such as that of Martinica, the action of Cape Finisterre, and before that the terrible battle close to Algeciras in July, 1801, and that off Cape Santa María on the 5th of October, 1804. He quitted the service at sixty-six years of age, not however for lack of spirit but because he was altogether "unmasted" and past fighting. On shore he and my master were the best of friends, and as the boatswain's only daughter was married to one of the servants of the house, of which union a small child was the token, Marcial had made up his mind to cast anchor for good, like a hulk past service, and even succeeded in making himself believe that peace was a good thing. Only to see him you would have thought that the most difficult task that could be set to this grand relic of a hero was that of minding babies; but, as a matter of fact, Marcial had no other occupation in life than carrying and amusing his grandchild, putting it to sleep with his snatches of sea-songs, seasoned with an oath or two—excusable under the circumstances.

But no sooner had he heard that the united fleets were making ready for a decisive battle than his moribund fires rose from their ashes, and he dreamed that he was calling up the crew in the forecastle of the *Santísima Trinidad.* Discovering in Don Alfonso similar symptoms of rejuvenescence, he confessed to him, and from that hour they spent the chief part of the day and night in discussing the news that arrived and their own feelings in the matter; "fighting their battles o'er again," hazarding conjectures as to those to be fought in the immediate future, and talking over their day-dreams like two ship's boys indulging in secret visions of the shortest road to the title of Admiral.

In the course of these *tête-à-tête* meetings, which occasioned the greatest alarm to Doña Francisca, the plan was hatched for setting out to join the fleet and be present at the impending battle. I have already told the reader what my mistress's opinion was and all the abuse she lavished on the insidious sailor; he knows too that Don Alonso persisted in his determination to carry out his rash purpose, accompanied by me, his trusty page, and I must now proceed to relate what occurred when Marcial himself appeared on the scene to take up the cudgels for war against the shameful *status quo* of Doña Francisca.

CHAPTER IV.

"SEÑOR MARCIAL," she began, with increased indignation, "if you choose to go to sea again and lose your other hand, you can go if you like; but my husband here, shall not."

"Very good," said the sailor who had seated himself on the edge of a chair, occupying no more space on it than was necessary to save himself from falling: "I will go alone. But the devil may take me if I can rest without looking on at the fun!"

Then he went on triumphantly: "We have fifteen ships and the French twenty smaller vessels. If they were all ours we should not want so many. Forty ships and plenty of brave hearts on board!"

Just as the spark creeps from one piece of timber to the next, the enthusiasm that fired Marcial's one eye lighted up both my master's, though dimmed by age. "But the *Señorito*" (Lord Nelson), added the sailor, "will bring up a great many men too. That is the sort of performance I enjoy: plenty of timbers to fire at, and plenty of gunpowder-smoke to warm the air when it is cold."

I forgot to mention that Marcial, like most sailors, used a vocabulary of the most wonderful and mongrel character, for it seems to be a habit among seamen of every nation to disfigure their mother tongue to the verge of caricature. By examining the nautical terms used by sailors we perceive that most of them are corruptions of more usual terms, modified to suit their eager and hasty temperament trained by circumstances to abridge all the functions of existence and particularly speech. Hearing them talk it has sometimes occurred to me that sailors find the tongue an organ that they would gladly dispense with.

Marcial, for instance, turned verbs into nouns and nouns into verbs without consulting the authorities. He applied nautical terms to every action and movement, and identified the ideas of a man and a ship, fancying that there was some analogy between their limbs and parts. He would say in speaking of the loss of his eye that his larboard port-hole was closed, and explained the amputation of his arm by saying that he had been left minus his starboard cat-head. His heart he called his courage-hold and his stomach his bread-basket. These terms sailors at any rate could understand; but he had others, the offspring of his own inventive genius of which he alone understood the meaning or could appreciate the force. He had words of his own coining for doubting a statement, for feeling sad; getting drunk he always called "putting on your coat" among a number of other fantastical idioms; and the derivation of this particular phrase will never occur to my readers without my explaining to them that the English sailors had acquired among the Spaniards the nickname of "great-coats," so that when he called getting drunk "putting your coat on" a recondite allusion was implied to the favorite vice of the enemy. He had the most extraordinary nicknames for foreign admirals; Nelson he called the *Señorito*, implying a certain amount of respect for him; Collingwood was *Rio Calambre*, (Uncle Cramp) which he believed to be an equivalent for the English name; Jervis he called—as the English did too—The old Fox; Calder was known as *Rio Perol* (Uncle Boiler) from an association of the name Calder with *caldera*, a kettle, and by an entirely different process he dubbed Villeneuve, the Admiral of the united fleets, with the name of*Monsieur Corneta*, borrowed from some play he had once seen acted at Madrid. In fact, when reporting the conversations I can recall, I must perforce translate his wonderful phraseology into more ordinary language, to avoid going into long and tiresome explanations.

To proceed, Doña Francisca, devoutly crossing herself, answered angrily:

"Forty ships! Good Heavens! it is tempting Providence; and there will be at least forty thousand guns for the enemies to kill each other."

"Ah! but *Monsieur Corneta* keeps the courage-hold well filled!" exclaimed Marcial, striking his breast. "We shall laugh at the great-coats this time. It will not be Cape St. Vincent over again."

"And you must not forget," added my master eagerly recurring to his favorite hobby, "that if Admiral Córdova had only ordered the *San José* and the *Mejicano* to tack to port, Captain Jervis would not now be rejoicing in the title of Earl St. Vincent. Of that you may be very certain, and I have ample evidence to show that if we had gone to port the day would have been ours."

"Ours!" exclaimed Doña Francisca scornfully. "As if you could have done more. To hear these fire-eaters it would seem as if they wanted to conquer the world, and as to going to sea—it appears that their shoulders are not broad enough to bear the blows of the English."

"No," said Marcial resolutely and clenching his fist defiantly. "If it were not for their cunning and knavery...! We got out against them with a bold front, defying them like men, with our flag hoisted and clean hands. The English never sail wide, they always steal up and surprise us, choosing heavy seas and stormy weather. That is how it was at the Straits, when we were made to pay so dearly. We were sailing on quite confidingly, for no one expected to be trapped even by a heretic dog of a Moor, much less by an Englishman who does the polite thing in a Christian fashion.—But no, an enemy who sneaks up to fight is not a Christian—he is a highwayman. Well now, just fancy, señora," and he turned to Doña Francisca to engage her attention and good-will, "we were going out of Cadiz to help the French fleet which was driven into Algeciras by the English.—It is four years ago now, and to this day it makes me so angry that my blood boils as I think of it. I was on board the *Real Cárlos*, 112 guns, commanded by Ezguerra, and we had with us the *San Hermenegildo*, 112 guns too, the *San Fernando*, the *Argonauta*, the *San Agustin*, and the frigate *Sabina*. We were joined by the French squadron of four men-of-war, three frigates and a brigantine, and all sailed out of Algeciras for Cadiz at twelve o'clock at noon; and as the wind was slack when night fell we were close under Punta Carnero. The night was blacker than a barrel of pitch, but the weather was fine so we could hold on our way in spite of the darkness. Most of the crew were asleep; I remember, I was sitting in the fo'castle talking to the mate, Pepe Débora, who was telling me all the dog's tricks his mother-in-law had played him, and alongside we could see the lights of the *San Hermenegildo*, which was sailing at a gun-shot to starboard. The other ships were ahead of us. For the very last thing we any of us thought of was that the 'great-coats' had slipped out of Gibraltar and were giving chase—and how the devil should we, when they had doused all their lights and were stealing up to us without our guessing it? Suddenly, for all that the night was so dark, I fancied I saw something—I always had a port-light like a lynx—I fancied a ship was standing between us and the *San Hermenegildo*, which was sailing at a gun-shot to starboard. 'José Débora,' says I, 'either I saw a ghost or there is an Englishman to starboard?' José Débora looks himself, and then he says: 'May the main-mast go by the board,' says he, 'if there is e'er a ship to starboard but the *San Hermenegildo*.' 'Well,' says I, 'whether or no I am going to tell the officer of the watch.'

"Well hardly were the words out of my mouth when, rub-a-dub! we heard the tune of a whole broadside that came rattling against our ribs. The crew were on deck in a minute, and each man at his post. That was a rumpus, señora! I wish you could have been there, just to have an idea of how these things are managed. We were all swearing like demons and at the same time praying the Lord to give us a gun at the end of every finger to fight them with. Ezguerra gave the word to return their broadside.—Thunder and lightning! They fired again, and in a minute or two we responded. But in the midst of all the noise and confusion we discovered that with their first broadside they had sent one of those infernal combustibles (but he called it 'comestibles') on board which fall on the deck as if it were raining fire. When we saw our ship was burning we fought like madmen and fired off broadside after broadside. Ah! Doña Francisca, it was hot work I can tell you!—Then our captain took us alongside of the enemy's ship that we might board her. I wish you could have seen it! I was in my glory then; in an instant we had our axes and boarding-pikes out, the enemy was coming down upon us and my heart jumped for joy to see it, for this was the quickest way of settling accounts. On we go, right into her!—Day was just beginning to dawn, the yards were touching, and the boarding parties ready at the gangways when we heard Spanish oaths on board the foe. We all stood dumb with horror, for we found that the ship we had been fighting with was the *San Hermenegildo* herself."

"That was a pretty state of things," said Doña Francisca roused to some interest in the narrative. "And how had you been such asses—with not a pin to choose between you?"

"I will tell you. We had no time for explanations then. The flames on our ship went over to the *San Hermenegildo* and then, Blessed Virgin! what a scene of confusion. 'To the boats!' was the cry. The fire caught the *Santa Bárbara* and her ladyship blew up with loud explosion.—We were all swearing, shouting, blaspheming God and the Virgin and all the Saints, for that seems the only way to avoid choking when you are primed to fight, up to the very muzzle...."

"Merciful Heavens how shocking!" cried my mistress. "And you escaped?"

"Forty of us got off in the launch and six or seven in the gig, these took up the second officer of the *San Hermenegildo*. José Débora clung to a piece of plank and came to shore at Morocco, more dead than alive."

"And the rest?"

"The rest—the sea was wide enough to hold them all. Two thousand men went down to Davy Jones that day, and among them our captain, Ezguerra, and Emparan, the captain of the other ship."

"Lord have mercy on them!" ejaculated Doña Francisca. "Though God knows! they were but ill-employed to be snatched away to judgment. If they had stayed quietly at home, as God requires...."

"The cause of that disaster," said Don Alonso, who delighted in getting his wife to listen to these dramatic narratives, "was this: The English emboldened by the darkness arranged that the *Superb*, the lightest of their vessels, should extinguish her lights and slip through between our two finest ships. Having done this, she fired both her broadsides and then put about as quickly as possible to escape the struggle that ensued. The two men-of-war, finding themselves unexpectedly attacked, returned fire and thus went on battering each other till dawn, when, just as they were about to board, they recognized each other and the end came as Marcial has told you in detail."

"Ah! and they played the game well," cried the lady. "It was well done though it was a mean trick!"

"What would you have?" added Marcial. "I never loved them much; but since that night!... If *they* are in Heaven I do not want ever to go there. Sooner would I be damned to all eternity!"

"Well—and then the taking of the four frigates which were coming from Rio de la Plata?" asked Don Alfonso, to incite the old sailor to go on with his stories.

"Aye—I was at that too," said Marcial. "And that was where I left my leg. That time too they took us unawares, and as it was in time of peace we were sailing on quietly enough, only counting the hours till we should be in port, when suddenly—— I will tell you exactly how it all happened, Doña Francisca, that you may just understand the ways of those people. After the engagement at the Straits I embarked on board the *Fama* for Montevideo, and we had been out there a long time when the Admiral of the squadron received orders to convoy treasure from Lima and Buenos Ayres to Spain. The voyage was a good one and we had no mishaps but a few slight cases of fever which only killed off a few of our men. Our freight was heavy—gold belonging to the king and to private persons, and we also had on board what we called the 'wages chest'—savings off the pay of the troops serving in America. Altogether, if I am not much mistaken, a matter of fifty millions or so of *pesos*, as if it were a mere nothing; and besides that, wolf-hides, vicuña wool, cascarilla, pigs of tin and copper, and cabinet woods. Well, sir, after sailing for fifty days we sighted land on the 5th of October, and reckoned on getting into Cadiz the next day when, bearing down from the northeast, what should we see but four frigates. Although, as I said, it was in time of peace, and though our captain, Don Miguel de Zapiain, did not seem to have any suspicion of evil, I—being an old sea-dog—called Débora and said to him that there was powder in the air, I could smell it. Well, when the English frigates were pretty near, we cleared the decks for action; the *Fama* went forward and we were soon within a cable's length of one of the English ships which lay to windward.

"The English captain hailed us through his speaking-trumpet and told us—there is nothing like plain-speaking—told us to prepare to defend ourselves, as he was going to attack. He asked a string of questions, but all he got out of us was that we should not take the trouble to answer him. Meanwhile the other three frigates had come up and had formed in such order that each Englishman had a Spaniard to the leeward of him."

"They could not have taken up a better position," said my master.

"So say I," replied Marcial. "The commander of our squadron, Don José Bustamante, was not very prompt; if I had been in his shoes.... Well, señor, the English commodore sent a little whipper-snapper officer, in a swallow-tail coat, on board the *Medea*, who wasted no time in trifling but said at once that though war had not been declared, the commodore had orders to take us. That is what it is to be English! Well, we engaged at once; our frigate received the first broadside in her port quarter; we politely returned the salute, and the cannonade was brisk on both sides—the long and the short of it is that we could do nothing with the heretics, for the devil was on their side; they set fire to the *Santa Bárbara* which blew up with a roar, and we were all so crushed by this and felt so cowed—not for want of courage, señor, but what they call demoralized—well, from the first we knew we were lost. There were more holes in our ship's sails than in an old cloak; our rigging was damaged, we had five feet of water in the hold, our mizzen-mast was split, we had three shots in the side only just above the water line and many dead and wounded. Notwithstanding all this we went on, give and take, with the English, but when we saw that the *Medea* and the *Clara* were unable to fight any longer and struck their colors we made all sail and retired, defending ourselves as best we could. The cursed Englishman gave chase, and as her sails were in better order than ours we could not escape and we had nothing for it but to haul our colors down at about three in the afternoon, when a great many men had been killed and I myself was lying half-dead on the deck, for a ball had gone out of its way to take my leg off. Those d——d wretches carried us off to England, not as prisoners, but as *détenus*; however, with despatches on one side and despatches on the other, from London to Madrid and back again, the end of it was that they stuck for want of money; and, so far as I was concerned, another leg might have grown by the time the King of Spain sent them such a trifle as those five millions of *pesos*."

"Poor man!—and it was then you lost your leg?" asked Doña Francisca compassionately.

"Yes, señora, the English, knowing that I was no dancer, thought one was as much as I could want. In return they took good care of me. I was six months in a town they called *Plinmuf* (Plymouth) lying in my bunk with my paw tied up and a passport for the next world in my pocket.—However, God A'mighty did not mean that I should make a hole in the water so soon; an English doctor made me this wooden leg, which is better than the other now, for the other aches with that d——d rheumatism and this one, thank God, never aches even when it is hit by a round of small shot. As to toughness, I believe it would stand anything, though, to be sure, I have never since faced English fire to test it."

"You are a brave fellow," said my mistress. "Please God you may not lose the other. But those who seek danger...."

And so, Marcial's story being ended, the dispute broke out anew as to whether or no my master should set out to join the squadron. Doña Francisca persisted in her negative, and Don Alonso, who in his wife's presence was as meek as a lamb, sought pretexts and brought forward every kind of reason to convince her.

"Well we shall go to look on, wife,—simply and merely to look on"—said the hero in a tone of entreaty.

"Let us have done with sight-seeing," answered his wife. "A pretty pair of lookers-on you two would make!"

"The united squadrons," added Marcial, "will remain in Cadiz—and they will try to force the entrance."

"Well then," said my mistress, "you can see the whole performance from within the walls of Cadiz, but as for going out in the ships—I say no, and I mean no, Alonso. During forty years of married life you have never seen me angry (he saw it every day)—but if you join the squadron I swear to you ... remember, Paquita lives only for you!"

"Wife, wife—" cried my master much disturbed: "Do you mean I am to die without having had that satisfaction?"

"A nice sort of satisfaction truly! to look on at mad men killing each other! If the King of Spain would only listen to me, I would pack off these English and say to them: 'My beloved subjects were not made to amuse you. Set to and fight each other, if you want to fight.' What do you say to that?—I, simpleton as I am, know very well what is in the wind, and that is that the first Consul—Emperor—Sultan—whatever you call him—wants to settle the English, and as he has no men brave enough for the job he has imposed upon our good King and persuaded him to lend him his; and the truth is he is sickening us with his everlasting sea-fights. Will you just tell me what is Spain to gain in all this? Why is Spain to submit to being cannonaded day after day for nothing at all? Before all that rascally business Marcial has told us of what harm had the English ever done us?—Ah, if they would only listen to me! Master Buonaparte might fight by himself, for I would not fight for him!"

"It is quite true," replied my master, "that our alliance with France is doing us much damage, for all the advantages accrue to our ally, while all the disasters are on our side."

"Well, then, you utter simpletons, why do you encourage the poor creatures to fight in this war?"

"The honor of the nation is at stake," replied Don Alonso, "and after having once joined the dance it would be a disgrace to back out of it. Last month, when I was at Cadiz, at my cousin's daughter's christening, Churruca said to me: 'This French alliance and that villainous treaty of San Ildefonso, which the astuteness of Buonaparte and the weakness of our government made a mere question of subsidies, will be the ruin of us and the ruin of our fleet if God does not come to the rescue, and afterwards will be the ruin of the colonies too and of Spanish trade with America. But we must go on now all the same....'"

"Well," said Doña Francisca, "what I say is that the Prince of Peace is interfering in things he does not understand. There you see what a man without learning is! My brother the archdeacon, who is on Prince Ferdinand's side, says that Godoy is a thoroughly commonplace soul, that he has studied neither Latin nor theology and that all he knows is how to play the guitar and twenty ways of dancing a gavotte. They made him prime minister for his good looks, as it would seem. That is the way we do things in Spain! And then we hear of starvation and want—everything is so dear—yellow fever breaking out in Andalusia.—This is a pretty state of things, sir,—yes, and the fault is yours; yours," she went on, raising her voice and turning purple. "Yes, señor, yours, who offend God by killing so many people—and if you would go to church and tell your beads instead of wanting to go in those diabolical ships of war, the devil would not find time to trot round Spain so nimbly, playing the mischief with us all."

"But you shall come to Cadiz too," said Don Alonso, hoping to light some spark of enthusiasm in his wife's heart; "you shall go to Flora's house, and from the balcony you will be able to see the fight quite comfortably, and the smoke and the flames and the flags.—It is a beautiful sight!"

"Thank you very much—but I should drop dead with fright. Here we shall be quiet; those who seek danger may go there."

Here the dialogue ended, and I remember every word of it though so many years have elapsed. But it often happens that the most remote incidents that occurred even in our earliest childhood, remain stamped on our imagination more clearly and permanently than the events of our riper years when our reasoning faculties have gained the upper hand.

That evening Don Alonzo and Marcial talked over matters whenever Doña Francisca left them together; but this was at rare intervals, for she was suspicious and watchful. When she went off to church to attend vespers, as was her pious custom, the two old sailors breathed freely again as if they were two giddy schoolboys out of sight of the master. They shut themselves into the library, pulled out their maps and studied them with eager attention; then they read some papers in which they had noted down the names of several English vessels with the number of their guns and men, and in the course of their excited conference, in which reading was varied by vigorous commentary, I discovered that they were scheming the plan of an imaginary naval battle. Marcial, by means of energetic gymnastics with his arm and a half, imitated the advance of the squadron and the explosion of the broadsides; with his head he indicated the alternate action of the hostile vessels; with his body the heavy lurch of each ship as it went to the bottom; with his hand the hauling up and down of the signal flags; he represented the boatswain's whistle by a sharp sibilation; the rattle of the cannon by thumping his wooden leg on the floor; he smacked his tongue to imitate the swearing and confusion of noises in the fight; and as my master assisted him in this performance with the utmost gravity I also must need take my share in the fray, encouraged by their example and giving natural vent to that irresistible longing to make a noise which is a master passion with every boy. Seeing the enthusiasm of the two veterans, I could no longer contain myself and took to leaping about the room—a freedom in which I was justified by my master's kind familiarity; I imitated with my head and arms the movements of a vessel veering before the wind, and at the same time making my voice as big as possible I shouted out all the most sonorous monosyllables I could think of as being most like the noise of a cannon. My worthy master and the mutilated old sailor, quite as childish as I in their own way, paid no attention to my proceedings, being entirely preoccupied with their own ideas.

How I have laughed since when I have remembered the scene! and how true it is—in spite of all my respect for my companions in the game—that senile enthusiasm makes old men children once more and renews the puerile follies of the cradle even on the very brink of the tomb!

They were deep in their discussion when they heard Doña Francisca's step returning from church.

"She is coming!" cried Marcial in an agony of alarm, and they folded up the maps and began to talk of indifferent matters. I, however, not being able to cool down my juvenile blood so rapidly or else not noticing my mistress's approach soon enough, went on, down the middle of the room in my mad career, ejaculating with the utmost incoherence, such phrases as I had picked up: "Tack to starboard! Now Port! Broadside to the leeward! Fire! Bang! bom! boom!..." She came up to me in a fury and without any warning delivered a broadside on my figure-head with her right hand, and with such effect that for a few moments I saw nothing but stars.

"What! you too?" she cried, battering me unmercifully. "You see," she added, turning on her husband with flashing eyes, "you have taught him to feel no respect for you!—You thought you were still in the *Caleta* did you, you little ne'er do weel?"

The commotion ended by my running off to the kitchen crying and disgraced, after striking my colors in an ignominious manner, before the superior force of the enemy; Doña Francisca giving chase and belaboring my neck and shoulders with heavy slaps. In the kitchen I cast anchor and sat down to cry over the fatal termination of my sea-fight.

CHAPTER V.

IN opposing her husband's insane determination to join the fleet, Doña Francisca did not rely solely on the reasons given in the last chapter; she had another and more weighty one which she did not mention in the course of that conversation, perhaps because it was wiser not. But the reader does not know it, and must be told.

I have mentioned that my master had a daughter; this daughter's name was Rosita; she was a little older than I was, that is to say scarcely fifteen, and a marriage had been arranged for her with a young officer of artillery named Malespina, belonging to a family of Medinasidonia and distantly related to my master. The wedding had been fixed for the end of October and, as may be supposed, the absence of the bride's father on so solemn an occasion would have been highly improper.

I must here give some account of my young lady, of her bridegroom, her love-affairs and her projected marriage; and alas! my recollections take a tinge of melancholy, recalling to my fancy many troublesome and far-away scenes, figures from another world—and stirring my weary old heart with feelings of which I should find it hard to say whether they were more pleasurable or sad. Those ardent memories which now lie withered in my brain, like tropical flowers exposed to a chill northern blast, sometimes make me laugh—but sometimes make me grave. However, to my tale, or the reader will be tired of these wearisome reflections which, after all, interest no one but myself.

Rosita was uncommonly pretty. I remember vividly how pretty she was, though I should find it difficult to describe her features. I fancy I see her now, smiling in my face; the curious expression of her countenance, unlike any other I ever saw, dwells in my mind—from the perfect distinctness with which it rises before me—like one of those innate ideas which seem to have come into the world with us from a former existence, or to have been impressed on our minds by some mysterious power while we were still in the cradle. And yet I cannot describe it, for what then was real and tangible remains now in my brain as a vague ideal; and while nothing is so fascinating as a beloved ideal, nothing so completely eludes all categorical description.

When I first went into the house I thought that Rosita belonged to some superior order of beings; I will explain my feelings more fully that you may form an idea of my utter simpleness. When we are little and a child comes into the world within our family the grown-up folks are apt to tell us that it has come from France, Paris, or England. I, like other children, having no notions as to the multiplication of the human race, firmly believed that babies were imported packed up in boxes like a cargo of hardware. Thus, gazing for the first time at my master's daughter, I argued that so lovely a being could not have come from the same factory as the rest of us, that is to say from Paris or from England, and I remained convinced that there must be some enchanted region where heaven-sent workmen were employed in making these choicer and lovelier specimens of humanity. Both of us being children, though in different ranks of life, we were soon on those terms of mutual confidence which were natural to our years, and my greatest joy was in playing with her, submitting to all her vagaries and insolence, which is not saying a little, for our relative position was never lost sight of in our games; she was always the young lady and I always the servant, so that I got the worst of it when slaps were going, and I need not say who was the sufferer.

My highest dream of happiness was to be allowed to fetch her from school, and when, by some unforeseen accident, some one else was entrusted with this delightful duty I was so deeply distressed that I honestly thought there could be no greater grief in life, and would say to myself: "It is impossible that I should ever be more miserable when I am a man grown." My greatest delight was to climb the orange-tree in the court-yard to pick the topmost sprays of blossom; I felt myself at a height far above the greatest king on earth when seated on his throne, and I can remember no pleasure to be compared to that of being obliged to capture her in that divinely rapturous game known as hide and seek. If she ran like a gazelle I flew like a bird to catch her as soon as possible, seizing her by the first part of her dress or person that I could lay my hand on. When we changed parts, when she was the pursuer and I was to be caught, the innocent delight of the blissful game was doubled, and the darkest and dingiest hole in which I might hide, breathlessly awaiting the grasp of her imprisoning hands, was to me a perfect paradise. And I may honestly say that during these happy games I never had a thought or a feeling that did not emanate from the purest and most loyal idealism.

Then her singing! From the time when she was quite little she used to sing the popular airs of Andalusia with the ease of a nightingale, which knows all the secrets of song without having been taught. All the neighbors admired her wonderful facility and would come to listen to her, but to me their applause and admiration were an offence; I could have wished her to sing to no one but me. Her singing was a sort of melancholy warbling, qualified by her fresh childlike voice. The air, which repeated itself with complicated little turns and trills like a thread of sound, seemed to be lost in distant heights and then to come back to earth again on the low notes. It was like the song of the lark as it rises towards heaven and suddenly comes down to sing close in our ears; the spirit of the hearer seemed to expand as it followed the voice, and then to contract again, but always following the swing of the melody and feeling the music to be inseparable from the sweet little singer. The effect was so singular that to me it was almost painful to hear her, particularly in the presence of others.

We were, as I have said, of about the same age, she being eight or nine months older than I was. But I was stunted and puny while she was well grown and vigorous, and at the end of my three years' residence in the house she looked much the elder of the two. These three years slipped by without our either of us suspecting that we were growing up; our games went on without interruption, for she was much livelier by nature than I, though her mother would scold her, trying to keep her in order and make her study—in which, however, she did not always succeed. At the end of these three years, however, my adored young mistress was a woman grown; her figure was round and well formed, giving the finishing touch to her beauty; her face had a tenderer blush, a softer form, a gentler look; her large eyes were brighter but their glance was less restless and eager; her gait was more sober; her movements were, I cannot say lighter nor less light, but certainly different, though I could not, either then or now, define in what the difference lay. But no change struck me so much as that in her voice, which acquired a gravity and depth very unlike the shrill gay tones in which she had been wont to call me, bewildering my common-sense and making me leave my various duties to join in her games. The bud, in short, had become a rose, the chrysalis was transformed into a butterfly.

Then, one day—one dreadful, dismal day—my young mistress appeared before me in a long dress. This alteration made such an impression on me that I could not speak a word the whole day. I felt like a man who has been cruelly imposed upon, and I was so vexed with her that in my secret soul I found fifty reasons for seriously resenting her rapid development. A perfect fever of argumentativeness was fired in my brain, and I debated the matter with myself in the most fervent manner during my sleepless nights. The thing that utterly confounded me was that the addition of a few yards of stuff to her skirts seemed altogether to have altered her character. That day—a thousand times unblessed—she spoke to me with the greatest formality, ordering me coldly and even repellently to do all the things I least liked doing—and she, who had so often been my accomplice and screen in idleness, now reproved me for it! and all this without a smile, or a skip, or a glance!—No more running, no more songs, no more hiding for me to find her, no making believe to be cross ending in a laugh—not a squabble, not even a slap from her sweet little hand! It was a terrible crisis in my life—she was a woman and I was still a child!

I need not say that this was an end to our pranks and games; I never again climbed the orange-tree, which henceforth blossomed unmolested by my greedy devotion, and unfolded its leaves and shed its luscious perfume at its own sweet will; we never again scampered across the court-yard, nor trotted too and from school—I, so proud of my responsibility, that I would have defended her against an army if they had tried to carry her off. From that day Rosita always walked with the greatest dignity and circumspection. I often observed that as she went up-stairs in front of me she took care not to show an inch, not a line, of her pretty ankles, and this systematic concealment I felt to be an insult to my dignity, for I had till lately seen a great deal more than her ankles! Bless me! I can laugh now when I remember how my heart was ready to burst over these things.

But worse misfortunes were in store. One day in the same year as that of this transformation old 'Aunt' Martina, Rosario the cook, Marcial, and other members of the kitchen society were discussing something very important. I made the best use of my ears and presently gathered the most alarming hints: My young mistress was to be married. The thing seemed incredible for I had never heard of a lover. However, the parents used to arrange all these matters and the strange thing is that sometimes they did not turn out badly. A young man of good family had asked her hand, and her parents had consented. He came to the house accompanied by his relatives, who were some kind of counts or marquises with a high-sounding title. The suitor wore a naval uniform, for he served his country as a sailor, but in spite of his elegant costume he was by no means attractive. This no doubt was the impression he made on my young mistress, for from the first she manifested a great dislike to the marriage. Her mother tried to persuade her, but all in vain though she drew the most flattering picture of the young man's excellent talents, ancient lineage and splendid wealth. The young girl was not to be convinced, and answered all these arguments with others no less cogent.

However, the sly baggage never said a word about the real reason, which was that she had another lover whom she really loved. This was a young artillery officer, Don Rafael Malespina, a fine-looking young fellow with a pleasing face. My young mistress had made his acquaintance in church, and the traitor Love had taken advantage of her while she was saying her prayers; but indeed a church has always seemed the fittest place, with its poetical and mysterious influences, for the doors of the soul to be opened for the admission of love. Malespina took to lurking round the house, in which I detected him on various occasions, and this love-affair became so much talked of in Vejer that the young naval officer came to know of it and challenged his rival. My master and mistress heard the whole story when news was brought to the house that Malespina had wounded his antagonist severely.

The scandal caused an immense commotion. My mistress's religious feelings were so much shocked by this deed that neither she nor my master could conceal their wrath, and Rosita was their first victim. However, months went by; the wounded man got well again, and as Malespina himself was a man of birth and wealth, there were evident indications in the political atmosphere of the house that Don Rafael was about to be admitted. The parents of the wounded man gave up the suit, and those of the conqueror appeared in their place to ask the hand of my sweet young mistress. After some discussion and demur the match was agreed upon.

I remember the first time old Malespina came. He was a very tall, dry-looking man with a gaudily-colored waistcoat, a quantity of seals and ornaments hanging to his watch, and a very large sharp nose with which he seemed to be smelling every one he talked to. He was terribly voluble and never allowed any one else to get a word in; he contradicted everything, and it was impossible to praise anything without his saying that he had something far better. From the first I felt sure he was a vain man and utterly untruthful, and my opinion was amply justified later. My master received him with friendly politeness, as well as his son who came with him. From that time the lover came to the house every day, sometimes alone and sometimes with his father.

Now a new phase came over my young mistress. Her coolness to me was so marked that it verged on utter contempt. It made me understand clearly, for the first time, the humbleness of my condition, and I cursed it bitterly; I tried to argue with myself as to the claims to superiority of those who really were my superiors, asking myself, with real anguish of mind, how far it was right and just that others should be rich and noble and learned, while my ancestry were of such low origin; my sole fortune was my skin, and I hardly knew how to read. Seeing what the reward of my devotion was, I fully believed that there was no ambition in this wide world that I dared aspire to; and it was not till long after that I acquired a rational conviction that, by a steady and vigorous use of my own powers, I might gain almost everything I was deficient in. Under the scorn with which she treated me I lost all confidence in myself; I never dared open my lips in her presence, and she inspired me with far greater awe than her parents. Meanwhile I attentively watched all the signs of the love that possessed her; I saw her sad and impatient when her lover was late; at every sound of an approaching footstep her pretty face flushed and her black eyes sparkled with anxiety and hope. If it was he who came in she could not conceal her rapture, and then they would sit and talk for hours together; but always under the eye of Doña Francisca, for she would not have allowed the young lady to have a *tête-à-tête* meeting with any one, even through iron bars.

However, they carried on an extensive correspondence, and the worst of it all was that I had to be the go-between and courier. That drove me mad!—The regular thing was that I should go out and meet the young gentleman at a certain place, as punctually as a clock, and he would give me a note to carry to my young mistress; having discharged this commission, she would give me one to take to him. How often have I felt tempted to burn those letters instead of delivering them. However, luckily for me, I always kept cool enough to resist this base temptation. I need hardly add that I hated Malespina; I no sooner saw him come into the house than my blood boiled, and whenever he desired me to do anything I did it as badly and sulkily as possible, wishing to betray my extreme disgust. This disgust, which to them seemed simply bad service, while to me it was a display of honest wrath worthy of a proud and noble heart, earned me many reprimands, and above all it once led my young lady to make a speech that pierced me to the heart like the thrust of an arrow. On one occasion I heard her say: "That boy is getting so troublesome that we shall have to get rid of him."

At last the day was fixed for the wedding, and it was only a short while before that event that all I have already related took place with reference to my master's project. It may therefore be easily understood that Doña Francisca had excellent reasons for objecting to her husband's joining the fleet, besides her regard for his safety.

CHAPTER VI.

I REMEMBER very well that the day after the cuffing bestowed on me by Doña Francisca in her wrath at my irreverent conduct and her intense aversion to all naval warfare, I went out to attend my master in his daily walk. He leaned upon my arm, and on the other side of him walked Marcial; we went slowly to suit Don Alonso's feeble pace and the awkwardness of the old sailor's wooden leg. It was like one of those processions in which a group of tottering and worm-eaten saints are carried along on a shaky litter, threatening to fall if the pace of the bearers is in the least accelerated. The two old men had no energy or motive power left but their brave hearts, which still acted as truly as a machine just turned out of a workshop; or like the needle of a ship's compass which, notwithstanding its unerring accuracy, could do nothing to work the crazy craft it served to guide! During our walk my master—after having asserted, as usual, that if Admiral Córdova had only tacked to port instead of starboard the battle of 'the 14th' would never have been lost—turned the conversation once more on their grand project, and though they did not put their scheme into plain words, no doubt because I was present, I gathered from what they said that they intended to effect their purpose by stealth, quietly walking out of the house one morning without my mistress's knowledge.

When we went in again indifferent matters were talked over. My master, who was always amiable to his wife, was more so, that day, than ever. Doña Francisca could say nothing, however trivial, that he did not laugh at immoderately. He even made her a present of some trifles, doing his utmost to keep her in a good humor, and it was no doubt as a result of this conspicuous complaisance that my mistress was crosser and more peevish than I had ever seen her. No accommodation was possible; she quarrelled with Marcial over heaven knows what trifle, and desired him to quit the house that instant; she used the most violent language to her husband; and during dinner, though he praised every dish with unwonted warmth, the lady was implacable and went on grumbling and scolding.

At last it was time for evening prayers, a solemn ceremony performed in the dining-room in the presence of all the household; and my master, who would not unfrequently go to sleep while he lazily muttered the*Paternoster*, was that evening unusually wide awake and prayed with genuine fervor, his voice being heard above all the rest. Another incident occurred which struck me particularly. The walls of the rooms were decorated with two distinct sets of prints: sacred subjects and maps—the hierarchy of Heaven on one hand and the soundings all round Europe and America on the other. After supper my master was standing in the passage, studying a mariner's chart and tracing lines upon it with his trembling forefinger, when Doña Francisca, who had gathered some hints of the plan for evasion, and who always appealed to Heaven when she caught her husband red-handed in any manifestations of nautical enthusiasm, came up behind him, and throwing up her arms, exclaimed:

"Merciful Heaven! If you are not enough to provoke a Saint!"

"But, my dear," my master timidly replied, "I was only tracing the course taken by Alcalá Galiano and Valdés in the schooners *Sutil* and *Mejicana* when we went to explore the straits of Magellan. It was a delightful expedition—I must have told you all about it."

"I shall come to burning all that paper trash!" cried Doña Francisca. "A plague on voyages and on the wandering dog of a Jew who invented them. You would do better to take some concern for the salvation of your soul, for the long and the short of it is you are no chicken. What a man! to be sure—what a man to have to take care of!"

She could not get over it; I happened to pass that way, but I cannot remember whether she relieved her fury by giving me a thrashing and demonstrating at once the elasticity of my ears and the weight of her hands. The fact is that these little endearments were so frequently repeated, that I cannot recollect whether I received them on this particular occasion; all I remember is that my master, in spite of his utmost amiability, entirely failed to mollify his wife.

Meanwhile I have neglected to speak of Rosita; she was in a very melancholy mood, for Señor de Malespina had not made his appearance all day nor written her a note; all my excursions to the market-place having proved vain. Evening came and with it grief fell on the young girl's soul, for there was no hope now of seeing him till next day—but suddenly, after supper had been ordered up, there was a loud knock at the door. I flew to open it, and it was he; before I opened it my hatred had recognized him.

I fancy I can see him now as he stood before me then, shaking his cloak which was wet with rain. Whenever I recall that man I see him as I saw him then. To be frankly impartial, I must say he was a very handsome young fellow, with a fine figure, good manners, and a pleasant expression; rather cold and reserved at first, grave and extremely courteous with the solemn and rather exaggerated politeness of the old school. He was dressed that evening in a frock-coat, with riding breeches and top boots; he wore a Portuguese hat and a very handsome cloak of scarlet cloth, lined with silk, which was the height of fashion with the gilded youth of that time.

As soon as he had come in I saw that something serious had happened. He went into the dining-room where all were much surprised to see him at so late an hour, for he never called in the evening; but my young mistress had hardly time to be glad before she understood that this unexpected visit was connected with some painful occasion.

"I have come to take leave of you," said Malespina. They all sat stupefied, and Rosita turned as white as the paper on which I am writing; then she turned scarlet and then again as pale as death.

"But what has happened? Where are you going Don Rafael?" asked my mistress. I have said that Malespina was an artillery officer, but I did not mention that he was stationed at Cadiz and at Vejer only on leave.

"As the fleet is short of men," he replied, "we are under orders to embark and serve on board ship. They say a battle is inevitable and most of the vessels are short of gunners."

"Christ, Mother Mary and Saint Joseph!" shrieked Doña Francisca almost beside herself. "And they are taking you too? That is too much. Your duties are on land, my friend. Tell them to manage as best they may; if they want men let them find them. Upon my soul this is beyond a joke!"

"But, my dear," said Don Alonso humbly, "do not you see that they must...." But he could not finish his sentence, for Doña Francisca, whose cup of wrath and grief was overflowing, proceeded to apostrophize all the potentates of the earth.

"You—" she exclaimed, "anything and everything seems right in your eyes, if only it is to benefit those blessed ships of war. And who, I say, who is the demon from hell who has ordered land forces on board ship? You need not tell me.—It is Buonaparte's doing. No Spaniard would have concocted such an infernal plot. Go and tell them that you are just going to be married. Come now," she added, turning to her husband, "write to Gravina and tell him that this young man cannot join the squadron." Then, seeing that her husband only shrugged his shoulders, she cried:

"He is of no use whatever! Mercy on me! If only I wore trousers I would be off to Cadiz and stop there till I had got you out of this mess."

Rosita said not a word. I who was watching her narrowly perceived how agitated she was. She never took her eyes off her lover, and if it had not been for good manners and to keep up her dignity, she would have cried and sobbed loudly to relieve the grief that was almost suffocating her.

"The soldier," said Don Alonso, "is the slave of duty, and our young friend is required by his country to serve on board ship in her defence. He will gain glory in the impending struggle, and make his name famous by some great deed which history will record as an example to future generations."

"Oh yes—this, that and the other!" said Doña Francisca mimicking the pompous tone in which her husband had made this speech. "We know—and all for what? To humor those ne'er-do-weels at Madrid. Let them come themselves to fire the cannons, and fight on their own account!—And when do you start?"

"To-morrow morning. My leave is cut short and I am under orders to proceed at once to Cadiz."

It would be impossible to describe the look that came into my young mistress's face as she heard these words. The lovers looked at each other, and a long and mournful silence fell after this announcement of Malespina's immediate departure.

"But this is not to be borne!" exclaimed Doña Francisca. "They will be calling out the peasantry next—and the women too, if the whim takes them. Lord of Heaven!" she went on looking up to the ceiling with the glare of a pythoness, "I do not fear to offend Thee by saying: Curses on the inventor of ships—Curses on all who sail in them, and Curses on the man who made the first cannon, with its thunder that is enough to drive one mad, and to be the death of so many poor wretches who never did any harm!"

Don Alonso looked at the young officer, expecting to read some protest in his face against these insults to the noble science of gunnery. Then he said:

"The worst of it is that the ships will lack material too and it would be...."

Marcial, who had been listening at the door to the whole conversation, could no longer contain himself. He came into the room saying:

"And why should they lack material?—The *Trinidad* carries 140 guns—32 thirty-six pounders, 34 twenty-four pounders, 36 twelve-pounders, 18 eighty-pounders, and 10 mortars. The *Príncipe de Astúrias* carries 118, the*Santa Ana* 120, the *Rayo* 100, the *Nepomuceno*, and the *San* ..."

"What business have you to interfere!" exclaimed Doña Francisca. "And what does it matter to us whether they carry fifty or eighty?" But Marcial went on with his patriotic list all the same, but in a lower voice and speaking only to my master, who dared not express his approbation. Doña Francisca went on:

"But for God's sake, Don Rafael, do not go. Explain that you are a landsman, that you are going to be married. If Napoleon must fight, let him fight alone: let him come forward and say: 'Here am I—kill me, you English—or let me kill you.' Why should Spain be subject to his lordship's vagaries?"

"I must admit," said Malespina, "that our alliance with France has proved most disastrous."

"Then why was it made? Every one says that this Godoy is an ignorant fellow. You might think a nation could be governed by playing the guitar!"

"After the treaty of Basle," the young man said, "we were forced to become the enemies of the English, who defeated our fleet off Cape St. Vincent."

"Ah! there you have it!" exclaimed Don Alonso, striking the table violently with his fist. "If Admiral Córdova had given the word to tack to port, to the vessels in front—in accordance with the simplest rules of strategy—the victory would have been ours. I consider that proved to a demonstration, and I stated my opinion at the time. But every man must keep his place."

"The fact remains that we were beaten," said Malespina. "The defeat might not have led to such serious consequences if the Spanish ministry had not signed the treaty of San Ildefonso with the French republic. That put us at the mercy of the First Consul, obliging us to support him in wars which had no aim or end but the furthering of his ambition. The peace of Amiens was no better than a truce; England and France declared war again immediately, and then Napoleon demanded our assistance. We wished to remain neutral, for that treaty did not oblige us to take any part in the second war, but he insisted on our co-operation with so much determination that the King of Spain, to pacify him, agreed to pay him a subsidy of a hundred millions of*reales*—it was purchasing our neutrality with gold. But even so we did not get what we had paid for; in spite of this enormous sacrifice we were dragged into war. England forced us into it by seizing, without any justification, four of our frigates returning from America freighted with bullion. After such an act of piracy the parliament of Madrid had no choice but to throw the country into the hands of Napoleon, and that was exactly what he wished. Our navy agreed to submit to the decision of the First Consul—nay, he was already Emperor—and he, hoping to conquer the English by stratagem, sent off the combined fleets to Martinique, intending to draw off the British naval forces from the coasts of Europe. Thus he hoped to realize his favorite dream of invading Great Britain; but this clever trick only served to prove the inexperience and cowardice of the French Admiral who, on his return to Europe would not share with our navy the glory of the battle off Finisterre. Then, in obedience to the Emperor's orders, the combined fleets were to enter Brest. They say that Napoleon is furious with the French Admiral and intends to supplant him immediately."

"But from what they say," Marcial began, putting his oar in again, as we say, "Monsieur Corneta wants to cancel it, and is on the look-out for some action which may wipe out the black mark against him. I am only too glad, for then we shall see who can do something and who cannot."

"One thing is certain," Malespina went on, "the English fleet is cruising in our waters and means to blockade Cadiz. The Spanish authorities think that our fleet ought not to go out of the bay, where they have every chance of conquering the foe; but it seems that the French are determined to go out to sea."

"We shall see," said my master. "It cannot fail to be a glorious battle, any way."

"Glorious! yes...." replied Malespina. "But who can promise that fortune shall favor us. You sailors indulge in many illusions and, perhaps from seeing things too closely, you do not realize the inferiority of our fleet to that of the English. They, besides having a splendid artillery have all the materials at hand for repairing their losses at once. As to the men, I need say nothing. The enemy's sailors are the best in the world—all old and experienced seamen, while only too many of the Spanish vessels are manned by raw recruits, indifferent to their work and hardly knowing how to serve a gun; our marines, again, are not all we could wish, for they have been supplemented by land-forces—brave enough, no doubt, but certain to be sea-sick."

"Well, well," said my master, "in the course of a few days we shall know the end of it all."

"I know the end of it all very well," said Doña Francisca. "All these gentlemen—though I am far from saying they will not have gained glory—will come home with broken heads."

"What can you know about it?" exclaimed Don Alonso, unable to conceal an impulse of vexation, which, however, lasted but a moment.

"More than you do," she retorted sharply. "But God have you in his keeping, Don Rafael, that you may come back to us safe and sound."

This conversation had taken place during supper, which was a melancholy meal, and after Doña Francisca's last speech no one said another word. The meal ended, Malespina took a tender leave of them all, and as a special indulgence on so solemn an occasion the kind-hearted parents left the lovers together, allowing them to bid each other adieu at their ease and unseen, so that nothing might prevent their indulging in any demonstration which might relieve their anguish. It is evident that I was not a spectator of the scene and I know nothing of what took place; but it may be supposed that no reticence on either side checked the expression of their feelings.

When Malespina came out of the room he was as pale as death; he once more bid farewell to my master and mistress, who embraced him affectionately, and was gone. When we went up to Rosita we found her drowned in tears, and her grief was so desperate that her devoted parents could not soothe her by any persuasion or argument, nor revive her energy by any of the remedies for which I was sent backwards and forwards to the apothecary. I must confess that I was so deeply grieved at the distress of these hapless lovers that my rancorous feelings against Malespina died away in my breast. A boy's heart is easily appeased, and mine was always open to gentle and generous impulses.

CHAPTER VII.

THE following morning had a great surprise in store for me, and my mistress was thrown into the most violent passion I suppose she can ever have known in her life. When I got up I perceived that Don Alonso was in the best of humors, and his wife even more ill-tempered than usual. While she was gone to mass with Rosita, I saw my master packing in the greatest haste, putting shirts, and other articles of clothing, and among them his uniform, into a portmanteau. I helped him and it made me suspect that he was about to steal away; still, I was surprised to see nothing of Marcial. However, his absence was presently accounted for; for Don Alonso, having made his rapid arrangements, became extremely impatient till the old sailor made his appearance, saying: "Here is the chaise. Let us be off before she comes in." I took up the valise, and in a twinkling Don Alonso, Marcial, and I had sneaked out of the back gate so as to be seen by nobody; we got into the chaise, which set off as fast as the wretched hack could draw it and the badness of the road allowed. This, which was bad enough for horses was almost impassable for vehicles; however, in spite of jolting that almost made us sick, we hurried as much as possible, and until we were fairly out of sight of the town our martyrdom was allowed no respite.

I enjoyed the journey immensely, for every novelty turns the brain of a boy. Marcial could not contain himself for joy, but my master, who at first displayed his satisfaction with even less reticence than I, became sadder and more subdued when we had left the town behind us. From time to time he would say: "And she will be so astonished! What will she say when she goes home and does not find us!"

As for me, my whole being seemed to expand at the sight of the landscape, with the gladness and freshness of the morning, and above all with the idea of soon seeing Cadiz and its matchless bay, crowded with vessels; its gay and busy streets and its creek (the Caleta) which remained in my mind as the symbol of the most precious gift of life—liberty; its Plaza, its jetty and other spots, all dear to my memory. We had not gone more than three leagues when there came in sight two riders mounted on magnificent horses, who were fast overtaking us and before long joined us. We had at once recognized them as Malespina and his father—the tall, haggard, and chattering old man of whom I have already spoken. They were both much surprised to see Don Alonso, and still more so when he explained that he was on his way to Cadiz to join a ship. The son took the announcement with much gravity; but the father, who as you will have understood was an arrant braggart and flatterer, complimented my master in high-flown terms on his determination, calling him the prince of navigators, the mirror of sailors, and an honor to his country.

We stopped to dine at the inn at Conil. The gentlemen had what they could get, and Marcial and I eat what was left, which was not much. I waited at table and heard the conversation, by which means I gained a better knowledge of the elder Malespina, who at first struck me as a boastful liar and afterwards as the most amusing chatterbox I ever in my life met with.

Don José Malespina, my young mistress's intended father-in-law—no relation to the famous naval officer of that name—was a retired colonel of artillery, and his greatest pride was founded on his perfect knowledge of that branch of military science and on his personal superiority in the tactics of gunnery. When he enlarged on that subject his imagination seemed to gain in vividness and in freedom of invention.

"Artillery," he said, without pausing for a moment in the act of deglutition, "is indispensable on board ships of war. What is a vessel without guns? But it is on land, Señor Don Alonso, that the marvellous results of that grand invention of the human mind are seen to the best advantage. During the war in Roussillon—you know of course that I took part in that campaign and that all our successes were due to my promptness in managing the artillery.—The battle of Masdeu—: How do you suppose that was won? General Ricardos posted me on a hill with four pieces, ordering me not to fire till he sent the word of command. But I, not taking the same view of the case, kept quiet till a column of the French took up a position in front of me, in such a way as that my fire raked them from end to end. Now the French troops form in file with extraordinary precision. I took a very exact aim with one of my guns, covering the head of the foremost soldier.—Do you see? The file was wonderfully straight.—I fired, and the ball took off one hundred and forty-two heads Sir! and the rest did not fall only because the farther end of the line swerved a little. This produced the greatest consternation among theenemy, but as they did not understand my tactics and could not see me from where they stood, they sent up another column to attack our troops on my right, and that column shared the same fate, and another and another, till I had won the battle."

"Well, señor, it was wonderful!" said my master, who, seeing the enormity of the lie, had no mind to trouble himself to contradict his friend.

"Then in the second campaign, under the command of the Conde de la Union, we gave the republicans a very pretty lesson. The defence of Boulou was not successful because we ran short of ammunition; but in spite of that I did great damage by loading a gun with the keys of the church—however, they did not go far, and as a last and desperate resource I loaded the cannon with my own keys, my watch, my money, a few trifles I found in my pockets and, at last, with my decorations. The strange thing is that one of the crosses found its billet on the breast of a French general, to which it stuck as if it had been glued there and did him no harm whatever. He kept it, and when he went to Paris, the Convention condemned him to death or exile—I forget which—for having allowed himself to accept an order from the hand of an enemy."

"The devil they did!" said my master, highly delighted with these audacious romances.

"When I was in England," continued the old soldier, "you know of course, that I was sent for by the English to make improvements in their artillery,—I dined every day with Pitt, with Burke, with Lord North, Lord Cornwallis, and other distinguished personages, who always called me 'the amusing Spaniard.' I remember that once, when I was at the Palace, they entreated me to show them what a bull-fight was like and I had to throw my cloak over a chair and to prick it and kill it, which vastly diverted all the court, and especially King George III., who was very great friends with me, and was always saying that I must send to my country to fetch some good olive-trees. Oh! we were on the best terms possible. All his anxiety was that I should teach him a few words of Spanish, and above all some of our beautiful Andalusian—but he could never learn more than '*otro toro*' (another bull) and '*vengan esos cinco*' (that makes five), and he greeted me with these phrases every day when I went to breakfast with him off pescadillas and a few *cañitas* of Manzanilla."

Pescadillas are a small fish peculiar to the south Atlantic coast of Spain. *Cañitas* is the name given to certain small glasses used only for drinking Manzanilla.

"That was what he took for breakfast?"

"That was what he preferred. I had some pescadillas bottled and brought from Cadiz. They kept very well by a recipe I invented and have at home."

"Wonderful! And you succeeded in reforming the English artillery?" asked my master, encouraging him to go on for he was greatly amused.

"Perfectly. I invented a cannon which could never be fired, for all London, including the ministers and parliament, came to entreat me not to attempt it, because they feared that the explosion would throw down a number of houses."

"So that the great gun has been laid aside and forgotten?"

"The Emperor of Russia wanted to buy it, but it was impossible to move it from the spot where it stood."

"Then you surely can get us out of our present difficulties by inventing a cannon to destroy the whole English fleet at one discharge."

"Yes," replied Malespina. "I have been thinking of it, and I believe I may realize my idea. I will show you the calculations I have made, not only with regard to increasing the calibre of guns to a fabulous degree, but also for constructing armor plates to protect ships and bastions. It is the absorbing idea of my life."

By this time the meal was ended. Marcial and I disposed of the fragments in less than no time, and we set out again; the Malespinas on horseback by the side of the chaise and we, as before, in the tumble-down vehicle. The effects of the dinner, and of the copious draughts of liquor with which he had moistened it, had stimulated the old gentleman's inventive powers and he went on all the way, pouring out a flood of nonsense. The conversation returned to the subject with which it had begun, the war in Roussillon, and as Don José was preparing to relate fresh deeds of valor, my master, weary of so many falsehoods, tried to divert him to something else, by saying: "It was a disastrous and impolitic war. We should have done better never to have undertaken it."

"Oh! the Conde de Aranda, as you know," exclaimed Malespina, "condemned that unlucky war with the Republic from the first. How often have we discussed the question—for we have been friends from our childhood. When I was in Aragon we lived together for six months at Moncayo. Indeed, it was for him that I had a very curious gun constructed...."

"Yes, Aranda was always opposed to it," interrupted Don Alonso, intercepting him on the dangerous ground of gunnery.

"So he did," said Don José to whom rodomontade was irresistible, "and I may say that when that distinguished man so warmly advocated peace with the republicans, it was because I advised it, being convinced from the first that the war was a mistake. But Godoy, who was then supreme, persisted in it, simply and solely to contradict me, as I have learnt since. But the best of it is that Godoy himself was obliged to put an end to the war in 1795, when he understood what it really was, and at the same time he adopted the high-sounding title of Prince of Peace."

"How much we want a good statesman, my worthy friend," said my master. "A man on a level with the times, who would not throw us into useless wars but who could maintain the dignity of the crown."

"Well, when I was at Madrid last year," continued Don José, "proposals were made to me to accept the post of Secretary of State. The Queen was most anxious for it—the King said nothing. I went with him every day to the Prado to fire a few shots.—Even Godoy would have agreed, recognizing my superior qualifications; and indeed, if he had not I should have had no difficulty in finding some snug little fortress where I might lock him up so that he might give me no trouble. However, I declined, preferring to live in peace in my own country-town; I left the management of public affairs in Godoy's hands. There you have a man whose father was a mule-boy on my father-in-law's estate in Estremadura...."

"I did not know that...." said Don Alonso. "Although he is a man of obscure origin I always supposed the Prince of Peace to belong to a family of good birth, whose fortune was impaired but whose ancestry was respectable."

And so the dialogue went on; Señor Malespina uttering his falsehoods as if they were gospel, and my master listening with angelic calmness, sometimes annoyed by them, and sometimes amused at listening to such nonsense. If I remember rightly, Don José Maria took the credit of having advised Napoleon to the bold deeds of the 18th Brumaire.

Talking of these and of other matters we reached Chiclana as night overtook us, and my master, who was utterly tired and worn out by the villainous chaise, remained in the town, while the others went on, being anxious to reach Cadiz the same night. While we were at supper Malespina poured out a fresh farrago of lies, and I could see that his son heard them with pain, as if he were horrified at having for his father the most romancing liar in the world probably. We took leave of them and rested there till next day when we proceeded on our journey by day-break, and as the road from Chiclana to Cadiz was much easier than that we had already traversed, we reached the end of our journey by about eleven o'clock in the morning, without adventure, safe in body and in excellent spirits.

CHAPTER VIII.

I CANNOT describe the enthusiasm that fired my mind at the sight of Cadiz. As soon as I had a moment to myself—as soon, that is to say, as my master was fairly settled in his cousin's house—I went out into the streets and ran to and fro without any fixed destination, intoxicated as it were by the atmosphere of my beloved native city. After so long an absence all I saw attracted my attention as though it were something new and beautiful. In how many of the passers-by did I recognize a familiar face? everything charmed me and appealed to my feelings—men, women, old folks, children—the dogs, nay the houses even; for my youthful imagination discovered in each a personal and living individuality; I felt towards them as towards intelligent creatures; they seemed to me to express, like all else, their satisfaction at seeing me, and to wear, in their balconies and windows, the expression of gay and cheerful faces. In short my spirit saw its own gladness reflected in every surrounding object.

I hurried through the streets with eager curiosity, as if I wanted to see them all at once. In the Plaza San Juan I bought a handful of sweetmeats, less for the satisfaction of eating them than for that of introducing myself under a new aspect to the sellers, whom I addressed as an old friend; some of them with gratitude as having been kind to me in my former misery and others as victims, not yet indemnified, to my childish propensity for pillage. Most of them did not remember me; some, however, received me with abusive language, bringing up the deeds of my youth against me and making ironical remarks on my new fit-out and the dignity of my appearance, reducing me to flight as quickly as possible and damaging my appearance by pelting me with the rind or husks of fruit, flung by skilful hands at my new clothes. However, as I was fully convinced of my own importance, these insults increased my pride more than they hurt my feelings.

Then I went to the ramparts, and counted all the ships at anchor within sight. I spoke to several sailors that I met, telling them that I too was about to join the fleet, and asking them with eager emphasis whether they had seen Nelson's fleet; and then I assured them that *Monsieur Corneta* was no better than a coward and that the impending fight would be a grand affair. At last I reached the creek and there my delight knew no bounds. I went down to the shore and, taking off my shoes, I leaped from rock to rock; I sought out my old comrades of both sexes but I found only a few, some who were now men had taken to some better mode of living, others had been impressed into the ships, and those who were left hardly recognized me. The undulating motion of the water excited my very senses; I could not resist the temptation—urged by the mysterious spell of the sea whose eloquent murmurs have always sounded to me—I know not why—like a voice inviting me to happiness or calling me with imperious threats to rave and storm. I stripped myself as quick as thought and threw myself into the water as if I were flying to the arms of a lover. I swam about for more than an hour, happy beyond all words, and then, having dressed myself, I continued my walk to the purlieus of *la Viña* where, in the taverns, I came across some of the most famous rascals of my young days. In talking with them I gave myself out to be a man of position, and as such, I wasted the few *cuartos* I possessed in treating them. I asked after my uncle but no one could give me any news of that gentleman, and after we had chatted for awhile they made me drink a glass of brandy which instantly went to my head and lay me prone on the floor. During the crisis of my intoxication I thought the scoundrels were laughing at me to their hearts' content; but as soon as I recovered a little I sneaked out of the tavern much ashamed of myself. I still had some difficulty in walking; I had to go by my own old home and there, at the door, I saw a coarse-looking woman frying blood and tripe. Much touched by recognizing the home of my childhood I could not help bursting into tears and the heartless woman, seeing this, took it for granted it was some jest or trick to enable me to steal her unsavory mess. However, I was able to take to my heels and so escape her clutches, postponing the expression of my emotion till a more favorable opportunity.

After this I thought I should like to see the old Cathedral, with which the tenderest memory of my childhood was inseparably linked, and I went into it; the interior seemed to me most beautiful; never have I felt a deeper impulse of religious veneration in any church. It gave me a passionate desire to pray, and I did in fact throw myself on my knees, before the very altar where my mother had offered an *ex-voto* for my escape from death. The waxen image which I believed to be an exact likeness of myself was still in its place which it filled with all the solemnity of sanctity, but it struck me as very like a chestnut-husk. And yet this trumpery doll, the symbol of piety and maternal devotion, filled me with tender respect. I said my prayers on my knees, in memory of my good mother's sufferings and death, and trying to realize that she was now happy in Heaven; but as my head was not yet very clear of the fumes of that accursed brandy, I stumbled and fell as I rose from my knees and an indignant sacristan turned me out into the street. A few steps took me back to the Calle del Fideo, where we were staying, and my master scolded me for being so long absent. If Doña Francisca had been cognizant of my fault I should not have escaped a sound drubbing, but my master was merciful and never beat me, perhaps because his conscience told him he was as much a child as I was.

We were staying at Cadiz in the house of a cousin of my master; and the reader must allow me to describe this lady somewhat fully, for she was a character deserving to be studied. Doña Flora de Cisniega was an old woman who still pretended to be young. She was certainly past fifty, but she practised every art that might deceive the world into believing her not more than half that terrible age. As to describing how she contrived to ally science and art to attain her object—that would be an undertaking far beyond my slender powers. The enumeration of the curls and plaits, bows and ends, powders, rouges, washes and other extraneous matters which she employed in effecting this monumental work of restoration, would exhaust the most vivid fancy; such things may be left to the indefatigable pen of the novelist—this, being History, deals only with great subjects and cannot meddle with those elegant mysteries. As far as her appearance was concerned what I remember best was the composition of her face, which all the painters of the Academy seemed to have touched up with rose color; I remember too that when she spoke she moved her lips with a grimace, a mincing prudery which was intended either to diminish the width of a very wide mouth, or to conceal the gaps in her teeth from whose ranks one or two proved deserters every year; but this elaborate attempt was so far a failure that it made her uglier rather than better looking. She was always richly drest, with pounds of powder in her hair, and as she was plump and fair—to judge from what was visible through her open tucker, or under the transparency of gauze and muslin—her best chance lay in the display of such charms as are least exposed to the injurious inroads of time, an art in which she certainly was marvellously successful.

Doña Flora was devoted to everything antiquated, and much addicted to piety, but not with the genuine devoutness of Doña Francisca; indeed she was in everything diametrically the opposite of my mistress; for while Doña Francisca hated even the glory that was won at sea, she was an enthusiastic admirer of all fighting-men and of the navy in particular. Fired by patriotic passion—since at her mature age she could not hope to feel the flame of any other—and intensely proud of herself as a woman and as a Spaniard, love of her country was symbolized in her mind by the roar of cannon, and she thought the greatness of a nation was measured by tons of gunpowder. Having no children her time was spent in gossip, picked up and passed round in a small circle of neighbors by two or three chatterboxes like herself; but she also amused herself by her indefatigable mania for discussing public affairs. At that time there were no newspapers, and political theories, like public news, were passed on from mouth to mouth, these being even more falsified then than now, in proportion as talk is less trustworthy even than print.

In all the large towns, and particularly in Cadiz, which was one of the foremost cities of Spain, there were a number of idle persons who made it their business always to have the latest news from Madrid and Paris, and to be diligent in distributing it, priding themselves, in fact, on a mission which gained them so much consideration. Some of these newsmongers would meet in the evening at Doña Flora's house, and this, seconded by excellent chocolate and still better cakes, attracted others eager to learn what was going on. Doña Flora, knowing that she could not hope to inspire a tender feeling or be quit of the burthen of her fifty years, would not have exchanged the part she was thus enabled to play for any other that could have been offered to her; for, at that time, to be the centre to which all news was conveyed was almost as precious a distinction as the majesty of a throne. Doña Flora and Doña Francisca could never get on together, as may easily be supposed when we consider the enthusiastic military tastes of one, and the pacific timidity of the other. Thus, speaking to Don Alonso the day we arrived, the good lady said:

"If you had always listened to your wife you might have been a common sailor to this day. What a woman! If I were a man and married to such a wife I should burst up like a bomb-shell. You did very rightly not to follow her advice but to come to join the fleet. Why you are not an old man yet, Alonsito; you may still rise to the rank of commodore, which you would have been sure of if Paca had not clipped your wings, as we do to chickens to prevent their straying."

When, presently, my master's eager curiosity made him press her for the latest news, she went on:

"The most important news is that all the naval men here are extremely dissatisfied with the French Admiral, who displayed his incapacity in the expedition to Martinique and the fight off Finisterre. He is so timid and so mortally afraid of the English that, when the combined fleets ran in here last August, he dared not seize the cruisers commanded by Collingwood though they were but three ships in all. All our officers are greatly disgusted at finding themselves obliged to serve under such a man; indeed Gravina went to Madrid to tell Godoy so, foreseeing some terrible disaster if the command were not placed in more able hands; but the minister gave him some vague answer as to why he could not venture to decide in the matter, and as Buonaparte is in Germany, dealing with the Austrians, he cannot be appealed to.—But it is said that he too is dissatisfied with Villeneuve and has determined to dismiss him; but meanwhile.... If only Napoleon would put the whole fleet under the command of some Spaniard—you, for instance, Alonso—promoting you at once as I am sure you richly deserve...."

"Oh! I am not fit for it!" replied my master, with his habitual modesty.

"Well, to Gravina, or to Churruca, who is said to be a very first-rate sailor. If not I am afraid mischief will come of it. You cannot see the French from here; only think, when Villeneuve's ships arrived they were short of victuals and ammunition, and the authorities here did not care to supply them out of the arsenal. They forwarded a complaint to Madrid, and as Godoy's one idea is to do what the French ambassador M. de Bernouville asks him, he sent orders that our allies should have as much of everything as they required. But this had no effect. The commandant of the navy yard and the commissary of the ordnance stores declared they would deliver nothing to Villeneuve till he paid for it money down and in hard cash. This seems to me very right and fair. The last misfortune that could come upon us was that these fine gentlemen should take possession of the little we had left! Pretty times we live in! Everything is ruinously dear, and yellow fever on one side and hard times on the other had brought Andalusia to such a state that she was not worth a doit—and now, to that you add all the miseries of war. Of course the honor of the nation is the first thing and we must go on now to avenge the insults we have received. I do not want to go back to the fight of Finisterre where, through the meanness of our allies, we lost the *Firme* and the *Rafael*, two splendid ships—nor of the piratical seizure of the *Real Cárlos*, which was such an act of treachery that the Barbary pirates would have been disgraced by it—nor of the plunder of the four frigates—nor of the battle off Cape St. ..."

"That was the thing," interrupted my master eagerly. "Every man must keep his own place, but if Admiral Córdova had given the word to tack...."

"Yes, yes—I know," exclaimed Doña Flora, who had heard the story a hundred times before. "We must positively give them a thorough beating and we will. You, I know, are going to cover yourself with glory. It will enfuriate Paca."

"I am of no use for fighting," said my master sadly. "I am only going to look on, for sheer love of it and devotion to the Spanish flag."

The day after our arrival my master received a visit from a naval officer, an old friend of his, whose face I can never forget though I saw him but that once. He was a man of about five and forty, with a really beautiful and gentle face and an expression of such tender melancholy that to see him was to love him. He wore no wig, but his abundant hair, untortured by the barber into the fashionable *ailes de pigeon*, was carelessly tied into a thick pigtail and heavily powdered, though with less elaborate care than was usual at that time. His eyes were large and blue, his nose finely chiselled, perfect in outline, rather wide, but not so wide as to disfigure him—on the contrary, it seemed to give distinction to his expressive countenance. His chin, which was carefully shaved, was somewhat pointed, and added to the melancholy charm of an oval face which was indicative of delicate feeling rather than of energetic determination. This noble exterior was well matched by the elegance of his manners—a grave courtesy of which the fatuous airs of the men of the present day retain no trace, any more than the modish graces of our *jeunesse dorée*. His figure was small, slight and even sickly looking. He looked more like a scholar than a warrior, and a brow, behind which lofty and subtle thoughts must have lain hid, looked ill-fitted to defy the horrors of battle. His fragile form, inhabited by a soul so far above the common, looked as though it must succumb to the first shock. And yet—as I afterwards learnt—this man's heart was as brave as his intellect was supreme. It was Churruca.

Our hero's uniform, though it was not in holes nor threadbare, bore the marks of long and honorable service; afterwards, when I heard it authoritatively stated that the Government owed him nine quarters' pay, I could account for this dilapidated appearance. My master asked after his wife, and I gathered from the answer that he was only lately married, which filled me with pity; it seemed to me so terrible a thing to be dragged off to battle in the midst of so much happiness. Then they talked of his ship, the *San Juan Nepomuceno*, which he seemed to love as much as his young wife; for, as was well known, he had had it planned and fitted to his own taste, under a special privilege, and had made it one of the finest ships in the Spanish fleet. Then of course they discussed the absorbing subject of the day: whether the squadrons would or would not put out to sea and the Commodore expressed his opinion at much length, in very much such words as these; for their substance had always remained in my memory so that now, by the help of dates and historical records, I can reconstruct his speech with considerable accuracy.

"The French admiral," said Churruca, "not knowing what course to pursue and being anxious to do something which might cast his errors into oblivion, has, ever since we arrived, manifested an inclination to go and seek the English. On the 8th of October he wrote to Gravina, saying that he wished to hold a council of war on board the *Bucentaure* (Villeneuve's ship) to agree on the best course of action. Gravina went to the council, taking with him the Vice-Admiral Alava, Rear-Admirals Escaño and Cisneros, Commodore Galiano and myself. Of the French there were present Rear-Admirals Dumanoir and Magon and Captains Cosmas, Maistral, Villiegries, and Prigmy.

"Villeneuve having expressed his wish to go out to sea, we Spaniards unanimously opposed it. The discussion was warm and eager, and Alcalá Galiano and Magon exchanged such hard words that it must have come to a duel if we had not intervened to pacify them. Our opposition greatly annoyed Villeneuve, and in the heat of argument he even threw out certain insolent hints to which Gravina promptly retorted.—And indeed these worthies display a curious anxiety to go forth to seek a powerful foe, considering that they forsook us at the battle off Cape Finisterre, depriving us of what would have been a victory if they had seconded us in time. But there are many reasons, which I fully explained to the council—such as the advanced season, which render it far more advantageous for us to remain in the bay, forcing them to form a blockade which they cannot maintain, particularly if at the same time they blockade Toulon and Cartagena. We cannot but admit the superiority of the English navy, as to the completeness of their armament, their ample supply of ammunition, and, above all, the unanimity with which they manœuvre.

"We—manned for the most part with less experienced crews, inadequately armed and provided, and commanded by a leader who dissatisfies everyone—might nevertheless act to advantage on the defensive, inside the bay. But we shall be forced to obey, to succumb to the blind submission of the ministry at Madrid and put our vessels and men at the mercy of Buonaparte, who, in return for this servility has certainly not given us a chief worthy of so much sacrifice. We must go if Villeneuve orders it, but if the result is a disaster our opposition to his insane resolution stands on record as our acquittal. Villeneuve in fact is desperate; his sovereign has used harsh language to him, and the warning that he will be degraded from his command is prompting him to the maddest acts, in the hope of recovering his tarnished reputation, in a single day, by death or victory."

So spoke my master's friend. His words impressed me deeply; child as I still was, I took an eager interest in the events going on around me, and since—reading in history all the facts to which I was then witness, I have been able to aid my memory by authenticated dates so that I can tell my story with considerable accuracy.

When Churruca left us, Doña Flora and my master sang his praises in the warmest terms; praising him especially for the expedition he had conducted to Central America to make charts of those seas. According to them Churruca's merits as a navigator and a man of learning were such that Napoleon himself had made him a magnificent present and heaped civilities upon him. But we will leave the sailor and return to Doña Flora.

By the end of the second day of our stay in her house I became aware of a phenomenon which disgusted me beyond measure, which was that my master's cousin seemed quite to fall in love with me; that is to say, that she took it into her head that I was made to be her page. She never ceased to load me with every sort of kindness, and on hearing that I too was to join the fleet she bewailed herself greatly, swearing that it would be a pity if I should lose an arm or a leg, or even some less important part of my person—even if I escaped with my life. Such unpatriotic pity roused my indignation, and I believe I even went so far as to declare, in so many words, that I was on fire with warlike ardor. My gasconade delighted the old lady and she gave me a heap of sweetmeats to recover her place in my good graces.

The next day she made me clean her parrot's cage—a most shrewd bird that talked like a preacher and woke us at all hours of the morning by shrieking "*perro inglés!*"—(dog of an Englishman.) Then she took me to mass with her, desiring me to carry her stool, and in church she was incessantly looking round to see if I were there. Afterwards she kept me to look on while her hair was dressed—an operation that filled me with dismay as I saw the catafalque of curls and puffs that the hair-dresser piled on her head. Observing the stupid astonishment with which I watched the skilful manipulation of this artist—a perfect architect of head-pieces—Doña Flora laughed very heartily, and assured me that I should do better to remain with her as her page than to join the fleet, adding that I ought to learn to dress her hair, and by acquiring the higher branches of the art I might earn my living and make a figure in the world. Such a prospect, however, had nothing seductive to my fancy, and I told her, somewhat roughly, that I would rather be a soldier than a hair-dresser. This pleased her mightily and as I was giving up the comb for something more patriotic and military she was more affectionate than ever. But notwithstanding that I was treated here with so much indulgence, I must confess that the lady annoyed me beyond measure, and that I really preferred the angry cuffing and slapping of Doña Francisca to Doña Flora's mawkish attentions. This was very natural; for her ill-timed caresses, her prudery, the persistency with which she invited my presence, declaring that she was delighted with me and my conversation, prevented my going with my master on his visits to the different ships. A servant of the house accompanied him on these delightful expeditions, while I, deprived of the liberty to run about Cadiz as I longed to be doing, was left at home, sick of life, in the society of Doña Flora's parrot and of the gentlemen who came every evening to announce whether or no the fleets would quit the bay, with other matters less to the purpose and far more trivial.

My vexation rose to desperation when I saw Marcial come to the house, and he and my master went out together, though not to embark finally; and when, after seeing them start, my forlorn spirit lost the last faint hope of being one of the party, Doña Flora took it into her head that she must have me to walk with her to the Alameda and then to church to attend vespers. This was more than I could bear and I began to dream of the possibility of putting a bold scheme into execution; of going, namely, on my own account to see one of the ships, hoping that, on the quay, I might meet some sailor of my acquaintance who would be persuaded to take me.

I went out with the old lady and as we went along the ramparts I tried to linger to look at the ships, but I could not abandon myself to the enjoyment of the spectacle for I had to answer the hundred questions with which Doña Flora persistently persecuted me. In the course of our walk we were joined by some young men and a few older ones. They all seemed very conceited, and were the most fashionable men of Cadiz, all extremely witty and elegantly dressed. Some of them were poets, or—to be accurate—wrote verses though sorry ones, and I fancied I heard them talking of some Academy where they met to fire shots at each other in rhyme, an amusement which could break no bones.

As I observed all that was going on round me, their extraordinary appearance fixed my attention—their effeminate gestures and, above all, their clothes, which to me looked preposterous. There were not many persons who dressed in this style in Cadiz; and, reflecting afterwards on the difference between their costume and the ordinary clothes of the people I was in the habit of seeing, I understood that it was that men in general wore the Spanish habit while Doña Flora's friends followed the fashions of Madrid or of Paris. The first thing to attract my attention were their walking-sticks, which were twisted and knotted cudgels, with enormous knobs. Their chins were invisible, being hidden by the cravat, a kind of shawl wrapped round and round the throat and brought across below the lips so as to form a protuberance—a basket, a dish, or, better still, a barber's basin—in which the chin was quite lost. Their hair was dressed with elaborate disorder, looking as if it had been done with a birch-broom rather than with a comb. The corners of their hats came down to their shoulders; their coats, extremely short-waisted, almost swept the ground with their skirts; their boots were pointed at the toes; dozens of seals and trinkets hung from their waistcoat pockets; their breeches, which were striped, were fastened at the knee with a wide ribbon, and to put the finishing stroke to these figures of fun, each carried an eye-glass which, in the course of conversation, was constantly applied to the right eye, half-closing the left, though they would have seen perfectly well by using both.

The conversation of these gentlemen, also, turned on the plans of the fleet, but they varied it by discussing some ball or entertainment which they talked of a great deal, and one of them was the object of the greatest admiration for the perfection with which he cut capers, and the lightness of his heels in dancing the gavotte.

After chattering for some time the whole party followed Doña Flora into the church *del Cármen*, and there, each one pulling out a rosary, they remained praying with much energy for some little time, and one of them, I remember, gave me a smart rap on the top of my head because, instead of attending devoutly to my prayers like them, I was paying too much attention to two flies that were buzzing round the topmost curl of Doña Flora's structure of hair. After listening to a tiresome sermon, which they praised as a magnificent oration, we went out again, and resumed our promenade; the chat was soon more lively than ever; for we were joined by some other ladies dressed in the same style and among them all there was such a noisy hubbub of compliments, fine speeches, and witticisms, with here and there an insipid epigram, that I could gather nothing from it all.

And all this time Marcial and my dear master were arranging the day and hour when they should embark! While I was perhaps doomed to remain on shore to gratify the whims of this old woman whom I positively loathed, with her odious petting! Would you believe that that very evening she insisted on it that I must remain forever in her service? Would you believe that she declared that she was very fond of me, and in proof of the fact kissed me and fondled me, desiring me to be sure to tell no one? Horrible spite of fate! I could not help thinking what my feelings would have been if my young mistress had treated me in such a fashion. I was confused to the last degree; however, I told her that I wished to join the fleet, and that when I came back she might keep me if it was her fancy, but that if she did not allow me to have my wish I should hate her as much as that—and I spread my arms out wide to express the immensity of my aversion.

Then, as my master came in unexpectedly, I thought it a favorable opportunity for gaining my purpose by a sudden stroke of oratory which I had hastily prepared; I fell on my knees at his feet, declaring in pathetic accents, that if he did not take me on board with him I should fling myself into the sea in despair.

My master laughed at this performance and his cousin, pursing her lips, affected amusement with a grimace which made her sallow wrinkled face uglier than ever; but, finally, she consented. She gave me a heap of sweetmeats to eat on board, charged me to keep out of the way of danger, and did not say another word against my embarking, as we did very early next morning.

CHAPTER IX.

IT was the 18th of October. I can have no doubt as to the date because the fleet sailed out of the bay next day. We rose very early and went down to the quay, where a boat was waiting to carry us on board.

Imagine if you can my surprise—nay surprise do I say?—my enthusiasm, my rapture, when I found myself on board the *Santísima Trinidad*, the largest vessel on the main, that floating fortress of timber which, seen from a distance, had appeared to my fancy some portentous and supernatural creature; such a monster as alone was worthy of the majesty of the seas. Each time our boat passed under the side of a ship I examined it with a sort of religious astonishment, wondering to see the hulls so huge that from the ramparts had looked so small; and in the wild enthusiasm that possessed me I ran the greatest danger of falling into the water as I gazed in ecstasy at a figure-head—an object which fascinated me more than anything else.

At last we reached the *Santísima Trinidad*. As we approached, the colossal mass loomed larger and larger, and when the launch pulled up alongside, lost in the black transparent void made where its vast shadow fell upon the water—when I saw the huge hulk lying motionless on the dark waves which gently plashed against the side—when I looked up and saw the three tiers of cannon with their threatening muzzles thrust through the port-holes—my excitement was changed to fear; I turned pale and sat silent and motionless by my master's side.

But when we went up the side and stood on deck my spirits rose. The intricate and lofty rigging, the busy scene on the quarter-deck, the open view of the sky and bay, the perfect order of everything on deck, from the hammocks lashed in a row to the bulwarks, to the capstans, shells, windsails and hatchways; the variety of uniforms—everything I saw, in short, amazed me to such a degree that for some time I stood blankly gazing at the stupendous structure heedless of all else. You can form no idea of any of those magnificent vessels, much less of the *Santísima Trinidad*, from the wretched prints I have seen of them. Still less, again, from the ships of war of the present day, covered with ponderous plates of iron, heavy looking, uninteresting and black, with no visible details on their vast sides, looking to me for all the world like enormous floating coffins. Invented by a materialistic age and calculated to suit the naval science of a time when steam has superseded manual labor, and the issue of a sea-fight is decided by the force and impetus of the vessels, our ships are now mere fighting-machines, while those of that day were literally Men-of-War, wielding all the implements of attack and defence but trusting mainly to skill and valor.

I, who not only see, but observe, have always been in the habit of associating—perhaps to an extravagant extent—ideas and images, things and persons, which in appearance seem most dissimilar or antagonistic. When, at a later period, I saw the cathedrals—Gothic, as they call them—of Castile and of Flanders, and noted the impressive majesty with which those perfect and elaborate structures stand up among the buildings of more modern style, built only for utility—such as banks, hospitals, and barracks—I could never help remembering all the various kinds of vessels that I have seen in the course of a long life, and comparing the old ones to those Gothic cathedrals. Their curves, so gracefully prolonged, the predominance of vertical over horizontal lines, a certain indefinable poetry about them—not historical only but religious too—underlying the complication of details and the play of colors brought out by the caprices of the sunshine, are, no doubt, what led to this far-fetched association of ideas—the result in my mind of the romantic impressions of my childhood.

The *Santísima Trinidad* had four decks; the largest ships in the World had but three. This giant, constructed at Havana, in 1769, of the finest woods of Cuba, could reckon thirty-six years of honorable service. She measured 220 feet from stem to stern, 58 feet in the waist, that is to say in width, and 28 feet deep from the keel to the deck, measurements which no other vessel at the time could approach. Her huge ribs, which were a perfect forest, supported four decks. When she was first built 116 port-holes gaped in her sides which were thick walls of timber; after she was enlarged in 1796 she had 130, and when she was newly fitted in 1805 she was made to carry 140 guns, cannons and carronades. The interior was a marvel of arrangement; there were decks for the guns, the forecastle for the crew, holds for stores of all kinds, state-cabins for the officers, the galley, the cock-pit and other offices. I was quite bewildered as I ran through the passages and endless nooks of this floating fortress. The stern cabins on the main deck were a little palace within, and outside like some fantastic castle; the galleries, the flag-turrets at the corners of the poop—exactly like the oriels of a Gothic tower—looked like huge cages open to the sea, whence the eye could command three quarters of the horizon.

Nothing could be grander than the rigging—those gigantic masts thrust up to heaven like a menace to the storm. It was difficult to believe that the wind could have strength enough to fill those vast sails. The eye lost its way and became weary in gazing at the maze of the rigging with the shrouds, stays, braces, halyards, and other ropes used to haul and reef the various sails.

I was standing lost in the contemplation of all these wonders when I felt a heavy hand on the nape of my neck; I thought the main-mast had fallen on the top of me. I turned round in alarm and gave a cry of horror at seeing a man who was now holding me by the ears as if he were going to lift me up by them. It was my uncle.

"What are you doing here, Vermin!" he asked, in the amiable tone that was habitual with him. "Do you want to learn the service? Hark ye Juan," he added, turning to a sailor of most sinister aspect, "send this landlubber up to the main-yard to take a walk there."

I excused myself as best I might from the pleasure of taking a walk on the main-yard, explaining that I was body-servant to Don Alonso Gutierrez de Cisniega and had come on board with him. Three or four sailors, my affectionate uncle's particular friends, wanted to torment me so I decided on quitting their distinguished society and went off to the cabin in search of my master. An officer's toilet is no less elaborate on board than on shore, and when I saw the valets busied in powdering the heads of the heroes they waited on, I could not help asking myself whether this was not, of all occupations, the least appropriate in a man-of-war, when every minute was precious and where everything that was not directly serviceable to the working of the ship was a hindrance. However, fashion was as tyrannical then as now, and even at such a moment as this enforced her absurd and inconvenient rules with inexorable rigor. The private soldiers even had to waste their valuable time in tying their pigtails, poor men! I saw them standing in a line, one behind another, each one at work on the pigtail of the man in front of him; by which ingenious device the operation was got through in a short space of time. Then they stuck on their fur hats, a ponderous head-piece the use of which no one was ever able to explain to me, and went to their posts if they were on duty or to pace the deck if they were not. The sailors did not wear this ridiculous queue of hair and I do not see that their very sensible costume has been altered to any great extent since that time.

In the cabin I found my master eagerly conversing with the captain in command of the ship, Don Francisco Xavier de Uriarte, and the commander of the squadron, Don Baltasar Hidalgo de Cisneros. From what I overheard I could have no doubt that the French admiral had ordered the fleets to put out to sea the next morning.

Marcial was highly delighted at this, and he and a knot of veteran sailors who held council on their own account in the forecastle, discoursed grandiloquently on the imminent fight. Their society suited me far better than that of my amiable uncle, for Marcial's companions indulged in no horse-play at my expense; and this difference was of itself enough to mark the difference of training in the two classes of sailors; for the old sea-dogs were of the pure breed originally levied as voluntary recruits; while the others were pressed men, almost without exception lazy, refractory, of low habits, and ignorant of the service.

I made much better friends with the former than with these and was always present at Marcial's conferences. If I did not fear to weary the reader, I might report the explanation he gave us that day of the diplomatical and political causes of the war—a most comical parody of all he had heard said, a few nights previously, by Malespina at my master's house. I learnt from him that my young mistress' lover was on board the*Nepomuceno*.

All these colloquies came round at last to the same point, the impending battle. The fleet was to sail out of the bay next morning—what joy! To ride the seas in this immense vessel—the largest in the world; to witness a fight at sea; to see what a battle was like, how cannon were fired, how the enemy's ships were taken—what a splendid triumph! and then to return to Cadiz covered with glory.—To say afterwards to all who cared to hear: "Yes, I was there, I was on board, I saw it all...." To tell Rosita too, describing the glorious scene, winning her attention, her curiosity, her interest.—To say to her: "Oh yes! I was in the most dangerous places and I was not afraid;"—and to see her turn pale with alarm, or faint, as she heard my tale of the horrors of the battle—and then to look down in contempt on all who would ask me: "Tell us, Gabrielito, was it so terrible after all?"—All this was more than enough to fire my imagination, and I may frankly say that I would not, that day, have changed places with Nelson himself.

The morning of the 19th dawned, the day I hailed so eagerly; indeed it had not yet dawned when I found myself at the stern of the vessel with my master, who wanted to look on at the working of the ship. After clearing the decks the business of starting the ship began. The huge topsails were hoisted, and the heavy windlass, turning with a shrill clatter, dragged the anchor up from the bottom of the bay. The sailors clambered along the yards, while others handled the braces, obedient to the boatswain's call; and all the ship's voices, hitherto mute, filled the air with threatening outcries. The whistles, the bell, the discordant medley of men's voices, mixed with the creaking of the blocks, the humming of the ropes, the flapping of the sails as they thrashed the mast before they caught the wind—all these various sounds filled the air as the huge ship got under way. The bright ripples seemed to caress her sides, and the majestic monster made her way out of the bay without the slightest roll or even lurch, with a slow and solemn advance which was only perceptible to those on board by watching the apparent motion of the merchantmen lying at anchor and the landscape beyond.

At this moment I stood looking back at the scene behind us. And what a scene it was! Thirty-two men-of-war, five frigates, and two brigantines, Spanish and French together—some in front, some behind, and some abreast of us—were bursting into sail, as it were, and riding before the light breeze. I never saw a lovelier morning. The sun flooded those lovely shores with light; a faint purple tinge colored the sea to the east, and the chain of hills which bound the horizon on the side of the town seemed to be on fire in the sunrise; the sky was perfectly clear excepting where, in the east, a few rose and golden clouds floated above the horizon. The blue sea was calm, and over that sea and beneath that sky the forty ships with their white sails rode forward, one of the noblest fleets that human eyes ever rested on.

The vessels did not all sail with equal speed. Some got ahead, others were slow to get under way; some gained upon us, while we passed others. The solemnity of their advance, the height of their masts, covered with canvas, and a vague and obscure harmony which my childish ears fancied they could detect proceeding from those glorious hulls—a kind of hymn, which was no doubt the effect of my own imagination—the loveliness of the day, the crispness of the air, the beauty of the sea, which seemed to be dancing with joy outside the gulf at the approach of the vessels—all formed the grandest picture that the mind of man can conceive of.

Cadiz, itself, like a moving panorama, unfolded itself before our eyes, displaying in turn every aspect of its vast amphitheatre. The low sun, illuminating the glass in its myriad windows, sprinkled it with living sparks of gold, and its buildings lay so purely white above the blue water that it looked as if it might have been that moment called into being, or raised from the sea like the fanciful city of San Genaro. I could see the wall extending from the mole as far as the fort of Santa Catalina; I could distinguish the bastions of Bonete and Orejon, and recognize the *Caleta*;

and my pride rose as I reflected what I had risen from and where I now was. At the same time the sound of the bells of the waking city came to my ear like some mysterious music, calling the inhabitants to early mass, with all the confused clamor of the bells of a large town. Now they seemed to me to ring gladly, and send good wishes after us—I listened to them as if they were human voices bidding us God-speed; then again they tolled sadly and dolefully—a knell of misfortune; and as we sailed further and further away their music grew fainter till it was lost in space.

The fleet slowly made its way out of the bay—some of the ships taking several hours in getting fairly to sea. Marcial meanwhile made his comments on each, watching their behavior, laughing them to scorn if they were clumsy, and encouraging them with paternal advice if they were swift and well-handled.

"What a lump that Don Federico is!" he exclaimed as he looked at the *Príncipe de Astúrias* commanded by Gravina. "There goes *Mr. Corneta*!" he exclaimed as he saw the *Bucentaure* with Villeneuve on board. "He was a clever man that called you the *Rayo*!" (Thunderbolt) he cried ironically, as he watched the ship so named, which was the least manageable of all the fleet. "Well done *Papá Ignacio*!" he added, pointing to the*Santa Ana* commanded by Alava.

"Hoist your topsail properly, senseless oaf!" he went on, addressing Dumanoir's ship, *Le Formidable*. "That Frenchman keeps a hair-dresser to crimp the topsail and to clew up the sails with curling tongs!"

Towards evening the sky clouded over, and as night fell we could see Cadiz, already at a great distance, gradually vanish in the mist till the last faint outline became one with the darkness. The fleet then steered to the Southward.

All night I kept close to Marcial, as soon as I had seen my master comfortably settled in his cabin. The old sailor, eagerly listened to by a couple of veteran comrades and admirers, was explaining Villeneuve's plan of battle.

"*Mr. Corneta*," said he, "has divided the fleet into four lines. The vanguard led by Alava consists of six vessels; the centre, likewise of six, is commanded by *Mr. Corneta* in person; the rear, again of six, is under Dumanoir, and the reserve of twelve ships is led by Don Federico. This seems to me not badly planned. I imagine that the French and Spanish ships are mixed, in order that they may not leave us impaled on the bull's horns as they did at Finisterre.

"From what Don Alfonso tells me the Frenchman says that if the enemy comes up to leeward we are to form in line of battle and attack at once.... This is very pretty talk in the state-room; but do you think the *Señorito* will be such a booby as to come up to leeward of us? Oh yes—his lordship has not much brains in his figure-head and is sure to let himself be caught in that trap! Well! we shall see—if we see, what the Frenchman expects!—If the enemy gets to windward and attacks us we are to receive him in line of battle, and as he must divide to attack if he does not succeed in breaking our line, it will be quite easy to beat him. Everything is easy to *Mr. Corneta* (applause). He says too that he shall give no signals, but expects every captain to do his best. If we should see what I have always prophesied, ever since that accursed subsidy treaty, and that is—but I had better hold my tongue.—Please God...! Well I have always told you that Mr. Corneta does not understand the weapons he has in his hands; there is not room in his head for fifty ships. What can you think of an admiral, who, the day before a battle, sends for his captains and tells each of them to do what he thinks will win the day.—After that! (Strong expressions of sympathy). However, we shall see what we shall see.—But do you just tell me: If we Spanish want to scuttle a few of those English ships, are we not strong enough and many enough to do it? Then why in the world need we ally ourselves with the French, who would not allow us to do anything we had a mind to, but would have us dancing attendance at the end of their tow-line? Whenever we have had to work with them they have got us into mischief and we have had the worst of it. Well—may God and the Holy Virgin *del Cármen* be on our side, and rid us of our French friends for ever and ever, Amen." (Great Applause.)

All his audience agreed heartily; the discussion was continued till a late hour, rising from the details of naval warfare to the science of diplomacy. The night was fine and we ran before a fresh breeze—I must be allowed to say "*We*" in speaking of the fleet. I was so proud of finding myself on board the *Santísima Trinidad* that I began to fancy that I was called to play some important part on this great occasion, and I could not forbear from swaggering about among the sailors to let them see that I was not there for nothing.

CHAPTER X.

ON the morning of the 20th there was a stiff breeze blowing and the vessels kept at some distance from each other; but as the wind had moderated soon after noon the admiral signalled that the ships were to form in five lines—the van, centre, and rear, and two lines of reserve. I was enchanted with watching the docile monsters, obediently taking their places; for, although the conditions of naval manœuvres did not admit of great rapidity nor of perfect uniformity in the line, it was impossible to see them without admiration. The wind was from the southwest, according to Marcial, and the fleet, catching the breeze on the starboard quarter, ran towards the straits. During the night a few lights were seen and by dawn on the 21st we saw twenty-seven ships to windward, among which Marcial pointed out three as three-deckers. By eight o'clock the thirty-three vessels of the enemy's fleet were in sight, forming two columns. Our fleet displayed a wide front, and to all appearance Nelson's two columns, advancing in a wedge, were coming down upon us so as to cut our lines through the centre and rear.

This was the position of the hostile fleets when the *Bucentaure* signalled that we were to put about; maybe you do not understand this. It means that we were to turn completely round and that whereas the wind was on our port side it would now be on the starboard, so that we should sail in the opposite direction. The ships' heads were now turned northwards and this manœuvre, which was intended to place us to windward of Cadiz so that we might reach it in case of disaster, was severely criticised on board the *Trinidad*, especially by Marcial, who said:

"The line of battle is all broken up; it was bad before and is worse now."

In point of fact what had been the vanguard was now in the rear and the reserve ships, which as I heard said, were the best, were hindmost of all. The wind had fallen and the ships, being of various tonnage and inefficiently manned, the new line could not form with due precision; some of the vessels moved quickly and rushed forward; others went slowly, hanging back or losing their course, and forming a wide gap that broke the line before the enemy took the trouble of doing it.

"Reform the line" was now the signal; but, though a good ship answers her helm with wonderful docility, it is not so easy to manage as a horse. As he stood watching the movements of the ships nearest to us, Marcial observed: "The line is wider than the milky-way. If the *Señorito* cuts through it, Heaven help us! we shall not be able to sail in any sort of order; they will shave our heads for us if they fire upon us. They are going to give us a dose through the centre and how can the *San Juan* and the *Bahama* come up to support us from the rear—or the *Neptuno* and the *Rayo* which are in front. (Murmurs of applause.) Besides, here we are to leeward and the 'great-coats' can pick and choose where they will attack us, while all we can do is to defend ourselves as best we may. All I have to say is: God get us well out of the scrape and deliver us from the French for ever and ever, Amen."

The sun had now nearly reached the meridian and the enemy was coming down upon us.

"And is this a proper hour to begin a battle?" asked the old sailor indignantly. "Twelve o'clock in the day!"

But he did not dare to express his views publicly and these discussions were confined to a small circle into which I, with my eternal and insatiable curiosity, had squeezed myself. I do not know why, but it seemed to me that there was an expression of dissatisfaction on every face. The officers on the quarter-deck, and the sailors and non-commissioned officers at the bows, stood watching the ships to leeward, quite out of the line of battle, four of which ought to have been in the centre.

I forgot to mention one preliminary in which I myself had borne a hand. Early in the morning the decks were cleared for action, and when all was ready for serving the guns and working the ship, I heard some one say: "The sand—bring the sand." Marcial pulled me by the ear, and taking me to one of the hatchways set me in a line with some of the pressed men, ship's boys, and other supernumeraries. A number of sailors were posted on the ladders from the hatchway to the hold and between decks, and in this way were hauling up sacks of sand. Each man handed one to the man next to him and so it was passed on without much labor. A great quantity of sacks were thus brought up from hand to hand, and to my great astonishment they were emptied out on the upper deck, the poop, and the forecastle, the sand being spread about so as to cover all the planking; and the same thing was done between decks. My curiosity prompted me to ask the boy who stood next to me what this was for.

"For the blood," he said very coolly.

"For the blood!" I exclaimed unable to repress a shudder. I looked at the sand—I looked at the men who were busily employed at this task—and for a moment I felt I was a coward. However, my imagination reverted to the ideas which had previously filled it, and relieved my mind of its alarms; I thought no more of anything but victory and a happy issue.

Everything was ready for serving the guns and the ammunition was passed up from the store-rooms to the decks by a chain of men, like that which had brought up the sand-bags.

The English advanced to attack us in two sections. One came straight down upon us, and at its head, which was the point of the wedge, sailed a large ship carrying the admiral's flag. This, as I afterwards learned, was the*Victory*, commanded by Nelson. At the head of the other line was the *Royal Sovereign*, commanded by Collingwood. All these names, and the strategical plan of the battle, were not known to me till later.

My recollections, which are vividly distinct as to all the graphic and picturesque details, fail me with regard to the scheme of action which was beyond my comprehension at the time. All that I picked from Marcial, combined with what I subsequently learnt, sufficed to give me a good idea of the arrangement of our fleets; and for the better intelligence of the reader I give in the next page a list of our ships, indicating the gaps left by those that had not come up, and the nationality of each.

It was now a quarter to twelve. The fatal moment was approaching. The anxiety was general, and I do not speak merely from what was going on in my own mind, for I was absorbed in watching the ship which was said to contain Nelson, and for some time was hardly aware of what was going on round me.

Suddenly a terrible order was given by our captain—the boatswains repeated it; the sailors flew to the tops; the blocks and ropes creaked, the topsails flapped in the wind.

"Take in sail!" cried Marcial, with a good round oath. "The infernal idiot is making us work back."

And then I understood that the *Trinidad* was to slacken her speed so as to run alongside of the *Bucentaure*, because the *Victory* seemed to be taking measures to run in between those two ships and so cut the line in the middle.

Ships	
Neptuno, Sp.	Front.
Le Scipion, Fr.	
Rayo, Sp.	
Le Formidable, Fr.	
—— Le Duguay Trouin, Fr.	
Le Mont Blanc, Fr.	

Asís, Sp.

San Augustin, Sp.
Le Héros, Fr.
Trinidad, Sp.
Le Bucentaure, Fr.
—— Neptune, Fr.

Le Redoutable, Fr.
L'Intrépide, Fr.
—— Leandro, Sp.

Victory
Nelson.
——————
—>

Centre.

—— Justo, Sp.

—— L'Indomptable, Fr.
Santa Ana, Sp.

Le Fougueux, Fr.
Monarca, Sp.
Le Pluton, Fr.

Royal Sovereign
Collingwood.
——————
—>

Rear.

Bahama, Sp.
—— L'Aigle, Fr.
Montañes, Sp.
Algeciras, Sp.
Argonauta, Sp.
Swiftsure, Fr.
—— L'Argonaute, Fr.
Ildefonso, Sp.
—— L'Achille, Fr.
Príncipe de Astúrias, Sp.
Le Berwick, Fr.
Nepomuceno, Sp.

Reserve.

In watching the working of our vessel I could see that a great many of the crew had not that nimble ease which is usually characteristic of sailors who, like Marcial, are familiar with war and tempests. Among the soldiers several were suffering from sea-sickness and were clinging to the ropes to save themselves from falling. There were among them many brave souls, especially among the volunteers, but for the most part they were impressed men, obeying orders with an ill-will and not feeling, I am very sure, the smallest impulse of patriotism. As I afterwards learnt, nothing but the battle itself made them worthy to fight. In spite of the wide differences in the moral stamp of all these men, I believe that during the solemn moments that immediately preceded the first shot a thought of God came to every mortal there.

So far as I am concerned, in all my life my soul has never gone through any experiences, to compare with those of that hour. In spite of my youth, I was quite capable of understanding the gravity of the occasion, and for the first time in my life, my mind was filled with grand ideas, lofty aspirations and heroic thoughts. A conviction that we must conquer was so firmly rooted in my mind that I felt quite pitiful towards the English, and wondered to see them so eagerly advancing to certain destruction. For the first time too I fully understood the ideal of patriotism, and my heart responded to the thought with a glow of feeling such as I had never experienced before. Until now my mother-country had been embodied in my mind in the persons of its rulers—such as the King and his famous minister, for whom I felt different degrees of respect. As I knew no more of history than I had picked up in the streets, it was to me a matter of course that everybody's enthusiasm must be fired by knowing that the Spaniards had, once upon a time, killed a great number of Moors, and, since then, swarms of French and of English. I considered my countrymen as models of valor; but valor, as I conceived of it, was as like barbarity as one egg is like another; and with such ideas as these, patriotism had been to me nothing more than boastful pride in belonging to a race of exterminators of Moors.

But in the pause that preceded the battle I understood the full significance of that divine word; the conception of nationality, of devotion to a mother-country, was suddenly born in my soul, lighting it up, as it were, and revealing a thousand wonderful possibilities—as the rising sun dissipates the darkness that has hidden a beautiful landscape. I thought of my native land as a vast place full of people all united in brotherly regard—of society as divided into families, married couples to be held together, and children to be educated—of honor, to be cherished and defended; I imagined an unspoken agreement among all these human beings to help and protect each other against any attack from without, and I understood that these vessels had been constructed by them all for the defence of their native land; that is to say, for the soil on which they lived, the fields watered by their sweat, the homes where their ancestors had dwelt, the gardens where their children played, the colonies discovered and conquered by their forefathers, the harbors where their ships found shelter after long voyages—the magazines where they stored their wealth—the Church which was the mausoleum of those they had loved, the dwelling-place of their saints, and the ark of their belief—the public places where they might take their pleasure, the private homes where the venerable household gods, handed down from generation to generation, seemed to symbolize the perpetuity of the nation—their family hearth round which the smoke-dyed walls seem still to re-echo with the time-honored legends with which the grand dame soothes the flightiness or the naughtiness of the little ones, the street where friendly faces meet and smile—the field, the sea, the sky—everything which from the moment of birth makes up the sum of existence, from the crib of a pet animal to the time-honored throne of the king; every object into which the soul seems to go forth to live, as if the body that clothes it were too narrow a shell.

I believed too that the disputes between Spain and France or England were always about something that those countries ought to give up to us, and in which Spain could not, on the whole, be wrong. Her self-defence seemed to me as legitimate as the aggression was brutal; and as I had always heard that justice must triumph, I never doubted of victory. Looking up at our red and yellow flag—the colors nearest to that of fire—I felt my bosom swell, and could not restrain a few tears of enthusiasm and excitement; I thought of Cadiz, of Vejer, of the whole Spanish nation assembled, as it were, on a vast platform and looking on with eager anxiety; and all this tide of emotion lifted up my heart to God to whom I put up a prayer, which was neither a *Paternoster* nor an *Ave*, but a gush of inspiration that came to me at the moment.

A sudden shock startled me from my ecstasy, terrifying me with its violent vibration. The first broadside had been fired.

CHAPTER XI.

A VESSEL in the rear had been the first to fire on the *Royal Sovereign*, commanded by Collingwood, and while that ship carried on the fight with the *Santa Ana* the Victory came down on us. On board the *Trinidad* every one was anxious to open fire; but our captain would not give the word till he saw a favorable opportunity. Meanwhile, as if the ships were in such close communication that a slow-match was lighted from one to the other, the fire ran along from the *Santa Ana* in the middle, to each end of the line.

The *Victory* fired first on the *Redoutable*, and being repulsed, came up to the windward of the *Trinidad*. The moment had come for us; a hundred voices cried "fire!"—loudly echoing the word of command, and fifty round-shot were hurled against the flank of the English man-of-war. For a minute I could see nothing of the enemy for the smoke, while he, as if blind with rage, came straight down upon us before the wind. Just within gun-shot he put the ship about and gave us a broadside. In the interval between our firing and theirs, our crew, who had taken note of the damage done to the enemy, had gained in enthusiasm. The guns were rapidly served, though not without some hitches owing to want of experience in some of the gunners. Marcial would have been only too glad to undertake the management of one of the cannon, but his mutilated body was not equal to the heroism of his spirit. He was forced to be satisfied with superintending the delivery of the charges and encouraging the gunners by word and gesture.

The *Bucentaure*, just at our stern, was, like us, firing on the *Victory* and the *Téméraire*, another powerful English vessel. It seemed as though the *Victory* must fall into our hands, for the *Trinidad's* fire had cut her tackle to pieces, and we saw with pride that her mizzen-mast had gone by the board.

In the excitement of this first onslaught I scarcely perceived that some of our men were wounded or killed. I had chosen a place where I thought I should be least in the way, and never took my eyes off the captain who stood on the quarter-deck, issuing his orders with heroic coolness; and I wondered to see my master, no less calm though less enthusiastic, encouraging the officers and men in his quavering voice.

"Ah!" said I to myself, "if only Doña Francisca could see him now!"

I am bound to confess that at times I felt desperately frightened, and would gladly have hidden myself at the very bottom of the hold, while, at others, I was filled with an almost delirious courage, when I longed to see the glorious spectacle from the most dangerous posts. However, I will set aside my own insignificant individuality and relate the most terrible crisis of our fight with the *Victory*. The *Trinidad* was doing her immense mischief when the *Téméraire*, by a wonderfully clever manœuvre, slipped in between the two vessels thus sheltering her consort from our fire. She then proceeded to cut through the line behind the *Trinidad*, and as the *Bucentaure*, under fire, had got so close alongside of the *Trinidad* that their yards touched, there was a wide space beyond into which the *Téméraire* rushed down and, going about immediately, came up on our lee and delivered a broadside on that quarter, till then untouched. At the same time the *Neptune*, another large English ship, ran in where the *Victory* had previously been, while the *Victory* veered round so that, in a few minutes, the *Trinidad*was surrounded by the enemy and riddled on all sides.

From my master's face, from Uriarte's heroic fury, and from a volley of oaths delivered by Marcial and his friends, I understood that we were lost and the idea of defeat was anguish to my soul. The line of the combined fleets was broken at several points, and the bad order in which they had formed after turning round, gave place to the most disastrous confusion. We were surrounded by the enemy whose artillery kept up a perfect hail of round and grape-shot on our ship, and on the *Bucentaure* as well. The *Agustin*, the *Héros*, and the *Leandro*were engaged at some distance from us where they had rather more sea-room, while the *Trinidad*, and the Admiral's ship, utterly hemmed in and driven to extremities by the genius of the great Nelson, were fighting heroically—no longer in hopes of a victory which was impossible but anxious, at any rate, to perish gloriously.

The white hairs which now cover my old head almost stand on end as I remember those terrible hours, from two to four in the afternoon. I think of those five ships, not as mere machines of war obeying the will of man, but as living giants, huge creatures fighting on their own account, carried into action by their sails as though they were active limbs and using the fearful artillery they bore in their sides for their personal defence. As I looked at them then, my fancy could not help personifying them and to this hour I feel as though I could see them coming up, defying each other, going about to fire a broadside, rushing furiously up to board, drawing back to gather more force, mocking or threatening the enemy;—I can fancy them expressing their suffering when wounded or loftily breathing their last, like a gladiator who in his agony forgets not the dignity which beseems him;—I can imagine that I hear the voices of the crews like the murmur of an oppressed sufferer, sometimes eager with enthusiasm, sometimes a dull roar of desperation the precursor of destruction, sometimes a hymn of triumph in anticipation of victory, or a hideous storm of voices lost in space and giving way to the awful silence of disgrace and defeat.

The scene on board the *Santísima Trinidad* was nothing short of infernal. All attempt at working the ship had been abandoned, for it did not and could not move. The only thing to be done was to serve the guns with the utmost rapidity, and to do as much damage to the enemy as they had done to us. The English small-shot rent the sails just as if huge and invisible nails were tearing slits in them. The splinters of timber and of masts, the stout cables cut through as if they were straws, the capstans, spindles, and other heavy machinery torn from their place by the enemy's fire, strewed the deck so that there was scarcely room to move. Every minute men, till then full of life, fell on deck or into the sea; the blasphemy of those who were fighting mingled with the cries of the wounded, till it was impossible to say whether the dying were defying God or the living crying to him for mercy while they fought.

I offered my services for a melancholy task, which was carrying the wounded into the cock-pit where the surgeons were busy doing their utmost. Some were dead before we could get them there, and others had to suffer painful operations before their exhausted bodies could be left to repose.

Then I had the extreme satisfaction of helping the carpenters who were constantly employed in repairing the holes made in the ship's sides; but my youth and inefficiency made me less useful than I would fain have been.

Blood was flowing in rivulets on the upper and lower decks and in spite of the sand the motion of the ship carried it from side to side making sinister patterns on the boards. The cannon-balls, fired at such a short range, mutilated those they killed in a terrible manner, and I saw more than one man still standing with his head blown away, the force of the shock not having been great enough to fling the victim into the sea, whose waters would have extinguished almost painlessly the last sensation of existence. Other balls struck a mast or against the bulwarks, carrying off a hail of hot splinters that pierced and stung like arrows. The rifle-shots from the tops and the round-shot from the carronades dealt a more lingering and painful death, and there was hardly a man to be seen who did not bear the marks, more or less severe, of the foe's iron and lead.

The crew—the soul of the ship—being thus thrashed by the storm of battle and utterly unable to deal equal destruction, saw death at hand though resolved to die with the courage of despair; and the ship itself—the glorious body—shivered under the cannonade. I could feel her shudder under the fearful blows; her timbers cracked, her beams creaked, her ribs groaned like limbs on the rack, and the deck trembled under my feet with audible throbs, as though the whole huge creature was indignant at the sufferings of her crew. Meanwhile the water was pouring in at a hundred holes in the riddled hull, and the hold was fast filling.

The *Bucentaure*, the Admiral's vessel, surrendered before our very eyes. Villeneuve struck to the *Victory*. When once the leader of the fleet was gone, what hope was there for the other ships? The French flag vanished from the gallant vessel's mast and she ceased firing. The *San Augustin* and the *Héros* still persevered, and the*Rayo* and *Neptuno*, of the van, made an effort to rescue us from the enemy that was battering us. I could see what was going on in the immediate neighborhood of the *Trinidad*, though nothing was to be seen of the rest of the line. The wind had fallen to a calm and the smoke settled down over our heads shrouding everything in its dense white wreaths which it was impossible for eye to pierce. We could catch a glimpse now and then of a distant ship, mysteriously magnified by some inexplicable optical effect; I believe indeed that the terror of that supreme moment exaggerated every impression.

Presently this dense cloud was dispersed for an instant—but in what a fearful manner! A tremendous explosion, louder than all the thousand guns of the fleet fired at once, paralyzed every man and filled every soul with dread; and just as the ear was stunned by the terrific roar an intense flash lighted up the two fleets, rending the veil of smoke and revealing the whole panorama of the battle. This catastrophe had taken place on the side towards the South where the rear line had been posted.

"A ship blown up!" said one to another. But opinion differed as to whether it was the *Santa Ana*, the*Argonauta*, the *Ildefonso*, or the *Bahama*. We afterwards learnt that it was a Frenchman, the *Achille*. The explosion scattered in a myriad fragments what had a few moments before been a noble ship of 74 guns and 600 men. But a few seconds after we had already forgotten the explosion in thinking only of ourselves.

The *Bucentaure* having struck, the enemy's fire was directed on us, and our fate was sealed. The enthusiasm of the first hour was by this extinct in my soul; my heart quaked with terror that paralyzed my limbs and smothered every other emotion excepting curiosity. This I found so irresistible that I could not keep away from places where the danger was greatest. My small assistance was of no great use now, for the wounded were too numerous to be carried below and the guns had to be served by those who had some little strength left. Among these was Marcial who was here, there, and everywhere, shouting and working to the best of his small ability, acting as boatswain, gunner, sailor, and carpenter all at once, doing everything that happened to be needed at this awful moment. No one could have believed that, with hardly more than half a body, he could have done the work of so many men. A splinter had struck him on the head and the blood had stained his face and given him a most horrible appearance. I could see his lips move as he licked the blood from them and then he spit it out viciously over the side, as if he thought he could thus punish the enemy.

What astonished me most, and indeed shocked me somewhat, was that Marcial even in this scene of horror could still cut a good-humored joke; whether to encourage his dejected comrades or only to keep his own courage up I do not know. The fore-mast fell with a tremendous crash, covering the whole of the fore-deck with rigging, and Marcial called out to me: "Bring the hatchets, boy; we must stow this lumber in Davy Jones' locker," and in two minutes the ropes were cut and the mast went overboard.

Then, seeing that the enemy's fire grew hotter, he shouted to the purser's mate, who had come up to serve a gun: "Daddy, order up some drink for those 'great-coats,' and then they will let us alone."

To a soldier, who was lying like a dead creature with the pain of his wounds and the misery of sea-sickness, he exclaimed as he whisked the slow-match under his nose: "Take a whiff of orange-flower, man, to cure your faintness. Would you like to take a turn in a boat? Nelson has invited us to take a glass of grog with him."

This took place amidships; looking up at the quarter-deck I saw that Cisneros was killed; two sailors hastily carried him down into his cabin. My master remained immovable at his post, but his left arm was bleeding severely. I ran up to help him, but before I could reach the spot an officer had gone to him to persuade him to retire to his state-room. He had not spoken two words when a ball shot away half his head and his blood sprinkled my face. Don Alonso withdrew, as pale as the corpse which fell on the quarter-deck. When my master had gone down the commander was left standing alone, so perfectly cool that I could not help gazing at him for a few minutes, astounded by such courage. His head was uncovered, his face very white, but his eyes flashed and his attitude was full of energy, and he stood at his post, commanding the desperate strife, though the battle was lost past retrieval. Even this fearful disaster must be conducted with due order, and the captain's duty was still to keep discipline over heroism. His voice still controlled his men in this struggle between honor and death. An officer who was serving in the first battery came up for orders, and before he could speak he was lying dead at the feet of his chief; another officer of marines who was standing by his side fell wounded on the deck, and at last Uriarte stood quite alone on the quarter-deck, which was strewn with the dead and wounded. Even then he never took his eyes off the English ships and the working of our guns—the horrible scene on the poop and in the round-house, where his comrades and subalterns lay dying, could not quell his noble spirit nor shake his firm determination to face the fire till he too should fall. As I recall the fortitude and stoical calmness of Don Francisco Xavier de Uriarte, I understand all that is told us of the heroes of antiquity. At that time the word Sublime was as yet unknown to me, but I felt that there must be, in every language under heaven, some human utterance to express that greatness of soul which I here saw incarnate and which revealed itself to me as a special grace vouchsafed by God to miserable humanity.

By this time most of our guns were silenced, more than half of our men being incapable of serving them. I might not, however, have been aware of the fact, but that being impelled by curiosity I went out of the cabin once more and heard a voice saying in a tone of thunder:

"Gabrielillo, come here."

It was Marcial who was calling me; I ran to his side and found him trying to work one of the guns which had been left silent for lack of men. A ball had shot away the half of his wooden leg, which made him exclaim: "Well! so long as I can manage to keep the one of flesh and bone...!"

Two sailors lay dead by the gun; a third, though horribly wounded, still tried to go on working it.

"Let be, mate!" said Marcial. "You cannot even light the match," and taking the linstock from his hand, he put it into mine, saying: "Take it, Gabrielillo.—If you are afraid you had better jump overboard."

He loaded the cannon as quickly as he was able, helped by a ship's boy who happened to come up; we ran it forward: "fire!" was the word, I applied the match and the gun went off.

We repeated this operation a second and a third time, and the roar of the cannon fired by my own hand produced an extraordinary effect on my nerves. The feeling that I was no longer a spectator but an actor in this stupendous tragedy for the moment blew all my alarms to the winds; I was eager and excited, or at any rate determined to appear so. That moment revealed to me the truth that heroism is often simply the pride of honor. Marcial's eye—the eyes of the world were upon me; I must bear myself worthy of their gaze.

"Oh!" I exclaimed to myself with an impulse of pride: "If only my young mistress could see me now!... Bravely firing cannon like a man!" Two dozen of English were the least I might have sent to the other world.

These grand visions, however, did not last long for Marcial, enfeebled by age, was beginning to sink with exhaustion; he breathed hard as he wiped away the blood which flowed profusely from his head, and at last his arms dropped by his side, and closing his eyes, he exclaimed: "I can do no more; the powder is rising to my head. Gabrielillo, fetch me some water."

I ran to obey him, and when I had brought the water he drank it eagerly. This seemed to give him fresh energy; we were just about to load once more when a tremendous shock petrified us as we stood. The main-mast, cut through by repeated shots, fell amidships and across the mizzen; the ship was completely covered with the wreck, and the confusion was appalling.

I happily was so far under shelter that I got no harm but a slight blow on the head which, though it stunned me for a moment, did not prevent my thrusting aside the fragments of rope and timber which had fallen above me. The sailors and marines were struggling to clear away the vast mass of lumber, but from this moment only the lower-deck guns could be used at all. I got clear as best I could and went to look for Marcial but I did not find him, and casting my eyes up at the quarter-deck, I saw that the captain was no longer at his post. He had fallen senseless, badly wounded in the head by a splinter, and two sailors were just about to carry him down to the state-room. I was running forward to assist when a piece of shell hit me on the shoulder, terrifying me excessively, for I made sure my wound was mortal and that I was at my last gasp. My alarm did not hinder me from going into the cabin; I tottered from loss of blood and for a few minutes lay in a dead faint. I was roused from my short swoon by hearing the rattle of the cannon below and then a voice shouting vehemently:

"Board her! bring pikes!—axes!"

And then the confusion was so complete that it was impossible to distinguish human voices from the rest of the hideous uproar. However, somehow—I know not how—without thoroughly waking from my drowsy state, I became aware that all was given up for lost and that the officers had met in the cabin to agree to strike; nor was this the work of my fancy, bewildered as I was, for I heard a voice exclaiming: "The *Trinidad* never strikes!" I felt sure that it was Marcial's voice; but at any rate some one said it.

When I recovered perfect consciousness, I saw my master sunk on one of the sofas in the cabin, his face hidden in his hands, prostrate with despair, and paying no heed to his wound.

I went to the heart-broken old man, who could find no way of expressing his grief but by embracing me like a father, as if we were both together on the brink of the grave. He, at any rate, was convinced that he must soon die of grief, though his wound was by no means serious. I comforted him as best I might, assuring him that if the battle were indeed lost it was not because I had failed to batter the English to the best of my power; and I went on to say that we should be more fortunate next time—but my childish arguments failed to soothe him.

Going out presently in search of water for my master, I witnessed the very act of lowering the flag which was flying at the gaff, that being one of the few spars, with the remains of the mizzen-mast, that remained standing. The glorious flag, the emblem of our honor, pierced and tattered as it was, which had gathered so many fighting-men under its folds, ran down the rope never to be unfurled again. The idea of stricken pride, of a brave spirit giving way before a superior force, can find no more appropriate symbol to represent it than that of a flying standard which sinks and disappears like a setting sun. And our flag thus slowly descending that fatal evening, at the moment when we surrendered, seem to shed a parting ray of glory.

The firing ceased, and the English took possession of the conquered vessel.

CHAPTER XII.

WHEN the mind had sufficiently recovered from the shock and excitement of battle, and had time to turn from "the pity of it" and the chill of terror left by the sight of that terrific struggle, those who were left alive could see the hapless vessel in all its majesty of horror. Till now we had thought of nothing but self-defence, but when the firing ceased we could turn our attention to the dilapidated state of the ship, which let in the water at a hundred leaks and was beginning to sink, threatening to bury us all, living and dead, at the bottom of the sea. The English had scarcely taken possession when a shout arose from our sailors, as from one man:

"To the pumps!"

All who were able flew to the pumps and labored hard at them; but these ineffectual machines turned out much less water than poured in. Suddenly a shriek even more appalling than any we had heard before filled us with horror. I have said that the wounded had been carried down into the hold which, being below the water line, was secure from the inroads of the cannon shot. But the water was fast gaining there, and some sailors came scrambling up the hatchways exclaiming that the wounded were being drowned. The greater part of the crew hesitated between continuing to pump and running down to rescue the hapless wretches; and God knows what would have happened if an English crew had not come to our assistance. They not only carried up the wounded to the second and third deck but they lent a hand at the pumps and their carpenters set to work to stop the leaks in the ship's sides.

Utterly tired out, and thinking too that Don Alonso might need my services, I returned to the cabin. As I went I saw some Englishmen hoisting the English flag at the bows of the *Trinidad*.

As I dare to believe that the amiable reader will allow me to record my feelings, I may say that this incident gave me something to think of. I had always thought of the English as pirates or sea-highwaymen, as a race of adventurers not worthy to be called a nation but living by robbery. When I saw the pride with which they hauled up their flag, saluting it with vociferous cheering; when I perceived the satisfaction it was to them to have made a prize of the largest vessel that, until then, had ever sailed the seas, it struck me that their country, too, was dear to them, that her honor was in their hands and I understood that in that land—to me so mysteriously remote—called England, there must be, as in Spain, honorable men, a paternal king, mothers, daughters, wives, and sisters of these brave mariners—all watching anxiously for their return and praying to God for victory.

I found my master in the cabin, somewhat calmer. The English officers who had come on board treated ours with the most distinguished courtesy and, as I heard, were anxious to transfer the wounded on board their own ship. One of these gentlemen went up to my master as if recognizing him, bowed to him, and addressing him in fairly-good Spanish, reminded him of an old acquaintanceship. Don Alonso responded gravely to his advances and then enquired of him as to some of the details of the battle.

"But what became of our reserve? What did Gravina do?" asked my master.

"Gravina withdrew with some of his ships," replied the English officer.

"Only the *Rayo* and *Neptuno* came to our assistance of all the front line?"

"Four French ships—the *Duguay-Trouin*, the *Mont Blanc*, the *Scipion*, and the *Formidable* were the only ones that kept out of the action."

"But Gravina—where was Gravina?" Don Alonso persisted.

"He got off in the *Príncipe de Astúrias*; but as he was chased I do not know whether he reached Cadiz in safety."

"And the *San Ildefonso*?"

"She struck."

"And the *Santa Ana*?"

"Struck too."

"Good God!" cried my master, unable to conceal his indignation. "But you did not take the *Nepomuceno*?"

"Yes, that too."

"Are you sure of that? With Churruca?"

"He was killed," said the Englishman with sincere regret.

"Killed—Churruca killed!" exclaimed Don Alonso in grievous bewilderment. "And the *Bahama*—she was saved—the *Bahama* must have been able to reach Cadiz in safety."

"She was taken too."

"Taken! And Galiano? He is a hero and a cultivated gentleman."

"He was," said the Englishman sadly, "but he too is dead."

"And the *Montañes* with Alcedo?"

"Killed, killed."

My master could not control his emotion and as, at his advanced age, presence of mind is lacking at such terrible moments, he suffered the slight humiliation of shedding a few tears as he remembered his lost friends. Nor are tears unbecoming to a noble soul; on the contrary, they reveal a happy infusion of delicate feeling, when combined with a resolute temper. My master's tears were manly tears, shed after he had done his duty as a sailor; but, hastily recovering from this paroxysm of grief, and anxious to retort on the Englishman by some pain equal to that he had caused, he said:

"You too have suffered, no doubt, and have lost some men of mark?"

"We have suffered one irreparable loss," said the English officer in accents as deeply sad as Don Alonso's. "We have lost our greatest man, the bravest of the brave—our noble, heroic, incomparable Nelson."

And his fortitude holding out no better than my master's he made no attempt to conceal his anguish of grief; he covered his face with his hands and wept with the pathetic frankness of incontrollable sorrow for his leader, his guardian, and his friend.

Nelson, mortally wounded at an early stage of the battle by a gun-shot—the ball piercing his chest and lodging in the spine—had simply said to Captain Hardy: "They have done for me at last, Hardy." He lingered till the evening, not losing any details of the battle, and his naval and military genius only failed him with the last breath of his shattered body. Though suffering agonies of pain, he still dictated his orders and kept himself informed of the manœuvres of both fleets; and when at length he was assured that victory was on the side of the English, he exclaimed: "Thank God, I have done my duty!" A quarter of an hour later the greatest sailor of the age breathed his last. The reader will forgive me this digression.

It may seem strange that we did not know the fate of many of the ships of the combined fleets. But nothing could be more natural than our ignorance, considering the great length of our front and the plan of isolated fights contrived and carried out by the English. Their vessels had got mixed up with ours and the ships fought at close quarters; the one which had engaged us hid the rest of the squadron from view, besides which the dense smoke prevented our seeing anything that was not quite close to us. Towards nightfall and before the firing had altogether ceased, we could distinguish a few ships in the offing, looking like phantoms; some with half their rigging gone, and others completely dismasted. The mist, the smoke and, indeed, our own wearied and bewildered brains, would not allow us to distinguish whether they were our own or the enemy's, and as, from time to time the glare of a broadside in the distance lighted up the lugubrious scene, we could see that the fight was still going on to a desperate end between detached groups of ships, while others were flying before the wind without aim or purpose, and some of ours were being towed by the English to the South.

Night fell, increasing the misery and horror of our situation. It might have been hoped that Nature at least would be on our side after so much disaster; but, on the contrary, the elements lashed us with their fury as though Heaven thought our cup of misfortune was not yet full. A tremendous storm burst and the winds and waves tossed and buffeted our ship in their fury and, as she could not be worked, she was utterly at their mercy. The rolling was so terrible that it was very difficult even to work the pumps, and this, combined with the exhausted condition of the men, made our condition grow worse every minute. An English vessel, which as we learnt was the *Prince*, tried to take us in tow; but her efforts were in vain and she was forced to keep off for fear of a collision which would have been fatal to both. Meanwhile it was impossible to get anything to eat, and I was dying of hunger, though the others seemed insensible to anything but the immediate danger and gave no thought to this important matter. I dared not ask for a piece of bread even, for fear of seeming greedy and troublesome; but at the same time, I must confess—and without shame—I looked out sharply to see if there were any place where I might hope to find any kind of eatable stores. Emboldened by hunger, I made free to inspect the hold where the biscuit-boxes were kept, and what was my astonishment at finding Marcial there before me, stowing himself with every thing he could lay his hands on. The old man's wound was not serious, and though a ball had carried away his right foot, as this was only the lower end of his wooden leg the mishap only left him a little more halt than before.

"Here, Gabrielillo," he said, giving me a heap of biscuits, "take these. No ship can sail without ballast." And then he pulled out a bottle and drank with intense satisfaction. As we went out of the biscuit-room we saw that we were not the only visitors who had made a raid upon it; on the contrary, it was very evident that it had been well pillaged not long since.

Having recruited my strength I could now think of trying to make myself useful by lending a hand at the pumps or helping the carpenters. They were laboriously repairing some of the damage done, aided by the English, who watched all our proceedings; indeed, as I have since learnt, they kept an eye on every one of our sailors, for they were afraid lest we should suddenly mutiny and turn upon them to recapture the vessel; in this, however, the enemy showed more vigilance than common-sense, for we must indeed have lost our wits before attempting to recover a ship in such a condition. However, the "great-coats" were everywhere at once, and we could not stir without being observed.

Night fell, and as I was perishing with cold I quitted the deck where I could scarcely bear myself besides incurring constant risk of being swept overboard by a wave, so I went down into the cabin. My purpose was to try to sleep a little while—but who could sleep in such a night? The same confusion prevailed in the cabin as on deck. Those who had escaped unhurt were doing what they could to aid the wounded, and these, disturbed by the motion of the vessel which prevented their getting any rest, were so pitiable a sight that it was impossible to resign one's self to sleep. On one side, covered with the Spanish flag, lay the bodies of the officers who had been killed; and in the midst of all this misery, surrounded by so much suffering, these senseless corpses seemed really to be envied. They alone on board the *Trinidad* were at rest, to them nothing mattered now: fatigue and pain, the disgrace of defeat, or physical sufferings. The standard which served them as a glorious winding-sheet shut them out, as it were, from the world of responsibility, of dishonor, and of despair, in which we were left behind. They could not care for the danger the vessel was in, for to them it was no longer anything but a coffin.

The officers who were killed were Don Juan Cisniega, a lieutenant in the navy, who was not related to my master, in spite of their identity of name; Don Joaquin de Salas and Don Juan Matute, also lieutenants; Don José Graullé, lieutenant-colonel in the army; Urias, lieutenant in command of a frigate, and midshipman Don Antonio de Bobadilla. The sailors and marines whose corpses lay strewn about the gun-decks and upper-deck amounted to the terrible number of four hundred.

Never shall I forget the moment when the bodies were cast into the sea, by order of the English officer in charge of the ship. The dismal ceremony took place on the morning of the 22nd when the storm seemed to be at its wildest on purpose to add to the terrors of the scene. The bodies of the officers were brought on deck, the priest said a short prayer for this was no time for elaborate ceremonial, and our melancholy task began. Each wrapped in a flag, with a cannon-ball tied to his feet, was dropped into the waves without any of the solemn and painful emotion which under ordinary circumstances would have agitated the lookers-on. Our spirits were so quelled by disaster that the contemplation of death had become almost indifference. Still, a burial at sea is more terribly sad than one on land. We cover the dead with earth and leave him there; those who loved him know that there is a spot where the dear remains are laid and can mark it with a slab, a cross, or a monument; but at sea—the body is cast into that heaving, shifting waste; it is lost forever as it disappears; imagination cannot follow it in its fall—down, down to the fathomless abyss; it is impossible to realize that it still exists at the bottom of the deep. These were my reflections as I watched the corpses vanish—the remains of those brave fighting-men, so full of life only the day before—the pride of their country and the joy of all who loved them.

The sailors were thrown overboard with less ceremony; the regulation is that they shall be tied up in their hammocks, but there was no time to carry this out. Some indeed were wrapped round as the rules require, but most of them were thrown into the sea without any shroud or ball at their feet, for the simple reason that there were not enough for all. There were four hundred of them, more or less, and merely to clear them overboard and out of sight every able-bodied man that was left had to lend a hand, so as to get it done as quickly as possible. Much to my horror I saw myself forced to offer my services in the dismal duty, and many a dead man dropped over the ship's side at a push from my hand helping other and stronger ones.

One incident—or rather coincidence—occurred which filled me with horror. A body horribly mauled and mutilated had been picked up by two sailors, and just as they lifted it one or two of the by-standers allowed themselves to utter some of those coarse and grim jests which are always offensive, and at such a moment revolting. I know not how it was that this poor wretch was the only one which moved them so completely to lose the sense of reverence due to the dead, but they exclaimed: "He has been paid out for old scores—he will never be at his tricks again," and other witticisms of the same kind. For a moment my blood rose, but my indignation suddenly turned to astonishment mingled with an indescribable feeling of awe, regret, and aversion, when, on looking at the mangled features of the corpse, I recognized my uncle. I shut my eyes with a shudder, and did not open them again till the splash of the water in my face told me that he had disappeared forever from mortal ken. This man had been very cruel to me, very cruel to his sister; still, he was my own flesh and blood, my mother's brother; the blood that flowed in my veins was his, and that secret voice which warns us to be charitable to the faults of our own kith and kin could not be silenced after what I had seen, for at the moment when I recognized him I had perceived in those blood-stained features some reminder of my mother's face, and this stirred my deepest feelings. I forgot that the man had been a brutal wretch, and all his barbarous treatment of me during my hapless childhood. I can honestly declare—and I venture to do so though it is to my own credit—that I forgave him with all my heart and lifted up my soul to God, praying for mercy on him for all his sins.

I learnt afterwards that he had behaved gallantly in the fight, but even this had not won him the respect of his comrades who, regarding him as a low sneak, never found a good word for him—not even at that supreme moment when, as a rule, every offence is forgiven on earth in the belief that the sinner is rendering an account to his Maker.

As the day advanced the *Prince* attempted once more to take the *Santísima Trinidad* in tow, but with no better success than before. Our situation was no worse, although the tempest raged with undiminished fury, for a good deal of the mischief had been patched up, and we thought that if the weather should mend the hulk, at any rate, might be saved. The English made a great point of it, for they were very anxious to take the largest man-of-war ever seen afloat into Gibraltar as a trophy; so they willingly plied the pumps by night and by day and allowed us to rest awhile. All through the day of the 22nd the sea continued terrific, tossing the huge and helpless vessel as though it were a little fishing-boat, and the enormous mass of timber proved the soundness of her build by not simply falling to pieces under the furious lashing of the waters. At some moments she rolled over so completely on her beam ends that it seemed as though she must go to the bottom, but suddenly the wave would fly off in smoke, as it were, before the hurricane, the ship, righting herself, rode over it with a toss of her mighty prow—which displayed the Lion of Castile—and we breathed once more with the hope of escaping with our lives.

On all sides we could see the scattered fleets; many of the ships were English, severely damaged and striving to gain shelter under the coast. There were Frenchmen and Spaniards too, some dismasted, others in tow of the enemy. Marcial recognized the *San Ildefonso*. Floating about were myriads of fragments and masses of wreck—spars, timbers, broken boats, hatches, bulwarks, and doors—besides two unfortunate sailors who were clinging to a plank, and who must have been swept off and drowned if the English had not hastened to rescue them. They were brought on board more dead than alive, and their resuscitation after being in the very jaws of death was like a new birth to them.

That day went by between agonies and hopes—now we thought nothing could save the ship and that we must be taken on board an Englishman then again we hoped to keep her afloat. The idea of being taken into Gibraltar as prisoners was intolerable, not so much to me perhaps as to men of punctilious honor and sensitive dignity like my master whose mental anguish at the thought must have been intolerable. However, all the torment of suspense, at any rate, was relieved by the evening when it was unanimously agreed that if we were not transferred to an English ship at once, to the bottom we must go with the vessel, which now had five feet of water in the hold. Uriarte and Cisneros took the announcement with dignified composure, saying that it mattered little to them whether they perished at once or were prisoners in a foreign land. The task was at once begun in the doubtful twilight, and as there were above three hundred wounded to be transferred it was no easy matter. The available number of hands was about five hundred, all that were left uninjured of the original crew of eleven hundred and fifteen before the battle.

We set to work promptly with the launches of the *Trinidad* and the *Prince*, and three other boats belonging to the English. The wounded were attended to first; but though they were lifted with all possible care they could not be moved without great suffering, and some entreated with groans and shrieks to be left in peace, preferring immediate death to anything that could aggravate and prolong their torments. But there was no time for pity, and they were carried to the boats as ruthlessly as the cold corpses of their comrades had been flung into the sea.

Uriarte and Cisneros embarked in the English captain's gig, but when they urged my master to accompany them he obstinately refused, saying that he wished to be last to leave the sinking ship. This I confess disturbed me not a little, for as by this time, the hardy patriotism which at first had given me courage had evaporated, I thought only of saving my life, and to stay on board a foundering vessel was clearly not the best means to that laudable end. Nor were my fears ill founded, for not more than half the men had been taken off when a dull roar of terror echoed through the ship.

"She is going to the bottom—the boats, to the boats!" shouted some, and there was a rush to the ship's side, all looking out eagerly for the return of the boats. Every attempt at work or order was given up, the wounded were forgotten, and several who had been brought on deck dragged themselves to the side in a sort of delirium, to seek an opening and throw themselves into the sea. Up through the hatchways came a hideous shriek which I think I can hear as I write, freezing the blood in my veins and setting my hair on end. It came from the poor wretches on the lowest deck who already felt the waters rising to drown them and vainly cried for help—to God or men—who can tell! Vainly indeed to men, for they had enough to do to save themselves. They jumped wildly into the boats, and this confusion in the darkness hindered progress. One man alone, quite cool in the midst of the danger, remained in the state cabin, paying no heed to all that was going on around him, walking up and down sunk in thought, as though the planks he trod were not fast sinking into the gulf below. It was my master. I ran to rouse him from his stupefaction. "Sir," I cried, "we are drowning!"

Don Alonzo did not heed me, and if I may trust my memory he merely said without looking round:

"How Paca will laugh at me, when I go home after such a terrible defeat!"

"Sir, the ship is sinking!" I insisted, not indeed exaggerating the danger, but in vehement entreaty.

My master looked at the sea, at the boats, at the men who were blindly and desperately leaping overboard; I looked anxiously for Marcial and called him as loudly as I could shout. At the same time I seemed to lose all consciousness of where I was and what was happening. I turned giddy and I could see nothing. To tell how I was saved from death I can only trust to the vaguest recollections, like the memory of a dream, for in fact I fairly swooned with terror. A sailor, as I fancy, came up to Don Alonso while I was speaking to him; in his strong arms I felt myself lifted up and when I somewhat recovered my wits I found myself in one of the boats, propped up against my master's knees, while he held my head in his hands with fatherly care and kindness. Marcial held the tiller and the boat was crowded with men.

Looking up I saw, apparently not more than four or five yards away, the black side of our ship sinking fast; but through the port-holes of the deck that was still above water I could see a dim light—that of the lamp which had been lighted at dusk and which still kept unwearied watch over the wreck of the deserted vessel. I still could hear the groans and cries of the hapless sufferers whom it had been impossible to remove and who were within a few feet of the abyss while, by that dismal lamp they could see each other's misery and read each other's agony in their eyes.

My fancy reverted to the dreadful scene on board—another inch of water would be enough to overweight her and destroy the little buoyancy that was left her. How far did those poor creatures understand the nearness of their fate? What were they saying in this awful moment? If they could see us safe in our boat—if they could hear the splash of our oars, how bitterly must their tortured souls complain to Heaven! But such agonizing martyrdom must surely avail to purify them of all guilt, and the grace of God must fill that hapless vessel, now when it was on the point of disappearing for ever!

Our boat moved away; and still I watched the shapeless mass—though I confess that I believe it was my imagination rather than my eyes that discerned the *Trinidad* through the darkness, till I believe I saw, against the black sky, a huge arm reaching down to the tossing waters—the effect no doubt of my imagination on my senses.

CHAPTER XIII.

THE boat moved on—but whither? Not Marcial himself knew where he was steering her to. The darkness was so complete that we lost sight of the other boats and the lights on board the *Prince* were as invisible through the fog, as though a gust of wind had extinguished them. The waves ran so high and the squalls were so violent that our frail bark made very little way, but thanks to skilful steering she only once shipped water. We all sat silent, most of us fixing a melancholy gaze on the spot where we supposed our deserted comrades were at this moment engaged in an agonizing death-struggle. In the course of this passage I could not fail to make, as was my habit, certain reflections which I may venture to call philosophical. Some may laugh at a philosopher of fourteen; but I will not heed their laughter; I will try to write down the thoughts that occupied me at this juncture. Children too can think great thoughts and at such a moment, in face of such a spectacle, what brain but an idiot's could remain unmoved.

There were both English and Spaniards in our boat—though most Spaniards—and it was strange to note how they fraternized, helping and encouraging each other in their common danger, and quite forgetting that only the day before they had been killing each other in hideous fight, more like wild beasts than men. I looked at the English who rowed with as good a will as our own sailors, I saw in their faces the same tokens of fear or of hope, and above all the same expression, sacred to humanity, of kindness and fellowship which was the common motive of all. And as I noted it I said to myself: "Good God! why are there wars? Why cannot these men be friends under all the circumstances of life as they are in danger? Is not such a scene as this enough to prove that all men are brothers?"

But the idea of nationality suddenly occurred to me to cut short these speculations, and my geographical theory of islands. "To be sure," said I to myself, "the islands must need want to rob each other of some portion of the land, and that is what spoils everything. And indeed there must be a great many bad men there who make wars for their own advantage, because they are ambitious and wish for power, or are avaricious and wish for wealth. It is these bad men who deceive the rest—all the miserable creatures who do the fighting for them; and to make the fraud complete, they set them against other nations, sow discord and foment envy—and here you see the consequences. I am certain"—added I to myself, "that this can never go on; I will bet two to one that before long the inhabitants of the different Islands will be convinced that they are committing a great folly in making such tremendous wars, and that a day will come when they will embrace each other and all agree to be like one family." So I thought then; and now, after sixty years of life, I have not seen that day dawn.

The launch labored on through the heavy sea. I believe that if only my master would have consented Marcial would have been quite ready to pitch the English overboard and steer the boat to Cadiz or the nearest coast, even at the imminent risk of foundering on the way. I fancy he had suggested something of the kind to Don Alonso, speaking in a low voice, and that my master wished to give him a lesson in honor, for I heard him say:

"We are prisoners, Marcial—we are prisoners."

The worst of it was that no vessel came in sight. The *Prince* had moved off, and no light on either side told us of the existence of an English ship. At last, however, we descried one at some distance and a few minutes later the vague outline came in sight of a ship before the storm, to our windward, and on the opposite tack to ours. Some thought it was a Frenchman, others said it was English; Marcial was sure she was a Spaniard. We pulled hard to meet her and were soon within speaking distance. Our men hailed her and the answer was in Spanish.

"It is the *San Agustin*" said Marcial.

"The *San Agustin* was sunk," said Don Alonso; "I believe it is the *Santa Ana* which was also captured." In fact, as we got close, we all recognized the *Santa Ana* which had gone into action under the command of Alava. The English officers in charge immediately prepared to take us on board, and before long we were all safe and sound on deck.

The *Santa Ana*, 112 guns, had suffered severely, though not to such an extent as the *Santísima Trinidad*; for, though she had lost all her masts and her rudder, the hull was fairly sound. The *Santa Ana* survived the battle of Trafalgar eleven years, and would have lived much longer if she had not gone to the bottom for want of repairs in the bay of Havana, in 1816. She had behaved splendidly in the fight. She was commanded, as I have said, by Vice-admiral Alava leader of the van which, as the order of battle was altered, became the rear. As the reader knows, the line of English ships led by Collingwood attacked the Spanish rear while Nelson took the centre. The *Santa Ana*, only supported by the *Fougueux*, a Frenchman, had to fight the *Royal Sovereign* and four other English ships; and in spite of their unequal strength one side suffered as much as the other, for Collingwood's ship was the first to retire and the *Euryalus* took her place. By all accounts the fighting was terrific, and the two great ships, whose masts were almost entangled, fired into each other for six hours until Alava and Gardoqui, both being wounded (Alava subsequently died), five officers and ninety-seven sailors being killed, besides more than 150 wounded, the *Santa Ana* was forced to surrender. The English took possession of her, but it was impossible to work her on account of her shattered condition, and the dreadful storm that rose during the night of the 21st; so when we went on board she was in a very critical, though not a desperate situation, floating at the mercy of the wind and waves and unable to make any course. From that moment I was greatly comforted by seeing that every face on board betrayed a dread of approaching death. They were all very sad and quiet, enduring with a solemn mien the disgrace of defeat and the sense of being prisoners. One circumstance I could not help observing, and that was that the English officers in charge of the ship were not by a great deal so polite or so kind as those sent on board the *Trinidad*; on the contrary, among those on the *Santa Ana* were some who were both stern and repellent, doing all they could to mortify us, exaggerating their own dignity and authority, and interfering in everything with the rudest impertinence. This greatly annoyed the captured crew, particularly the sailors; and I fancied I overheard many alarming murmurs of rebellion which would have been highly disquieting to the English if they had come to their ears.

Beyond this there is nothing to tell of our progress that night—if progress it can be called when we were driven at the will of the wind and waves, sailless and rudderless. Nor do I wish to weary the reader with a repetition of the scenes we had witnessed on board the *Trinidad*, so I will go on to other and newer incidents which will surprise him as much as they did me.

I had lost my liking for hanging about the deck and poop, and as soon as we got on board the *Santa Ana* I took shelter in the cabin with my master, hoping to get food and rest, both of which I needed sorely. However, I found there many wounded who required constant attention and this duty, which I gladly fulfilled, prevented my getting the sleep which my wearied frame required. I was engaged in placing a bandage on Don Alonso's arm when a hand was laid on my shoulder. I turned round and saw a tall young officer wrapped in a large blue cloak whom I did not immediately recognize; but after gazing at him for a few seconds, I exclaimed aloud with surprise; it was Don Rafael Malespina, my young mistress's lover.

My master embraced him affectionately and he sat down by us. He had been wounded in the shoulder, and was so pale from fatigue and loss of blood that his face looked quite altered. His presence here filled me with strange sensations—some of which I am fain to own were anything rather than pleasing. At first I felt glad enough indeed to see any one I knew and who had come out alive from those scenes of horror, but the next moment my old aversion for this man rose up, as strong as ever in my breast, like some dormant pain reviving to torment me after an interval of respite. I confess with shame that I was sorry to see him safe and sound, but I must do myself the justice to add that the regret was but momentary, as brief as a lightning flash—a flash of blackness, as I may say, darkening my soul; or rather a transient eclipse of the light of conscience which shone clearly again in the next instant. The evil side of my nature for a moment came uppermost; but I was able to suppress it at once and drive it down again to the depths whence it had come. Can every one say as much?

After this brief mental struggle I could look at Malespina, glad that he was alive and sorry that he was hurt; and I remember, not without pride, that I did all I could to show him my feelings. Poor little mistress! How terrible must her anguish have been all this time. My heart overflowed with pitiful kindness at the thought—I could have run all the way to Vejer to say: "Señorita Doña Rosa, your Don Rafael is safe and sound."

The luckless Malespina had been brought on board the *Santa Ana* from the *Nepomuceno*, which had also been captured, and with so many wounded on board that it had been necessary, as we learnt, to distribute them or they must have perished of neglect. When the father and his daughter's *fiancé* had exchanged the first greetings and spoken of the absent ones on shore, the conversation turned on the details of the battle. My master related all that had occurred on board the *Trinidad* and then he added: "But no one has told me exactly what has become of Gravina. Was he taken prisoner, or has he got off to Cadiz?"

"The Admiral," said Malespina, "stood a terrific fire from the *Defiance* and the *Revenge*. The *Neptune*, a Frenchman, came to her assistance with the *San Ildefonso* and the *San Justo*; but our enemies were reinforced by the *Dreadnought*, the *Thunderer*, and the *Polyphemus*; so that resistance was hopeless. Seeing the *Príncipe de Astúrias* with all her tackle cut, her masts overboard and her sides riddled with balls, while Gravina himself and Escaño, his second in command, were both wounded, they resolved on giving up the struggle which was quite in vain for the battle was lost. Gravina hoisted the signal to retire on the stump of a mast and sailed off for Cadiz, followed by the *San Justo*, the *San Leandro*, the *Montañes* and three others; only regretting their inability to rescue the *San Ildefonso* which had fallen into the hands of the enemy."

"But tell us what happened on board the *Nepomuceno*," said my master, deeply interested. "I can hardly believe that Churruca can be dead; and, though every one tells me that he is, I cannot help fancying that that wonderful man must still be alive somewhere on earth."

But Malespina told him that it had been his misfortune to see Churruca killed and said he would relate every detail. A few officers gathered round him while I, as curious as they could be, was all ears in order not to lose a syllable.

"Even as we came out of Cadiz," said Malespina, "Churruca had a presentiment of disaster. He had voted against sailing out to sea, for he knew the inferiority of our armament, and he also had little confidence in Villeneuve's skill and judgment. All his predictions were verified—all, even to his own death: for there is no doubt that he had foreseen it as surely as he did our defeat. On the 19th he had said to Apodaca, his brother-in-law, before going on board: 'Sooner than surrender my ship, I will blow her up or go to the bottom. That is the duty of every man who serves his king and country.' And the same day, writing to a friend, he said: 'If you hear that my ship is taken you will know that I am dead.'

"Indeed it was legible in his sad grave face that he looked forward to nothing but a catastrophe. I believe that this conviction, and the absolute impossibility of avoiding defeat while feeling himself strong enough for his own part, seriously weighed upon his mind, for he was as capable of great deeds as he was of noble thoughts.

"Churruca's was a religious as well as a superior mind. On the 21st, at eleven in the morning, he called up all the soldiers and crew; he bid them all kneel and said to his chaplain in solemn tones: 'Fulfil your function, holy Father, and absolve these brave souls that know not what this fight may have in store for them.' When the priest had pronounced absolution Churruca desired them to stand up, and speaking in friendly but audible tones he added: 'My children all:—In God's name I promise heavenly bliss to all who die doing their duty. If one of you shirks it he shall be shot on the spot; or, if he escapes my notice or that of the gallant officers I have the honor to command, his remorse shall pursue him so long as he crawls through the rest of his miserable and dishonored days.'

"This harangue, as eloquent as it was wise, combining the ideas of religion and of military duty, filled every man on board with enthusiasm. Alas for all these brave hearts!—wasted like gold sunk at the bottom of the ocean! Face to face with the English, Churruca watched Villeneuve's preliminary manœuvres with entire disapproval, and when the signal was given for the whole fleet to turn about—a manœuvre which, as we know, reversed the order of battle—he told his captain in so many words that this blunder had lost us the day. He immediately understood the masterly plan struck out by Nelson of cutting our line through the centre from the rear, and engaging the whole fleet at once, dealing with our ships in separate divisions so that they could not assist each other.

"The *Nepomuceno* was at the end of the line. The *Royal Sovereign* and the *Santa Ana* opened fire and then all the ships in turn came into action. Five English vessels under Collingwood attacked our ship; two, however, passed on and Churruca had only three to deal with.

"We held out bravely against these odds till two in the afternoon, suffering terribly, however, though we dealt double havoc on the foe. Our Admiral seemed to have infused his heroic spirit into the crew and soldiers, and the ship was handled and the broadsides delivered with terrible promptitude and accuracy. The new recruits had learnt their lesson in courage in no more than a couple of hours' apprenticeship, and our defence struck the English not merely with dismay but with astonishment.

"They were in fact forced to get assistance and bring up no less than six against one. The two ships that had at first sailed past now returned, and the *Dreadnought* came alongside of us, with not more than half a pistol-shot between her and our stern. You may imagine the fire of these six giants pouring balls and small shot into a vessel of 74 guns. But our ship seemed positively to grow bigger in proportion to the desperate bravery of her defenders. They themselves seemed to grow in strength as their courage mounted, and seeing the dismay we created in an enemy six times as strong, we could have believed ourselves something more than men.

"Churruca, meanwhile, who was the brain of us all, directed the action with gloomy calmness. Knowing that only care and skill could supply the place of strength he economized our fire, trusting entirely to careful aim, and the consequence was that each ball did terrible havoc on the foe. He saw to everything, settled everything, and the shot flew round him and over his head without his ever once changing color even. That frail and delicate man, whose beautiful and melancholy features looked so little fitted to dare such scenes of terror, inspired us all with unheard-of courage, simply by a glance of his eye.

"However, it was not the will of God that he should escape alive from that storm of fire. Seeing that no one could hit one of the enemy's ships which was battering us with impunity, he went down himself to judge of the line of fire and succeeded in dismasting her. He was returning to the quarter-deck when a cannon ball hit his right leg with such violence as almost to take it off, tearing it across the thigh in the most frightful manner. We rushed to support him and our hero sank into my arms. It was a fearful moment. I still fancy I can feel his heart beating under my hand—a heart which, even at that terrible moment, beat only for his country. He sank rapidly. I saw him make an effort to raise his head, which had fallen forward on his breast; I saw him try to force a smile while his face was as white as death, and he said, in a voice that was scarcely weaker than usual: 'It is nothing—go on firing.'

"His spirit revolted against death and he did all he could to conceal the terrible sufferings of his mutilated frame, while his heart beat more feebly every instant. We wanted to carry him down into the cabin, but nothing would persuade him to quit the quarter-deck. At last he yielded to our entreaties and understood that he must give up the command. He called for Moyna, his lieutenant, and was told that he was dead; then he called for the officer in command of the first battery, and the latter though himself seriously wounded at once mounted the quarter-deck and assumed the command.

"But from that moment the men lost heart; from giants they shrank to pigmies; their courage was worn out and it was plain that we must surrender. The consternation that had possessed me from the instant when our hero fell into my arms had not prevented my observing the terrible effect that this disaster had produced in the minds of all. A sudden paralysis of soul and body seemed to have fallen on the crew; they all stood petrified and speechless and the grief of losing their beloved leader quite overpowered the disgrace of surrender.

"Quite half of the men were dead or wounded; most of the guns were past serving; all the masts except the main-mast were gone by the board and the rudder could not be used. Even in this deplorable plight we made an attempt to follow the *Príncipe de Astúrias* which had given the signal to retreat, but the *Nepomuceno* was mortally wounded and could not move nor steer. Even then, in spite of the wrecked state of the ship, in spite of the dismayed condition of the men, in spite of a concurrence of circumstances to render our case hopeless, not one of the six English captains attempted to board us. They respected our ship even when she was at their mercy.

"Churruca, in the midst of his agony, ordered that the flag should be nailed to the mast, for the ship should never surrender so long as he breathed. The delay alas! could be but brief, for Churruca was going rapidly, and we who supported him only wondered that a body so mangled could still breathe; it was his indomitable spirit that kept him alive added to a resolute determination to live, for he felt it his first duty. He never lost consciousness till the very end, nor complained of his sufferings, nor seemed to dread his approaching death; his sole care and anxiety was that the crew should not know how dangerous his condition was, so that no one should fail in his duty. He desired that the men should be thanked for their heroic bravery, spoke a few words to his brother-in-law, Ruiz de Apodaca, and, after sending a message to his young wife he fixed his thoughts on God, whose name we heard frequently on his parched lips, and died with the calm resignation of a just man and the fortitude of a hero; bereft of the satisfaction of victory but with no angry sense of defeat. In him duty and dignity were equally combined, and discipline was second only to religion. As a soldier he was resolute, as a man he was resigned, and without a murmur or an accusing word he died as nobly as he had lived. We looked at his body, not yet cold, and it seemed all a delusion—he must surely wake to give us our orders; and we wept with less fortitude than he had shown in dying, for in him we had lost all the valor and enthusiasm that had borne us up.

"Well, the ship struck; and when the officers from the six vessels that had destroyed her came on board each claimed the honor of receiving the sword of our dead hero. Each exclaimed: 'He surrendered to me!'—and for a few minutes they eagerly disputed the victory, each for the ship he represented. Then they asked the officer who had taken the command to which of the Englishmen he had struck. 'To all,' he replied. 'The *Nepomuceno*would never have surrendered to one.'

"The English gazed with sincere emotion on the body of the hapless Churruca, for the fame of his courage and genius was known to them and one of them spoke to this effect: 'A man of such illustrious qualities ought never to be exposed to the risks of battle; he should be kept to live and serve the interests of science and navigation.' Then they prepared for dropping him overboard, the English marines and seamen forming a line of honor alongside of the Spaniards; they behaved throughout like noble-minded and magnanimous gentlemen.

"The number of our wounded was very considerable, and they were transferred on board other English or captured ships. It was my lot to be sent to this one which has suffered worse than most; however, they count more on getting her into Gibraltar than any other, now that they have lost the *Trinidad* which was the finest and most coveted of our ships."

Thus ended Malespina's narrative which was attentively listened to as being that of an eye-witness. From what I heard I understood that a tragedy just as fearful as that I myself had seen had been enacted on board every ship of the fleet. "Good God!" said I to myself, "what infinite misery! and all brought about by the obstinacy of a single man!" And child as I was, I remember thinking: "One man, however mad he may be, can never commit such extravagant follies as whole nations sometimes plunge into at the bidding of a hundred wise ones."

CHAPTER XIV.

A LARGE part of the night was spent in listening to Malespina's narrative and the experiences of other officers. They were interesting enough to keep me awake and I was so excited that I found great difficulty afterwards in going to sleep at all. I could not get the image of Churruca out of my mind as I had seen him, handsome and strong, at Doña Flora's house. On that occasion, even, I had been startled by the expression of intense sadness on the hero's features, as if he had a sure presentiment of his near and painful death. His noble life had come to an untimely end when he was only forty-four years old, after twenty-nine years of honorable service as a soldier, a navigator, and a man of science—for Churruca was all of these, besides being a noble and cultivated gentlemen. I was still thinking of all these things when, at length, my brain surrendered to fatigue and I fell asleep on the morning of the 23rd, my youthful nature having got the better of my excitement and curiosity. But in my sleep, which was long if not quiet, I was still haunted by nightmare visions, as was natural in my overwrought state of mind, hearing the roar of cannon, the tumult of battle and the thunder of billows; meanwhile I fancied I was serving out ammunition, climbing the rigging, rushing about between decks to encourage the gunners and even standing on the quarter-deck in command of the vessel. I need hardly say that in this curious but visionary battle I routed all the English past, present, or to come, with as much ease as though their ships were made of paper and their cannon-balls were bread-pills. I had a thousand men-of-war under my command, each larger than the *Trinidad*, and they moved before me with as much precision as the toy-ships with which I and my comrades had been wont to play in the puddles of *la Caleta*.

At last, however, all this glory faded away, which, as it was but a dream, is scarcely to be wondered at when we see how even the reality vanishes. It was all over when I opened my eyes and remembered how small a part I had actually played in the stupendous catastrophe I had witnessed. Still—strange to say—even when wide awake I heard cannon and the all-dreadful tumult of war, with shouts and a clatter that told of some great turmoil on deck. I thought I must still be dreaming; I sat up on the sofa on which I had fallen asleep; I listened with all my ears, and certainly a thundering shout of "God save the King" left no doubt in my mind that the*Santa Ana* was fighting once more.

I went out of the cabin and studied the situation. The weather had moderated; to the windward a few battered ships were in sight, and two of them, Englishmen, had opened fire on the *Santa Ana* which was defending herself with the aid of two others, a Frenchman and a Spaniard. I could not understand the sudden change in the aspect of affairs. Were we no longer prisoners of war? I looked up—our flag was flying in the place of the Union Jack. What could have happened?—or rather what was happening? For the drama was in progress.

On the quarter-deck stood a man who, I concluded, must be Alava, and though suffering from several wounds he still had strength enough to command this second action, which seemed likely enough to recover the honor his good ship had lost in the disaster of the first. The officers were encouraging the sailors who were serving those guns that could still be worked, while a detachment kept guard over the English, who had been disarmed and shut up in the lower deck. Their officers who had been our jailers were now become our prisoners.

I understood it all. The brave commander of the *Santa Ana*, Don Ignacio de Alva, seeing that we were within hail of some Spanish ships, which had come out of Cadiz in hope of rescuing some of our captured vessels and to take off the survivors from such as might be sinking, had addressed a stirring harangue to his disheartened crew who responded to his enthusiasm by a supreme effort. By a sudden rush they had disarmed the English who were in charge and hoisted the Spanish flag once more. The *Santa Ana* was free, but she had to fight for life, a more desperate struggle perhaps than the first had been.

This bold attempt—one of the most honorable episodes of the battle of Trafalgar—was made on board a dismasted ship, that had lost her rudder, with half her complement of men killed or wounded, and the other half in a wretched condition both moral and physical. However, the deed once done we had to face the consequences; two Englishmen, considerably battered no doubt, fired on the *Santa Ana*; but the *Asís*, the*Montañes*, and the *Rayo*—three ships that had got off with Gravina on the 21st—opportunely came to the rescue, having come out with a view to recapturing the prizes. The brave cripples rushed into the desperate action, with even more courage perhaps than into the former battle, for their unhealed wounds spurred them to fury and they seemed to fight with greater ardor in proportion as they had less life to lose.

All the incidents of the dreadful 21st were repeated before my eyes; the enthusiasm was tremendous, but the hands were so few that twice the will and energy were needed. This heroic action fills indeed but a brief page in history, for, by the side of the great event which is now known as the Battle of Trafalgar, such details are dwarfed or disappear altogether like a transient spark in a night of gloom and horror.

The next thing that happened to me personally cost me some bitter tears. Not finding my master at once I felt sure he was in some danger, so I went down to the upper gun-deck and there I found him, training a cannon. His trembling hand had snatched the linstock from that of a wounded sailor and he was trying, with the feeble sight of his right eye, to discover to what point in the foe he had better send the missile. When the piece went off he turned to me trembling with satisfaction, and said in a scarcely audible voice:

"Ah ha! Paca need not laugh at me now. We shall return to Cadiz in triumph."

Finally we won the fight. The English perceived the impossibility of recapturing the *Santa Ana* when, besides the three ships already mentioned, two other Frenchmen and a frigate came up to her assistance in the very thick of the fray.

We were free, and by a glorious effort; but at the very moment of victory we saw most clearly the peril we were in, for the *Santa Ana* was now so completely disabled that we could only be towed into Cadiz. The French frigate *Themis* sent a cable on board and put her head to the North, but what could she do with such a deadweight in tow as the *Santa Ana*, which could do little enough to help herself with the ragged sails that still clung to her one remaining mast? The other ships that had supported her—the *Rayo*, the *Montañes*, and the *San Francisco de Asís*, were forced to proceed at full sail to the assistance of the *San Juan* and the *Bahama*, which were also in the hands of the English. There we were, alone, with no help but the frigate that was doing her best for us—a child leading a giant. What would become of us if the enemy—as was very probable—recovering from their repulse, were to fall upon us with renewed energy and reinforcements? However, Providence thought good to protect us; the wind favored us, and our frigate gently leading the way, we found ourselves nearing Cadiz.

Only five leagues from port! What an unspeakable comfort! Our miseries seemed ended; ere long we should set foot on *terra firma*, and though we brought news no doubt of a terrible disaster, we were bringing relief and joy to many faithful souls who were suffering mortal anguish in the belief that those who were returning alive and well had all perished.

The valor of the Spaniards did not avail to rescue any ships but ours, for they were too late and had to return without being able to give chase to the English ships that kept guard over the *San Juan*, the *Bahama*, and the*San Ildefonso*. We were still four leagues from land when we saw them making towards us. A southerly gale was blowing up and it was clear to all on board the *Santa Ana* that if we did not soon get into port we should have a bad time of it. Once more we were filled with anxiety; once more we lost hope almost in sight of safety, and when a few hours more on the cruel sea would have seen us safe and sound in harbor. Night was coming on black and angry; the sky was covered with dark clouds which seemed to lie on the face of the ocean, and the lurid flashes which lighted them up from time to time added terror to the gloom. The sea waxing in fury every instant, as if it were not yet satiated, raved and roared with hungry rage, demanding more and yet more victims. The remnant of the mighty fleet which a short time since had defied its fury combined with that of the foe was not to escape from the wrath of the angry element which, implacable as an ancient god and pitiless to the last, was as cruel to the victor as to the conquered.

I could read the signs of deep depression in the face not only of my master but of the Admiral, Alava, who, in spite of his wounds, still kept on his feet and signalled to the frigate to make all possible speed; but, instead of responding to his very natural haste, the *Themis* prepared to shorten sail so as to be able to keep before the gale. I shared the general dismay and could not help reflecting on the irony with which Fate mocks at our surest calculations and best founded hopes, on the swiftness with which she flings us from happy security to the depth of misery. Here we were, on the wide ocean, that majestic emblem of human life. A gust of wind and it is completely transformed, the light ripple which gently caressed the vessel's side swells into a mountain of water that lashes and beats it, the soft music of the wavelets in a calm turns to a loud, hoarse voice, threatening the frail bark which flings itself into the waters as though its keel were unable to balance it, to rise the next moment buffeted and tossed by the very wave that has lifted it from the abyss. A lovely day ends in a fearful night, or, on the other hand, a radiant moon that illumines an infinite sky and soothes the soul, pales before an angry sun at whose light all nature quakes with dismay.

We had experienced all these viscissitudes, and in addition, those which are the result of the will of man. We had suffered shipwreck in the midst of defeat; after escaping once we had been compelled to fight again, this time with success; and then, when we thought ourselves out of our troubles, when we hailed Cadiz with delight, we were once more at the mercy of the tempest which had treacherously deluded us only to destroy us outright. Such a succession of adverse fortune seemed monstrous—it was like the malignant aberrations of a divinity trying to do all the harm he could devise to us hapless mortals—but it was only the natural course of things at sea, combined with the fortune of war. Given a combination of these two fearful forces and none but an idiot can be astonished at the disasters that must ensue.

Another circumstance contributed to my master's distress of mind, and to mine too, that evening. Since the rescue of the *Santa Ana* Malespina had disappeared. At last, after seeking him everywhere, I discovered him lying in a heap on a sofa in the cabin. I went up to him and saw that he was very pale; I spoke to him but he could not answer. He tried to move but fell back gasping.

"Are you wounded?" I asked. "I will fetch some one to attend to you."

"It is nothing," he said. "Can you get me some water?"

I went at once for my master.

"What is the matter—this wound in your hand?" said he, examining the young officer.

"It is more than that," replied Don Rafael sadly, and he put his hand to his right side close by his sword-belt. And, then, as if the effort of pointing out his wound and speaking those few words had been too much for his weakened frame, he closed his eyes and neither spoke nor moved for some minutes.

"This is serious," said my master anxiously.

"It is more than serious," said a surgeon who had come to examine him. Malespina, deeply depressed by finding himself in so evil a plight, and believing himself past all hope, had not even reported himself as wounded, but had crept away to this corner where he had given himself up to his reflections and memories. He believed that he was killed and he would not have the wound touched. The surgeon assured him that though it was dangerous it need not prove mortal, though he owned that if he did not get into port that night so that he might be properly treated on shore, his life, like that of the rest of the wounded, was in the greatest danger. The*Santa Ana* had lost ninety-seven men killed on the 21st, and a hundred and forty wounded; all the resources of the surgery were exhausted and many indispensable articles were altogether wanting. Malespina's catastrophe was not the only one during the rescue, and it had been the will of Heaven that another man very near and dear to me should share his fate. Marcial had been wounded; though at first his indomitable spirit had kept him up and he hardly felt the pain and depression, before long he submitted to be carried down into the cock-pit, confessing that he was very badly hit. My master sent a surgeon to attend to him, but all he would say was that the wound would have been trifling in a man of five-and-twenty—but Marcial was past sixty.

Meanwhile the *Rayo* passed to leeward and we hailed her. Alava begged her to enquire of the *Themis* whether the captain thought he could get us into Cadiz, and when he roundly said, No, the Admiral asked whether the*Rayo*, which was almost unharmed, expected to get in safely. Her captain thought she might and it was agreed that Gardoqui, who was severely wounded, and several others, should be sent on board her, among them Don Rafael Malespina. Don Alonso obtained that Marcial should also be transferred to her in consideration for his age which greatly aggravated his case, and he sent me, too, in charge of them as page or sick-nurse, desiring me never to lose sight of them for an instant till I saw them safe in the hands of their family, at Cadiz, or even at Vejer. I prepared to obey him, though I tried to persuade my master that he too ought to come on board the*Rayo* for greater safety, but he would not even listen to such a suggestion.

"Fate," he said, "has brought me on board this ship, and in it I will stay till it shall please God to save us or no. Alava is very bad, most of the officers are more or less hurt, and I may be able to be of some service here. I am not one of those who run away from danger; on the contrary, since the defeat of the 21st I have sought it; I long for the moment when my presence may prove to be of some use. If you reach home before me, as I hope you will, tell Paca that a good sailor is the slave of his country, that I am very glad that I came—that I do not regret it—on the contrary. Tell her that she is to be glad, too, when she sees me, and that my comrades would certainly have thought badly of me if I had not come. How could I have done otherwise? You—do you not think that I did well to come?"

"Of course, certainly," I replied, anxious to soothe his agitation, "who doubts it?" For his excitement was so great that the absurdity of asking the opinion of a page-boy had not even occurred to him.

"I see you are a reasonable fellow," he went on, much comforted by my admission. "I see you have a noble and patriotic soul. But Paca never sees anything excepting through her own selfishness, as she has a very odd temper and has taken it into her head that fleets and guns are useless inventions, she cannot understand why I.... In short, I know that she will be furious when she sees me and then—as we have not won the battle, she will say one thing and another—oh! she will drive me mad! However, I will not mind her. You—what do you say? Was I not right to come?"

"Yes, indeed, I think so," I said once more: "You were very right to come. It shows that you are a brave officer."

"Well then go—go to Paca, go and tell her so, and you will see what she will say," he went on more excited than ever. "And tell her that I am safe and sound, and my presence here is indispensable. In point of fact, I was the principal leader in the rescue of the *Santa Ana*. If I had not trained those guns—who knows, who knows? You—what do you think? We may do more yet; if the wind favors us to-morrow morning we may rescue some more ships. Yes sir, for I have a plan in my head.... We shall see, we shall see. And so good bye, my boy. Be careful of what you say to Paca."

"I will not forget," said I. "She shall know that if it had not been for you we should not have recaptured the*Santa Ana*, and that if you are lucky you may still bring a couple of dozen ships into Cadiz."

"A couple of dozen!—no man; that is a large number. Two ships, I say—or perhaps three. In short, I am sure I was right to join the fleet. She will be furious and will drive me mad when I get home again; but I was right, I say—I am sure I was right." With these words he left me and I saw him last sitting in a corner of the cabin. He was praying, but he told his beads with as little display as possible, for he did not choose to be detected at his devotions. My master's last speech had convinced me that he had lost his wits and, seeing him pray, I understood how his enfeebled spirit had struggled in vain to triumph over the exhaustion of age, and now, beaten in strife, turned to God for support and consolation. Doña Francisca was right; for many years my master had been past all service but prayer.

We left the ship according to orders. Don Rafael and Marcial with the rest of the wounded officers were carefully let down into the boats by the strong-armed sailors. The violence of the sea made this a long and difficult business, but at last it was done and two boat loads were pulled off to the *Rayo*. The passage, though short was really frightful; but at last, though there were moments when it seemed to me that we must be swallowed up by the waves, we got alongside of the *Rayo* and with great difficulty clambered on board.

CHAPTER XV.

"OUT of the frying-pan into the fire," said Marcial, when they laid him down on deck. "However, when the captain commands the men must obey. *Rayo* is an unlucky name for this cursed ship. They say she will be in Cadiz by midnight, and I say she won't. We shall see what we shall see."

"What do you say, Marcial? we shall not get in?" I asked in much alarm.

"You, master Gabrielito, you know nothing about such matters," said he.

"But when Don Alonso and the officers of the *Santa Ana* say that the *Rayo* will get in to-night.... She must get in when they say she will."

"Do not you know, you little landlubber, that the gentlemen of the quarter-deck are far more often mistaken than we are in the fo'castle? If not, what was the admiral of the fleet about?—*Mr. Corneta*—devil take him! You see he had not brains enough to work a fleet. Do you suppose that if *Mr. Corneta* had asked my advice we should have lost the battle?"

"And you think we shall not get into Cadiz?"

"I say this old ship is as heavy as lead itself and not to be trusted either. She rides the sea badly and will not answer her helm. Why, she is as lop-sided and crippled as I am! If you try to put her to port off she goes to starboard."

In point of fact the *Rayo* was considered by all as bad a ship as ever sailed. But in spite of that, in spite of her advanced age—for she had been afloat nearly fifty-six years—as she was still sound she did not seem to be in any danger though the gale increased in fury every minute, for we were almost close to port. At any rate, did it not stand to reason that the *Santa Ana* was in greater jeopardy, dismasted and rudderless, in tow of a frigate?

Marcial was carried to the cock-pit and Malespina to the captain's cabin. When we had settled him there, with the rest of the wounded officers, I suddenly heard a voice that was familiar to me though for the moment I could not identify it with any one I knew. However, on going up to the group whence the stentorian accents proceeded, drowning every other voice, what was my surprise at recognizing Don José Maria Malespina! I ran to tell him that his son was on board, and the worthy parent at once broke off the string of rodomontade that he was pouring forth and flew to the wounded man. His delight was great at finding him alive; he had come out of Cadiz because he could no longer endure the suspense and he must know what had become of his boy at any cost.

"Why your wound is a mere trifle," he said, embracing his son. "A mere scratch! But you are not used to wounds; you are quite a mollycoddle, Rafael. Oh, if only you had been old enough to go with me to fight in Rousillon! You would have learnt there what wounds are—something like wounds! Do you know a ball hit me in the fleshy part of the arm, ran up to my shoulder and then right round the shoulder blade and out by the belt. A most extraordinary case, that was. But in three days I was all right again and commanding the artillery at Bellegarde." He went on to give the following account of his presence on board the *Rayo*.

"We knew the issue of the battle at Cadiz, by the evening of the 21st. I tell you, gentlemen—no one would listen to me when I talked of reforming our artillery and you see the consequences. Well, as soon as I knew the worst and had learnt that Gravina had come in with a few ships I went to see if the *San Juan Nepomuceno*, on board which you were, was one of them; but they told me she had been captured. You cannot imagine my anxiety; I could hardly doubt that you were dead, particularly when I heard how many had been killed on board your ship. However, I am one of those men who must follow a matter up to the end, and knowing that some of the ships in port were preparing to put out to sea in hope of picking up derelicts and rescuing captured vessels, I determined to set out without a moment's delay and sail in one of them. I explained my wishes to Solano and then to the Admiral in command, my old friend Escaño, and after some hesitation they allowed me on board. I embarked this morning, and enquired of every one in the *Rayo* for some news of you and of the *San Juan*, but I could get no comfort; nay, quite the contrary, for I heard that Churruca was killed and that his ship, after a glorious defence, had struck to the enemy. You may fancy my anxiety. How far was I from supposing this morning, when we rescued the *Santa Ana*, that you were on board! If I had but known it for certain I would have redoubled my efforts in the orders I issued—by the kind permission of these gentlemen; Alava's ship should have been free in two minutes."

The officers who were standing round us looked at each other with a shrug as they heard Don José's last audacious falsehood. I could gather from their smiles and winks that he had afforded them much diversion all day with his vainglorious fictions, for the worthy gentleman could put no bridle on his indefatigable tongue, even under the most critical and painful circumstances.

The surgeon now said that his patients ought to be left to rest and that there must be no conversation in their presence, particularly no reference to the recent disaster. Don José Maria, however, contradicted him flatly, saying that it was good to keep their spirits up by talking to them.

"In the war in Rousillon," he added, "those who were badly wounded—and I was several times—sent for the soldiers to dance and play the guitar in the infirmary; and I am very certain that this treatment did more to cure us than all your plasters and dosing."

"Yes, and in the wars with the French Republic," said an Andalusian officer who wanted to trump Don José's trick, "it was a regular thing that a *corps de ballet* should be attached to the ambulance corps, and an opera company as well. It left the surgeons and apothecaries nothing to do, for a few songs, and a short course of pirouettes and capers set them to rights again, as good as new."

"Come, come!" cried Malespina, "this is too much. You do not mean to say that music and dancing can heal a wound?"

"You said so."

"Yes, but that was only once and it is not likely to occur again. Perhaps you think it not unlikely that we may have such another war as that in Rousillon? The most bloody, the best conducted, the most splendidly planned war since the days of Epaminondas! Certainly not. Every thing about it was exceptional; and you may believe me when I say it, for I was in the thick of it, from the Introit to the last blessing. It is to my experience there that I owe my knowledge of artillery—did you never hear me spoken of? I am sure you must recognize my name. Well, you must know that I have in my head a magnificent scheme, and if one of these days it is only realized we shall hear of no more disasters like that of the 21st. Yes, gentlemen," he said, looking round at the three or four officers who were listening, with consummate gravity and conceit: "Something must be done for the country. Something must be devised—something stupendous, to recoup us at once for our losses and secure victory to our fleets for ever and ever, Amen."

"Let us hear, Don José," said one of the audience. "Explain your scheme to us."

"Well, I am devoting my mind to the construction of 300-pounders."

"Three-hundred-pounders!" cried the officers with shouts of laughter and derision. "Why, the largest we carry is a 36-pounder."

"Mere toys! Just imagine the ruin that would be dealt by a 300-pound gun fired into the enemy's fleet," said Malespina. "But what the devil is that?" he added putting out his hand to keep himself from falling, for the*Rayo* rolled so heavily that it was very difficult for any one to keep his feet.

"The gale is stiffening and I doubt our getting into Cadiz to-night," said one of the officers moving away. The worthy man had now but two listeners, but he proceeded with his mendacious harangue all the same.

"The first thing must be to build a ship from 95 to 100 yards in length."

"The Devil you will! That would be a snug little craft with a vengeance!" said one of the officers. "A hundred yards! Why the *Trinidad*—God rest her—was but seventy and everybody thought her too long. She did not sail well you know and was very difficult to handle."

"It does not take much to astonish you I see," Malespina went on. "What is a hundred yards? Why, much larger ships than that might be built. And you must know that I would build her of iron."

"Of iron!" and his listeners went into fits of laughter.

"Yes sir, of iron. Perhaps you are not familiar with the science of hydrostatics? There can be no difficulty in building an iron ship of 7000 tons."

"And the *Trinidad* was of 4000! and that was too big. But do you not see that in order to move such a monster you would want such gigantic tackle that no human power could work it?"

"Not a bit of it!—Besides, my good sir, who told you that I was so stupid as to think that I could trust to the wind alone to propel my ship? If you knew—I have an idea.—But I do not care to explain my scheme to you for you would not understand me."

At this point of his discourse Don José was so severely shaken that he fell on all fours. But not even this could stop his tongue. Another of his audience walked away, leaving only one who had to listen and to keep up the conversation.

"What a pitching and tossing," said the old man. "I should not wonder if we were driven on shore.—Well, as I was saying—I should move my monster by an invention of my own—can you guess what?—By steam. To this end I should construct a peculiar kind of machine in which the steam, expanding and contracting alternately inside two cylinders, would put certain wheels in motion; then...."

The officer would listen no longer, and though he had no commission on board the ship nor any fixed duty, being one of the rescued, he went off to assist in working the ship, which was hard enough to do as the tempest increased. Malespina was left alone with me for an audience, and at first I thought he would certainly cease talking, not thinking me capable of sustaining the conversation. But, for my sins, it would seem that he credited me with more merit than I could lay claim to, for he turned to me and went on:

"You understand what I mean? Seven thousand tons, and steam working two wheels, and then...."

"Yes señor, I understand you perfectly," I replied, to see if he would be silent, for I did not care to hear him, nor did the violent motion of the ship which threatened us with immediate peril at all incline my mind to dissertations on the aggrandizement of the Spanish navy.

"I see," he continued, "that you know how to appreciate me and value my inventions. You see at once that such a ship as I describe would be invincible, and as available for attack as for defence. With four or five discharges it could rout thirty of the enemy's ships."

"Would not their cannon do it some damage?" I asked timidly, and speaking out of civility rather than from any interest I felt in the matter.

"Your observation is a very shrewd one my little gentleman, and proves that you really appreciate my great invention. But to avoid injury from the enemy's guns I should cover my ship with thick plates of steel. I should put on it a breastplate, in fact, such as warriors wore of old. With this protection it could attack the foe, while their projectiles would have no more effect on its sides than a broadside of bread-pills flung by a child. It is a wonderful idea I can tell you, this notion of mine. Just fancy our navy with two or three ships of this kind! What would become of the English fleet then, in spite of its Nelsons and Collingwoods?"

"But they might make such ships themselves," I returned eagerly and feeling the force of this argument. "The English would do the same, and then the conditions of the battle would be equal again."

Don José was quite dumbfounded by this suggestion and for a minute did not know what to say, but his inexhaustible imagination did not desert him for long and he answered, but somewhat crossly:

"And who said, impertinent boy, that I should be such a fool as to divulge the secret so that the English might learn it? These ships would be constructed in perfect secrecy without a word being whispered even to any one. Suppose a fresh war were to break out. We should defy the English: 'Come on, gentlemen,' we should say, 'we are ready, quite ready.' The common ships would put out to sea and begin the action when lo and behold! out come two or three of these iron monsters into the thick of the fight, vomiting steam and smoke and turning here and there without troubling themselves about the wind; they go wherever they are wanted, splintering the wooden sides of the enemy's ships by the blows of their sharp bows, and then with a broadside or two.... It would all be over in a quarter of an hour."

I did not care to raise any further difficulties for the conviction that our vessel was in the greatest danger quite kept my mind from dwelling on ideas so inappropriate to our critical situation. In fact, I never thought again of the monster ship of the old man's fancy till thirty years after when we first heard of the application of steam to purposes of navigation; and again when, half-way through the century, our fine frigate the *Numancia* actually realized the extravagant dreams of the braggart of Trafalgar.

Half a century later I remembered Don José Maria Malespina and I said: "He seemed to us a bombastic liar; but conceptions which are extravagant in one place and time, when born in due season become marvellous realities! And since living to see this particular instance of the fact, I have ceased to think any Utopia impossible, and the greatest visionaries seem to me possible men of genius."

I left Don José in the cabin and ascended the companion-way, to see what was going forward, and as soon as I was on deck I understood the dangerous situation of the *Rayo*. The gale not only prevented her getting into Cadiz, but was driving her towards the coast where she must inevitably be wrecked on the rocky shore. Melancholy as was the fate of the abandoned *Santa Ana* it could not be more desperate than ours. I looked with dismay into the faces of the officers and crew to see if I could read hope in any one of them, but despair was written in all. I glanced at the sky—it was black and awful; I gazed at the sea—it was raging with fury. God was our only hope—and He had shown us no mercy since the fatal 21st!

The *Rayo* was running northwards. I could understand, from what I heard the men about me saying, that we were driving past the reef of Marajotes—past Hazte Afuera—Juan Bola—Torregorda, and at last past the entrance to Cadiz. In vain was every effort made to put her head round to enter the bay. The old ship, like a frightened horse, refused to obey; the wind and waves carried her on, due north, with irresistible fury and science could do nothing to prevent it.

We flew past the bay, and could make out to our right, Rota, Punta Candor, Punta de Meca, Regla and Chipiona. There was not a doubt that the *Rayo* must be driven on shore, close to the mouth of the Guadalquivir. I need hardly say that the sails were close reefed and that as this proved insufficient in such a furious tempest the topmasts were lowered; at last it was even thought necessary to cut away the masts to prevent her from foundering. In great storms a ship has to humble herself, to shrink from a stately tree to a lowly plant; and as her masts will no more yield than the branches of an oak, she is under the sad necessity of seeing them amputated and losing her limbs to save her life.

The loss of the ship was now inevitable. The main and mizzen-masts were cut through and sent overboard, and our only hope was that we might be able to cast anchor near the coast. The anchors were got ready and the chains and cables strengthened. We were now running right on shore, and two cannon were fired as a signal that we wanted help; for as we could clearly distinguish fires we kept up our hope that there must be some one to come to our rescue. Some were of opinion that a Spanish or English ship had already been wrecked here and that the fires we saw had been lighted by the destitute crew. Our anxiety increased every instant, and as for myself I firmly believed that I was face to face with a cruel death. I paid no attention to what was doing on board, being much too agitated to think of anything but my end, which seemed inevitable. If the vessel ran on a rock, what man could swim through the breakers that still divided us from the coast? The most dangerous spot in a storm is just where the waves are hurled revolving against the shore, as if they were trying to scoop it out and drag away whole tracts of earth into the gulfs below. The blow of a wave as it dashes forward and its gluttonous fury as it rushes back again, is such as no human strength can stand against.

At last, after some hours of mortal anguish, the keel of the *Rayo* came upon a sand bank and there she stuck. The hull and the remaining masts shivered as she struck; she seemed to be trying to cut her way through the obstacle; but it was too much for her; after heaving violently for a few moments, her stern went slowly down with fearful creaks and groans, and she remained steady. All was over now, nothing remained to be done but to save ourselves by getting across the tract of sea which separated us from the land. This seemed almost impossible in the boats we had on board; our best hope was that they might send us help from the shore, for it was evident that the crew of a lately wrecked vessel was encamped there, and one of the government cutters, which had been placed on the coast by the naval authorities for service in such cases, must surely be in the neighborhood. The *Rayo* fired again and again, and we watched with desperate impatience, for if some succour did not reach us soon we must all go down in the ship. The hapless crippled mass whose timbers had parted as she struck seemed likely to hasten her end by the violence of her throes, and the moment could not be far off when her ribs must fall asunder and we should be left at the mercy of the waves with nothing to cling to but the floating wreck.

Those on shore could do nothing for us, but by God's mercy our signal guns were heard by a sloop which had put to sea at Chipiona and which now approached us, keeping, however, at a respectful distance. As soon as her broad mainsail came in view we knew that we were saved, and the captain of the *Rayo* gave orders to insure our all getting on board without confusion in such imminent peril. My first idea, when I saw the boats being got out, was to run to the two men who most interested me on board: Marcial and young Malespina, both wounded, though Marcial's was not a serious case. I found the young officer in a very bad way and saying to the men around him: "I will not be moved—leave me to die here."

Marcial had crawled up on deck and was lying on the planks so utterly prostrate and indifferent that I was really terrified at his appearance. He looked up as I went near him and taking my hand said in piteous tones: "Gabrielillo, do not forsake me!"

"To land!" I cried trying to encourage him, "we are all going on shore." But he only shook his head sadly as if he foresaw some immediate disaster.

I tried to help him up, but after the first effort he let himself drop as if he were dead. "I cannot," he said at length. The bandages had come off his wound and in the confusion of our desperate situation no one had thought of applying fresh ones. I dressed it as well as I could, comforting him all the time with hopeful words; I even went so far as to laugh at his appearance to see if that would rouse him. But the poor old man could not smile; he let his head droop gloomily on his breast, as insensible to a jest as he was to consolation. Thinking only of him, I did not observe that the boats were putting off. Among the first to be put on board were Don José Malespina and his son; my first impulse had been to follow them in obedience to my master's orders, but the sight of the wounded sailor was too much for me. Malespina could not need me, while Marcial was almost a dead man and still clung to my hand with his cold fingers, saying again and again: "Gabrielillo, do not leave me."

The boats labored hard through the breakers, but notwithstanding, when once the wounded had been moved the embarkation went forward rapidly, the sailors flinging themselves in by a rope or taking a flying leap. Several jumped into the water and saved themselves by swimming. It flashed through my mind as a terrible problem, by which of these means I could escape with my life, and there was no time to lose for the *Rayo* was breaking up; the after-part was all under water and the cracking of the beams and timbers, which were in many places half rotten, warned me that the huge hulk would soon cease to exist. Every one was rushing to the boats, and the sloop, which kept at a safe distance, very skilfully handled so as to avoid shipping water, took them all on board. The empty boats came back at once and were filled again in no time.

Seeing the helpless state in which Marcial was lying I turned, half-choked with tears, to some sailors and implored them to pick him up and carry him to a boat; but it was as much as they could do to save themselves. In my desperation I tried to lift him and drag him to the ship's side, but my small strength was hardly enough to raise his helpless arms. I ran about the deck, seeking some charitable soul; and some seemed on the point of yielding to my entreaties, but their own pressing danger choked their kind impulses. To understand such cold-blooded cruelty you must have gone through such a scene of horror; every feeling of humanity vanishes before the stronger instinct of self-preservation which becomes a perfect possession, and sometimes reduces man to the level of a wild beast.

"Oh the wretches! they will do nothing to save you, Marcial," I cried in bitter anguish.

"Let them be," he said. "They are the same at sea as on shore. But you child, be off, run, or they will leave you behind." I do not know which seemed to me the most horrible alternative—to remain on board with the certainty of death, or to go and leave the miserable man alone. At length, however, natural instinct proved the stronger and I took a few steps towards the ship's side; but I turned back to embrace the poor old man once more and then I ran as fast as I could to the spot where the last men were getting into the boat. There were but four, and when I reached the spot I saw that all four had jumped into the sea and were swimming to meet the boat which was still a few yards distant.

"Take me!" I shrieked, seeing that they were leaving me behind. "I am coming too!—Take me too!"

I shouted with all my strength but they either did not hear or did not heed me. Dark as it was, I could make out the boat and even knew when they were getting into it, though I could hardly say that I saw them. I was on the point of flinging myself overboard to take my chance of reaching the boat when, at that very moment, it had vanished—there was nothing to be seen but the black waste of waters. Every hope of escape had vanished with it. I looked round in despair—nothing was visible but the waves preying on what was left of the ship; not a star in the sky, not a spark on shore—the sloop had sailed away.

Beneath my feet, which I stamped with rage and anguish, the hull of the *Rayo* was going to pieces, nothing remained indeed but the bows, and the deck was covered with wreck; I was actually standing on a sort of raft which threatened every moment to float away at the mercy of the waves.

I flew back to Marcial. "They have left me, they have left us!" I cried. The old man sat up with great difficulty, leaning on one hand and his dim eyes scanned the scene and the darkness around us.

"Nothing...." he said. "Nothing to be seen; no boats, no land, no lights, no beach.—They are not coming back!"

As he spoke a tremendous crash was heard beneath our feet in the depths of the hold under the bows, long since full of water; the deck gave a great lurch and we were obliged to clutch at a capstan to save ourselves from falling into the sea. We could not stand up; the last remains of the *Rayo* were on the point of being engulfed. Still, hope never forsakes us; and I, at any rate, consoled myself with the belief that things might remain as they were now till day-break and with observing that the fore-mast had not yet gone overboard. I looked up at the tall mast, round which some tatters of sails and ends of ropes still flapped in the wind, and which stood like a dishevelled giant pointing heavenward and imploring mercy with the persistency of despair; and I fully determined that if the rest of the hull sank under water I would climb it for a chance of life.

Marcial laid himself down on the deck.

"There is no hope, Gabrielillo," he said. "They have no idea of coming back, nor could they if they tried in such a sea. Well, since it is God's will, we must both die where we are. For me, it matters not; I am an old man, and of no use for any earthly thing.—But you, you are a mere child and you...." But here his voice broke with emotion. "You," he went on, "have no sins to answer for, you are but a child. But I.... Still, when a man dies like this—what shall I say—like a dog or a cat—there is no need, I have heard, for the priest to give him absolution—all that is needed is that he should make his peace himself with God. Have you not heard that said?"

I do not know what answer I made; I believe I said nothing, but only cried miserably.

"Keep your heart up, Gabrielillo," he went on. "A man must be a man, and it is at a time like this that you get to know the stuff you are made of. You have no sins to answer for, but I have. They say that when a man is dying and there is no priest for him to confess to, he ought to tell whatever he has on his conscience to any one who will listen to him. Well, I will confess to you Gabrielillo; I will tell you all my sins, and I expect God will hear me through you and then he will forgive me."

Dumb with terror and awe at the solemnity of his address, I threw my arms round the old man who went on speaking.

"Well, I say, I have always been a Christian, a Catholic, Apostolic Roman; and that I always was and still am devoted to the Holy Virgin del Cármen, to whom I pray for help at this very minute; and I say too that though for twenty years I have never been to confession nor received the sacrament, it has not been my fault, but that of this cursed service, and because one always puts it off from one Sunday to the next. But it is a trouble to me now that I failed to do it, and I declare and swear that I pray God and the Virgin and all the Saints to punish me if it was my fault; for this year, if I have never been to confession or communion, it was all because of those cursed English that forced me to go to sea again just when I really meant to make it up with the Church. I never stole so much as a pin's head, and I never told a lie, except for the fun of it now and then. I repent of the thrashings I gave my wife thirty years ago—though I think she rightly deserved them, for her temper was more venomous than a scorpion's sting. I never failed to obey the captain's order in the least thing; I hate no one on earth but the 'great-coats,' and I should have liked to see them made mince-meat of. However, they say we are all the children of the same God, so I forgive them, and I forgive the French who brought us into this war. I will say no more, for I believe I am going—full sail. I love God and my mind is easy. Gabriel hold me tight and stick close to me; you have no sins to answer for, you will go straight away to Heaven to pipe tunes with the angels. Ah well, it is better to die so, at your age, than to stay below in this wicked world. Keep up your courage, boy, till the end. The sea is rising and the *Rayo* will soon be gone. Death by drowning is an easy one; do not be frightened—stick close to me. In less than no time we shall be out of it all; I answering to God for all my shortcomings, and you as happy as a fairy, dancing through the star-paved heavens—and they tell us happiness never comes to an end up there because it is eternal, or, as they say, to-morrow and to-morrow and to-morrow, world without end...."

He could say no more. I clung passionately to the poor mutilated body. A tremendous sea swept over the bows and I felt the water dash against my shoulder. I shut my eyes and fixed my thoughts on God. Then I lost consciousness and knew no more.

CHAPTER XVI.

WHEN, I know not how long after, the idea of life dawned once more on my darkened spirit, I was conscious only of being miserably cold; indeed, this was the only fact that made me aware of my own existence, for I remembered nothing whatever of all that had happened and had not the slightest idea of where I was. When my mind began to get clearer and my senses recovered their functions I found that I was lying on the beach; some men were standing round me and watching me with interest. The first thing I heard was: "Poor little fellow!—he is coming round."

By degrees I recovered my wits and, with them, my recollection of past events. My first thought was for Marcial, and I believe that the first words I spoke were an enquiry for him. But no one could tell me anything about him; I recognized some of the crew of the *Rayo* among the men on the beach and asked them where he was; they were all agreed that he must have perished. Then I wanted to know how I had been saved, but they would tell me nothing about that either. They gave me some liquor to drink, I know not what, and carried me to a neighboring hut, where, warmed by a good fire and cared for by an old woman, I soon felt quite well, though still rather weak. Meanwhile I learnt that another cutter had put out to reconnoitre the wreck of the *Rayo* and that of a French ship which had met with the same fate, and that they had picked me up still clinging to Marcial; they found that I could be saved but my companion was dead. I learnt too that a number of poor wretches had been drowned in trying to reach the coast. Then I wanted to know what had become of Malespina, but no one knew anything either of him or of his father. I enquired about the *Santa Ana* which, it appeared, had reached Cadiz in safety, so I determined to set out forthwith to join my master. We were at some distance from Cadiz, on the coast to the north of the Guadalquivir, I wanted therefore to start at once to make so long a journey. I took two days' rest to recover my strength, and then set out for Sanlúcar, in the company of a sailor who was going the same way. We crossed the river on the morning of the 27th and then continued our walk, keeping along the coast. As my companion was a jolly, friendly fellow the journey was as pleasant as I could expect in the frame of mind I was in, grieved at Marcial's death and depressed by the scenes I had so lately witnessed. As we walked on we discussed the battle and the shipwrecks that had ensued.

"A very good sailor was that old cripple," said my companion. "But what possessed him to go to sea again with more than sixty years on his shoulders? It served him right to come to a bad end."

"He was a brave seaman," said I, "and had such a passion for fighting that even his infirmities could not keep him quiet when he had made up his mind to join the fleet."

"Well, I have had enough of it for my part," said the sailor. "I do not want to see any more fighting at sea. The King pays us badly, and then, if you are maimed or crippled—good-bye to you—I know nothing about you—I never set eyes on you in my life.—Perhaps you don't believe me when I tell you the King pays his men so badly? But I can tell you this: most of the officers in command of the ships that went into action on the 21st had seen no pay for months. Only last year there was a navy captain at Cadiz who went as waiter in an inn because he had no other way of keeping himself or his children. His friends found him out though he tried to conceal his misery, and they succeeded at last in getting him out of his degrading position. Such things do not happen in any other country in the world; and then we are horrified at finding ourselves beaten by the English! As to the arsenals, I will say nothing about them; they are empty and it is of no use to hope for money from Madrid—not a *cuarto* comes this way. All the King's revenues are spent in paying the court officials, and chief among them the Prince of Peace; who gets 40,000 dollars as Counsellor of the Realm, Secretary of State, Captain-General, and Sergeant-Major of the Guards.—No, say I, I have had enough of serving the King. I am going home to my wife and children, for I have served my time and in a few days they must give me my papers."

"But you have nothing to complain of friend," said I, "since you were on board the *Rayo* which hardly did any fighting."

"I was not in the *Rayo* but in the *Bahama*, one of the ships that fought hardest and longest."

"She was taken and her captain killed, if I remember rightly."

"Aye, so it was," he said. "I could cry over it when I think of him—Don Dionisio Alcalá Galiano, the bravest seaman in the fleet. Well, he was a stern commander; he never overlooked the smallest fault, and yet his very severity made us love him all the more, for a captain who is feared for his severity—if his severity is unfailingly just—inspires respect and wins the affection of his men. I can honestly say that a more noble and generous gentleman than Don Dionisio Alcalá Galiano was never born. And when he wanted to do a civility to his friends he did not do it by halves; once, out in Havana he spent ten thousand dollars on a supper he gave on board ship."

"He was a first-rate seaman too, I have heard."

"Ah, that he was. And he was more learned than Merlin and all the Fathers of the Church. He made no end of maps, and discovered Lord knows how many countries out there, where it is as hot as hell itself! And then they send men like these out to fight and to be killed like a parcel of cabin-boys. I will just tell you what happened on board the *Bahama*. As soon as the fighting began Don Dionisio Alcalá Galiano knew we must be beaten on account of that infernal trick of turning the ships round—we were in the reserve and had been in the rear. Nelson, who was certainly no fool, looked along our line, and he said: 'If we cut them through at two separate points, and keep them between two fires, hardly a ship will escape me.' And so he did, blast him; and as our line was so long the head could never help the tail. He fought us in detachments, attacking us in two wedge-shaped columns which, as I have heard say, were the tactics adopted by the great Moorish general, Alexander the Great, and now used by Napoleon. It is very certain, at any rate, that they got round us and cut us in three, and fought us ship to ship in such a manner that we could not support or help each other; every Spaniard had to deal with three or four Englishmen.

"Well, so you see the *Bahama* was one of the first to be under fire. Galiano reviewed the crew at noon, went round the gun-decks, and made us a speech in which he said: 'Gentlemen, you all know that our flag is nailed to the mast.' Yes, we all knew the sort of man our Captain was, and we were not at all surprised to hear it. Then he turned to the captain of the marines, Don Alonso Butron, 'I charge you to defend it,' he said. 'No Galiano ever surrenders and no Butron should either.'

"'What a pity it is,' said I, 'that such men should not have had a leader worthy of such courage, since they could not themselves conduct the fleet.'

"Aye, it is a pity, and you shall hear what happened. The battle began, and you know something of what it was like if you were on board the *Trinidad*. The ships riddled us with broadsides to port and starboard. The wounded fell like flies from the very first, and the captain first had a bad bruise on his foot and then a splinter struck his head and hurt him badly. But do you think he would give in, or submit to be plastered with ointment? Not a bit of it; he staid on the quarter-deck, just as if nothing had happened, though many a man he loved truly fell close to him never to stand up again. Alcalá Galiano gave his orders and directed his guns as if we had been firing a salute at a review. A spent ball knocked his telescope out of his hand and that made him laugh. I fancy I can see him now; the blood from his wound stained his uniform and his hands and he cared no more than if it had been drops of salt-water splashed up from the sea. He was a man of great spirit and a hasty temper; he shouted out his orders so positively that if we had not obeyed them because it was our duty, we should have done so out of sheer alarm.—But suddenly it was all over with him.—He was struck in the head by a shot and instantly killed.

"The fight was not at an end, but all our heart in it was gone. When our beloved captain fell the officers covered his body that we men might not see it, but we all knew at once what had happened, and after a short and desperate struggle for the honor of our flag, the *Bahama* surrendered to the English who carried her off to Gibraltar if she did not go to the bottom on the way, as I rather suspect she did."

After giving this history and telling me how he had been transferred from the *Bahama* to the *Santa Ana*, my companion sighed deeply and was silent for some time. However, as the way was long and dull I tried to reopen the conversation and I began telling him what I myself had seen, and how I had at last been put on board the *Rayo* with young Malespina.

"Ah!" said he. "Was he a young artillery officer who was transferred to the sloop to be taken to shore on the night of the 23d?"

"The very same," said I. "But no one has been able to tell me for certain what became of him."

"He was one of a party in the second boat which could not get to shore; some of those who were whole and strong contrived to escape, and among them that young officer's father; but all the wounded were drowned, as you may easily suppose, as the poor souls of course could not swim to land."

I was shocked to hear of Don Rafael's death, and the thought of the grief it would be to my hapless and adored little mistress quite overcame me, choking every mean and jealous feeling.

"What a dreadful thing!" I exclaimed. "And is it my misfortune to have to carry the news to his sorrowing friends? But, tell me, are you certain of the facts?"

"I saw his father with my own eyes, lamenting bitterly and telling all the details of the catastrophe with such distress it was enough to break your heart. From what he said he seemed to have saved everybody on board the boat, and he declared that if he had saved his son it would have been at the cost of the lives of all the others, so he chose, on the whole, to preserve the lives of the greatest number, even in sacrificing that of his son, and he did so. He must be a singularly humane man, and wonderfully brave and dexterous." But I was so deeply distressed that I could not discuss the subject. Marcial dead, Malespina dead! What terrible news to take home to my master's house. For a moment my mind was almost made up not to return to Cadiz; I would leave it to chance or to public rumor to carry the report to the sad hearts that were waiting in such painful suspense. However, I was bound to present myself before Don Alonso and give him some account of my proceedings.

At length we reached Rota and there embarked for Cadiz. It is impossible to describe the commotion produced by the report of the disaster to our fleet. News of the details had come in by degrees, and by this time the fate of most of our ships was known, though what had become of many men and even whole crews had not been ascertained. The streets were full of distressing scenes at every turn, where some one who had come off scot-free stood telling off the deaths he knew of, and the names of those who would be seen no more. The populace crowded down to the quays to see the wounded as they came on shore, hoping to recognize a father, husband, son or brother. There were episodes of frantic joy mingled with shrieks of dismay and bitter cries of disappointment. Too often were hopes deceived and fears confirmed, and the losers in this fearful lottery were far more numerous than the winners. The bodies thrown up on the shore put an end to the suspense of many families, while others still hoped to find those they had lost among the prisoners taken to Gibraltar.

To the honor of Cadiz be it said never did a community devote itself with greater willingness to the care of the wounded, making no distinctions between friends and foes but hoisting the standard, as it were, of universal and comprehensive charity. Collingwood, in his narrative, does justice to this generosity on the part of my fellow-countrymen. The magnitude of the disaster had deadened all resentment, but is it not sad to reflect that it is only in misfortune that men are truly brothers?

In Cadiz I saw collected in the harbor the whole results of the conflict which previously, as an actor in it, I had only partially understood, since the length of the line and the manœuvring of the vessels would not allow me to see everything that happened. As I now learnt—besides the *Trinidad*—the *Argonauta*, 92 guns, Captain Don Antonio Pareja, and the *San Augustin*, 80 guns, Don Felipe Cagigal, had been sunk. Gravina had got back into Cadiz with the *Príncipe de Astúrias*, as well as the *Montañes*, 80 guns, commanded by Alcedo, who with his second officer Castaños, had been killed; the *San Justo*, 76 guns, Captain Don Miguel Gaston; the *San Leandro*, 74, Captain Don José Quevedo; the *San Francisco*, 74, Don Luis Flores; and the *Rayo*, 100, commanded by Macdonell. Four of these had gone out again on the 23d to recapture the vessels making for Gibraltar; and of these, two, the *San Francisco* and the *Rayo* were wrecked on the coast. So, too, was the*Monarca*, 74 guns, under Argumosa, and the *Neptuno*, 80 guns; and her heroic commander, Don Cayetano Valdés, who had previously distinguished himself at Cape St. Vincent, narrowly escaped with his life. The*Bahama* had surrendered but went to pieces before she could be got into Gibraltar; the *San Ildefonso*, 74 guns, Captain Vargas, was taken to England, while the *San Juan Nepomuceno* was left for many years at Gibraltar, where she was regarded as an object of veneration and curiosity. The *Santa Ana* had come safely into Cadiz the very night we were taken off her.

The English too lost some fine ships, and not a few of their gallant officers shared Nelson's glorious fate.

With regard to the French it need not be said that they had suffered as severely as we had. With the exception of the four ships that withdrew under Dumanoir without showing fight—a stain which the Imperial navy could not for a long time wipe out—our allies behaved splendidly. Villeneuve, only caring to efface in one day the remembrance of all his mistakes, fought desperately to the last and was carried off a prisoner to Gibraltar. Many of their officers were taken with him, and very many were killed. Their vessels shared all our risks and dangers; some got off with Gravina, some were taken and several were wrecked on the coast. The *Achille* blew up, as I have said, in the midst of the action.

But in spite of all these disasters, Spain had paid dearer for the war than her haughty ally. France had lost the flower of her navy indeed, but at that very time Napoleon had won a glorious victory on land. His army had marched with wonderful rapidity from the shores of the English Channel across Europe, and was carrying out his colossal schemes in the campaign against Austria. It was on the 20th of October, the day before Trafalgar, that Napoleon, at the camp at Ulm, looked on as the Austrian troops marched past, while their officers delivered up their swords; only two months later, on the 2d of December, he won, on the field of Austerlitz, the greatest of his many victories.

These triumphs consoled France for the defeat of Trafalgar; Napoleon silenced the newspapers, forbidding them to discuss the matter; and when the victory of his implacable enemies, the English, was reported to him he simply shrugged his shoulders and said: "I cannot be everywhere at once."

CHAPTER XVII.

I POSTPONED the fatal hour when I must face my master as long as possible, but at last my destitute condition, without money and without a home, brought me to the point. As I went to the house of Doña Flora my heart beat so violently that I had to stop for breath at every step. The terrible shock I was about to give the family by announcing young Malespina's death weighed so terribly on my soul that I could not have felt more crushed and guilty if I had myself been the occasion of it. At last however, I went in. My presence in the court-yard caused an immense sensation. I heard heavy steps hurrying along the upper galleries and I had not been able to speak a word before I felt myself in a close embrace. I at once recognized Doña Flora, with more paint on her face than if it had been a picture, but seriously discomposed in effect by the good old soul's delight at seeing me once more. But all the fond names she lavished on me—her dear boy, her pet, her little angel—could not make me smile. I went up stairs, every one was in a bustle of excitement. I heard my master exclaim: "Oh! thank God! he is safe." I went into the drawing-room, and there it was Doña Francisca who came forward, asking with mortal anxiety—"And Don Rafael?—Where is Don Rafael?"

But for some minutes I could not speak; my voice failed me, I had not courage to tell the fatal news. They questioned me eagerly and I saw Doña Rosita come in from an adjoining room, pale, heavy-eyed, and altered by the anguish she had gone through. At the sight of my young mistress I burst into tears, and there was then no need for words. Rosita gave a terrible cry and fell senseless; her father and mother flew to her side, smothering their own grief, while Doña Flora melted into tears and took me aside to assure herself that I, at any rate, had returned whole in every part.

"Tell me," she said, "how did he come by his death? I felt sure of it—I told Paca so; but she would only say her prayers and believed that so she could save him. As if God could be troubled with such matters.—And you are safe and sound—what a comfort! No damage anywhere?"

It is impossible to describe the consternation of the whole household. For a quarter of an hour nothing was to be heard but crying, lamentation, and sobbing; for Malespina's mother had come to Cadiz and was also in the house. But how mysterious are the ways of Providence in working out its ends! About a quarter of an hour, as I say, had elapsed since I had told them the news when a loud assertive voice fell on my ear. It was that of Don José Maria, shouting in the court-yard, calling his wife, Don Alonso, and Rosita. That which first struck me was that his tones seemed just as strident and cheerful as ever, which I thought very indecorous after the misfortune that had happened. We all ran to meet him, and I stared to see him radiant and smiling.

"But poor Don Rafael...." said my master.

"Safe and sound," replied Don José. "That is to say not exactly sound, but out of danger, for his wound is nothing to be anxious about. The fool of a surgeon said he would die, but I knew better. What do I care for surgeons! I cured him, gentlemen—I, I myself, by a new treatment which no one knows of but myself."

These words, which so suddenly and completely altered the aspect of affairs, astounded the audience. The greatest joy took the place of grief and dismay; and to wind up, as soon as their agitation allowed them to think of the delusion they had suffered under, they scolded me soundly for the fright I had given them. I excused myself by saying that I had only repeated the tale as it was told to me, and Don José flew into a great rage, calling me a rascal, an imposter, and a busybody.

It was happily true that Don Rafael was alive and out of danger; he had remained with some friends at Sanlúcar while his father had come to Cadiz to fetch his mother to see him. My readers will hardly believe in the origin of the mistake which had led me to announce the young man's death in such perfect good faith; though a few may have been led to suspect that some tremendous fib of the old man's must have given rise to the report that reached me. And so it was, neither more nor less. I heard all about it at Sanlúcar whither I went with the family. Don José Maria had invented a whole romance of devotion and skill on his own part, and had related more than once the history of his son's death, inventing so many dramatic details that for a few days he figured as a hero, and had been the object of universal admiration for his humanity and courage. His story was that the boat had upset, and that as the choice lay between rescuing his son and saving all the others he had chosen the latter alternative as the most magnanimous and philanthropical. This romance he dressed up in so many interesting, and at the same time probable circumstances that it could not fail to be believed. The falsehood was of course very soon found out, and his success was of brief duration, but not before the story had come to my ears and put me under the necessity of reporting it to the family. Though I knew very well how absolutely mendacious old Malespina could be, I had never dreamed of his lying about so serious a matter.

When all this excitement was over my master sank into deep melancholy; he would scarcely speak and seemed as though his soul, having no illusions left, had closed accounts with the world and was only waiting to take its departure. The absence of Marcial was to him the loss of the only companion of his childish old age; he had no one now to fight mimic battles with, and he gave himself up to dull sorrow. Nor did Doña Francisca spare him any drop of mortification, seeing him in this crest-fallen state. I heard her the same day saying spitefully:

"A pretty mess you have made of it! What do you think of yourself now? Now are you satisfied? Go, oh go by all means and join the fleet! Was I right or was I wrong? If you would only have listened to me. But you have had a lesson I hope; you see now how God has punished you."

"Woman, leave me in peace," said my master sadly.

"And now we are left without any fleet at all, and without sailors, and we shall soon find ourselves ruined out of hand if we keep up our alliance with the French.—Please God those gentry may not pay us out for their misfortunes. Señor Villeneuve!—he has covered himself with glory indeed! And Gravina again! If he had opposed the scheme of taking the fleet out, as Churruca and Alcalá Galiano did, he might have prevented this heartbreaking catastrophe."

"Woman, woman—what do you know about it? Do not annoy me," said Don Alonso quite vexed.

"What do I know about it? More than you do. Yes—I repeat it: Gravina may be a worthy gentleman and as brave as you please; but in this case, much good he has done!"

"He did his duty. You would have liked us all to be set down as cowards, I suppose?"

"Cowards, no—but prudent. It is as I say and repeat: the fleet ought never to have gone out of Cadiz just to humor the whims and conceit of Villeneuve.

"Every one here knew that Gravina, like the others, was of opinion that it ought to stop in the bay. But Villeneuve had made up his mind to it, intending to hit a blow that might restore him to his master's favor, and he worked on our Spanish pride. It seems that one of the reasons Gravina gave was the badness of the weather, and that he said, looking at the barometer in the cabin: 'Do you not see that the barometer foretells foul weather? Do you not see how it has gone down?' And then Villeneuve said drily: 'What is gone down here is courage!' At such an insult Gravina stood up, blind with rage, and threw the French Admiral's own conduct at Finisterre in his teeth. Some angry words were spoken on both sides and at last our Admiral exclaimed: 'To sea then to-morrow morning.'

"But I say that Gravina ought to have taken no notice of Villeneuve's insolence—none whatever; that prudence is an officer's first duty, and particularly when he knew—as we all knew—that the fleet was not in a condition to fight the English."

This view, which at the time seemed to me an insult to our national honor, I understood later was well-founded. Doña Francisca was right. Gravina ought not to have given way to Villeneuve's obstinacy, and I say it almost dims the halo of prestige with which the popular voice crowned the leader of the Spanish forces on that disastrous occasion. Without denying Gravina's many merits, in my opinion there was much exaggeration in the high-flown praises that were lavished upon him, both after the battle, and again when he died of his wounds a few months later. Everything he did proved him to be an accomplished gentleman and a brave sailor, but he was perhaps too much of a courtier to show the determination which commonly comes of long experience in war; he was deficient too in that complete superiority which, in so learned a profession as the Navy, can only be acquired by assiduous study of the sciences on which it relies. Gravina was a good commander of a division under superior orders, but nothing more. The foresight, coolness, and immovable determination, which are indispensable elements in the man whose fortune it is to wield such mighty forces, he had not; Don Cosme Damian Churruca had—and Don Dionisio Alcalá Galiano.

March, 1806.

My master made no reply to Doña Francisca's last speech and when she left the room I observed that he was praying as fervently as when I had left him in the cabin of the *Santa Ana*. Indeed, from that day Don Alonso did nothing else but pray; he prayed incessantly till the day came when he had to sail in the ship that never comes home.

He did not die till some time after his daughter's marriage with Don Rafael Malespina, an event which took place two months after the action which the Spanish know as "the 21st," and the English as the battle of Trafalgar. My young mistress was married one lovely morning, though it was winter time, and set out at once for Medina-Sidonia where a house was ready and waiting for the young couple. I might look on at her happiness during the days preceding the wedding but she did not observe the melancholy that I was suffering under; nor, if she had, would she have guessed the cause. She thought more of herself every day, as I could see, and I felt more and more humiliated by her beauty and her superior position in life. But I had taught myself to understand that such a sweet vision of all the graces could never be mine, and this kept me calm; for resignation—honest renunciation of all hope—is a real consolation, though it is a consolation akin to death.

Well, they were married, and the very day they had left us for Medina-Sidonia Doña Francisca told me that I was to follow them and enter their service. I set out that night, and during my solitary journey I tried to fight down my thoughts and my feelings which wavered between accepting a place in the house of the bridegroom or flying from them forever. I arrived very early in the morning and found out the house. I went into the garden but on the bottom step I stopped, for my reflections absorbed all my energies, and I had to stand still to think more clearly; I must have stood there for more than half an hour.

Perfect silence prevailed. The young couple were sleeping untroubled by a care or a sorrow. I could not help recalling that far-off time when my young mistress and I had played together. To me she had then been my first and only thought. To her, though I had not been the first in her affections, I had been something she loved and that she missed if we were apart for an hour. In so short a time how great a change!

I looked round me and all I saw seemed to symbolize the happiness of the lovers and to mock my forlorn fate. Although it was winter time, I could picture the trees in full leaf, and the porch in front of the door seemed suddenly overgrown with creepers to shade them when they should come out. The sun was warmer, the air blew softer round this nest for which I myself had carried the first straws when I served as the messenger of their loves. I seemed to see the bare rose-bushes covered with roses, the orange-trees with blossoms and fruit pecked by crowds of birds thus sharing in the wedding feast. My dreams and reflections were at last interrupted by a fresh young voice breaking the silence of the place and which made me tremble from head to foot as I heard it. It thrilled me with an indescribable sensation, that clear, happy, happy voice—whether of fear or shame I can hardly say; all I am sure of is that a sudden impulse made me turn from the door, and fly from the spot like a thief afraid of being caught.

My mind was made up. I quitted Medina-Sidonia forthwith, quite determined never to be a servant in that house, nor to return to Vejer. After a few minutes reflection I set out for Cadiz intending to get from thence to Madrid; and this was what I ultimately did, in spite of the persuasions of Doña Flora who tried to chain me to her side with a wreath of the faded flowers of her affection!

But since that day how much I have gone through; how much I have seen, well worthy of record. My fate, which had taken me to Trafalgar, led me subsequently through many glorious and inglorious scenes, all in their way worth remembering. If the reader cares to hear the story of my life I will tell him more about it at a future opportunity.

The Novel on the Tram

I

The tram left the end of the Salamanca district to pass through the whole of Madrid in the direction of Pozas. Motivated by a selfish desire to sit down before others with the same intention, I put my hand on the handrail of the stair leading to the upper deck, stepped onto the platform and went up. At the same time (a fateful meeting!) I collided with another passenger who was getting on the tram from the other side. I looked at him and recognized my friend Don Dionisio Cascajares y de la Vallina, a man as inoffensive as he was discreet, who had at this critical juncture the goodness to greet me with a warm and enthusiastic handshake. The shock of our unexpected meeting did not have serious consequences apart from the partial denting of a certain straw hat placed on top of the head of an English woman who was trying to get on behind my friend, and who suffered, no doubt for lack of agility, a glancing blow from his stick. We sat down without attaching exaggerated importance to this slight mishap and started to chat.

Don Dionisio Cascajares is a famous doctor, although not for the depth of his knowledge of pathology, and a good man, since it could never be said of him that he was inclined to take what did not belong to him, nor to kill his fellow men by means other than those of his dangerous and scientific vocation. We can be quite sure that the leniency of his treatment and his complacency in not giving his patients any other treatment than the one they want are the root cause of the confidence he inspires in a great many families, irrespective of class, especially when, in his limitless kindness, he also has a reputation for meting out services over and above the call of duty though always of a rigorously honest nature. Nobody knows like he does interesting events which are not common knowledge, and no-one possesses to a higher degree the mania of asking questions, though this vice of being overly inquisitive is compensated for in him by the promptness with which he tells you everything he knows without others needing to take the trouble to sound him out. Judge then if such a fine exemplar of human flippancy would be in demand with the curious and the garrulous. This man, my friend as he is everyone's, was sitting next to me when the tram, slipping smoothly along its iron road, was going down the calle de Serrano, stopping from time to time in order to fill the few seats that still remained empty. We were so hemmed in that the bundle of books I was carrying with me became a source of great concern to me, and I was putting it first on one knee, then on the other. Finally I decided to sit on it, fearing to disturb the English lady, whose seat just happened to be next to me on my left.

"And where are you going?" Cascajares asked me, looking at me over the top of his dark glasses, which made me feel that I was being watched by four eyes rather than two. I answered him evasively and he, not wanting to lose any time before finding something out, insisted on asking questions: "And what's so-and-so up to? And that woman, what's-her-name, where is she?" accompanied by other inquiries of the same ilk which were not fully replied to either. As a last resort, seeing how useless his attempts were to start a conversation, he set off on a path more in keeping with his expansive temperament and began to spill the beans:

"Poor countess!" he said, expressing with a movement of his head and facial features his disinterested compassion. "If she had followed my advice, she would not be in such a critical situation."

"Quite clearly," I replied mechanically, doing compassionate homage also to the aforementioned countess. "Just imagine," he continued, "that they've let themselves be dominated by that man! And that man will end up being master of the house. Poor woman! She thinks that with tears and lamentations all can be remedied, but it isn't so. She must make a decision, for that man is a monster; I believe he has it in him to commit the most heinous crimes."

"Yes, he'll stop at nothing," I said, unconsciously participating in his indignation.

"He's like all those low-born men who follow their base instincts. If they raise their station in life, they become insufferable. His face is a clear indication that nothing good can come out of all this."

"It hits you in the face. I believe you."

"I'll explain it to you in a nutshell. The countess is an excellent woman, angelic, as discreet as she is beautiful and deserving of something far better. But she is married to a man who does not understand the value of the treasure he possesses and he spends his life given over to gambling and to all sorts of illicit pastimes. She in the meantime gets bored and cries. Is it surprising that she tries to dull her pain honestly, here and there, wherever a piano is being played? Moreover I myself give her this advice and say it loud and clear: Madam, seek diversion. Life's too short. The count in the end will have to repent of his follies and your sufferings will then be over. It seems to me I'm right."

"No doubt about it," I replied off the cuff, although, in my heart of hearts, as indifferent as I had been to begin with to the sundry misfortunes of the countess. "But that's not the worst of it," Cascajares added, striking the floor with his stick, "for now the count, in the prime of life, has started to be jealous, yes, of a certain young man who has taken to heart the enterprise of helping the countess to enjoy herself."

"The husband will be to blame if he succeeds."

"None of that would matter as the countess is virtue incarnate; none of that would matter, I say, if there was not a terrible man whom I suspect of being about to cause a disaster in that house."

"Really? And who is he, this man?" I asked with a spark of curiosity.

"A former butler, well-liked by the count, who has set himself to make a martyr of the countess as unhappy as she is sensitive. It seems that he is now in possession of a certain secret which could compromise her, and with this weapon he presumes to do God knows what. It's infamous!"

"It certainly is and he merits an exemplary punishment," I said, discharging in turn the weight of my wrath on that man.

"But she is innocent, she is an angel. But enough said! We've reached Cibeles. Yes, on the right I can see Buenavista Park. Have them stop, boy. I'm not one of those who jump off while the tram is still moving to split open their heads on the cobbles. Farewell, my friend, farewell."

The tram stopped and Don Dionisio Cascajares y de la Vallina got off after shaking my hand again and inflicting more slight damage on the hat of the English lady who had not yet recovered from her original scare.

II

The tram carried on and, strange to relate, I in turn continued to think about the unknown countess, of her cruel and suspicious consort and above all of the sinister man who, according to the doctor's emphatic expression, was on the point of causing a disaster in the house. Consider, reader, the nature of human thought: when Cascajares started to relate those events to me, I was annoyed at his importunity and heaviness, but my mind wasted little time in taking hold of that same subject, turning it upside down and right side up, a psychological process which did not cease to be stimulated by the regular motion of the tram and the dull and monotonous noise of its wheels polishing the iron of the rails.

But in the end I stopped thinking about what was of such little interest to me and, scanning with my eyes the inside of the tram, I examined one by one my travelling companions. What distinctive faces and what expressions! Some appeared not to be bothered in the least about those who were next to them. Some were happy, some were sad, this one was yawning, that one was laughing, and in spite of the journey's shortness, there was not a single one who did not want it to be over quickly, for among the thousand and one annoyances of our existence, none exceeds the one that consists in being a dozen people gazing at one another's faces without saying a word and mutually musing over their wrinkles, their moles or some anomaly noticed in a face or in clothing.

It is strange this short acquaintance with people that we have not seen before and will in all likelihood not see again. We already meet someone on entering and others arrive while we're still there. Passengers get off leaving us alone and finally we too alight. It's a mirror of human life itself in which birth and death are like the entrances and exits I've just mentioned for new generations of passengers come to populate the little world that lives inside the tram. They get on, they get off; they are born and they die. How many have passed through here before we have! How many more will succeed us! And for the resemblance to be even more complete there is also a small world of passions in miniature inside that big box.

Many go there that we feel instinctively to be excellent people and their appearance pleases us and we are even upset to see them go. Others, on the contrary, annoy us as soon as we look at them. We examine with a certain rancour their phrenological characteristics and feel a real pleasure when we see them go. And meanwhile the vehicle, an imitation of life, keeps going, always receiving and letting go, uniform, indefatigable, majestic, oblivious to what is happening inside it, without being moved very much by the barely stifled passions of dumb show. The tram is running, always running over the two interminable iron tracks, wide and slippery as centuries. I was thinking about this while the tram was going up the calle de Alcalá until the noise of my bundle of books falling on the floor pulled me back from the gulf of so many mixed up ruminations. I picked it up immediately and my eyes focused on the sheet of newspaper that was serving as a wrapper to the volumes and mechanically took in half a line of what was printed there. All of a sudden my curiosity was well and truly aroused. I had read something that interested me and certain names scattered through that scrap of a newspaper serial affected both my vision and my memory. I looked for the beginning and did not find it: the paper was torn and I could only read, with curiosity at first and afterwards more and more eagerly, what follows:

The countess felt indescribably agitated. The presence of Mudarra, the insolent butler, who had forgotten his humble beginnings to dare to cast his gaze on such a noble personage, was a continual source of anxiety to her. The scoundrel never stopped spying on her, watching her as a prison guard watches a prisoner. He already showed no deference to her and nor were the sensitivity and delicacy of such an excellent lady an obstacle to his entrapment of her. Mudarra made an untimely entrance into the private quarters of the countess, who, pale and agitated, feeling at one and the same time both shame and terror, did not have the strength to dismiss him.

"Don't be frightened, Your Ladyship," he said with a forced and sinister smile, which made the lady even more alarmed. "I haven't come to do you any harm."

"Oh my God! When will this agony be over?" the lady exclaimed, dropping her arms in discouragement. "Leave. I cannot accede to your desires. What infamy! To make use in this way of my weakness and the indifference of my husband, the source of so many of my misfortunes!"

"Why so surly, countess?" the fierce butler added. "If I did not have in my hands the secret that could lead to your perdition, if I could not apprise the count of certain particulars with reference to that young nobleman. But I will not use these terrible weapons against you. One day you will understand me and know how selfless is the great love that you have been able to inspire in me."

As he said this Mudarra moved a few steps nearer to the countess who distanced herself with horror and repugnance from that monster. Mudarra was a man of around fifty, dark-skinned, thickset and knock-kneed, with rough, untidy hair and a big mouth full of teeth. His eyes, half hidden behind the luxuriant growth of wide, black and very thick eyebrows, expressed at moments like these the most bestial concupiscence.

"Ah porcupine!" he angrily exclaimed on seeing the lady's natural reticence. "How unfortunate I am not to be a dapper young chap! Such prudery knowing full well I can tell the count and have no doubt that he'll believe me, Your Ladyship: the count has so much trust in me that he takes what I say as gospel and he'll be full of jealousy if I show him the paper."

"Scoundrel!" shouted the countess with a noble display of righteous indignation. "I am innocent and my husband will not give credence to such vile slanders. And even if I were guilty I would prefer a thousand times over for my husband and the whole world to despise me than to buy peace of mind at that price. Leave here at once."

"I too have a temper, countess," said the butler swallowing his rage. "I too can lose it and get angry and since Your Ladyship is making a big thing of this, let's make a big thing of it. I already know what I have to do and I've been until now far too affable. One last time I put it to Your Ladyship that we should be friends and don't make me do something you'll regret, and so my lady."

On saying this Mudarra contracted the parchment-like skin and the rigid tendons of his face making a grimace like a smile and took a few more steps as if to sit down on the sofa next to the countess. The latter jumped up shouting: "No! Leave! Scoundrel! And not to have anyone here to defend me. Leave!"

The butler then was like a wild animal that lets go of the prey it was holding a moment before in its claws. He breathed heavily, made a threatening gesture and slowly left with soft footfalls. The countess, trembling and out of breath, having taken refuge in a corner of the room, heard the footfalls which faded away on the carpet of the room next door and finally breathed when she judged him to be far away. She closed the doors and tried to sleep, but sleep eluded her, her eyes still full of terror at the image of the monster.

Mudarra, on leaving the countess's room, went in the direction of his own and, dominated by a strong feeling of nervous anxiety, started to search for letters and papers muttering to himself: "I can't stand it anymore. You'll pay me back for all of this." Then he sat down, took up his pen, and, putting in front of him one of those letters and examining it closely, he began to write another, trying to copy the writing. He moved his eyes feverishly from the model to the copy and finally, after a great deal of work, he wrote with writing totally identical to that of the model, the following letter, the sentiments in which were of his own making: I promised to meet with you and I'm hastening to carry out that promise.

The newspaper in which this serial appeared was torn and I could read no further.

III

Without taking my eyes off the bundle of books I started to think about the relationship between the news I had had from the mouth of Don Cascajares and the scene I had just read in that scandal sheet, a roman feuilleton no doubt translated from some silly novel by Ponson du Terrail or Montépin. It may be silly I said to myself, but the fact is I'm interested in this countess who has fallen victim to the nastiness of an insufferable butler who only exists in the disturbed mind of some novelist born to terrify simple souls. And what will he do to take his revenge? He'd be capable of framing some atrocity to bring to an end in sensational style such a chapter. And what will the count do? And that young man Cascajares mentioned on the tram and Mudarra in the serial, what will he do? Who is he? What is there between the countess and that unknown gentleman? I'd give my eye teeth to know.

These were my thoughts when I raised my eyes and looked over the inside of the tram with them. To my horror I saw a person who made me shake with fear. While I was engrossed in the interesting reading of the feuilleton, the tram had stopped several times to take on or let off passengers. On one of these occasions this man had got on whose sudden presence now produced such a strong impression on me. It was him, Mudarra, the butler in person, sitting opposite me, with his knees touching my knees. I took a second to examine him from head to toe and saw in him the features I had already read about. He could be no-one else: even the most trifling details of his clothing clearly indicated it was him. I recognized his dark and lustrous complexion, his unruly hair, the curls of which sprang up in opposite directions like the snakes of Medusa. His deep-sunk eyes were covered by the thickness of his bushy eyebrows and his beard was no less unkempt than his hair, while his feet were twisted inwards like those of parrots. The same look in a nutshell, the same man in his appearance, in his clothes, in the way he breathed and in the way he coughed, even in the way he put his hand into his pocket to pay his fare.

Suddenly I saw him take out a letter writing case and I noticed that this object had on its cover a great gilded M, the first letter of his surname. He opened it, took out a letter and looked at the envelope with a demonic smile and I even thought I heard him mutter: "How well I've imitated the handwriting!" The letter was indeed a small one with the envelope addressed in a feminine scrawl. I watched him closely as he took pleasure in his infamous action until he saw that I had indiscreetly and discourteously stretched my face in order to read the address. He gave me a stare that hit me like a blow and put the letter back in the case.

The tram kept going and in the short time it had taken me to read an extract from the novel, to reflect on such strange occurrences and to see Mudarra in the flesh, a character out of a book, hard to believe in, made human and now my companion on this journey, we had left behind the calle de Alcalá, were currently crossing the Puerta del Sol and making a triumphal entrance into the calle Mayor, making a way for ourselves between other vehicles, making slow-moving covered waggons speed up and frightening pedestrians who, in the tumult of the street and dazed by so many diverse noises, only saw the solid outline of the tram when it was almost on top of them. I continued to look at that man as one looks at an object of whose existence one is uncertain and I did not take my eyes from his repugnant face till I saw him get up, ask for the tram to stop and get off, losing sight of him then among the crowd on the street.

Various passengers got off and got on and the living décor of the tram changed completely. The more I thought of it, the more alive was the curiosity that event aroused in me, which I had to begin with considered as forced into my head exclusively by the juxtaposition of various feelings occasioned by my erstwhile conversation and subsequent reading, but which I finally imagined as indubitably true.

When the man in whom I thought to see the awful butler got off the tram, I was still thinking about the incident with the letter and I explained it to myself as best I could, hoping not to have on such a delicate matter an imagination less fertile than the novelist who had written what only moments before I had read. Mudarra, I thought, desirous of taking his revenge on the countess, that unfortunate lady, had copied her writing and written a letter to a certain gentleman of her acquaintance. In the letter she had given him a rendezvous in her own home. The young man had arrived at the time indicated and shortly afterwards the husband, whom the butler had warned so that he would catch his unfaithful wife in flagrante which was in itself an admirable idea! An action, which in life has points for and against, fits snugly in a novel like a ring on a finger. The lady would faint, the lover would panic and the husband would commit an atrocity and, lurking behind a curtain, the face of the butler would light up diabolically.

As an avid reader of numerous bad novels, I gave that twist to what was unconsciously developing in my imagination on the basis of the words of a friend, the reading of a piece of torn-off paper and the sight of someone I had never laid eyes on before.

IV

The tram kept on going and going and whether because of the heat that could be felt inside it or the slow and monotonous movement of the vehicle that gives rise to a certain amount of dizziness which then turns into sleep, what is certain is that I felt my eyelids droop, leaned to my left-hand side, placing my elbow on the bundle of books, and closed my eyes. While in this position I continued to see the row of faces of both sexes in front of me, some bearded, some shaven, some laughing, some very stiff and serious. Afterwards it seemed to me that, obeying the contraction of a single muscle, all those faces winked and grimaced, opening and closing their eyes and their mouths, and showing me in turn a series of teeth that varied from whiter than white to yellowish, some as sharp as knives, others broken and worn. Those eight noses set under sixteen eyes varying in colour and expression, got bigger or smaller and changed shape; the mouths opened in a horizontal line producing silent laughter or stretched forward forming sharp-pointed snouts similar to the interesting face of a certain distinguished animal which has brought down on itself the anathema of being unnameable.

Behind those eight faces, whose horrendous traits I have just depicted, and through the windows of the tram, I could see the street, the houses and the passers-by, all speeding past as if the tram were travelling at a vertiginous speed. I at least thought that it went faster than the trains on our railroads, faster than its French, English and North American counterparts. It ran as fast as might be imagined when it came to displacing solid objects.

As this state of lethargy increased, I was able to imagine that houses, streets and the whole of Madrid were gradually disappearing. For a moment I thought that the tram was running through oceanic depths: through the windows could be seen the bodies of enormous cetaceans and the sticky appendages of a multitude of polyps of various sizes. Small fish were shaking their slippery tails against the glass and some of them were looking inside with great and gilded eyes. Crustaceans of an unfamiliar shape, large molluscs, madrepores, sponges and a scattering of big and misshapen bivalves which I had never seen before, swam ceaselessly past. The tram was being pulled by monstrous swimming creatures, whose oars, fighting with the water, sounded like the blades of a propeller churning it up with their ceaseless rotation.

This vision started to fade. Then it seemed to me that the tram was flying through the air, always in the same direction and without being blown off course by winds. Through the windows only empty space was visible. Clouds sometimes enveloped us and a sudden downpour drummed against the upper deck. All at once we came out into pure space flooded with sunshine, only to go back to the nebulous presence of huge flashes, now red, now yellow, sometimes opal, sometimes amethyst, which were being left behind us as we made our way forward. We passed then through a point in space where shining forms floated in a very fine golden dust: further on this dust storm, which I took to be produced by the movement of the wheels grinding the light, was silver, then green like flour made from emeralds, and finally red like flour made from rubies. The tram was being dragged by some apocalyptic bird, stronger than a hippogryph and more daring than a dragon, and the noise of the wheels and the driving force made me think of the whirring of the great sails of a windmill, or rather the buzz of a bumblebee the size of an elephant. We were flying through infinite space without ever arriving anywhere. In the meantime the earth fell away several leagues below our feet, and the things of earth—Spain, Madrid, the Salamanca district, Cascajares, the Countess, the Count, Mudarra, the gallant young man, all of them together.

I soon fell into a deep sleep and then the tram stopped moving, stopped flying and the sensation that I felt of travelling in such a tram disappeared and all that was left was the deep and monotonous bass of the wheels which never abandons us even in our nightmares, be it in a train or in the cabin of a steamship. I slept. Oh unhappy countess! I saw her as clearly as I now see the paper that I'm writing on. I saw her sat next to a night light, hand on cheek, sad and pensive like a statue depicting Melancholy. At her feet a lapdog lay curled up that seemed to me just as sad as his as his interesting mistress.

Then I was able to examine at my leisure the woman I had come to see as misfortune personified. She was tall and fair with big and expressive eyes, an aquiline nose that was actually quite prominent, though not out of proportion to the rest of her face, and set off by the twin curves of her fine and arched eyebrows. She was casually groomed and from this, as from her dress, it was possible to surmise that she did not intend to go out again that night. A night of marvels truly! I observed with increasing anxiety the beautiful form I so much wanted to know better and it seemed to me that I could read her mind behind that noble brow in which the habit of reflexion had traced scarcely visible lines which would soon become wrinkles. Suddenly the door to her room opened to let a man in. The Countess gave a yelp of surprise and got up in a state of great agitation.

"What's this?" she said. "Rafael. You. What barefaced cheek! How did you get in?"

"Madam," answered the one who had just entered, a young man of noble bearing. "Weren't you expecting me? I received a letter from you."

"A letter from me!" exclaimed the Countess even more agitated. "I wrote no such letter. And what reason would I have for writing it?"

"Madam, look," the young man responded, taking out the letter and showing it to her. "It's in your own handwriting."

"Good God! What devilry is this?" said the lady in despair. "It was not I who wrote this letter. They're setting a trap for me."

"Madam, calm down. I'm very sorry."

"Yes. I understand everything now. That infamous man. I have a strong suspicion as to what he had in mind. Leave this instant. But it's already too late. I can already hear my husband's voice."

Indeed a deafening voice could be heard in the room next door and, after a short interval, the Count came in the room. He feigned surprise at seeing the gallant visitor and, subsequently laughing somewhat affectedly, spoke to him:

"Ah Rafael! You're here. Long time no see! You came to accompany

Antonia on the piano. You'll take tea with us."

The Countess and her spouse exchanged a meaningful glance. The young man in his perplexity hardly managed to return the Count's greeting. I saw them entering the living room and servants coming out to meet them. I saw that the servants were carrying tea things and afterwards they disappeared, leaving the three main characters alone.

Something terrible was going to happen.

They sat down. The Countess looked mortified. The Count affected a dazed hilarity like drunkenness and the young man spoke only in monosyllables. Tea was served and the Count passed to Rafael one of the cups, not just any cup, but one he'd singled out. The Countess looked at that cup so fearfully it seemed that her soul had left her body. They drank in silence ballasting the brew with a tasty assortment of Huntley and Palmers biscuits and other nibbles appropriate to this type of supper. Then the Count burst out laughing again with the outrageous and noisy demonstrativeness that was peculiar to him that night, and said:

"How bored we all are! You, Rafael, haven't said a word. Antonia, play something. We haven't heard you play for such a long time. This piece by Gorschack, for instance, entitled Death. You used to play it wonderfully. Come on. Sit down at the piano."

The Countess tried to speak, but could not say a word. The Count looked at her in such a way that the unhappy woman quailed before the terrible expression in his eyes like a dove hypnotized by a boa constrictor. She got up to go to the piano and again there the husband must have said something that terrified her even more, subjecting her to his devilish dominion. The piano sounded with several strings struck at once and, running from the low notes to the high notes, the lady's hands awoke in a second hundreds of sounds that were lying dormant in among the strings and hammers. At first the music was a confused mixture of sounds that stunned rather than pleased, but then that storm blew over and a funereal and timorous dirge like the Dies irae came out of such disorder. It seemed to me I heard the sad sound of a choir of Carthusians accompanied by the hoarse bellow of the bassoons. After could be heard pitiful sighs like those that we imagine souls exhale, condemned in purgatory to ceaselessly beg for a pardon that is a long time in coming.

Then came loud and extended arpeggios and the notes reared up as if arguing about which of them would could there first. Chords came together and broke up like the foam on waves which forms and is then effaced. The harmonies boiled and fluctuated in an endless heavy swell, fading into silence and then coming back more strongly in great and hasty eddies. I carried on entranced by the majestic and impressive music. I could not see the face of the countess, sat with her back to me, but I imagined it to be in such a state of bewilderment and fright that I started to think that the piano was playing itself. The young man was behind her, the count to her right, leaning on the piano. From time to time she raised her eyes to look at him, but she must have seen something dreadful in the eyes of her companion as she went back to lowering hers and kept on playing. Suddenly the piano stopped sounding and the Countess cried out.

Just at that moment I felt an extremely strong blow to my shoulder, shook myself violently and woke up.

V

In my agitated dream I had changed position and had allowed myself to fall on the venerable English lady who was travelling next to me. "Aah! You—sleeping—disturb me," she said, making a sour face, while she pushed away from her my bundle of books which had fallen onto her knees.

"Madam, it's true. I fell asleep," I replied, embarrassed to see that all the passengers were laughing at this scene.

"Oh! I tell driver—you disturb me—very shocking," the English woman added in her incomprehensible gibberish: "Oh! You think my body is your bed for you to sleep. Oh! Gentleman, you are a stupid ass."

On saying this, this daughter of Britannia, who already had a ruddy complexion, blushed red as a tomato. You might have thought that the blood that had rushed to her cheeks and her nose was flowing from her incandescent pores. She showed me four sharp and very white teeth as if she wanted to bite me. I asked of her a thousand pardons for the discourtesy of falling asleep, picked up my bundle and reviewed the new faces that there now were in the tram.

Imagine, oh calm and kind reader, when I saw facing me—guess who? the young man I had just finished dreaming about, Don Rafael in the flesh. I rubbed my eyes to convince myself that I was not still asleep and found myself awake, as awake as I am now. He it was and he was talking to someone else who was travelling with him. I paid attention and listened as hard as I could:

"But didn't you suspect anything?" the other person said to him.

"Something, yes. But I held my tongue. She looked petrified with terror. Her husband ordered her to play the piano and she did not dare to resist. She played, as always, admirably, and, as I listened to her, I managed to forget the dangerous situation in which we found ourselves. Despite the efforts she was making to look calm, a moment came when she was no longer able to pretend any more. Her arms relaxed and slipped off the keys. She threw her head back and cried out. Then her husband took out a dagger and, taking a step towards her, shouted furiously: "Play or I'll kill you this instant." When I saw this my blood boiled. I wanted to throw myself at that wretch, but I felt in my body a sensation that I cannot describe to you. A furnace had lit up in my stomach. Fire was running through my veins. My lungs were hyperventilating and I fell on the floor senseless."

"And before that did you not recognize the symptoms of poisoning?" asked the other. "I noticed a certain feeling of uneasiness and had a vague suspicion, but nothing more than that. The poison had been well prepared. It had a delayed effect on me and did not kill me, though it's left me with a physical impairment for life."

"And after you passed out, what happened?"

Rafael was going to answer and I was hanging on his every word as if it were a matter of life and death when the tram halted.

"Ah, here we are already at Consejos. Let's get off here," said

Rafael.

What a nuisance! They were getting off and I would not know how the story ended.

"Sir, sir, a word," I said on seeing them get off. The young man stopped and looked at me.

"And the Countess? What became of her?" I asked eagerly.

Loud laughter was my only response. The two young men laughed too and left without saying a word. The only living being to keep her sphinx-like calm at such a comic scene was the English woman who, indignant at my outlandish behaviour, turned to the other passengers saying: "Oh! A lunatic fellow!"

VI

The tram continued on its way and I was burning with curiosity to know what had happened to the unfortunate Countess. Had her husband killed her? I understood how that villain's mind worked. Desirous of enjoying his revenge, like all cruel souls, he wanted his wife to be present, without pause in playing, at the death of that unwary young man brought there by a spiteful trick on the part of Mudarra. But the lady could not continue making desperate efforts to keep calm, knowing that Rafael had swallowed the poison. A tragic and horrifying scene I thought, more convinced than ever of the reality of that event—and now you'll say that such things only happen in novels!

On passing in front of Palacio the tram halted and a woman got on who was carrying a small dog in her arms. I immediately recognized the dog I had seen reclining at the feet of the Countess. This was the same dog with the same white and fine fur, the same black patch on one of his ears. As luck would have it the woman sat down next to me. Unable to resist being curious, I put the following question to her:

"Is this nice dog your dog?"

"Who else could he belong to? Do you like him?"

I fondled one of the ears of the intelligent animal to show him affection, but he, oblivious to my blandishments, jumped and put his paws on the knees of the English woman, who showed me her two teeth again as if wanting to bite me, and exclaimed:

"Oh! You are unsupportable!"

"And where did you acquire this dog?" I asked without taking notice of the latest explosion of righteous indignation on the part of the British lady. "Can you tell me?"

"My mistress gave it me."

"And what became of your mistress?" I asked most anxiously.

"Ah! Did you know her?" the woman replied.

"She was a good woman, wasn't she?"

"An excellent woman. But may I know how that bad business ended?"

"So you know about it, you've had news of it."

"Yes, madam. I know what happened, including the tea that was served. And tell me—did your mistress die?"

"Yes, sir. She's gone to a better place."

"And what happened? Was she murdered or did she die of fright?"

"What murder? What fright?" she said with a mocking expression. "You're not in the know after all. She ate something that disagreed with her that night and it harmed her. She had a fainting fit that lasted till dawn."

This one, I thought, knows nothing about the incident with the piano and the poison or doesn't want to make me think she does. Afterwards I said in a loud voice:

"So she died of food poisoning?"

"Yes, sir. I warned her not to eat those shellfish, but she took no notice of me."

"Shellfish, eh?" I said incredulously. "I know what really happened."

"Don't you believe me?"

"Yes. Yes," I replied, pretending to believe her. "And what about the Count, her husband, the one who pulled the dagger on her while she was playing the piano?"

The woman looked at me for a moment and then laughed in my face.

"You're laughing, are you? Don't you think I know what took place? You don't want to tell me what really happened. There'd be grounds for a criminal prosecution if you did."

"But you mentioned a count and a countess."

"Was not this dog's mistress the Countess wronged by the butler
Mudarra?"

The woman burst out laughing again so uproariously that I muttered to myself distractedly: She must be Mudarra's accomplice and naturally she'll hide as much as she can.

"You're mad," the unknown woman added.

"Lunatic, lunatic. I'm suffocated. Oh! My God!"

"I know everything. Come now. Don't hide it from me. Tell me what the Countess died of."

"For crying out loud, what countess?" exclaimed the woman, laughing even more loudly.

"Don't think you fool me with your laughter!" I replied. "The Countess was either poisoned or murdered. There's no doubt about it in my mind."

At this juncture the tram arrived at Pozas and I had reached the end of my journey. We all got off. The English woman gave me a look indicative of her elation at finding herself free of me and each of us went in our several directions. I followed the woman with the dog, plying her with questions, until she reached her home still laughing at my determination to know better about other people's lives. Once alone in the street, I remembered the object of my journey and set off to visit the house where I was due to hand over those books. I gave them to the person who had asked for them in order to read them, and I started to walk up and down opposite Buen Suceso, waiting for the tram to reappear so I could then return to the opposite end of Madrid again.

I waited a long time and finally, just as it was getting dark, the tram prepared to leave.

I got on and the first thing I saw was the English lady sitting where she had sat before. When she saw me get on and sit down next to her, the expression on her face beggared description. She went as red as a beetroot and exclaimed:

"Oh! You again. I complain to driver—you are for high jump this time."

I was so preoccupied with my own emotions that, without paying attention to what the English lady was saying in her laborious utterances, I answered her thus:

"Madam, there is no doubt that the Countess was either poisoned or killed. You have no idea of that man's ferocity."

The tram continued on its way and every now and then stopped to take on passengers. Near the royal palace three got on, occupying seats opposite me. One of them was a tall, thin and bony man with very stern eyes and a bell-like voice that imposed respect.

They hadn't been on ten minutes when this man turned to the others and said:

"Poor thing! How she cried out in her dying moments! The bullet went in above her right shoulder-blade and penetrated down to her heart."

"What?" I exclaimed all of a sudden. "She died of a shot and not a stab wound?"

The three of them looked at me in amazement.

"Of a shot, sir, yes," the tall, thin and bony one said with a certain amount of surliness.

"And that woman maintained she had died of food poisoning," I said, more interested in this affair by the minute. "Tell me how it came about."

"And what concern is it of yours?" said the other with an offhand gesture.

"I'm very interested indeed to know the end of this horrific tragedy.

Does it not seem to be straight from the pages of a novel?"

"Where do novels and dead people come into it? Either you're mad or you're trying to make fun of us."

"Young man, be careful what you joke about," added the tall and thin one.

"Don't you think I know what happened? I know it all from start to finish. I witnessed all the various scenes of this horrendous crime. But you're saying that the Countess died of a pistol shot."

"Good God. We weren't talking about a Countess, but about my female dog that we inadvertently shot while out hunting. If you want to make a joke of it, meet me outside and I'll answer you as you deserve."

"I see where you're coming from. Now you're determined to keep the truth hidden," I said, thinking that these men wanted to lead me astray in my inquiries, transforming that unfortunate lady into a female dog.

One of my interlocutors was doubtless preparing his answer, more physical than the case required, when the English woman put her finger to her temple as if to indicate to them that my head did not function properly. They calmed down at this and spoke not a single word more for the whole of their journey, which finished for them at the Puerta del Sol. No doubt they had been afraid of me.

I was so fixated on the idea that a crime had been committed that it was in vain that I tried to calm down as I reasoned out the threads of such a complicated question. But each time I did so my confusion grew and the image of the poor lady refused to leave me. In all the countenances that succeeded one another inside the tram, I thought I might see something that would contribute to an explanation of the enigma. I felt a frightful overheating of my brain and no doubt this inner disturbance was reflected in my face as everyone looked at me as at something that you don't see every day.

VII

There was yet another incident which would turn my head during that fateful journey. On passing through the Calle de Alcalá a man got on with his wife. He sat down next to me. He was a man who seemed affected by some strong and recent emotion and I could even believe that, from time to time, he raised his handkerchief to his eyes to wipe away invisible tears which were no doubt being shed behind the dark green lenses of his unusual spectacles. After a short time he said in a low voice to the person I took to be his wife:

"They suspect that she was poisoned, there's no doubt about it. Don

Mateo's just told me. Poor woman!"

"How terrible! That's what I thought too," answered his wife.

"What else can you expect from such savages?"

"I won't leave a stone unturned till I get to the bottom of this business."

I, who was all ears, also said in a low voice: "Yes, sir, she was poisoned. There's proof of it."

"What? You know? Did you know her too?" said the man with the green specs, turning towards me.

"Yes, sir. And I do not doubt that her death was a violent one, no matter how hard they try to make us believe it was food poisoning."

"I'm of the same opinion. What an excellent woman! But how do you know all this for a fact?"

"I know, I know," I replied, extremely pleased that this man at least did not think I was mad.

"You'll make a declaration to the court then, for the judge has already started to sum up."

"I'll be happy just to see these rascals get what's coming to them.

I'll make that declaration, yes, I will, sir."

My moral blindness had reached such a point that I ended up completely taken in by this event half dreamed, half read about, and believed it as I now believe I'm writing with a pen.

"Indeed I will, sir, for it is necessary to clear up this mystery so that the perpetrators of this crime can be punished. I will declare that she was poisoned by a cup of tea, the same as the young man."

"Did you hear that, Petronila?" said the bespectacled man to his wife.

"By a cup of tea."

"Yes, it surprises me," the lady answered. "What terrible things those monsters were capable of!"

"It's true, sir. With a cup of tea. The Countess was playing the piano."

"What countess?" the man asked, interrupting me. "The countess. The woman who was poisoned."

"The woman in question was no countess."

"Come off it. You too are one of those determined to hide the facts in this case."

"This was no countess or duchess, but simply the woman who did my laundry for me, the wife of the pointsman at Madrid North station."

"A laundress, eh?" I said roguishly. "You won't make me swallow that one."

The man and his wife looked at me quizzically and muttered some words to each other. From a gesture that I saw the woman make I understood that she had formed the deep conviction I was drunk. I opted not to argue and said nothing, content to despise such an irreverent supposition in silence as befits great souls. My anxiety knew no bounds. The Countess was not absent for a moment from my thoughts and she had started to interest me by reason of her sinister end as if all that had not been a morbid expression of my own impulse to fantasize, forged by successive visions and conversations. Finally, to understand to what extreme my madness carried me, I am going to relate the ultimate occurrence on this journey of mine. I shall say with what extravagance I put an end to the painful combat of my understanding caught in a battle with an army of shadows.

The tram was entering the calle de Serrano when I chanced to look through the window opposite where I was sitting into the street, weakly lit by street lights, and I saw a man go by. I shouted with surprise and foolishly exclaimed the following:

"There he goes. It's him, Mudarra, the principal author of so many crimes."

I ordered the tram to stop and alighted or rather jumped through the door, colliding with the feet and legs of the passengers. I descended to the street and ran after that man, shouting:

"Stop him! Stop him! Murderer!"

You can imagine what the effect of these words would have been in such a tranquil neighbourhood. The man in question, the same one I had seen in the tram that afternoon, was arrested. I, for my part, did not stop shouting:

"He's the one who prepared the poison for the Countess, the one who murdered the Countess."

There was a moment of indescribable confusion. He affirmed that I was mad, but we were both placed in police custody. Afterwards I lost all notion of what was happening around me. I do not remember what I did that night in the place where they locked me up. The most vivid recollection that I have of such a strange event was to have awoken from the deep sleep I fell into, a veritable drunken stupor morally produced, I know not how, by one of the passing phenomena of alienation that science now studies with great care as one of the heralds of madness.

As you can surmise the event did not have consequences because the unsympathetic person I baptized with the name of Mudarra was an honourable grocer who had never in his life poisoned any countess. But for a long time afterwards I persisted in my self-deception and was wont to exclaim: "Poor countess. Whatever they say, I'll stick to my guns. No-one will persuade me that you did not end your days at the hand of your irate husband."

Months needed to pass for the shadows to return to the unknown place from whence they had come forth driving me mad and for reality to gain the ascendance in my head. I always laugh when I remember that journey and all the consideration I had lavished beforehand on my dreamed-of victim I now devoted to—who do you think?—my travelling companion on that anguished expedition, the irascible English woman, whose foot I dislocated when I hastily left the tram to run after the alleged butler.

Made in the USA
Middletown, DE
08 October 2022